CHRONICLES OF THE XANDIM

~ VOLUME 2 ~

EXODUS OF THE XANDIM

MAGGIE FUREY

GOLLANCZ

LONDON

The right of Maggie Furey to be identified as the author of
this work has been asserted by her in accordance with the
Copyright, Designs and Patents Act 1988.

First published in Great Britain in 2013 by Gollancz
An imprint of the Orion Publishing Group
Orion House, 5 Upper St Martin's Lane, London WC2H 9EA
An Hachette UK Company

A CIP catalogue record for this book
is available from the British Library

ISBN (Trade Paperback) 978 0 575 07663 1

1 3 5 7 9 10 8 6 4 2

Typeset by Deltatype Ltd, Birkenhead, Merseyside
Printed in Great Britain by CPI Group (UK) Ltd,
Croydon, CRO 4YY

www.maggiefurey.co.uk
www.orionbooks.co.uk

Dedicated with love to my sister, Lin Stockley,
Canine Behaviourist and Dog Trainer beyond compare.
May your future hold nothing but happiness.

1

~

THE MAGIC OF AIR

Many momentous events took place in the winter when the Wild Hunt was ambushed by mortals and the Forest Lord Hellorin was lost to the world, betrayed by the malice of Ferimon. In Eliorand, Tiolani, the Forest Lord's daughter, was seduced by the same evil traitor as part of his plan to rule the Phaerie, and the grey mare Corisand discovered her responsibilities as Windeye of the Xandim. In Tyrineld, the Archwizard Cyran's broodings over his dread visions of war and destruction were supported by the premonitions of his fellow Archmages, and the blind Wizard Iriana's dreams of freedom and adventure were finally realised, though she never could have guessed what would lie in store for her before the summer's end.

While in the north the strands of the approaching crisis were spinning out thick and fast upon the web of fate, circumstances were moving towards another crisis elsewhere, in the far lands of the south: in the ocean deeps for the Leviathan; in the glittering glory of the Jewelled Desert for the Dragonfolk; and in beautiful Aerillia, the soaring mountain city of the Skyfolk.

The Winged Folk of Aerillia were generous to visitors, thought Yinze. The chambers set aside for guests were high up on the pinnacle of the mountain, just below the complex of buildings that formed the Royal Palace, and the view from the landing platform was stunning. To a Wizard's eye, the city looked utterly alien but very beautiful, with some of its buildings suspended from the precipitous crags and others carved out of the mountain peak itself. He had been here over half a year now and was used to the view, but the slender spires and turrets of pale, almost translucent stone, and the delicately crafted structures that seemed to cling like coral to the steep rock face, still

I

filled him with amazement. There were no angles in Aerillia; no hard corners to form awkward air currents, or hurt an unwary flier who'd been hit by an unexpected gust of wind. Everything looked stream-lined, fluid, organic: a miracle wrought, by magic and tremendous labour, from the mountain's very bones.

It was spectacular. It was beautiful. It was no place for someone without wings. Though it was possible to access some places by going through a labyrinth of intervening buildings, the routes were tortuous and inconvenient, for the simple reason that the Winged Folk never used those routes except during the worst of the stormy weather, and many places were completely inaccessible except by flight. It was for this very reason that the Skyfolk, unlike the Phaerie, the Wizards and the Dragonfolk, did not possess human slaves – at least, not in Aerillia itself, though they were used down in the valleys to cultivate crops, and to mine the jewels and precious metals with which these mountains abounded.

To fulfil the domestic functions in the city itself the Skyfolk used instead a special low caste of their own kind, known as the Forsaken, who were barred from any existence other than obedience and drudgery. Yinze had been allocated some of these to be his own staff during his stay here. As well as Kereru, a motherly winged woman to clean and cook for him, he had four sturdy young men whose function it was to transport him wherever he wanted to go, strapped into a carrying sling and suspended below them like a piece of cargo as they soared effortlessly across the gulfs of empty air.

It was inconvenient, terrifying, and worst of all, utterly humiliat-ing. Though it was sometimes unavoidable, the Wizard used that mode of transport as little as possible, and therefore his movements were circumscribed and he suffered limitations that he had never known before. Always vigorous and active at home, here Yinze ached from lack of exercise. Sometimes he felt so bad that he'd be forced to get his bearers to take him down the mountain to the valleys and terraces where crops were grown and sheep and goats were bred. He would walk and run himself into a state of exhaustion, thinking wistfully of Tyrineld's olive groves and sparkling blue bays, its warm, herb-scented breezes and the laughter and company of his friends.

Beyond Aerillia the eye was led across the breathtaking vista of lower, snow-covered peaks beyond, right to the glittering line on the far horizon which marked the beginning of the Jewelled Desert. It was almost worth freezing for. Now, at sunset, the mountains were tinted with amethyst and rose, and shadows darkened the pale stone of the city's buildings. At this time of year, everyone in the city went to bed early. The temperature plunged after nightfall, and even the hardy Skyfolk found it more pleasant to snuggle beneath the bedclothes. Supper hour had passed, and Yinze was standing on the landing platform of his room, taking his customary last look out before retiring.

The Wizard shivered, and tried to bury himself deeper into his thick woollen cloak. In Tyrineld, even the winter nights were a great deal warmer than this, but Aerillia, though situated further south, was set high in the mountains, and the season's chill bit deep. The Winged Folk had a tremendous tolerance of the freezing conditions, but the cold was beginning to wear upon their guest. Though Yinze felt a pang of sadness at the thought of parting from the new friends that he'd made, he was desperately missing the sunlit warmth of his home. Even supposing he stayed here all his life (perish the thought), he would never grow accustomed to this temperature!

He stamped his freezing feet on the pale stone of the landing platform, and began to walk up and down to try to keep warm. Under his cloak he was wearing layers of clothing: a sleeveless fleece-lined sheepskin tunic, and beneath it a baggy knitted overshirt. Beneath *that* he had a thick flannel shirt, sturdy woven pants of wool, and finally, under everything else, two pairs of thick socks and long, thick, winter underwear. A knitted cap in knock-your-eyes-out purple, a contribution from his mother Zybina, was crammed over his dark curls and pulled well down to cover his ears, and a matching scarf was wound twice around his neck. Sturdy knee-length leather boots and big leather gauntlets with a secret pair of purple woollen gloves worn beneath them completed the outfit. 'And I *still* can't get warm,' he muttered to himself through chattering teeth. 'Guardians preserve us! I'm so glad I'll be going home soon.'

And yet …

How could he bear to go home a failure?

In four months his time here would be up and he would return to Tyrineld with the shame of being the only one who had not fulfilled his mission. Thanks to the sporadic messages that had reached him in this isolated place, he knew that his friend Chathak had made enormous strides in the Fire magic he was studying with the Dragonfolk, and that good old brainy Ionor had mastered the tricky magic of Water and gained the respect of the Leviathan in the process.

It was all very well for them. The Dragonfolk Fire magic was a singularly versatile branch of the arcane arts, with a multitude of uses. Water magic, too, could be used in all sorts of practical ways. But the magic of Air – when you came right down to it – was no bloody use at all. Air was an incredibly elusive substance, and Yinze was finding it impossible to find a place where his powers could connect. With other elements Air could be fine: put it together with Water magic, for instance, and you got Weather magic, unite it with Fire and you could heat a building or perform all sorts of clever tricks with light. But like Fire and Water, Earth and Air were opposites; two powers very difficult to combine.

It was too cold to stay outside any longer. Yinze had been lingering, frustrated after another difficult day, in the hope that he might catch a glimpse of Kea. The winged girl, apprentice to Crombec, the city's foremost harp maker, was the closest friend he'd made since he'd come to Aerillia, and her pretty face was just what he needed to cheer him ...

His thoughts broke off in a scream as a heavy weight cannoned into him from the side, knocking him off the platform. As he fell, arms and legs flailing in panic, the freezing air blasted into his face, snatching his breath away. Terror – pure, mindless terror – squeezed his heart in an iron fist as he plummeted. He saw his purple cap go whirling away on the wind. Sky, city, mountains cartwheeled around him – and the ground, so far away, was hurtling closer every second.

Something clamped around his ankle, cruelly wrenching his leg but, for a mercy, slowing his fall. As his arms and other leg were caught, he realised that strong hands had him, arresting his terrifying plunge. Relief swept over him, and though his strained muscles hurt like a rotten tooth, Yinze did not care. The drumming of four sets of mighty wings and the purr of wind through feathers made the sweetest music he had ever heard as he was borne upwards, back to safety, back to life.

'Here,' he heard a voice say. 'Put him well back from the edge.' The rescuers set him gently down on his own landing platform. There was a solid surface beneath him and he could no longer see the dizzying fall. Collapsing like a puppet whose strings had been cut, he threw up his recently-finished supper then curled into a shivering ball, his eyes screwed tight shut and his fingers trying to dig into the stone.

He heard someone swearing, and recognised Kea's voice, sharp with anxiety. 'Yinze, are you all right? Come on, we'll help you indoors.'

The Wizard was all for that. Though his common sense told him that the platform on which he lay had borne the weight of generations of Skyfolk, it seemed, right now, to be all too fragile a barrier between himself and the abyss. He opened his eyes to see his team of sturdy bearers; Parea, who was Kereru's brother, Dunlin, Tinamou and Chukar, all clustering around him, and Kea's anxious face looking down. The winged girl knelt beside him to help him up. He caught the scent of her, warm and spicy, like cinnamon – but before he could move, cruel laughter, harsh and mocking, made him look up at last. There, perched in a row on the edge of the roof like malign gargoyles, were Incondor, a young, black-winged aristocrat who had an evil reputation as a bully, and his friends, Milvus and Torgos.

Incondor laughed again, his handsome features marred by his usual expression of haughty contempt. 'What a shame,' he said. 'The Wizard didn't seem to like his flying lesson.'

Kea was on her feet in a flash. 'You filthy monster,' she blazed. 'You pushed him. I saw you.'

Incondor shrugged. 'I gave the earthbound slug a chance to see what it was like to fly,' he drawled. 'I knew his minions would catch him before he hit the ground – it's their function, after all.'

'You tried to kill him! This time you've gone too far. I'm reporting this to Ardea.'

A scowl darkened Incondor's face, and his eyes grew hard. 'If you know what's good for you, Kea, you'll keep your mouth shut,' he snarled. 'It would be my word against yours, and my friends will back me up. Do you think I fear Ardea? A mere teacher? A nobody? My family is closely related to Queen Pandion herself. Who is *she* going to believe? One of her own blood, or you, a common harp maker's apprentice whose grandmother was nothing but a lowly drudge?' He turned away from her with a sneer.

'Blood has nothing to do with it.' Yinze scrambled up from his prone position. 'Master Crombec says that Kea is the finest apprentice he has ever trained, and Ardea is the most respected teacher in all Aerillia.'

'Is that so?' Incondor lifted an eyebrow. 'She doesn't seem to be making any progress with you. You're about as much use at our magic as you are at flying.' With that he and his friends flew off, leaving an echo of mocking laughter.

Yinze snarled a curse and drove his fist at the wall, but Kea, with the whip-fast reflexes of her kind, knocked his arm aside before it could hit. 'Don't,' she said. 'He's not worth hurting yourself over.'

'I wish I could hurt him.' Yinze clenched his fists. 'I'd like to kill him. I'm sick and tired of him making my life a misery. If it wasn't for the Archwizard, and those accursed restrictions he set on me, I would never have let things get this far.'

Before he had come to Aerillia, Yinze had been taken aside by Cyran and subjected to a long, tiresome lecture about his responsibilities as the sole representative of the Wizards among another race of Magefolk. 'You must keep a rein on your temper, Yinze,' he'd said. 'Though I am sending you to Aerillia because I feel you are the candidate most likely to succeed, my one misgiving is your occasional tendency to be hot-headed. Make no mistake about the grave responsibility that rests on your shoulders. It has taken me a great deal of time and endless discussions, debates and arguments to persuade the other Magefolk leaders to participate in my plan for disseminating our knowledge more widely. This project is of the utmost importance, both to me personally, and, if my concerns are correct, to the entire future of the Magefolk at large. You must *not*, under any circumstances, place it in jeopardy by hasty words or inappropriate actions. I am placing all my trust in you, Yinze. Do not let me down by any impetuous, ill-advised behaviour – or I will be most seriously displeased.'

For light-hearted, sociable Yinze, as quick to laugh as to anger, such sober behaviour did not come easily. For months now, he had been forced to suppress the natural peaks and troughs of his emotions, always striving to stay on an even keel; well-mannered, polite, and circumspect in his speech. As far as Incondor and his friends were concerned, this mild behaviour had made him a very obvious target. During most of his stay in Aerillia, Yinze had been the butt of endless bullying and nasty pranks – and every time he'd failed to defend himself, Incondor had pushed the persecution to a more vicious level, culminating in tonight's potentially deadly attack.

Matters were rapidly reaching the point where Yinze would be forced to defend himself, and then what would happen? It was true that Incondor was closely related to Queen Pandion – his grandfather was the brother of her father. She was almost certain to take his word over that of an outsider and a newcomer. What if she sent him home in disgrace? What would Cyran say if Yinze ruined this scheme that was so dear to his heart?

'Yinze?' Kea's voice broke into his circling thoughts. 'Are you all right?' She looked so concerned that the Wizard forced himself to smile.

'Of course I am. Don't worry – it would take more than that arrogant pig to bother me.'

She gave him that odd, wry little smile of hers that told him she saw right through him. 'You need to work on that lying, my friend, if you mean to make a habit of it.' She clenched her fists in frustration. 'We should report the brute. Surely Ardea could make Queen Pandion believe us.' She shuddered. 'Thank all Creation Parea and your other bearers were there.'

'Yes.' Yinze smiled at the bearers, who still stood in a protective group nearby. 'Had it not been for you, I hate to think what might have happened.'

'I'm pretty sure Incondor and his cronies would have caught you before you hit the ground,' Parea said. 'Not even a relative of Queen Pandion would dare go so far as the killing of a foreign Mage.'

'Probably not,' Yinze agreed, glad that Parea had given him an excuse to make light of the situation. The last thing he wanted was for Kea to go tattling to Ardea about the incident. 'Even Incondor would stop short of actual murder, wouldn't he? Being related to the Queen wouldn't help him if he was implicated in the death of a visiting delegate sent by the Archwizard himself. Nonetheless, I'm more grateful to all of you than I can say.'

Parea grinned. 'All in a day's work. Besides, my sister would never have forgiven me if I'd let you fall.' He glanced up at the darkening sky, and stretched out his wings. 'Well, if you don't need us any more Yinze, we'll be off for the night.'

'Believe me, I don't feel like going anywhere right now – apart from bed. Thank you, Parea. Thank you, Dunlin, Tinamou and Chukar. I'll see you in the morning.'

When the bearers had gone, Kea tucked an arm through his. 'It's dreadfully cold tonight, and I'm sure you'll be feeling it far more than I do. Shall we go inside, and I'll make you a hot drink?' Despite the delicacy of her fine-boned features, she looked beautiful and bold, her hair blowing back in the strengthening wind, wearing her extraordinary colours like a banner that said: 'Here I am, world! Deal with me on my terms, or not at all.' It had become the fashion among some of the younger generation to augment the traditional shades of their elders, the browns, whites, blacks, greys and golds, and use magic to tint their hair and wings in a rainbow of hues. Most were content with flashes of brilliance, with streaks and splashes of colour, but Kea had gone all the way, changing her hair and the backs of her wings into a medley of greens ranging from silvery sage to the vivid emerald of new leaves. The inner surface of her wings was the glowing, red-gold of fire, so that when she opened them to fly, she looked as if she was bursting into flame. Though the traditionalists in Aerillia's society regarded her with frowning, purse-lipped dismay, her master Crombec simply smiled, and encouraged her to channel her creativity into the harps she made.

She was delightful to look at, and always good company, but Yinze shook his head. 'Not tonight thanks, Kea. I really am very tired.' Though he was very fond of her, and grateful that she had cared enough about him to stand up to the bullies, he just wanted to be alone. Today Incondor had heaped further humiliation on him, in addition to that which he already felt over his continued inability to perform even the simplest Air magic. He just wanted to be left to lick his wounds in peace.

'All right,' the winged girl replied, but there was a forced edge of cheerfulness in her voice, and he knew that he had hurt her.

Cursing his own clumsiness, Yinze took her hands. 'I'm sorry, Kea. There's no one I'd rather be with than you. But tonight I just need to be alone with my thoughts. I'm no fit company for anyone just now. All my attempts at your magic have been such a failure, and I hate myself for being so useless.' He couldn't believe he had finally said it out loud. She was the only person in Aerillia to whom he could confess such a thing.

'I think you underestimate yourself.' Kea kissed him lightly on the cheek. 'Don't worry, Yinze. You'll work it out. I have every confidence in you.' With that she flew off to her own quarters, leaving him alone with the starlight blazing down through the frosty air.

The Wizard watched her launch herself across the void, then turned and went indoors, closing his door against the chill, for dark clouds had smothered the glowing western sky, and there was a smell of snow in the air. Perhaps because he had been thinking so longingly of home his chambers, now so familiar, looked as strange as they had when he had first come here. The slightly curving walls with their heavy, woollen hangings to help conserve the heat and the tall, wide doorways that were designed to accommodate the folded wings of the usual inhabitants seemed alien to him, and he felt rootless and lost, and very far from home. The spindly furnishings were, for the most part, crafted of exquisite wrought iron, which was far easier than wood to obtain in these mineral-rich mountains, so high above the treeline. They were sparse and close to the wall, allowing plenty of turning space in the centre of the chamber for the sweeping Skyfolk wings. Also because of the wings, the braziers that heated the rooms were tucked safely away in the corners, and there was little clutter that could be knocked over or down. Any loose items were stored away in deep wall niches concealed behind the hangings. The chairs were backless stools, with cushioned seats of padded leather or wool, on which the natives of Aerillia could perch for hours with every appearance of comfort – unlike Yinze, who had been forced to purchase some of the rare, expensive wood and make a chair of his own, with arms and a back to support his aching spine.

Yinze lit the lamps, added more charcoal to the brazier that heated the room, and sat as close to it as he dared until the shivering had subsided a little, and he could shed his outer layers of clothing. Suddenly he regretted sending Kea away, and almost went after her, but he didn't want to risk running into Incondor and his cronies again. If he were to encounter them now, he might just forget Cyran's restrictions, he thought grimly. How immensely satisfying it would be to pulverise those too-handsome features beyond all recognition. By pushing him off the ledge, the bullies had given him a real scare. His face burned with humiliation as he remembered how he had screamed as he fell, and disgraced himself by throwing up after he was rescued. He must have looked like a pathetic fool. But worse than Incondor's actions had been his words about the Wizard's failure to master Air magic, which had lodged in Yinze's mind like a poisoned dagger.

There was no defence against the truth.

Right now, what he really wanted was a glass of wine – or something stronger. But brewed, distilled and fermented drinks were forbidden, and for the most part unwanted, among the Skyfolk. Flying required skill, precision and razor-sharp reflexes, because the slightest misjudgement could mean death. There was no place for fuddled wits in the sky.

In every society, however, there were always rebels. Yinze had not been in Aerillia for very long when he first heard the rumours that there was covert use of the prohibited drug by some of the younger generation of the Skyfolk, and it had not been long before he discovered the truth of them for himself. Incondor, who had initially been very friendly and welcoming, had approached him covertly and asked him if, on his return to Tyrineld, he would be willing to provide a smuggled supply of wine and spirits. 'We have many things of value here in these mountains,' the young aristocrat had urged. 'Jewels, gold, furs ... I could make you very wealthy.'

Yinze, with Cyran's warnings ringing through his mind, had refused to become involved in such a scheme, and Incondor's animosity had originated from that rebuttal. From that day onwards the bullying had begun, and it had continued, and escalated, ever since.

So his goblet of wine was out of the question, but the Wizard suspected that it was just as well. He felt a gnawing in his stomach; partly strain and anxiety, but partly hunger. The meal he had eaten earlier with Ardea's other students was gone. It was a long time until breakfast, and he craved the comfort of something warm in his belly. He went to the door that led into the small kitchen and his housekeeper's quarters, and called, 'Kereru, are you there?'

'And where else would I be on a cold night like this, with a blizzard in the offing?'

She was plump for one of the Winged folk, and her grey hair and wings had a sheen of iridescence in the lamplight. Her kindly smile was, as always, a balm for his wounded feelings. 'Kereru, I—'

'I have some soup ready,' she interrupted. 'It'll be just what you need – considering.'

'You saw?'

'Out of the window.' She frowned. 'You mark my words, one of these days that boy is going to come to a bad end.'

'The sooner the better, if you ask me,' Yinze said ruefully. 'Oh,' he suddenly remembered. 'I'm sorry, Kereru, I never cleared up the mess I made on the platform.'

'Don't you worry about that now. The storm will scour it all away.' She smiled at him. 'Aerillia housekeeping at its best – oh, and while I remember, Parea found your woollen hat for you. I know how attached you are to it.'

She took the damp purple cap from her pocket and laid it on the table, then went off to fetch his soup, reappearing moments later bearing a tray loaded with a steaming bowl, a plate of bread and the delicious sheep-milk cheese made by the Skyfolk, and a pot of fragrant liafa, a bitter, stimulating drink made from berries, that was the Aerillian equivalent of taillin.

Not for the first time, Yinze thanked providence that Kereru had been allotted to him. She always had a way of making him feel better. He thanked her with a smile. 'I think I'll have to take you back with me to Tyrineld,' he told her.

The smile dropped from Kereru's face. 'Just to make me a servant in a different place? And what possible good would that do me? No, wait – I forgot. It wasn't me you were thinking of, was it?'

Shamefaced, Yinze looked at her, as if seeing her for the first time. 'Kereru, I'm sorry. I'm dismayed that I never thought … I've been too busy adapting here and settling in, too caught up with my own problems to think much about the Forsaken. Coming as an outsider to Aerillia, I just accepted the way things were.' He reached over and took her work-roughened hand. 'Please, Kereru – will you stay and have some liafa with me? Tell me how it is that some of the Skyfolk are forced to labour so hard for others?'

Gently but firmly, Kereru removed her hand from his. 'I don't have to sit down. I can tell you in two minutes. About six hundred years ago, there were no Forsaken – until a group of Skyfolk got religion. One of them claimed to have had visions which told him that one day there would come a Dark God who would raise the Children of the Skies to a position of dominion over all the other Magefolk, and that his coming would change the world for ever.' She shrugged. 'You can see, can't you, why that would seem a very attractive proposition to a lot of folk? The prophet – Malkoha, his name was – soon rose to a position of eminence. People flocked to him, and his followers overthrew the King of that time, and built their dark temple right on the pinnacle, where the palace stands now.'

Pulling out a chair, Kereru sat down after all, as if barely aware of what she was doing. 'And that was where Malkoha made his mistake. He got carried away with his success, I suppose, and he must have been a twisted soul. Out of the blue, he declared that the Dark God required human sacrifices, and before long, that temple of his was swimming in blood. That certainly had a way of bringing most folk to their senses,' she added wryly. 'The old king and his followers suddenly found themselves very popular again. The people of Aerillia fought Malkoha's followers, and dreadful battles raged across the skies. Eventually, the prophet was defeated and executed – though to the very last, he insisted that the Dark God would strike his enemies down and restore him to eminence.'

Again, there was that wry expression. 'His miracle didn't happen of course. He was beheaded on the steps of his own temple, and his body thrown to the great cats who inhabit the Shattered Peak to the north. But what became of his faithful followers? Well might you ask. They, and all their descendants, were sentenced to an eternity of labour for the good of the other Skyfolk, to expiate their crimes, and their first task was to tear down Malkoha's temple. Henceforth, and ever after, they were to be known as the Forsaken. Each child born to them was taken by so-called healers, powerful telepaths who could alter those infantile minds from within, blocking their magic for ever.'

'But that's so unfair,' Yinze protested. 'Why do they still allow it?'

'Mostly, I think, because it's convenient. No society can function without people to do the drudge work. The only way for one of us to escape our lot is to wed with someone who is not of the Forsaken – though such cases happen only rarely, and do not meet with approval in our society. Then our children will become normal members of the Skyfolk, with all their magic, but we will not. That is what happened to your Kea's forebears – her grandmother was one of the Forsaken, noted for her beauty, who had the good fortune to wed with a young artisan. But though we will escape servitude in such a joining, and our children will have their powers, we will not. They have gone for ever.'

When Kereru had gone, Yinze found he had little appetite for his cooling soup. For the thousandth time, he considered the ways in which the Winged Folk used their Air magic. On a large scale, they could herd clouds for considerable distances, to bring rain for their crops, or give dry and sunny weather for their harvest; and on a small, domestic level, they could send warm air from around their braziers wherever they wished inside their dwellings. They could make large, fast changes in air pressure to blast tunnels in the mountains so that their human slaves could mine metals and jewels. They could use their magic to hunt, giving an extra impetus to arrows or spears, or simply knocking down earthbound game with very localised, high-pressure waves, or creating fast-moving swirls of air to trap their winged prey.

Unlike Earth magic, the powers of Air held no particular healing applications, but the Skyfolk could keep the lungs of a very sick or injured individual working, and change the composition of the air so that the patient could breathe more easily. On the other side of the scale, air could be used in battle, either using powerful concussive blasts to take out a large number of enemies at once, or using high-pressure jabs of air to knock a foe out of the sky. Indeed, this was a favourite form of entertainment, with hotly contested tournaments taking place in the High Arena.

Which was interesting, but none of it was getting Yinze any closer to his goal. In all his life, he had never felt so beaten down. He, who had always succeeded in his aims, was staring failure squarely in the face. Outside, the stars had vanished and it had started to snow. He could hear the wind picking up, whistling and whining around the walls of his dwelling. It had a nasty, sneering sound, as though it was mocking his failure to master it. It occurred to him that sound, carried as it was on the air, had the effect of making the air manifest, giving it a presence and almost a personality ... For an instant the wisp of an idea touched his thoughts, and he tried to follow it through before it slipped away.

In how many ways did air actually make its presence known? He could feel it against his skin as he shivered in the draught that blew under the door; he could see it interact with physical objects, such as driving the snow past his window, or blowing Kea's hair out behind her like a banner ...

Forget about Kea.

It really was alarming how fond of her Yinze had become; how attractive he was finding her nowadays. She's not even the same species as you, he told himself firmly. Yet the physical similarities between all races of humanoid form – Wizards, Winged Folk, Phaerie and even the despised sub-race of mortals – were sufficiently pronounced to permit sexual congress, and sometimes actual cross-breeding ...

Don't even think about it!

Yinze rubbed his hands over his face, as if to scrub away such thoughts. He'd been here too long, that was the problem. He was going native. If punching Incondor's smug face would cause trouble, he hardly dared imagine what a scandal there would be if he slept with the talented apprentice of the foremost harp maker in Aerillia. The Wizard let out a low whistle of dismay at the thought of what Cyran would say, and – there it was again! That connection between air and sound. Experimentally, Yinze repeated the whistle, glad of a chance to distract himself from Kea's dangerous charms. Again, that nebulous hint of an idea touched the edges of his thoughts, then flitted away like a butterfly – which put the image of wings into his head.

Wings? Was that how he could make the connection between the tangible and intangible? Wings needed the air to function, yet they, in turn, acted upon the air and moved it, and as they did there was sound … Yinze cursed. The inspiration, so close, had slid beyond his grasp once more. He sighed with frustration, and noticed the soft whisper of sound it made. Sound? Why did his thoughts keep circling back to sound?

And Kea. He just couldn't keep her out of his head. With another sigh, Yinze gave up the unequal struggle. No wonder he was a failure. It seemed that he couldn't concentrate on the magical conundrum before him for two minutes together. For all the progress he was making without her, he might as well have let the winged girl stay tonight. Perhaps talking through his frustrations with her might have helped to clear his mind. And failing all else, she could have played for him.

He pictured her sitting in the lamplight, her wings like a cloak of shadows behind her, her long hair falling forward over her shoulder, that endearing little frown of concentration on her face as her nimble fingers moved effortlessly over the beautifully crafted instrument of her own making, coaxing a waterfall of delicate, evocative sound from the shining strings …

And suddenly the answer was staring him in the face. Music. Or more precisely, a musical instrument. Wood and metal – substances of the Earth element which he could imbue with his own powers. The music he produced with them would provide his tangible link to the magic of Air.

Excitement drove Yinze to his feet, and he began to pace. Could it work? Would it? Such a technique was unheard of among his own people, and the Skyfolk had never needed aids to manipulate their magic. Yet it might just give him the crucial link he had been needing so badly. Of course he'd have to learn a lot about harp making really fast, but didn't he have the best possible person in the world to help him with that?

With a whoop of joy, Yinze summoned his net bearers and ran to wrap up in his outdoor clothes once more. In less than ten minutes, plastered from head to foot with snow but grinning like a maniac, he was knocking on Kea's door. She opened it, wrapped in her sleeping robe, blinking sleepy eyes against the wind-driven snowflakes. 'Yinze! Do you know how late it is?'

Ignoring her protests he took her in his arms and danced her around the landing platform in a dizzy whirl. 'I've got it!' He covered her startled face in kisses. 'At last I have the answer.'

2
~

WINDSINGER

'What do you think?' Uncharacteristically nervous, Yinze held the harp out to his mentor. Ardea, tall and bony, her hair a shock of white, looked down her long, thin nose at his creation, turning it from side to side to examine it more closely. The instrument glowed with the warm hues of polished wood in the bright sunshine of early summer that was pouring through the window. Looking at it, Yinze felt a surge of pride. These last few months of intense work, which had kept him so busy through the bleak winter and the promise-filled days of spring, had all been worthwhile. It was a lap harp, and beautifully wrought; light enough to be played on the move. Yinze of the dextrous, clever hands had carved the frame with all manner of birds, from the mighty eagle down to the tiniest wren. Wrapped about with spells, the warm gleam of its wood overlaid with the silver-blue shimmer of magic, it thrummed with power.

Ardea raised her eyebrows as she continued her scrutiny and, though she was not one to throw compliments about lightly, Yinze could see that she was impressed. She stroked long, knob-knuckled fingers across the silver cascade of strings, producing a shower of pure and perfect notes, and he caught his breath as a wave of energy rippled across the room. The scrolls shifted and rustled in their racks, a cup and a quill went skittering across the surface of the table, and the weighty metal furniture shifted slightly across the floor, resounding with a deep, bell-like tone.

'Hmmm ...' Ardea's dark, gimlet eyes flicked up towards the Wizard. 'This is good work, and I can see how much thought and care you've put into it. You must have had help – or did the Wizards train you in the art of harp making?'

'I almost wish they had,' Yinze admitted, 'for I discovered a fascination with the craft. But no, I had no training in such work as this.
Crombec taught me the basics, but without his considerable aid, I
would have lacked the skill to complete such a project. And—' He
felt his face growing warm. 'Without Kea's help I would never have
managed.'

His teacher raised a feathery eyebrow, and the Wizard caught the
shadow of a smile. 'I dare say,' Ardea said. 'The question is – does
your harp work for you? Does it do what you intended?'

Relief washed over Yinze. He knew how sceptical his mentor had
been about this project. Now it seemed that she was prepared to give
him a chance to prove himself. 'Indeed it does, Master Ardea,' he
said eagerly. 'In my natural powers of Earth magic we deal with such
concrete factors all the time, and I had begun to wonder if I would
ever be able to grasp – literally as well as figuratively – the more abstract energies of Air. But this harp allows me to use a solid object to
make the air vibrate, forming sounds and giving me a bridge between
Earth and Air, between the seen and the unseen. I'm still working
out all of the ramifications, but I already know that it's finally giving
me the control I've been lacking.'

'Demonstrate.' Ardea thrust the harp back into his hands.

Almost limp with relief, for he had not been sure that his mentor
would accept what must seem to her like a radical and unnecessary
scheme, Yinze took back his creation and, because he preferred to
play standing rather than sitting, looped its strap around his right
shoulder and under his left arm to hold the instrument in playing
position in front of him, so that the soundboard rested on his chest.
The power he had poured into it during its making vibrated through
his arms and into his body.

He had thought long and hard about what would make a good,
dramatic demonstration of his control, and the potential of the harp.
Taking a deep breath, he sharpened his focus on the instrument,
feeling the smooth curve of the wood beneath his hands. Then he
touched the strings, the sleek pressure of the tensioned strands cool
against his fingertips, and called forth a glissade of silvery notes.
Mingling his newly learned Air magic with his native powers of
Earth, and using the music to form a conduit between both, he made
the notes visible: a drifting rain of many-hued, crystalline flowers that
opened in the vault of the ceiling and floated gently down through
the air, their glittering petals opening as they fell. They touched

the ground lightly and lay there for a moment, glistening like frost, before vanishing in a waft of glorious perfume.

Ardea applauded. 'Very pretty,' she said drily, 'but can it do anything *useful*?'

What use is any of this blasted Air magic? Yinze thought sourly, but was careful to hide the thought too deep for her to find. Instead he smiled easily. 'Of course,' he said. He began to play again, making the tempo more lively and forceful this time. Jaw rigid with concentration, he moulded the music, not making it visible, as he had done in his previous demonstration, but using it as a focus for the Air magic. He let the power coil around him and tightened it until it formed a network around his body, then he let it spiral upwards, lifting him gently off the ground and raising him up towards the ceiling.

Yinze fought down the instinctive clutch of fear in his stomach and kept his attention fast upon the music, looking down at the open-mouthed Ardea with what he hoped was a casual smile. 'See? With my harp, even a wingless Wizard can fly.'

His moment of triumph was spoiled by a perilous wobble in the air which jolted his teacher out of her trance. 'Yinze! Get down here at *once*.'

The Wizard descended, somewhat faster than he had intended, and hit the ground with a jolt.

'Do you have any idea how dangerous that was?' Ardea blazed. 'Air magic is a tricky business, even for an expert. What if you had lost control of the magic and it had smashed you into the ceiling? Or if you had drifted out of the door and then fallen to your death? Don't ever do this again, do you hear me? And don't tell anyone what you did today.'

'But I—'

His teacher pierced him with her gaze. 'How many people know about this, Yinze?'

The Wizard looked at his feet. 'Only Kea,' he muttered.

'Well, thank Providence for that.'

She thought for a moment. 'Well, maybe you could do it just once more,' she said. 'I'll arrange a demonstration for Queen Pandion and her Council, as soon as possible.'

Yinze went cold all over, and his palms were suddenly clammy on the smooth, carved wood of his harp. 'But—'

'You aren't ready?' There was a twinkle in Ardea's eye. 'Of course you are – as ready as you'll ever be. You can go on developing your skills, of course, but all the Queen needs to know is that you've mastered and understood the basics of our powers. Then she might finally be persuaded that there's some point in sending a representative to the other Magefolk, and stop procrastinating. She never really believed it was possible, you know, that our magic could cross the boundary of race like this.' Her grin transformed her face into an expression of youthful mischief. 'I can't wait to see her face. I've been telling her for months that you have it in you.'

Yinze, consumed with nerves at the thought of having to demonstrate his newly mastered powers before the Queen, desperately hoped that there would be some form of delay. Maybe Pandion would be too busy to witness the antics of her visitor, and he would gain a reprieve in which to keep practising with his harp, which he had rather fancifully named Windsinger. He was out of luck, however. Before he knew what was happening, his demonstration was scheduled for the following day, in the High Arena, before the Queen, her family, and various counsellors.

The rest of the day passed in a blur of preparations, working with Kea, Crombec and Ardea in the High Arena to prepare and rehearse his demonstration for the following day. They left him in his quarters at sunset, telling him to rest and get a good night's sleep – as if *that* was ever going to happen. After a night spent staring wide-eyed into the darkness, imagining an endless succession of things that could go wrong, the Wizard picked at his breakfast and went out, on a bright morning with a brisk wind, to meet his fate.

The High Arena was a natural volcanic crater in the neighbouring mountain to Aerillia Peak. It was a breathtaking sight, with its soaring, craggy walls that provided so many natural perches for the Skyfolk spectators, and its vast stretch of smoothly polished, almost level floor, from which all debris and dust had been removed. It was normally used for tournaments, in which individuals or teams tried to knock one another out of the sky, or vied in contests of skill such as fast-paced races on the wing to pick up the most strips of cloth attached to high poles, or hit the most targets with spears while on the move. They also played a popular game called Yttril, in which teams of three per side competed over a light wooden ring which was skimmed through the air from player to player and, to score a point, was looped over a tall post with a short crosspiece a little way down, which stopped the hoop from falling all the way to the ground.

Today the arena was empty of spectators, save for Queen Pandion, various members of her family and the Royal Council, Yinze's teacher Ardea, and the harp maker Crombec, with his apprentice Kea. The Wizard's net bearers dropped him off in front of the Royal Balcony, and he felt very small against the immensity of his surroundings. He trembled as he slung the harp into position on its strap. His hands were clenched and slippery on the sleek carved wood, and he knew he had to speak before nervousness paralysed his voice completely. He looked up at Kea, sitting above him in the Royal Balcony, and saw pride and encouragement in her eyes. Steadied and bolstered by her presence, Yinze took a deep breath, and began to introduce the wondrous device he had created.

He told them, honestly, of his difficulties in reconciling his natural powers with their own, and how he had almost succumbed to despair. He spoke of the dark night when he had almost given up hope, and of the sudden inspiration that had come to him in the howling storm. He gave a brief account of the actual making of the harp and all the help that Crombec and Kea had given him, and spoke in more detail of the way he had imbued it with his magic, so that it could form a bridge between the powers of Earth and those of Air. Then he ran out of words, and could defer the inevitable no longer. It was time for him to finally prove that he had learned what he had come here to learn. Again he looked up at Kea, and was buoyed by the shining confidence in her face.

'Your Majesty,' he said, 'and all of my other kind winged hosts in this beautiful mountain city ...'

'Get on with it,' called a cold, contemptuous voice from the back of Queen Pandion's family group. The Wizard cursed under his breath, suddenly more nervous than ever. He had not realised that Incondor would be there. Then anger won out. He was damned if he would let that slimy bully ruin the culmination of all his months of hard work and learning. If Incondor wanted a demonstration then that, by all Creation, was what he would get.

'First,' he said coldly, 'I will demonstrate that I can use Air magic as a weapon.' He began to play – not the tune he had intended to use, but a strident, martial song. Using the music to focus the magic, he formed a blunt spear of air, and hurled it at his tormenter. With a squawk, Incondor tumbled from his seat in a flurry of flapping wings and flying feathers.

There was a split second's startled silence, then the spectators burst into gales of laughter. All but one. During the storm of applause that followed, Incondor picked himself up and resumed his perch. His face was bone-white with rage and, if Yinze had been looking, he might have quailed at the sight of such naked fury. But the Wizard was enjoying himself now. He did his trick with the scented blossoms, showering them around the startled and delighted watchers, then he moved smoothly into the rest of his demonstration.

The previous day, Kea had tied long, silken pennants on the Yttril posts around the arena, so that they streamed out in the brisk wind. The Wizard used his Air magic to make them change direction, so that they blew out the other way – first singly, one by one, then all together. Kea threw Yttril hoops from her balcony, and he caught them up in his newfound powers, and looped them neatly over the posts. Progressing to more difficult feats, the Wizard used compressed air to break a small boulder into pieces, cleaving it neatly in half with great precision then shattering it into fragments. To follow, he herded clouds to produce a small, localised shower of rain within the confines of the arena.

By this time, Yinze was trembling with fatigue, and his fingers were stiff and aching from having played so long without respite. Though he had practised all these individual spells before, he had never performed them in quick succession. Using any form of magic was tiring to a certain extent, but the powers of Air did not come naturally to him, and required far greater effort than usual. Most of the spectators had applauded his efforts, and if only the Queen had done the same he might have been buoyed and encouraged, but Queen Pandion had watched his demonstration in stony and, he felt, judgemental silence, greatly increasing the tension and pressure of the occasion.

The Wizard, however, had one last trick up his sleeve, to *make* her sit up and take notice. What followed would be the finale and climax of the entire performance – the most difficult and dangerous spell of all. As he had done in Ardea's chambers, he sent the music, and the power, coiling around him, to propel him upwards through the air.

His feet left the ground, and Yinze again felt his stomach clench. Out in the open air, on top of a mountain, he became aware of the dangers of this spell as he never had when performing it in a smaller, enclosed environment. The wind grew stronger as he rose, pushing him off course, and he had to control his rate of ascent very carefully, so as not to get above the level of the crater's encircling walls. Beyond their shelter the wind would be far too strong for him, blowing him off course and out of control, to be dashed to his death against the rocks.

Though he had mastered simple levitation and gentle descent, he had not yet had time to work out how to manoeuvre effectively in the horizontal plane. To his horror, Yinze felt himself beginning to drift, moving away from the Royal Balcony and picking up speed. This had never happened before! Though he tried with all the strength of his will, he could not push himself back on course and, what was worse, he couldn't stop rising at an increasing speed. Fighting panic, the Wizard kept on playing the harp. If he lost his hold on the spell, he would fall straight to the rocky floor of the arena, which now seemed a very long way away.

Yinze knew he should have better control than this. Once again he tried to halt his speeding rate of ascent, and reverse it to bring himself down quickly, but nothing happened. Briefly he considered calling for help, but the thought of the cringing humiliation, should he have to be rescued, flicked through his mind, at war with the terror. In another moment, the fear had won out. He looked down to the Royal Balcony, intending to shout to Kea and Ardea, but instead his eyes locked on those of Incondor whose stare burned with concentration – and triumph.

Not the wind then! This disaster was neither the harp's fault nor his own. It was deliberate, malicious sabotage.

The Wizard was consumed by incandescent fury. Fixing all his concentration on his enemy's smug, sneering features, he threw his total being, all his strength, and all the powers of both Air and Earth, into a vision of himself planting his fist square into that hated face. Beneath his fingers the harp shrilled an angry, discordant tune, almost playing itself as the magic, fuelled by his anger, grew stronger.

The smugness dropped from the winged man's face as his spell was shattered against the combined powers of Yinze and the harp. Playing faster, the Wizard shot down towards him like a vengeful comet – but before he could reach the Royal Balcony, Incondor was gone.

Yinze came to a shuddering halt only inches in front of Queen Pandion, barely managing to stop in time. Ardea's face was white with anger – clearly she thought that the entire episode had been nothing more than her pupil showing off – but Kea was pale with fear. Everyone else, however, including the Queen, were on their feet, applauding him and calling out their praise and appreciation.

Pandion, normally so stern of face, was actually smiling. She held up a hand for silence. 'An interesting display, young Wizard,' she said drily. 'And now, having almost frightened the lives out of some of my counsellors, do you feel that you have accomplished what Archwizard Cyran sent you here to do?'

Yinze bowed. 'The powers of Air are as complex as they are fascinating, Your Majesty, and it would take many years to study all their possibilities; but to the best of my ability, I feel that I have at least mastered the basic concepts.'

'I agree with you. You may return to Cyran and tell him he was right. It would appear that the magical disciplines can cross species – at least, after a fashion. But this is not the time for such matters. Let us all return to the palace now, and there you may rest, for I can see that the use of such unfamiliar power has taken its toll on you. When the sun goes down we will feast, and celebrate your triumph in a proper style.'

Yinze had never been particularly keen on being transported in a net, like a piece of inanimate cargo. It was inconvenient and embarrassing, in a land where everyone else soared gracefully through the air without a thought, not to mention uncomfortable, cold, nauseating and desperately scary. But today he was incredibly grateful for his sturdy bearers, and got into their sling without a murmur of complaint, letting himself sink down to the ground on top of the slack meshes before his knees gave way completely.

In the labyrinthine palace, Yinze was given a set of warm and comfortable chambers in which to rest. Aching and bleary from lack of sustenance and sleep, his thoughts were fixed on food and bed, but he was out of luck. Scarcely had the respectful servitor closed the door behind him, leaving the Wizard alone, when it banged open again and there were Ardea and Crombec, with Kea behind them, and judging from their stormy expressions, the next few minutes were about to be unpleasant. They all spoke at once.

'Just what did you think you were playing at out there?' Ardea demanded. 'How dare you act in a stupid, thoughtless—'

'It wasn't me.'

'Dangerous, irresponsible—' Crombec's voice was cold.

'It wasn't me.'

'Did you make a mistake?' Kea demanded. 'Was it the harp?'

'IT WASN'T ME!'

Finally they all shut up, and Yinze spoke into the shocked silence that followed. 'It was Incondor.'

23

Bedlam broke out again. And in the end, Yinze was forced to tell them everything.

Queen Pandion's feast took place in the dazzling great hall with its lofty arched ceiling, and jewelled hangings of gold and silver thread on the walls. Sitting at the Queen's right hand, Yinze basked in the compliments that were showered upon him. Though, according to the Skyfolk laws, there was no strong drink served at the feast, Yinze felt drunk on all the attention. Due to the furore that afternoon with Kea and his mentors he had lost his chance of a meal, but now, though he finally could, and did, eat like a famished wolf, he couldn't help but notice that Kea and Ardea, the two he loved best in all Aerillia, only picked at their food. The winged girl was pale and her eyes were haunted, and he knew she couldn't help imagining the horrible death he might so easily have met that day. His teacher, her face taut and unsmiling, had the look of one who had been forced to lock up her anger until later. Incondor had spoiled for them this hour of triumph, which Yinze could never have achieved without their help. The bully kept adding to what he owed.

Incondor was conspicuous by his absence, and to the Wizard that crowned the entire evening. He looked around at the jewelled surroundings glittering in the lamplight, the sumptuous feast and the bright, smiling faces, all there for him. He heard all the plaudits that came from every side, and basked in his position of honour at Queen Pandion's right hand. Suddenly, in a moment of absolute clarity, he remembered the day Incondor had pushed him off the landing platform and remembered what his winged foe had said when Kea had threatened to tell Ardea.

'If you know what's good for you, Kea, you'll keep your mouth shut. It would be my word against yours, and my friends will back me up. Do you think I fear Ardea? A mere teacher? A nobody? My family is closely related to Queen Pandion herself. Who is she going to believe? One of her own blood, or you, a common harp maker's apprentice whose grandmother was nothing but a lowly drudge?'

Well, things had certainly changed since then. Who would the Queen believe now? Some skulking braggart, or the hero of the hour? The next time their paths crossed, Incondor had better watch out.

*

24

After the feast was finally over, Ardea and Crombec sat up for most of the night in the harp maker's cluttered quarters, discussing what Yinze had told them, and sharing their dismay at the implications of Incondor's cowardly attack in the arena. 'That youth always has been wild,' Crombec said, 'but this time he has gone too far.' Small and spry, his grey hair clipped short, the harp maker lacked his customary twinkle of good humour, and looked worried and tired. 'Wine and spirits are forbidden here for a whole number of good reasons. This is more than mere youthful rebellion, Ardea. This is dangerous.'

'And this feud with my pupil is completely out of hand.' Ardea took a sip of her cold liafa, neglected while they talked, and set it down with a grimace. 'I know Yinze doesn't want us to tell Queen Pandion, and I can understand why, as an emissary sent by the Archwizard himself, he doesn't want to become embroiled in any trouble. But we must do something, now that we know.'

She sighed, and rubbed her tired eyes. 'The blame has got to lie with me, Crombec. I should have been more vigilant. Surely I should have noticed that something was seriously amiss. What that poor boy must have been going through, these last few months! I can't believe he could have managed to stay so close-mouthed about his problems all this time, choosing to suffer in silence instead of coming to us for help. Why, without Kea's intercession, I don't think we would have dragged it out of him yet.'

Crombec's gloomy expression softened for a moment at the mention of his favourite pupil. 'That girl is the joy of my old age. She might look a little strange, but beneath that colourful exterior she has plenty of common sense.'

'Sadly, Crombec, this problem is far beyond the scope of plain common sense. This time Incondor has gone too far. He could have killed Yinze today. Even now we could have been trying to draft a message to Cyran to tell him of the tragedy—' She broke off with a shudder.

'Don't think of that.' Crombec laid a comforting hand over hers. 'It didn't happen, and instead, somehow, that young idiot pupil of ours came out looking like a hero. It's what will happen now that concerns me, however. Incondor's plan backfired on him today, and if things have already deteriorated so far between the two of them, I can only imagine his chagrin and anger tonight. I fear that the problem will only escalate from here.'

'You're right.' Ardea rubbed a tired hand over her face. 'Goodness knows I'm going to miss that boy when he leaves, but I think we should persuade the Queen to send him home as soon as possible. It may avert a tragedy.'

'Come along, then.' Crombec got to his feet. 'We still have an hour or two before the sun rises, so let's get some rest. We'll see Queen Pandion in the morning and tell her everything.'

Ardea went to the door and paused, with one hand poised on the latch. She looked back over her shoulder. 'She's not going to like it.'

She was right about that. Ardea and Crombec were long-lived and well-respected members of the Aerillian community. They had known the Queen for all her life, and had always been on very friendly terms with her. Nonetheless, they found themselves quailing at the look on her face when they told her of Incondor's misdemeanours, and his cowardly attacks on Yinze that had put the Wizard in such danger.

'Are you absolutely certain this is true?' she demanded.

Though they were usually friends, Ardea sensed that this was no time to be friendly. She decided it was best to adhere to strict formality, and sat up a little straighter on her chair. 'Were we not absolutely certain, we would never have come to you with this, Your Majesty. Yinze did not willingly volunteer this information to us. We only extracted the truth from him with the greatest of difficulty, after what happened yesterday in the arena. He is keenly – almost too keenly – aware of his responsibilities as a representative of his people, and the last thing he wants is any trouble or stigma to be attached to the Wizardfolk over his personal troubles. Kea corroborated his story, as did his housekeeper Kereru, who witnessed a previous attack by Incondor and his friends.'

Pandion's mouth was a grim line. 'I cannot thank you for bringing this news to me. Incondor's behaviour brings shame on us all.' She rose, and walked to the window, her wings, dark brown with each feather exquisitely edged with a narrow band of white, sweeping out behind her. Ardea and Crombec waited in silence while she stared out at the wild mountain landscape.

'Rightly or wrongly, I cannot bring disgrace upon my family by making Incondor's aberrations public.' Pandion kept her golden eyes firmly fixed on the view outside, almost as if she was reluctant to face them.

When Ardea hesitated in her reply, Crombec stepped in with the words she'd been reluctant to say. 'Your Majesty, it is our opinion that if this situation is allowed to continue it will end in tragedy. I appreciate how hard it is to discover that one of your own family is acting so rashly, but can you truly afford to let that prevent you from taking action?'

Pandion turned back to face them. 'You are right, of course,' she said with a sigh. 'Yinze must be protected at all costs.' Her wings rustled as she straightened her shoulders. 'In your opinion, Ardea, has he learned what he came here to learn?'

A pang of sadness struck deep into Ardea's heart. 'Yes indeed, Your Majesty. He has acquitted himself diligently and well and I am proud to call him my pupil.'

'Very well then.' Pandion's voice was clipped and decisive. 'Cyran has been pressing all the Archmages to send his delegates home, for since the death of Hellorin he is becoming increasingly concerned about the threat of the Phaerie on his doorstep. I was reluctant to part with Yinze before he mastered our magic, but now that he has done so, he must go home as soon as possible, and in all honour. Also, I will accede to Cyran's wishes and send one of our own people back with him to learn what they may of the Wizards' Earth magic.

'In the meantime, until arrangements can be made, it is important that we keep your student and Incondor apart. I will send the troublemaker out with a party to hunt the great cats of Steelclaw. On his return, once Yinze is safely out of the way, he will be dealt with.' She took a deep breath. 'That is my decision. Tell the young Wizard to start packing. Within the next few days he will be leaving us.'

3
~

READ THE WHIRLWIND

'Why do I have the feeling I'm being punished for something I did wrong?' Yinze complained to his teacher, who had come to his quarters so early that he had barely finished eating. 'Yesterday I was being feted and feasted by the Queen, then out of the blue she's sending me packing in what feels very much like disgrace.'

'Do *you* think you've done something wrong?' Ardea's face was expressionless.

'I told you yesterday when you dragged the truth about Incondor out of me!' Yinze said exasperatedly, too anxious to remember the usual terms of respect between pupil and teacher. 'I've practically turned myself inside out over the last few months to keep out of trouble. I don't want to drag the good name of the Wizards through the mire – let alone what Cyran would do to me if I did.'

'There you are, then,' Ardea said briskly. 'You've just answered your own question. You know perfectly well that you've done nothing wrong. You're guilty of nought but stupidity for worrying yourself over nothing. The Queen is very pleased with you, and so is Crombec, and so am I.' Her voice softened. 'We're all very proud of you, Yinze, and what you've achieved here. But you've learned all you need now.'

'But if I stayed I could learn more.'

'Then the Skyfolk student who is accompanying you to Tyrineld can continue to teach you. What's wrong with you, boy?' She flung out her arms in exasperation. 'You never actually said anything, but all during the winter I got the very distinct impression that you were desperate to go home.'

'That was then. At that time I was still very homesick, the weather

28

was absolutely dreadful, and I wasn't making any progress. But now that I am, and I have friends—'

'Kea, you mean?'

Yinze, to his horror, actually felt his face ▓▓▓▓ go hot. 'I have other friends here,' he protested.

'But you weren't talking about them, were you?' Ardea took a deep breath. 'Yinze, I will be frank with you. I want you to be very careful about getting too close to Kea. Such a coupling is against the laws of both the Wizard and Winged Folk. You must know that it would result in a great deal of trouble for you both.'

Horrified at how close he'd come to revealing his most secret yearnings, Yinze forced himself to laugh. 'Couple with Kea? I can get enough girls of my own kind, thank you. And you're right. The female population of Tyrineld must be pining for me, and it's time I was getting back to them.'

On the same day, not very far away, Kea, having just received a similar warning, was giving a very similar reply to her own mentor. 'Mate with Yinze?' She looked guilelessly – she hoped – at Crombec, her eyes wide open in surprise. 'Why in all the wide skies would I want to do that?'

She hoped that he couldn't hear her heart hammering. If she failed to convince him now, her plan, her dearest dream, would come to nothing. Kea's scheme – or maybe she should call it a hope – had been born while she and Yinze had been working together on his harp. Ever since he'd first arrived she had liked the Wizard, with his handsome face and those laughing eyes that, until he'd finally developed the notion of using sound to give him control over Air magic, had become ever more sombre. She had been delighted to play a part in helping him to solve his problems and master the powers of her people, but while they worked together her bond with him had grown ever stronger. She had found herself thinking:

What if he succeeds? There'll be no need for him so stay here any longer.

As the harp took shape and they had closed in on their goal, Yinze looked happier and happier, while Kea's unhappiness had grown. She couldn't possibly be in love with him of course, she kept telling herself. That was taboo between their people. If she loved him, then she'd be honour bound to stay away from him – and she couldn't bear the thought of that. No, she told herself, they were *friends*, that was all. It was the notion of losing a friend that was making her feel so sad and restless. But if he was a friend, and therefore safe, maybe

she didn't have to lose him after all. By now it was common knowledge that Queen Pandion would be selecting a representative from
the Skyfolk to return with Yinze to Tyrineld and learn the Wizards'
Earth magic. If only Kea could get herself chosen, then she wouldn't
have to be parted from him after all.

She had a great deal going in her favour, for she had already been
helping Yinze to form a bridge between the powers of Earth and Air.
Surely that must put her ahead of any other candidate? So confident
had she been, that Crombec's question had taken her completely by
surprise. She only hoped her reply would sound sincere enough to
convince him.

'Well, it's just that – you've been working so closely together
these last months,' Crombec floundered. 'That is, you're such good
friends, I'd begun to wonder ...'

Kea looked at him reprovingly. 'Master Crombec, you've taught
me everything I know. You of all people must surely realise that my
work is my all-consuming passion right now. In the future, when we
both feel I've attained sufficient mastery of my skills, there will be
time enough to start looking around for a suitable young man. In the
meantime – well, I'm just too busy for such nonsense.'

'Oh. Good. Er ... good.' For once, the harp maker seemed at a
loss for a reply. Kea slanted a glance at him out of the corner of her
eye. Had she convinced him? As his shoulders relaxed and he turned
away, whistling, to his work, she realised that she had, and her heart
beat a little faster with excitement. The scheme that she had been
hugging to her heart for some time was safe for a little while longer.

While Kea drifted off to sleep that night, confident that her plan
was still safe and secret, she had no idea that the very same proposition was being discussed at the palace, between Crombec, Ardea,
Queen Pandion and the Royal Council of advisers. Though she had
dared to hope, however, it still came as a shock when, first thing in
the morning, and barely out of bed, she found herself summoned
before the Queen. All at once, it appeared that her dream stood a
chance of becoming reality.

Kea's hands were shaking as she dressed, and she barely noticed
the brilliant sunshine sparkling on the white buildings of Aerillia as
she flew across to the palace. Pandion was waiting for her, not in the
imposing hall of Audience but outside in the sunshine, on a wide
balcony that overlooked the city, and Crombec and Ardea sat beside

her, at a table on which were set a steaming pot of liafa and a platter of sweet cakes.

Kea made her obeisance, and the Queen nodded graciously. 'Come and sit down, child,' she said. 'Break your fast with us.'

To be in the presence of the Queen was awe-inspiring. To be sitting here, in the palace, drinking liafa with her, was just unbelievable. Kea, for once lost for words, sat down and took the cup in unsteady hands, hoping desperately that she wouldn't slop the hot, dark liquid all over the place and disgrace herself. Ardea and Crombec, sitting one on either side of her, came to the rescue. Yinze's mentor tipped a generous spoonful of honey into Kea's liafa. 'Take a drink and steady yourself,' she said. Crombec put one of the little cakes on her plate. 'Eat,' he said out loud, his eyes twinkling kindly. 'If your usual habits are anything to go by, I'll wager you had no breakfast.'

'The girl is here for more than breakfast,' Pandion said briskly, making Kea drop the cake back to her plate, untasted. 'I don't have all day to dawdle over this business. Kea' – she turned to the winged girl – 'as you may have heard, I am sending one of our students back to Tyrineld with Yinze, when he goes home. The chosen person will study the Wizards' Earth magic, as Cyran's delegate has done with our magic during his time here. After considerable discussion with Ardea, Crombec, and my advisers in the Royal Council, I have decided that you will be the one to go.'

'Oh! Oh, thank you.' Wild with excitement Kea leapt to her feet, almost sending her liafa flying. Suddenly realising she was about to hug the Queen, an unpardonable breach of protocol, she sat down quickly and composed herself, but inside her heart was singing. It had really happened! Her secret plan, her dearest wish and hope, had come to pass.

If Pandion had looked intimidating before, she was even more so when she frowned. 'When you go you will constantly bear in mind that you are representing the Winged Folk – representing me – in a foreign land. You will comport yourself with dignity and decorum at all times. Is that absolutely clear?'

Kea quailed. 'Yes, Your Majesty,' she whispered.

'You must be aware that there was considerable doubt about choosing you. You have worked very closely with Yinze on his project these past few months, and the two of you have become friends – very close friends, it seems to me. Dangerously close.' Pandion's gaze seemed to be drilling right into Kea's head, as if she was trying to see what thoughts were concealed within. 'For this reason, we came very close to deciding against you, for I was not prepared to risk the intolerable scandal of a coupling between our race and the Wizards. But your mentors, I gather, have spoken to both you and Yinze very seriously about this matter, and both of you have protested very strongly against the possibility.'

Yinze said that? Kea felt a stab of sadness at the thought, but there was no time to dwell on it, for the Queen was still speaking.

'Ironically, the very situation which prompted my uneasiness has weighed in your favour. While helping the Wizard, you have shown that you can work well with his kind. Also you, of all the Skyfolk, have the greatest experience in integrating Earth magic with our own. Therefore I have set my doubts aside. But bear in mind, Kea, that your friendship with Yinze must go no further than it already has. I will be in regular communication with the Archwizard, and at the faintest hint of a scandal, you will be recalled to Aerillia.' Her eyes grew hard as flint. 'And you will be punished.' Then her expression softened. She rose, and held out a hand to Kea. 'Go with my blessings, child. You have already made the Skyfolk proud. Go now, and make me prouder still.'

Clearly the interview was over. Once Pandion had left the balcony, Kea could hardly wait to tear herself away from Ardea and Crombec, and their congratulations that she knew would all too soon turn into more warnings about good behaviour – as if she hadn't heard enough of that today. She was bursting to tell Yinze her news, and she didn't want to waste a minute. She sped across to his quarters, flying recklessly fast, and hurled herself through the door as soon as he opened it. 'Yinze, Yinze, you'll never guess …'

His delight at her news was all she had imagined, all that she could have wished. 'Why that's wonderful, Kea. Congratulations. I couldn't be more happy.' He whirled her round in an embrace, as he had done once before, and as they spun to a halt, their eyes met; held. Kea's heart beat faster. Yet, when he lowered his head to kiss her, the Queen's dire warnings resounded in her mind. She ducked her face away hastily, and the moment turned to dust and ashes.

Inside Yinze's dwelling was a scene of absolute chaos, as he tried to sort out the essentials and pack. His bearers were standing by to take his baggage outside and load it into cargo nets, ready for transport in the morning, but he couldn't see that happening any time soon.

Looking at it all, the Wizard felt like tearing his hair out. How the blazes had he managed to accumulate so much *stuff* during his stay here? He'd thought he had managed to sort out the essentials, but unless he wanted to take a dozen winged bearers with him, it looked as though he was going to have to think again.

Kereru, moving at her usual rapid pace, whisked in with a tray containing a pot of fragrant liafa, bread, cold slices of roast mutton from the mountain sheep that roamed the lower slopes, cheese from the same animals, and some dried apricots. With her elbow she swept a pile of Yinze's clothing off the table and put down her burden.

'Hey! I just folded those.'

'Not from where I'm standing.' Kereru shrugged, her glossy feathers rustling, and began to fold the garments again, making a much better job of it in half the time.

'I'll never be ready,' Yinze said disconsolately. It was very late, he had to get up early in the morning, and it looked as though he wouldn't make it to bed tonight at all.

Kereru laid a motherly hand on his shoulder. 'Sit. Eat. Let me help you.' As Yinze, his mouth full of bread and meat, looked on in astonishment, the room began to organise itself, as if by magic, beneath her capable hands.

'The climate in Tyrineld is very warm, isn't it? Well, you won't be wanting all this cold weather gear any longer, will you? Pick out what you'll need for the journey and anything else you're particularly attached to, and I'll put the rest aside.' She ran her hands over the furs that had covered his bed, the thick, heavy pelts of bear and the great cats that roamed the nearby Steelclaw mountain. 'Do you want to keep any of these?'

Yinze thought of Iriana. 'No. Definitely not.'

'Well, you'll need to take a couple with you for travelling or you'll freeze in that net, but if you don't want to keep them the bearers will bring them back. We can always use them here.'

On she went, sorting, organising, helping him with practical suggestions and, when he had finished eating, directing him in the best ways to pack. Within an hour the chaos had been reduced to two large bundles, a sack containing gifts for all his friends and family in Tyrineld and a roll of furs for the journey. Everything he was leaving behind was put away neatly or stacked against the wall.

'Kereru, I love you.' Yinze hugged her. Even though he was longing to see his home again, his mother, his friends and Iriana, he was sad to be leaving. His entire day had been spent in farewells, and he had felt his spirits growing heavier with each one, but this was one too many.

'I'll miss you very much, Yinze.' The winged woman's eyes were bright with unshed tears. 'Wherever they send me to work next, I'm sure it won't be nearly so entertaining.'

When she had left him, the Wizard looked around at the strangely altered room. The traces of his presence, all the little personal belongings, were gone now, and he felt peculiarly unreal and displaced, as though he had ceased to exist. Like a compass needle, every thought turned unerringly northward now, towards home. For the last time, he went to his bedchamber, turned out the lamp, and curled up beneath the tickling furs in his uncomfortable, scoop-shaped bed. By this time tomorrow, he would be at the northern borders of the mountain range, and well on his way home.

Except that he wasn't.

In the depths of the night, the Wizard was awakened by a screaming gale outside, and the staccato clatter of hail hitting his shutters. He swore, long and inventively. He was used by now to these violent mountain storms that blew up so fast and unexpectedly. When they were as bad as this one sounded, they could go on for several days. At a fresh blast of wind, he snarled another curse. This just wasn't fair. He'd said his farewells, he'd packed, he was *ready*, damn it. A wild thought entered his mind of taking his harp and trying to turn the bad weather away, but he knew it was impossible. It would take many experienced Air Mages working in concert to disperse such ferocity, and the Winged Folk had learned long ago that it was a pointless waste of energy to try to tamper with the violent tempests of the mountains. Stoically, they would secure their homes and stay inside, passing the time with study, music, games and conversation, until the worst was over. With a savage jerk, Yinze pulled the covers over his head and tried to shut out the noise of the howling blasts. Might as well go back to sleep. He wouldn't be going anywhere in a hurry.

It took two full days for the storm to blow itself out, and by the time it was over Yinze was almost climbing the walls through boredom and frustration. But the third day dawned with high, scudding clouds, watery sunlight, and a blustery wind that still gusted, but would at least permit strong, experienced flyers to travel. Though he had half-expected the Queen to err on the side of caution, and make him wait an extra day, the word came while he was eating breakfast:

his bearers and porters were on their way, and he should be ready to leave within the hour.

Kereru, whose brother Parea had brought the message, said, 'I'll prepare some food for the journey,' and vanished in the direction of her kitchen, but not before Yinze had seen her surreptitiously wipe away a tear. Bolting the last of his breakfast, he leapt from his seat and dragged his bundles outside, ready to be loaded into the cargo net that the two porters would bring. The thought of Kea, in her home across the city, doing the same thing flashed through his mind, and he wondered how she must be feeling. He remembered how he had reacted on his departure from Tyrineld: that churning mix of pride, excitement, and fear. What would the new city be like? Would the inhabitants be welcoming to one of a different race, or hostile? Would he succeed in mastering the skills he had been sent to learn, or would he return home a failure? For an instant, Yinze both envied and pitied his friend. 'Don't worry, Kea,' he murmured under his breath, 'I'll take care of you.'

With that, he left the platform and went back inside to dress in all the layers of cold-weather clothing he could cram on. His Skyfolk companions had their race's resistance to the cold, and would be flying besides. The exercise would keep them warm, but he would be an inanimate piece of cargo, swinging ignominiously in his net. He remembered the bitter, bone-piercing chill when he'd been brought here from Tyrineld, and his blood had still been thin from the temperate climate of home. He'd thought he would die before he reached his destination. Well, he had adapted since them, and had learned a lot about dressing against the cold. Maybe the journey home would not be quite so bad.

When I get home, he thought, I'm going to see everyone: Mother, Iriana and my friends – and Cyran, of course, he's bound to want a report – and I'll made sure that Kea is settled in. Then I'm going swimming. His head filled with happy thoughts of floating in those warm, silken blue waters, he headed back outside, to find the platform crowded with Kea, Ardea and Crombec, two strange Skyfolk porters busy loading his bundles into a net, and his own four personal bearers, Kereru's brother Parea, Dunlin, Tinamou, and Chukar, who were waiting with another net, its bottom padded thickly with furs, that would be his transport home.

The porters flew off with his belongings, heading for the High Crown Pass, some five miles to the north of the city, where they would be meeting Kea's two porters, who had gone on ahead with her baggage. That left a little more space for farewells. As Kereru brought out mugs of liafa to warm them for the journey, Yinze embraced Crombec, and his mentor Ardea, sad that he wouldn't be seeing them again.

'Maybe you will.' Ardea had always been good at picking up stray thoughts from his mind. 'You never know, Crombec and I might just come to pay you a visit one of these days.'

'I truly hope you will,' Yinze told her. 'I would love to see you again, and show you my city. I can't thank you enough – both of you – for everything you've done for me.'

'Just take good care of my Kea, if you please,' Crombec said. 'She's as dear as a daughter to me.'

'I will, I promise. It will be my pleasure.' Yinze smiled at the winged girl.

'Ha! I can take care of myself,' Kea snorted, then her expression softened. 'All the same, it means a lot to me, knowing that I'll have one friend in a strange place.'

'You'll soon have lots of friends,' Yinze promised. 'They're going to love you in Tyrineld.'

Finally all the farewells had been said, and Yinze climbed into his net, bundling himself in the furs that Kereru had handed to him. His bearers took the strain and lifted from the ground with a great beating of wings, heading north towards the pass with Kereru circling around them to keep pace. Yinze watched Aerillia recede behind him, storing memories until it vanished from sight. It felt like the end of an era. With a gloved hand he touched his precious harp, tucked safely beside him in its fur-lined case. At least he hadn't come away empty-handed. He would return to Tyrineld a success.

The Wizard left the past behind him and began to think of home. Of the future. But his past was not ready to let go of him yet.

The great cats of Steelclaw Mountain had proved, as always, to be worthy opponents, intelligent, cunning and fierce, but they stood little chance against a hunter armed with a crossbow and attacking from the air. Incondor's hunting party were heading back home with their two porters carrying a net full of pelts, and their belt pouches filled with fangs and claws. The storm that had lashed Aerillia had not reached into the northern parts of the mountain range, so they had made good time, and hoped to be back within the hour. They had been passing a flask of contraband brandy between them as they flew, and his companions, Milvus and Torgos, were jubilant at their success, but Incondor's thoughts were dark. He knew full well that the Queen had dispatched him off to Steelclaw to keep him away from that worm Yinze. He realised that she planned to send the Wizard away in his absence, cheating him of his revenge. Yinze – or Kea, he wasn't sure which, for the pair of them were constantly in each other's pockets – had told Crombec and Ardea about the liquor, and Pandion had made it clear that there would be consequences to face on his return.

No wonder Incondor's mood was black.

Still, he had one last hope of placating the Queen. On his hunt he had been incredibly lucky, and had found a white cub. These aberrations, known as ghost cats by the Skyfolk, were incredibly rare among the great cats, which tended to be marked in various combinations of black and gold. Their pelts were said to bring good fortune to the owner, and when Incondor gave this one to the Queen, that luck should spill out over the entire Skyfolk race. Surely that would be enough to save him from her wrath?

He had left the cub alive. This treasure would be skinned by experts back in the city, who could make sure that the precious hide was undamaged. Unfortunately, the creature was young – only about the size of the white foxes that hunted on the lower slopes – but it was a precious ghost cat, nonetheless. He had insisted on carrying it himself, and it swung beneath him in a net, mewling with fear. Its lack of size would not diminish its value.

The High Crown Pass hove into sight, and Incondor knew he would soon be home. Milvus flew up beside him. 'Do you want to stop here and rest for a little while, or shall we press on?'

'Press on. I plan to get back as soon as possible, before this stupid animal dies on me. I want the pelt to be as fresh as possible.'

Then Incondor saw a group of figures below, resting in the pass. The Winged Folk had excellent vision. Even though it was summer there was still snow at this altitude, and Yinze's purple cap stood out clearly against the white background.

The winged man looked at his companions with a feral grin, and gestured them downward. 'I've just changed my mind,' he said.

The Wizard and his companions were making a brief stop in the pass, to rendezvous with their porters and make sure all their baggage was organised, before they set off on the long journey north. Yinze had dusted the snow off a boulder and was sitting down, with his harp case open on his lap. In the final scramble to leave Aerillia he had packed the precious instrument rather hastily, and he wanted to make sure it was safe and secure before continuing on his way.

Kea, dressed in snug travelling clothes of a tunic and leggings, came over to him. 'Are you finished yet? We're all ready to—' Her words were cut off by the thundering of wings. Snow whirled up, blinding them, and as it cleared Yinze found himself confronting Incondor and his henchmen.

The Wizard's heart sank. He'd thought he'd seen the last of his foe. Ardea had made no secret of the fact that Pandion had sent him home while Incondor was away hunting, in the hope of keeping the two of them apart. Had it not been for the storm which had delayed him, the plan would have worked perfectly. His bearers, under orders from the Queen to protect the Wizard at all costs, closed ranks around him, outnumbering the interlopers.

Incondor's eyes glinted nastily. 'Well, well. If it isn't the Wizard and his little friend. I'm so glad I didn't miss the chance to say fare-well.'

Kea's attention was on the mewling bundle. 'What are you doing with that cub?'

'It's a gift for the Queen.' Again, that feral grin. 'I killed its mother and siblings yesterday, but this is the only white kit that has been seen on Steelclaw for many years. Won't it look lovely when it's skinned? That pelt is going to make me very popular with Pandion for some time to come, I suspect.'

Yinze looked at the wretched little creature, pity stirring in his heart. He thought of Iriana, so far away, and knew that she would want him to save it. Yinze, with a half-formed plan of promising Incondor liquor in trade for the cub, stepped closer – and smelled the brandy on the winged man's breath. 'If I were you, I'd take some time to sober up before meeting her,' he said with a grin. 'If she smells that liquor on you, all the scrawny cubs in the world won't save your hide.'

'She won't catch me,' Incondor sneered. 'I'm far too clever.'

'You're clever enough to let a number of witnesses see you in this state, including some of the Queen's own bearers, sent along by her to make sure we met no trouble.'

Incondor turned white as he realised that he had trapped himself.

For a moment his brash pose crumpled, and his arrogant expression was replaced by a sick, furtive look. Then the panic disappeared, as anger won out. Dropping the cub he lunged, and smashed his fist into the Wizard's face, catching him beneath the left eye. Yinze reeled back, cursing, and impacted hard against the cliff face. Fuelled by blazing rage, he used the ròck as a springboard to launch himself at his foe, and crashed into the winged man, knocking him off his feet.

The pair rolled on the ground, kicking, pummelling and gouging at one another. Yinze's entire focus was on the battle. He was bigger and heavier, but his opponent was lightning-fast, and was possessed of a wiry strength that the Wizard had not suspected. Also, the Winged Folk had sharp, curved, talon-like fingernails, which Incondor used as a weapon in addition to his fists, tearing at Yinze's face and coming perilously close to his eyes. Nevertheless, as the pair scrambled back to their feet, the Wizard was more than holding his own. This fight had been a long time coming, and he had months of taunts, pranks, and downright bullying to avenge. With a black savagery completely at odds with his usual, sunny nature, he began to press home his advantage, driving Incondor back.

The winged man's eyes were swollen, his face was scraped and bruised. Blood flooded from his nose as he choked and gasped for breath. Yinze pulled back his fist for one last blow to finish it, but suddenly hands were grasping him from behind, pulling him back from his foe. With a jolt of anger at such betrayal, he realised that his own bearers had intervened – and then another shock, of horror this time – turned his wrath to black terror as he saw that Incondor's companions had hold of Kea, and Torgos was pressing a blade against her throat.

'This has gone far enough, Wizard,' Milvus said. 'Take your bearers and your Skyfolk trull and leave these lands. Never come back, for if you do – we'll be waiting.'

'Gladly.' Yinze spat blood onto the ground. Part of him, seeing Kea's face bone-white with fear, revolted against retreating from these cowardly louts, but despite his temper he had intelligence enough to realise that this was the most sensible option. Having managed to avoid any dishonour or disgrace all these months, he must not fail at the final hurdle. 'Let her go. We're leaving.'

Torgos pushed Kea away from him, hard. Yinze caught her as she stumbled, and saw that her eyes were blazing with anger. He bit down on his own fury, though it nearly strangled him, and put an arm around her shoulders. 'Come on, let's go. The sooner we're far away from these scum, the better.'

Incondor, however, had other ideas. While the Wizard was distracted he scrambled to his feet and his eye fell on the harp, resting atop the rock in its open case. Before anyone could react he darted past Yinze, snatched up the instrument, and rocketed into the sky.

'Come near me and I'll drop it,' he screamed, spittle flying, as Kea and the porters prepared to take wing. Helpless, they all watched in dismay as he flew higher. 'If you're going to ruin me, I'll pay you back. See how you manage the powers of Air without your little toy.'

'For pity's sake be careful,' Yinze shouted. 'That's no toy, you fool, and you don't understand it. It's loaded with strange magic.'

'Magic, my backside,' Incondor jeered. 'A child could master this trinket.' To Yinze's horror, he slung the strap over his shoulder and began to play.

It happened with terrifying speed. The gusting wind screamed into a tempest, and the clouds came swirling down into a vortex of spinning air that centred on the harp. Snow and stones flew up into Yinze's face and the gale flattened him back against the cliff. He snatched at Kea's hand as she was whirled helplessly past him, her wings catching the wind like sails, and pulled her against him, trying to shelter her with his body.

Then a shriek, loud enough to be heard over the screaming of the storm, drew his eyes upwards. Through streaming eyes he saw the titanic forces snatch at Incondor, hurling him like a stone from a slingshot, tumbling him over and over in the air like an autumn leaf. Once more he shrieked hideously, and Yinze saw his wings crumple like paper as the dreadful forces snapped the delicate bones like kindling. Then the gale hammered down like a fist, smashing the winged man into the harsh rocks of the pass.

He was dead. He had to be. Yinze rushed forward, sick with horror, but Kea was faster, and knelt over the broken, bloodied form. 'Don't move him,' she said. 'He's still breathing, but he's smashed up so badly … We need a healer here.' Wildly she looked around for their bearers, but they had all suffered the same fate as she would have done had Yinze not protected her, with the wind catching their wings and bowling them over. They had been scattered further down the pass, and even now were picking themselves up and limping back, their flesh covered in cuts and abrasions, and already darkening with bruises. Two of them, it was clear, had dragging, damaged wings;

another was bleeding from a jagged tear in his scalp, and yet another needed help from his comrades to walk.

Kea beckoned to them. 'Are any of you fit to fly?' Parea and Incondor's friend Milvus were the first to step forward. 'Then return to Aerillia as fast as you can, and fetch help,' the winged girl told them. 'We'll try to keep Incondor alive until you get back.'

Sick with dismay, Yinze dropped to the ground beside Kea. While they had been working on the harp they had become adept at melding their two very different sorts of power, and now, as she laid her hand gently on the winged man's breast, he put his own hand over hers, lending her his energy and magic to help hold his enemy to life. Nearby, the harp lay on the ground, as mangled and shattered as Incondor's wings, and the Wizard felt a stab of anger at the waste, the destruction. Surely this disaster must spell the end for all his hopes and plans?

Queen Pandion looked down at Incondor, her expression very grave. The healers had cleaned him up as best they could, and straightened his broken limbs, holding them in place with casts of stiffened rawhide, but even Yinze, who knew little about healing, was sure that even if the winged man survived, he would be hopelessly crippled and would never fly again. He felt sick and sorry and, even though he had not initiated the confrontation, his stomach was knotted with guilt.

'Come,' the Queen said, and motioned the Wizard and Kea from the room. The corridors of the palace were hushed and empty around the sickroom, apart from the swift, padding tread of the healers going back and forth. Pandion led the way into another chamber, where food and liafa were set out on a table. Outside, the sun had set, and the room was growing dark. 'Sit,' she said wearily. 'Rest. Neither of you have eaten anything all day.'

Gratefully, Yinze sank down onto a stool, and took a sip of liafa sweetened with honey, wincing at the sting from his bruised mouth where Incondor had hit him. The hot liquid was both comforting and reviving, but his stomach still revolted at the thought of food.

'Have the healers looked at you, Yinze?' Pandion asked.

'It's not important,' he mumbled.

'It is important. Get those scrapes and bruises treated, Wizard. Cyran would never forgive me if I sent you home in that state. I already feel guilty that one of my own subjects should have caused such damage.'

'Your Majesty, I'm sorry,' Yinze blurted. 'I'm just so dreadfully sorry. All these months of keeping the peace with Incondor, then I failed the final test.'

'That you are sorry says a great deal for your character, but as far as I am concerned, you have absolutely no reason to feel guilty,' Pandion said firmly. 'I have spoken to your bearers, and Kea, and Incondor's companions. It seems clear to me that the blame lies with him. He initiated the confrontation. He struck the first blow, his friends threatened Kea's life, and he stole and destroyed your harp, almost destroying himself in the process.'

Her eyes went once again to Yinze's battered face. 'I will speak with Archwizard Cyran, and make it clear that no blame is attached to you for this regrettable incident. Nevertheless, I feel that you should return home as soon as possible. Our physicians have suggested that I send Incondor with you, to see what the healers of Tyrineld can salvage, for his injuries are beyond our skills.'

'So they think he'll live?' Relief washed over the Wizard.

'Our healers believe they can hold him to life – but he will be terribly crippled. But the Wizards, with their Earth magic, are far more adept at healing than we. Perhaps the damage can at least be minimised.'

The terrible fear that Incondor would die, that had haunted him over the last few hours, finally subsided, leaving Yinze weak and shaking. When the Queen spoke again, he saw sympathy in her eyes. 'Be comforted, my children,' she said, looking from Kea's tear-stained face to Yinze's pale and battered one. 'As I said, this tragedy was not your fault. It was my duty to keep you safe while you were here, Yinze, and because I failed you have been injured, and all of your hard work of these last months has been destroyed by one of my subjects. Crombec is repairing the structure of your broken harp – all that remains for you is to imbue it with your magic once more. But is there any way in which I can make recompense?'

The Wizard was stunned. Despite his involvement in the tragedy, the Queen was apologising to him. Enough guilt still lingered to make that seem very wrong. 'Your Majesty, I don't deserve ...'

'I mean it,' Pandion insisted. 'The honour of the Skyfolk, of Aerillia, is at stake here. I ask again, is there any way in which I can compensate you?'

Suddenly, Yinze thought of the little white creature that had mewled in panic in Incondor's hands. 'Does the cub still survive?'

he asked. 'The white cub that Incondor found? If it lives, may I be permitted to keep it? To take it home as a gift for my sister Iriana? Though she is blind, her skill with animals is unsurpassed, and if anyone can raise it, she can. I know she would love one of the great cats of the mountains.'

Pandion looked grave. 'Yinze, do you realise how dangerous those creatures are? How big it will grow?'

'I have no fear for Iriana, Your Majesty,' Yinze said proudly. 'Perhaps to compensate for her blindness, she has formed a special, close connection with the minds of beasts, and has even raised and tamed one of the great eagles of the northern ranges. She would be in no danger.'

Queen Pandion thought for a moment, then nodded. 'Very well. So be it. If the cub survives it will be yours. Such rare creatures are said by my people to bring great fortune, but after the events of this day, I doubt it greatly. May it bring better fortune to your sister.'

She got to her feet, suddenly looking old and weary. 'Go now. Rest. As soon as the healers say that Incondor is fit to travel, you will be going home.'

4
~

FRIENDSHIP

It was sunset, and at last the Archwizard Cyran had reached the edge of the forest. He was bone weary after a long day of galloping across the moors, desperate to discover what disaster had befallen his ill-starred emissaries, and now, at the insistence of his escort, Nara and Baxian, who were anxious about the well-being of their horses, they had stopped to make camp. The Archwizard did not help them with their chores of setting up tents, lighting a fire and seeing to the poor, exhausted mounts. He sat alone beneath a tree, lost in dark and wretched thought. He was mourning the lost ones: those whose passing he'd felt this morning, his only son Avithan, poor blind Iriana, who had so longed for adventure, and brave Esmon, the warrior he had sent to guard them. His heart was rent by grief, remorse and guilt, and the terrible pangs of their ending would haunt him to the end of his days. He dreaded the reaction of his soulmate Sharalind. He, and no other, had sent them to their deaths. How could she ever forgive him?

He would never forgive himself.

All he could do was bring their bodies home, and try to discover what dreadful fate had befallen them. He clenched his fists. If the Phaerie had been responsible for Avithan's death, he would wreak bloody war upon them such as the world had never seen. A shiver went through him as he recalled the terrible visions that had tormented him for so long – but now, instead of dread, they brought forth a feeling of resolution. If it was his fate to bring about the horrors that he had tried for so long to avoid, if all that ruin and bloodshed must be on his hands, then so be it. Justice must be done. Avithan must be avenged.

Then, even as his mind wrapped itself in such dreadful darkness, a strange sensation swept over him. It felt like the lift of spirits that accompanied the first day of spring, the approach of dawn after a long and troubled night, a door opening to let in sunlight. It was as if the missing piece of a puzzle had clicked back into place, and without question, without doubt, he knew that one of his own had come back.

For one heady instant Cyran thought that Avithan had returned. Then that mysterious blaze of life, that sense of an unknown presence, steadied and clarified, and he knew the truth. Emotions warred within him: amazement and disbelief that such a miracle could have happened, joy and relief that one of the young Wizards had been saved, followed swiftly by disappointment, black and bitter.

Why Iriana? Why did *she* have to be the one who had survived?

Why couldn't it have been Avithan?

The Archwizard hated himself for harbouring such shocking and unworthy thoughts. He had known the girl all her life, because his soulmate Sharalind had been such close friends with Iriana's foster mother Zybina. He was very fond of her, and he admired the cleverness and courage with which she had surmounted the disadvantages of her blindness. Yet she was not, and never could be, his son, and her return could in no way compensate for the loss of Avithan.

Cyran suddenly roused from his thoughts to see Nara and Baxian hovering expectantly, close by. From their expressions, it was plain that they too had sensed Iriana's impossible return, and were bursting to ask him about it. He was glad they had been sensitive enough to allow him a moment to get his emotions under control. Even as Baxian opened his mouth to speak, the Archwizard held up a hand, stilling the words. 'No, I cannot understand it either,' he said shortly. 'It appears that we have been vouchsafed a miracle today – yet how, why and whence has Iriana returned? Our first step must be to find her quickly, for she may need our help, and there are many questions we must ask her.'

He rose to his feet, brushing leaf litter from his robes. 'Come,' he said. 'Let us eat and sleep, and we will set off at dawn to start our search. There is no time to lose.'

If the others noticed him frowning, though they had been granted such seeming good fortune, they forbore to mention it. Though Iriana had returned, she had appeared to be alone. Cyran had a right to grieve.

*

The group of young Wizards left behind in Tyrineld thought of themselves as the survivors now, a change in circumstances that had left shadows of sorrow on their faces and a heaviness in their steps. Before Yinze, Chathak and Ionor had gone away, it had been their habit to meet together every evening. In the summer, their favourite place had been at the women's house, in Thara's lovely garden. All seven of them: Chathak, Yinze, Ionor, Iriana, Thara, Melisanda and Avithan, would sit around the long wooden table near the fountain; eating, drinking cool, sparkling starwine and endlessly talking. Somehow, no matter how many times they met like this, they never ran out of things to say, their words well seasoned with laughter and smiles. While the stars came out and the moon cast a shining silver track across the ocean they would linger, giddy with the scent of the datura flowers that glowed in the moonlight on the bush beside the wall, and watching the flickering flights of the bats as they flashed by, feeding on the moths that were attracted by the shimmering globes of magelight that Avithan suspended in the trees.

Tonight they were together again; hopeful, perhaps, that this scene of such good memories would give them some comfort in these dark and sorrowful times, for their happy group had been fractured, and what should have been joy at their reunion after being separated for so long had been replaced by worry and sorrow. There were two spaces at the table now. Avithan and Iriana had been snatched away from them without warning, leaving them grieving, anxious and confused.

The first death they had experienced had been that of Esmon. They had all felt it: the brief, wrenching stab of agony that all Wizards experienced at the passing of another. Chathak and his Dragon counterpart, Atka, had arrived later that same night. Because Chathak had been utterly devastated by the passing of his brother, they had been teleported to Tyrineld by a concerted effort of the Dragonfolk. Ionor, speeding through the night with the Leviathan, had reached the city the following morning with his fellow Leviathan Mage Lituya, to find out that Cyran had already left at dawn with a force of warriors to search for his son and Iriana. Then a few days later, only this morning, Yinze had arrived with Kea, in time to feel the passing of Iriana and Avithan. Though the blow had been faint and muted with distance, they had all known when their friends had left the world, and had mourned them as gone for ever.

They were absolutely stunned when, near sunset, they felt Iriana return from death. This was something that had never happened in the history of the Wizards, and the companions' joy in her mysterious regeneration was greatly tempered by concern. Surely no one could go through such an experience unscathed and unchanged. What would they find when they met Iriana again? One thing was for sure – she would never be the same.

Whatever had become of Iriana, however, one thing was certain. Avithan had not come back with her, and they were grieving for the loss of a beloved brother.

It had always been natural for the group to share their joys and triumphs, and now they did the same with their sorrow. The other Magefolk that Yinze, Chathak and Ionor had brought back with them from far-off lands all understood and respected this, and had formed a group of their own, gathering together elsewhere in the city, united in their strangeness, though they could not be physically present in the same location.

Lituya, the Leviathan, had made his home in the quieter northern bay, away from the busy harbour. A special, heated house for Atka of the Dragonfolk had been built nearby, with a flat rooftop that could be screened from the wind, so that she could go up there to catch the sun and feed. The Skyfolk Mage Kea, having discovered an immediate rapport with Thara and Melisanda, was staying with the Wizards in Iriana's house but, respecting her hosts' grief, she had spent a lot of time that afternoon with Lituya and Atka, sitting on the roof of the Dragon's new home while the Leviathan sported in the bay below, and Atka sunned herself during the daylight, and curled up in her heated quarters at sundown.

Their conversations were, of necessity, conducted at a distance, in mindspeech, but the strangers needed such a bond. All three felt a little lonely and out of place here in Tyrineld. There had been no Archwizard Cyran to welcome them, his soulmate was closeted away, mourning the loss of Avithan, and only a scant handful of people apart from the Heads of the Luens knew of the visitors' existence at all. The entire city seemed to be in a state of sorrow, unsettled and confused, and until Cyran came back they were simply marking time, their thoughts with their Wizard friends across the bay, for they were worried about their counterparts, who had become close friends over the past months while the Wizards had worked with them in Aerillia, in Dhiammara and beneath the ocean.

'I wish we could do something to help them.' Kea glanced down

47

through the glass skylight at the golden dragon, cosily curled up on her bed in her heated building, and picked moodily at a piece of yellow lichen on the roof.

'I agree.' Atka lifted her great head to look up at the winged Mage above her. 'I hate to see Chathak so devastated. He was always so cheerful and lively back in Dhiammara, but now he won't even talk to me. I have never seen this side of him before, and I'm deeply concerned.'

'His Wizard friends are worried about him too,' Kea told her. 'He's acting the same way with them. It must be hard to lose a brother the way he has lost Esmon. Melisanda has been trying to get him to open up and talk about his grief, but so far without any luck.'

'At least he agreed to join them tonight.' Lituya turned over lazily in the silvery waters of the bay. 'Maybe the tide of his feelings will turn at last. I hope so, for his sake. For my part, I could wish that Ionor had never been called back here to face such sorrow.' He heaved a great, gusting sigh, and a fountain of spray shot up, glittering in the moonlight. 'He was going to make an excuse, you know, so that he could have stayed with us all summer. We were so looking forward to going north with the rest of the Leviathan. Somehow, in the time he spent with us, I began to think of him more as one of us, than one of his own kind. I am sorry to lose him back to the Wizards again – and see what has become of it!'

'It seems that all three of them fitted in with our own respective people,' Kea said, thrusting away the thought of the one exception, Incondor, who even now was languishing near death within the halls of the Wizard Luen of Healers. 'But I suppose they need to be with their own kind, though it fills my heart with sadness to think that I will be parted from Yinze when I leave here.'

'Maybe we should never have come,' Atka said suddenly. 'Maybe it was all a mistake.'

In mindspeech it was less easy to conceal emotion, and there was an uneasy, troubled edge to her words that set Kea's instincts on full alert. 'Atka? What's wrong? Has something happened that we don't know about?'

'Nothing,' the Dragon said hastily. 'Only concern for our friends, that's all. Nothing else.'

Kea wasn't having that. 'Now listen,' she said sternly, 'we may not have known each other very long, but I thought the three of us were friends. Don't tell me there's nothing wrong, because I know better. How can we help you, Lituya and I, if you won't tell us what the problem is? We've just been discussing how bad it is for Chathak not to open up to his friends. Don't you go making the same mistake. We're strangers here, and far from home. We have to stick together.'

The Dragon hesitated. Then, through the skylight, Kea saw her lower her head to the floor, a picture of abject misery. 'Kea, I'm so worried,' she moaned. 'I've made a terrible mistake, and I don't know what to do. I wanted to be here with Chathak so much, but a few months ago I needed to mate, and I knew I wouldn't be able to travel, bearing an egg. So I altered one of our healing spells, just a little, so that the mating would not take and I'd be free to come to Tyrineld.'

Her distress was so palpable that the other two had no trouble guessing what had happened. 'And now you've found out that your spell didn't work, and you are carrying an egg after all,' Lituya said softly.

'Oh, you poor, poor thing.' Kea scrambled through the open sky-light and glided down to settle beside the Dragon's head, stroking her shining scales in sympathy. 'I know it would be a wrench to leave here, especially when Chathak is so unhappy, but is there no way you can get back home before you're ready to lay your egg? We would be very sorry to lose you, Atka, but if your people could apport you here, surely they could do the same to get you back?'

'I can't go home that way. It took all the Dragonfolk in Dhiammara, working in concert, to apport us so far, and they only risked such a difficult and dangerous thing because it was an emergency. Chathak was desperate to get back when his brother died. Esmon was the experienced traveller and warrior in the group that the Archmage had sent out. If he had been slain, then Chathak knew that his friends Avithan and Iriana must be in desperate straits. He felt that he must be here in Tyrineld, and my people were happy to help. However, it takes a long time to recover from the working of such powerful and intense magic, and the Dragonfolk will be weak and exhausted for some time, until they can recover their strength. They could not bring me home so soon. By the time they can, the young one will already be here, and it will be too late, for a hatchling could not withstand the stresses and strains of such a great apport, or even a sea voyage, until it is older. And if there is no time for an apport, there would certainly be no time to get me back by sea.'

Her voice rose to a wail. 'I don't know what to do. This is my first child, and I will be all alone here. And how can I tell my people? I told them the mating hadn't taken, and I really thought it was true at the time, but I was wrong. I had no right to come. I've let everybody down, and Aizaiel, the Dragonfolk Matriarch, will be so angry with me. And what will happen to my hatchling? It's so cold here, compared to home. How will I even hatch the egg, let alone care for a little one?'

While Atka had been speaking, Kea's brain had been racing. 'Now listen, Atka,' she said sternly, 'you simply cannot keep this to yourself. If the Wizards know of your predicament, I'm certain they'll do everything in their power to help you – but you must tell them first.'

'But Chathak is the only person in the city I know, and right now he's in no fit state to be interested in my difficulties.'

But Kea, because she had moved in with Yinze's friends, knew the Wizards a little better than the others, and thought differently. 'You know, my dear, this might be exactly what Chathak needs. A distraction to take his mind off his own unhappiness. Atka, you must tell him. I'll stay with you if you like. I'll fly over in the morning and tell him you need to talk to him, and Melisanda too. From what you were saying, it sounds as if we've no time to waste.'

While the visiting Magefolk held their conclave and Atka shared her worries, Avithan's companions were gathered in their usual place, with food in front of them which no one had touched, though they all were drinking wine.

They had all been dealing with the loss of their companions in their different ways. Melisanda had thrown herself into her work; she had recently been promoted to the position of second-in-command to Tinagen, Head of the Luen of Healers, and was just getting used to her new responsibilities. She was sharing the care of the white cub that Yinze had brought back for Iriana with Thara, who had sought comfort from her garden and the growing things all around her. Ionor had spent most of the day at sea, spending time with Lituya out in the bay and submerging his sorrow in the great group mind of the Leviathan.

Yinze and Chathak had found it harder to cope, for their losses were more intimate. Iriana, though a fosterling in his family, was the sister of Yinze's heart. They had grown up together and a special bond had developed between them. Chathak had not only lost friends but also a brother, Esmon, and he seemed to be taking the deaths worst of all. Yinze was angry, and had found an outlet for his rage by training with the Luen of Warriors, who were themselves mourning the loss of their leader. They understood his needs and were glad to help him. Chathak, however, had turned his grief and anger inward, and was silent and morose. The others, seeing how pale and haggard he looked and knowing that he had been neither eating nor sleeping since Esmon's death, had tried to draw him out and help him express the painful emotions that gnawed at his heart and mind, but so far he had turned away their every attempt. It had been a great triumph for Melisanda that he had finally joined the others tonight, for he had shut himself away alone all day. Now that he was with them, in the hope of persuading him to communicate, they began to recount their own experiences of Esmon's passing.

Ionor had started it, telling of his arrival back in Tyrineld the morning after Esmon had died. 'Fortunately, I was already close to home when I felt it,' Ionor said in his quiet voice. 'Lituya and I were already heading north with the Leviathan on their summer migration when I got Cyran's message to return to Tyrineld due to the situation with the Phaerie.' He grimaced. 'I might as well tell you now that I wasn't going to come back, initially. I was having such a wonderful time and learning so much with the Leviathan, and I was really looking forward to seeing the northern fjords and mountains with them. I was going to make some excuse to the Archwizard about not having learned enough yet – then Esmon's death changed everything. We headed back here with all speed.'

He sighed. 'When we came in sight of Tyrineld, it looked so peaceful. I remember surfacing, blinking in the bright moonlight and coughing out water as my lungs changed from breathing underwater to breathing air. I'd made this transformation so very many times over the past months that it was second nature now, with none of the choking and panic I felt when I first joined the Leviathan.

'I came with mixed feelings. It would be good to be home, of course, and to see all of you again – but I felt so dreadful that it had taken such a terrible thing as the loss of Esmon to bring me back.' He glanced at Chathak, to see if his friend would take this opportunity to speak, but Chathak looked away, refusing to meet his eye, so he continued, 'I'd been missing you, and so many other things I'd always taken for granted. Candlelight. Sunshine. Making toast in front of a glowing fire. Snuggling into a warm, soft bed at night. Hot food. Flowers, their colours, textures and perfumes. The smell and taste of spices. The feel of grass underfoot. Dry hair, dry clothing, dry *everything*.'

'We can all breathe underwater, but you're the only one who has ever stayed down there for such a length of time,' Melisanda said, with one eye also on Chathak. 'I'm very interested in this spell you used. Tinagen, the Head of my Luen, had a part in creating it.'

'It was an incredible spell,' Ionor agreed. 'Without it I could never have lived with the Leviathan all that time. My skin would have sloughed off, for a start. But the magic did far more than that. It protected me from the immense pressures of the depths, and prevented me from feeling the chill of the water.'

'They were very advanced enchantments,' said Yinze.

'They certainly were – and it took me a long time to learn to trust them, to trust my own powers and those of the Leviathan who were helping me maintain the magic. I learned so much from them. They became my brothers and sisters, my friends, my family, as close as you dear friends on shore. I'm going to miss them desperately, just as I missed you all while I was away. I might still call Tyrineld home, but the vast green oceans of the north and the warm blue seas of the south have captured my heart, and so have the Magefolk of the boundless waters.'

'You said that you were already heading north,' Thara said. 'How far were you going?'

'A good deal further than Tyrineld. We were going up to where the mountains north of the Phaerie realm drop into the sea. The coastline is very broken up there, with inlets, fjords and islands where each year the seas turn emerald green with the summer plankton bloom.' He sighed. 'I'd wintered with the Leviathan in the warm southern ocean with its coral reefs and brightly coloured fish, and that was beautiful, but I was so looking forward to seeing their summer grounds; the mountains, the sea otters and the soaring eagles. But sadly, it wasn't to be. And then we lost Esmon, and my own disappointment meant nothing.'

'I was just planning to leave.' Chathak spoke out abruptly. Ionor and Melisanda exchanged a glance. Their plan seemed to be working.

'I was so far away in Dhiammara,' Chathak continued. 'It's amazing that I felt it at all – yet Esmon was my brother, and when I felt him go, when I felt that tie between us break, it almost brought me to my knees.'

Without being aware of what he was doing, he was crumbling a piece of bread on his plate, his tense, fretful fingers shredding it into fragments. 'It was night, and I was packing to leave the city. Atka was with me, laughing at me because I had managed to accumulate so much stuff in such a short time. I can even remember what she was saying: that Wizards are such packrats. Our soft, frail little bodies need so many aids to keep them alive. Then apart from all the clothes and blankets and knives and so on, there are all the mementos and trinkets we feel we must drag around with us; all the books, the writing materials ... She was most amused by it all.

'Then suddenly it hit me – that shocking jolt of loss and pain and emptiness. That was when I knew Esmon was gone.

'Atka was a true friend that night, conferring with the Dragonfolk Elders and even the Matriarch herself, and talking them into changing their plans and arranging things so I could come home as quickly as possible. It took the coordinated efforts of the entire Dragon race to perform the apport that sent us back here, using the images they gleaned from my mind, but it was the only way.'

He shuddered. 'It was a horrible way to travel. We were never designed to apport that far. Instead of being instantaneous, it actually seemed to take time, and for the space of a few heartbeats we were lost in a dreadful, lightless, airless void. I've never been so terrified – I actually thought that something had gone wrong, and we'd be trapped in there for eternity.' He looked down at the scattering of crumbs on his plate, all that remained of his mangled piece of bread, as if he had no idea how they'd come to be there. 'Then after I got back here, I found that Avithan and Iriana had been with Esmon when he died. When we felt their passing this morning, I just didn't think I could bear any more grief.'

'And then Iriana returned again at sunset, and who knows what has happened to her in the meantime; where she went, or what we'll find when we meet her again. To all appearances she certainly died, but if that's true, how could she have come back? And how could anyone not be changed by an experience like that?' With a face that was hollow-cheeked and pale, Thara was not looking her usual self. 'What I also don't understand,' she went on thoughtfully, 'is how Cyran knew that something else was going to go wrong. He had set off to find Iriana and Avithan a couple of days before – before we lost them. There was a rumour going around that there had been some kind of message or warning, but no one seems to have noticed a messenger arrive.'

'I don't care how he knew.' Yinze picked up his knife, his fingers clenching around the handle as though he wanted to plunge it into the Archwizard's heart. 'I want to know what that stupid son of a whore was thinking when he sent our friends on such a fool's errand in the first place. It was bad enough sending Chathak's brother and his own son into danger, but a blind, inexperienced girl like Iriana ...' His words ended in a growl. 'The bastard should have done his own stinking dirty work. *He* should have been the one to go off into the forest to be killed.'

'Yinze,' Melisanda said gently. 'Though we all share your anger, such disrespectful words and thoughts about the Archwizard are dangerous.'

'Do you think I care?' Yinze snapped. That morning, when they had experienced the passing of their friends, he had been distraught. He'd been all for setting out north after Cyran then and there, but had been preoccupied with his mother at first, who was also grieving the loss of Iriana. Then, out of the blue, had come the extraordinary knowledge of Iriana's return.

'I can't rest, knowing she's out there; not knowing what has happened to her, or if she needs help.' Yinze spoke into the silence. 'I intend to go and find her, and if Cyran can't do it, or if Sharalind won't send out a search party from Tyrineld, then I'll go myself. Who's coming with me?'

'I am,' Chathak said. 'I can't stand not knowing. What did go on up north in the forest today? What happened to our friends?'

5
~

KALDATH

Some hours earlier, far away to the north, in the realm of the Phaerie, Aelwen was wondering what had happened to herself. She came awake slowly. She felt dazed, exhausted, and she ached in every inch of her body, right down to her bones. The landscape – trees and bushes – was spinning around her in a nauseating fashion, and she felt unsteady and fragile, as if her hold on the solid world had shaken loose.

Casting her mind back with difficulty, she remembered the tower where she had found her long lost lover Taine after so many years apart; where the powerful and enigmatic Creator, Athina, had given sanctuary to a motley band of fugitives including Tiolani, daughter of Hellorin the Phaerie Lord, the blind Wizard Iriana and the escaped human slave Dael. And after a lifetime of caring for the Phaerie steeds, Aelwen had discovered, to her profound shock, that they were the Xandim, an ancient race of shapeshifters, enslaved in their equine form by Hellorin's magic.

Corisand, the Windeye, or shaman, of the Xandim, had travelled into the magical otherworld of the Elsewhere with Iriana to attempt to recover the Stone of Fate, which she needed to free her people from the Forest Lord's spells. Meanwhile Aelwen, Taine and Tiolani had gone back to the Phaerie city of Eliorand, so that Tiolani could rule in her father's continued absence and prepare the way for Corisand's return. On their arrival, however, they had been arrested by Hellorin's Chief Counsellor Cordain. Then – it all came back to her! She had grabbed hold of Taine and apported, a fearfully danger-ous move even in the most ideal of circumstances, which these were certainly not, for she'd had no idea of a destination in her mind, but had simply made a blind and desperate leap into nowhere.

Why, she thought with a shudder, we could have materialised any-where. In the middle of a tree trunk, or underground – *anywhere*. But it appeared that luck had been with her. She vaguely remembered hitting something hard with her shoulder and stumbling, tangling her feet with those of Taine, who came down in a heap beside her. Then blank nothingness, until now. She sat up, looking around her wildly, but to her relief her lover lay beside her. He looked very pale but was breathing easily, apparently in the same deep sleep from which she had just awakened. She could only assume that the stresses of the apport had shocked their systems so badly that they'd needed this rest to recover. Still dazed and disoriented from her immense ef-fort, she knew little more for a few moments save that her heart was still beating, and that Taine was safely with her. Gently, she reached down and shook his shoulder. 'Taine? Taine, wake up.'

With a groan he opened his eyes and looked at her blearily. 'What in the name of perdition just happened?'

'Tell you in a minute,' Aelwen said, and dropped her head between her knees. Everything was still whirling and she felt sick, but after a while the landscape settled down around her, and she saw that they had ended up in some bushes. *Thorny* bushes, Aelwen thought, as she pulled twigs out of her dishevelled red braid, and carefully dis-entangled a briar that had hooked itself, all along its length, into her sleeve. Beyond the tangle of undergrowth she could see a tall, dark wall of trees with pale sunlight flashing through the occasional gap in the branches.

She felt bruised and shaken, and the huge expenditure of energy, both physical and magical, that she'd used in the apport had left her muscles weak and her head swimming with weariness. Taine looked no better. His long dark hair had come loose from the thong that tied it. Blood trickled from a deep scratch on his cheek, perilously close to his eye. His face was bone-white, his eyes wide and dark with shock. He said nothing yet, but simply held out his arms to her. The jolt of their landing had knocked them apart, but now, without getting to her feet – she couldn't risk it yet – she moved gladly into his embrace.

It was only then that she noticed that both of them were shaking. They had come so close to dying! If they had not materialised in these bushes, but in the forest beyond, they might easily have had a fatal encounter with a tree trunk. As it was, their bodies had simply broken brittle twigs, and pushed flexible briars aside. Aelwen was appalled by the narrowness of their escape. 'I'm sorry,' she murmured into Taine's shoulder. 'That was an insane thing to do. We're lucky I didn't kill us both.'

Taine kissed her gently. 'Don't be sorry. Far from killing us, you saved our lives.' There had been a death sentence on his head, imposed by the Phaerie Lord long ago, that Tiolani had intended to remove on their return, but she was now Cordain's prisoner and he was determined to carry out his master's will. Aelwen too would have fared badly, having committed the extremely grave crime of stealing several of the Xandim steeds, and she'd acted on instinct to take the only way out, apporting herself and Taine – who knew where? They could have ended up anywhere.

'Don't think about what might have been, my love. Right now we need to concentrate on what is.' Taine's words helped calm her, almost as much as his closeness did. Oh, how she had missed him all these years. What an unbelievable joy it was, to have him back!

'We'll just take a minute or two to recover,' he continued, 'then we should move on and find a better hiding place than these bushes. Have you any notion of where we are, or how far we've come?'

'I've no idea.' Aelwen shook her head. 'There was certainly no time to pick a destination. I acted on pure impulse. When those guards came at you I just grabbed you – and went.'

'They were coming at you, too,' he reminded her gently, 'but trust you not to think of that. You got us out of there, so now it's my turn. One way and another, I've learned a lot about wilderness survival over the years. I don't suppose you're carrying any food and water with you?'

'A little.' Aelwen felt quite smug to be able to say it.

'You are?' His eyebrows went up in surprise.

'When I escaped from Eliorand, the night of that tremendous storm, I got stranded alone in the forest with nothing to eat or drink. I swore I'd never make that mistake again. Of course everything is probably squashed out of all recognition.' So far they had not moved from their sprawled embrace, but now she spared an arm to feel gingerly for the pouch that she'd tied to her belt when they had set out – it seemed so long ago now – from Athina's tower. It was still there. The jerky it contained would survive anything, and though the bread had been flattened, the contents would nourish them nonetheless. The leather water bottle, slung over her shoulder and across her body on its long strap, was also intact, its contents still in place.

'Good.' Taine sounded pleased. 'I have some basic rations too. Are you ready to find out where we've landed? Let's hope we're far enough away from the city that they won't find us too soon. Though Cordain has seized the reins of power in the realm, he is still the Forest Lord's Chief Counsellor. Hellorin put a death sentence on my head, so Cordain will carry it out if he can – and you will meet the same fate for stealing Xandim. You know the law, Aelwen. We can't let them catch us. We've got to get moving.'

Though Aelwen didn't feel like moving for the next century or so, Taine was already clambering to his feet, with a speed and ease which made her envious and faintly annoyed. It was all very well for him, she thought. *He* had just been the passenger in the apport. She had done all the hard work.

'Come on, you can do it.' He grinned at her and held out a hand. Unable to resist grinning back, she took it and let him haul her up. For a moment her head spun and she lurched against him.

'Are you all right?' She heard the concern in Taine's voice.

'I feel as if I've been stamped on very hard, by a giant boot, but it'll pass.'

'Here, take my arm – no, not the sword arm, the other one – and I'll help you.'

'Just for a little while, until I pull myself together.' With a flash of pain, she thought of her black stallion Taryn, the bay Alil and the pretty skewbald mare Halira, all left behind in Eliorand when she had apported out of there. 'I wish I could have brought the horses, too. It would have helped both of us.' She was very aware that Taine had recently suffered some dreadful injuries, after being mauled by a bear. First Iriana and then Athina had done first-rate jobs of healing him, but his body would still need time to recover its full energy, strength and balance.

Taine, as he did so often, seemed to pick up on her thoughts. 'It can't be helped about our mounts, love,' he said. 'Or Tiolani. There was nothing you could have done. Even *you* couldn't apport the two of us, Tiolani and three horses too – though knowing how you love them, I'm surprised you didn't try. Come on, we'll help each other.'

As they emerged from the undergrowth, Aelwen gave a gasp of surprise. There in front of them was a torrent of fast-moving water, so broad that the great trees on the opposite bank seemed to be no bigger than the bushes they had just left. 'It's the Carnim, that flows between Hellorin's lands and the realm of the Wizards. I brought us all the way back to the border!'

'By the Light, Aelwen! How did you manage that? No wonder you're so exhausted. I see I shall have to watch my step in future.' He smiled at her. 'You don't know your own strength.'

'It must have been pure instinct,' Aelwen said, 'to get as far from the Phaerie as I could. At least we'll be safe from search parties for quite a while, since they no longer have the flying spell.'

Taine frowned. 'Unless Tiolani betrays us to save herself. If that has happened, they could have the flying spell right now.'

'She wouldn't—' Aelwen's protest died away. Try as she might, she couldn't deny the possibility.

'I think she would.' His voice took on a hard edge. 'Remember that, to Tiolani, it will seem as if we abandoned her.'

'But I couldn't have apported three people,' Aelwen protested, horrified. 'And we were the ones whose lives were at stake.'

'Of course you couldn't.' He put a comforting arm around her shoulder. 'And you're right – we were the ones in peril. I don't know what Cordain plans for Tiolani, but he won't risk hurting Hellorin's daughter and angering the Forest Lord, should Hellorin come back. And if the Forest Lord cannot return to his body, then Tiolani is the last remaining scion of his line, and the only one who can perform the flying spell. Cordain cannot harm her. As you say, we are the ones whose lives were at stake. But Tiolani might not see things that way, and the worst of it is, she knows all our plans.'

The plans, such as they were, had been made in haste back at Athina's tower, before they had all taken their leave of one another. If all had been well in Eliorand, and Tiolani had taken up the reins of power, as they had expected, Aelwen and Taine had planned to meet Corisand and her companions – supposing *their* plans worked out, and they won the Fialan and found a way to return from the Elsewhere to their own world – at a hidden place that Taine had discovered during his life of spying and concealment.

This location, closer to the border than the city, was where another river, the Snowstream, descended from the northern mountains and flowed down to join with the Carnim. Just before the confluence the Snowstream plunged through a narrow gorge, and it was in this shadowy and secret place, filled with the roar and power of the constricted torrent, that Taine had found a cave, partway up the cliff. It was far from easy to reach, but that only made it more secret and safe for the conspirators.

Since the Windeye and the Wizard would be forced to travel on horseback with no flying spell, it would take them a few days longer to reach the cave than Tiolani's party. Had the plan worked out, that would have given Hellorin's heir time to assemble all the Xandim, on the pretext of taking a count of all the herds and studs, so that Corisand would be able to take them all together when the time came to free them. When they met at the cave, Aelwen and Taine would be able to tell Corisand of the current conditions in Eliorand, and they could make further arrangements from there.

That had been the plan – until Hellorin's Chief Counsellor Cordain had ruined everything. Tiolani was now his prisoner, and she knew everything, including the location of their meeting place. Would she use the information to purchase her freedom? When Corisand and the others arrived at the cave, would there be a mounted patrol of Phaerie warriors waiting to trap them?

'We need to move, and fast,' Taine continued, 'but which way shall we go? Back towards Eliorand? To the cave? Or should we return to our friends at the tower and warn them of the danger? Right now, we don't know whether Iriana and Corisand succeeded, or if they're even alive.'

Aelwen saw the shadow of worry pass across him: the sag of his shoulders; the biting of his lower lip; the fleeting frown. 'They'll be all right,' she reassured him. 'Look what they went through before we met them. They're survivors, and between them they have a lot of resources to draw on. If anyone can bring the Fialan back from the Elsewhere, they can.'

Taine took a deep breath and straightened. 'You're right, of course. Together, combining their two different sets of powers, they're a force to be reckoned with. But if they do get the Fialan, we can't risk them being ambushed when they come to meet us. Because if Tiolani exposes the rest of us to save herself, Corisand and Iriana could walk straight into a trap.'

Aelwen stared at him, appalled. Unaccustomed to intrigue, her mind had been concentrating on their own present peril, not the future risks to their other companions. 'Whichever way we go, I can't get us there yet,' she said. 'Not with another apport. I expended too much energy bringing us all the way here.'

'You're right,' Taine agreed. 'You ought to eat, and then sleep for a little while, supposing we can find somewhere safe. Besides, we need to think things through very carefully before you take us on another jump. We were lucky last time. Next time we need to know exactly where we're heading, and we should probably do it in stages, so it doesn't exhaust you so much. If you'd burned yourself out last time, attempting so much …'

'Don't.' Aelwen shuddered. 'We might never have materialised at all, either of us. Would we have died? Or been caught for all eternity in some endless limbo? It doesn't bear thinking about.'

'We won't think about it. It didn't happen and it won't happen next time, because we'll plan it out and take greater care, making several small jumps.'

Easy for you to say, Aelwen thought. But she said nothing, because she knew that he was right. It would be difficult, time-consuming and downright dangerous to try to get anywhere on foot in this vast forest full of predators. Her apport skills at least provided a way out, and the river gave them a very rough idea of their location. She studied the direction of the flow. 'If I'm right, it looks as though we're on the Phaerie side of the border,' she said.

'You are right,' Taine replied. 'We are on the Phaerie side. And it looks as though we were asleep, or unconscious, or whatever it was, for quite a while.'

While they had been talking the sun had gone down, and a shadowy dusk had crept around them as stealthily as the swirls of mist that were rising from the river and curling around their feet. Aelwen pulled her cloak tightly around her shoulders and shivered – but not just from the evening chill. Something had changed. Something was very wrong. Now that the daylight had gone this place felt different; an uneasy, uncomfortable atmosphere surrounded her like a miasma, as though she was being watched by hostile eyes. A profound silence had fallen. There was no sound of wind in the trees, no sleepy chirrups as the birds settled down for the night, no rustle of small creatures in the undergrowth. Even though she could see the river quite clearly, she could no longer hear it running.

She looked around to see if Taine had noticed the alteration in the atmosphere, but he was still talking, thinking aloud, absorbed in their plans. 'Maybe we should head back towards the tower. But we would probably miss the others in the forest. So the cave is probably best. If we—'

Then the nightmare broke loose. Without warning, they were engulfed in darkness – then a horde of terrifying ghostly forms exploded into existence all around them: speeding towards them from the forest's edge, rising from the river mist, falling from the murky skies above. The air was pierced by the shrilling of angry shrieks and howls in strange, inhuman voices, and there seemed to be words in the screeching, though they did not understand the language. An odd shivering in the air, like the heat rising from a courtyard on a summer day, made the apparitions visible against the surrounding gloom, and in these roiling shadows, flashing out like lightning through storm clouds, was the deadly glitter of fangs and claws, and eyes that burned with a white-hot rage.

Aelwen and Taine took in this horror in the space of a single heartbeat. They whirled back to back; his sword came whistling out with fearsome speed while she drew hers more clumsily. Though she had learned the basics long ago, she had little interest in swordplay, and had not drawn a blade in years. It made no difference. The terror struck them first, a blood-chilling miasma that surged in front of the phantoms like a wave. A breath behind it came the ghosts themselves.

Aelwen swung her sword to spit the first leaping shape: the blade clove through thin air and the *thing* plunged on as before, inexorable and unchanged. Yet the claws and fangs were all too sharp and solid, and buried themselves deep in Aelwen's shoulder. She screamed as the pain tore through her, and dropped the useless weapon as other beings from the uncanny throng attached themselves to her legs and leapt to sink their claws into her arms.

Suddenly there was a dazzling blaze. Taine, the Wizard half-blood, had conjured magelight, and for a heartbeat the attackers halted, shocked and frozen in the glare. In the actinic light they were haloed with a translucent, bluish glimmer, and the trees and ground behind them could be seen, blurred and distorted, through their bodies. No human apparitions, these. Those that poured out of the forest to leap on their prey, going for arms, throats and faces, were small, about the size of a fox, but long, lithe and sinuous, and deathly quick. Those that emerged from the ground to attack legs and feet were different: a sleek, domed shape with horny carapaces, scaly faces and limbs, and great, strong, sturdy forelimbs armed with formidable claws.

The frozen instant passed in an eyeblink, and the ghosts attacked again.

Taine had managed to hold on to his blade, but it did him no good. By now both he and Aelwen were bleeding in a number of places, their clothing shredded to tatters, their lifeblood running down in rivulets to mingle on the ground. Overwhelmed, they sank beneath the onslaught. Aelwen felt talons scrabbling at her upraised arms, trying to reach her throat, and knew the end had come …

'Hai renya! Zintavaral istolan!' The voice rang out like a thunder-clap, and though Aelwen could not understand the language, the authority in the words smote her like a fist. Abruptly, instantly, the phantoms fell back a little way, surrounding Taine and Aelwen in a snarling, gibbering circle, their palpable fury blasting across the intervening space.

'Come,' said the voice. 'I will take you to safety. Hurry, for not even I can hold back the wrath of the ghosts for ever.' A hand came down, knotted with age, yet when Aelwen took it, its grasp was surprisingly firm and strong. She looked up and saw that its owner had the look of a Phaerie half-blood, like herself and Taine, but old – old! His sleek cap of hair was pewter grey, his face a mass of lines and wrinkles and he leant upon a heavy staff, though his stance was upright for one so aged. His eyes were hooded, piercing, dark and wise, as befitted one of his venerable years, yet his engaging smile belonged to the youth he once had been.

'Come,' he said again, more urgently this time. 'Trust me. Your lives depend upon it. There is a shelter of sorts nearby that we can reach if you are stout of heart.' He smiled wryly. 'And I have no doubt that you are. You need not fear the ghosts. As long as you are with me, you will be protected.'

He lifted his hand and a glimmer of light appeared around him, illuminating their immediate surroundings with a faint golden radi-ance. They scrambled to their feet and limped after him as quickly as they could, though Aelwen noticed that Taine still had his sword drawn. Moving faster than they had expected, the ancient one led them away from the river and into the trees. The phantom horde fell back before them, but one glance over her shoulder told Aelwen that they were following, crowding behind the travellers and dogging their footsteps. She did not dare look again, and despite the pain of her many wounds she quickened her steps.

The forest here was dense and dark, dwarfing them beneath the massive trees. All the undergrowth had been choked off for want of light, and they moved as if traversing the gigantic, pillared hall of some ancient king. Behind them and close on either side flowed the ghosts, their gibbering hushed now; stalking, waiting. Suddenly there was a glimmer of white through the trees, and a few more steps brought Aelwen into a small, cramped clearing, in the centre of which sat a most peculiar structure. It was a simple dome, a perfect hemisphere hewn from white marble, carved with a multitude of runes, some recognisably Phaerie, others incomprehensible and strange, all of them shimmering with power. It stood no taller than Aelwen at its apex and had no doors or windows that she could see.

The phantoms had fallen back now, unable or unwilling to enter the clearing, but Aelwen could still feel their hatred and hostility gnawing at her like iron teeth. The ancient guide turned back to his companions. 'This is my dwelling,' he said simply. 'In a manner of speaking, and such as it is. Now, before I permit you to enter, I wish to know why and how you came here.'

Taine looked at him suspiciously. 'And I wish to know more about *you*. Is this truly a shelter? Or a trap? Who are you, and what do you want with us?'

Aelwen turned to her lover in astonishment. Somehow, it had never occurred to her to doubt their benefactor. Something in his demeanour, in his eyes, had made her trust him at once. 'Taine,' she protested. 'He wants to help us. He saved us from the ghosts.'

'How do we know he's not in league with them? It would be easy enough to have them attack us so that he could pretend to rescue us and lure us here.'

'It is no trap,' the old one replied, 'though I understand your suspicion, for there is nothing in this haunted place that breeds trust, or indeed any good feelings. Though your instincts for survival have no doubt stood you in good stead through the years, in this case your lady's intuition will serve you better.'

Seeing the scowl on Taine's face, Aelwen took the initiative before he could speak again. 'We are cautious because we are fugitives,' she explained, 'fleeing from the Phaerie. We are under a sentence of death in Eliorand, so every stranger must seem a threat – even one who has just saved our lives.'

A keen light kindled in those wise old eyes. 'You are fleeing Hellorin? Then all is well, my friends. If you are foes of the Forest Lord you will have nothing to fear from me, for he is my enemy also.'

Aelwen could see the struggle taking place in Taine's eyes. *What happened to you, my love, in all our years apart, to make you so wary?* she thought. For the first time, it occurred to her that they were no longer the Taine and Aelwen of their youth, full of innocence and high ideals. Time and absence had made changes in them both.

A frisson of unease went through her. Then, to her relief, Taine exhaled with a sigh and his tense posture relaxed a little. 'Forgive my suspicion, sir,' he said. 'For many years my life has depended on wariness and vigilance. Such is the price for enmity with Hellorin.'

The ancient one nodded. 'I understand all too well the bitter price you have paid, my friend, for I too have paid, and still am paying now. But let us go inside. The ghosts cannot enter this place. Though it is not exactly comfortable, at least you can rest and, if you will, we can relate why and how we all came to be here.' He stepped forward and laid his hand on the curved stone of the strange structure and spoke a word in a language Aelwen did not understand. Beneath his hand a doorway appeared, a narrow archway with utter darkness beyond. 'Come,' he said, gesturing them to follow. 'I will lead the way so that you may have light.'

Aelwen ducked inside, leaving Taine no option but to follow. Whatever was inside, could it be worse than what awaited them out here in this haunted forest? She could only take the chance that it would not.

6
~

THE SORROW OF THE DWELVEN

Aelwen followed the old man quickly, ducking under the low arch, eager to be out of the clearing. Taine followed, sword still in his hand. Once they were safely inside, the door closed behind them, vanishing as if it had never been.

She felt the change as soon as she had crossed the threshold. The waves of fury and menace fell away as though they had been cut off with a knife. The pain from Aelwen's many wounds vanished abruptly, and when she looked down at herself in the light that surrounded the old one, she realised with a shock that the injuries had gone too. The bleeding had stopped. Her skin was smooth, whole and unblemished, and even the rents in her tattered clothing had somehow disappeared, the cloth and supple leather just as they had been before the attack. Wonderingly, she looked at Taine, and found him as uninjured as herself, though the expression of utter bafflement on his face must, she thought, be a mirror image of her own.

It was as though the attack had never happened.

It was as though the ghosts had never been.

Aelwen turned wondering eyes towards the ancient one, but before she could do more than draw in a breath to frame her question, he had answered her. 'You see these runes? This place is protected by very powerful spells. The ghosts may not enter here, and nor can any evil that they have done.'

'But – but what about when we leave? Will all those hurts come back?'

'No, my dear. Your injuries have been healed by the spells set about this place, and after I have told you the tragic history of those phantoms, it may be that your fear will be diminished also. And if you truly do not fear them, they will never be able to harm you again.'

Much as she liked this old one, Aelwen felt that she'd be reluctant to put his statement to the test. Curiously, she looked around this chamber that held such power, finally taking in all the details. Another shock ran through her like a cold, bright bolt of lightning. 'It's a tomb!'

The curving walls were the same grey stone as the exterior, carved all over with more of the glimmering runes – but in the centre stood a raised tomb of pure white marble. Incised into the lid was a complex symbol bordered by more of the incomprehensible runes, and carved beneath in Phaerie letters were two words:

'KALDATH. TRAITOR.'

Taine and Aelwen moved closer together, and the stranger sighed. 'I suppose I cannot fault your unease, after what you have experienced tonight, but you can rest easy, my children. There are no dead here. This tomb is empty, and nothing more than Hellorin's idea of a cruel jest. You see, long ages ago, he consigned me to a living death here on this island, as a warder of the ghosts you have seen and felt tonight. I am Kaldath, and this is my tomb, set here to remind me daily of my fate.'

Now it was Taine's turn to gasp. 'I've just realised where we are – or I think I have. And we both would have realised sooner, when we saw those spectres, if they had left us any chance to think. Is this the Haunted Isle?'

Kaldath gave a deprecating shrug. 'Could it be anywhere else? There are precious few other islands on this river.'

'So the legends are true.' Without thinking, Aelwen sat down on the edge of the tomb. This news, coming on top of all the shocks and alarms of the past hour, left her feeling a little shaky – and it was hardly surprising. All the Phaerie, Hemifae and Pureblood alike, had grown up with the horrific tales of this place, a long, narrow island in the middle of the border river. It was said to have been formed from thousands of corpses, the mound of flesh and blood and bone turned into stone and soil, by Hellorin's magic. Thus the Forest Lord had dealt with his enemies – though who they had been or what they had done had been hidden, forgotten or lost. It was said, however, that no Phaerie could survive a night on the island, for after dark all the ghosts of the slaughtered ones would come forth, thirsting for vengeance. Aelwen had always thought the whole legend nothing more than a tale to frighten gullible children. Tonight, she had learned the truth.

'But where do you fit into the story, sir?' Taine asked. 'If you are not a ghost, why are you imprisoned here?'

'First of all we should tell Kaldath who we are,' Aelwen interrupted, ignoring Taine's almost imperceptible shake of the head. 'My name is Aelwen and my companion is Taine, and as you already know, we have become enemies of the Forest Lord. How that happened, and the reason we apported so abruptly onto your island – well, that is a long and complicated tale.'

'Then you must make yourselves as comfortable as you can, Aelwen and Taine,' Kaldath said, 'for I can see that you are weary. For all these centuries I have needed neither sustenance nor sleep, though I have missed them greatly, but unless I miss my guess, you need both food and rest. Do you have any provisions?'

'Enough to get by,' Taine answered. 'And as for comforts, this place will serve us just as it is. We are only too glad to be safe.' Aelwen noticed the change in his attitude. He was beginning to warm to Kaldath, and she was glad.

The two travellers did their best to settle themselves. Fortunately, the air within the tomb was not cold, for the structure had no ventilation, so they were unable to make a fire. They sat with their backs to the tomb, stretching their legs out gratefully, and began to unwrap their provisions. Aelwen took a long drink from her water flask. While the ghosts had been attacking, fear had dried her mouth and throat, and now she was safe, she was suddenly conscious of a raging thirst.

Kaldath sat opposite them, with his back against the curving wall of the mausoleum. For a moment he said nothing. His head was bowed, as though he was concentrating on the hands that were folded in his lap, but his gaze was inward, seeing people and places that had vanished long ago. Then, seemingly with a great effort, he came back to the present, raised his eyes and looked at Taine and Aelwen.

'I am extremely old,' he began. 'So old that you would find it impossible to imagine all the years I have lived. My father was with Hellorin before the Phaerie even came to this mundane world, when we dwelt in another dimension of existence known as the Elsewhere.'

'*The Elsewhere?*' Aelwen had not intended to interrupt, but the question burst out of her in sheer surprise.

Kaldath, slightly put out at her interjection, looked at her sharply. 'How do you know of the Elsewhere? Our origins ceased to be common knowledge among the Phaerie long ago. Hellorin wished it to be so.'

Aelwen took a deep breath to explain, then thought better of it. Maybe Taine's wariness was contagious, but she found herself reluctant to tell Kaldath about the Windeye of the Xandim and her search for the Fialan, until she knew more about him. 'The explanation is long and complicated, and I fear it must wait for our part of the tale,' she said, 'but suffice it to say that a friend of ours has been there before, and returned there just before we came to this place, with another of our companions.'

Her brows drew together as a spasm of worry gripped her. In the shocks and dangers of the past few hours, she had almost forgotten Corisand and Iriana. Were they all right? Had they succeeded in their mission? Had they been able to return from the Elsewhere? So much of the sketchy plan that had been thrown together in haste in Athina's tower depended on them.

Kaldath's voice pulled her out of her reverie. 'I cannot believe this to be possible, and my mind is a whirl of questions.' He sighed. 'I said I would tell you my history first, however, and I will hold to that.'

'It may make the telling easier if I say that we know how the Phaerie came here from the Elsewhere. We know about the Moldai, and the Stone of Fate.'

Kaldath's mouth fell open. 'But how ...?' With an effort he collected himself. 'I am beginning to realise that more than chance brought you here to me. Maybe your desperate apport was not as random as you thought, Aelwen. I believe that fate, or some other influence, has played a part.'

The image of Athina immediately flashed into Aelwen's mind – but surely that couldn't be – could it? The kindly Creator who'd broken all the laws of her own kind to befriend the Windeye and her companions had been exiled from this world by her brethren, for meddling with its fate. And yet ... Aelwen knew how much the Cailleach had cared about this world she had created; had cared about – nay, loved – Dael, the mortal slave she'd rescued and adopted, for a brief, doomed, happy time, as her own son. If there was any chance that she could reach out and help she would, disregarding the risks to herself.

Kaldath was still speaking, and Aelwen wrenched her thoughts back to concentrate on the here and now.

'That you know of these matters will certainly shorten my tale,' he said, 'for it will save us a number of tedious explanations. There is one race you have not mentioned, however. You say you are aware of the Elsewhere and the Moldai, but do you also know of the Dwelven?'

Taine swallowed a mouthful of jerky and shook his head. 'That part of the tale we have not heard.' He turned aside to Aelwen with a smile, and pointed at the untouched food in her lap. 'Don't forget to eat.'

It was as if his words had unleashed her hunger. She took a huge bite of bread, but her eyes never left Kaldath as he continued. 'I suspected you might not. No one will speak of them, neither the Phaerie, the Magefolk nor the Moldai, for there is blame and shame on all sides. The Moldai failed to protect their companions, permitting Hellorin to snatch them away into slavery, and the Magefolk and Phaerie – well, you will hear that presently.

'The Dwelven and the Moldai had close ties, like the Phaerie and the mortals, save for one fundamental difference: the Dwelven were not slaves. The relationship was far more complex; symbiotic, if you will, based much more on love than power. And just as the Moldai were not shaped like the Phaerie, the Dwelven had different forms from mortals. They were – well, you saw their spectres here tonight. You know what they looked like.'

'Those creatures?' Taine said. 'But as far as I could see there seemed to be two entirely different types, the quick, lithe ones and the heavy ones with the rounded carapaces. Surely they cannot be the same race.'

'Yet they are. As they grow older they change from one form to the other. The quick, lithe ones, as you call them, are known as the Sidrai. They are the younger Dwelven. This is how they start their lives. They are the warriors, the foragers, the artisans. When they reach a certain age – about a hundred and fifty years, in our terms – they metamorphose.

'When a group is ready to make the transformation, for siblings from the same hatching tend to change more or less at the same time, they find themselves becoming sleepy and slow. Then there is a ceremony, and all their friends come, both to celebrate and perhaps weep a little too for, as with any of the great transformations in our existence, there is some sorrow for what is being left behind, as well as joy in the expectation of what is to come. The Oredai, the other type of Dwelven, are there also. They dig special chambers, one for each of the Sidrai, deep within the rock underground, and the Sidrai are sealed within. They sink into oblivion for a long time – almost a year – and when they awake they have transformed. They dig their way out of the chambers to where the other Oredai are waiting to welcome them, and help them begin their new lives.

'The Oredai are the miners, who can dig through solid rock with their powerful claws and forelimbs. It is they who make the underground dwellings and shelters for themselves and their Sidrai brethren, and they who mine metals and gems for the Sidrai to work and trade. They also bear the young. Before it metamorphoses, a Sidran will mate many times – they are hermaphrodite, both male and female together, so that all of them can form eggs, and all can fertilise. The eggs remain within them, very small and undeveloped, until the Sidrai transform. Then each of the Oredai will dig a nursery, wall itself up inside, and tend the eggs until they hatch – as Sidrai. They are then returned to the Sidrai community to learn and grow, and the whole cycle begins all over again.' While Kaldath had been speaking of the Dwelven he had been looking far away into his memories. Now he raised his head and looked at his new companions.

Aelwen had been utterly absorbed in his tale, and now found herself sitting with her partly eaten chunk of bread in her hand, half-lifted to her mouth. She took a bite, wondering how long she'd been holding it there. Taine was frowning. 'You said that neither the Phaerie nor Magefolk nor Moldai would talk about the Dwelven because there was shame on both sides,' he said. 'So tell me, how were the Magefolk involved in this? What did Hellorin do to the Dwelven and why did the Moldai permit it? Or was it that they simply couldn't stop him?'

A mirthless smile, almost a grimace, passed across Kaldath's face. 'I see you know the Forest Lord well.'

'Too well, and to my cost,' Taine said grimly.

Aelwen was about to protest that Hellorin was not all bad: he could be good-humoured, charming and generous, he was protective of his people and a good ruler of the Phaerie, for under his auspices his people had flourished. One only needed to observe the chaos that had befallen his realm in his absence to see that. He had loved his lifemate, Estrelle, Aelwen's Pureblood half-sister, beyond everything, and his son and daughter too. He'd loved and nurtured his horses ...

His slaves.

At that moment, she realised that the driving force behind Hellorin, his real love, was power. He could afford to be kind and generous to those in his sway, but if they opposed him, another, darker side of his character emerged. Power was what he craved, to the point of enslaving entire races. With a shudder she realised that though he had been content for a time within the realm he had carved out in the mundane world, that state of affairs would not, could not last, especially now that he'd come so close to regaining the Fialan. A chill struck her heart as she finally understood that he would never stop now until he had regained the Stone – and if he succeeded, he would stretch out his hand to enslave the Wizards, then the other Magefolk, only ceasing when he held the whole world in his grasp.

He had to be stopped.

Someone had to stop him, and that staggering responsibility had landed squarely on the shoulders of herself and her companions.

'Aelwen?' Taine touched her face gently, and she came out of her dreadful thoughts to see the concern in his eyes. 'Are you all right? You went absolutely white. Are you still hurt somehow?'

'I'm all right. I'm sorry. I was thinking about Hellorin, and ...' She shuddered. 'Never mind. It's just that I suddenly realised exactly what we were up against.'

'The Forest Lord is a formidable enemy, as we all know to our cost,' Kaldath said. 'Even to beings as mighty as the Moldai. You know that when the Stone of Fate was made, the Moldai included a spell that the Phaerie could never complete, so the Fialan would never be completely in Hellorin's power?'

Taine and Aelwen nodded.

'In his rage, the Phaerie Lord swore to be revenged upon them. When he brought his own people into this world he cast a spell to bring the Dwelven also, sundering them for ever from the Moldai. Ghabal, to his credit, even though he was driven insane as the titanic forces of the Fialan opened a portal between the Elsewhere and this realm, tried to protect them, wresting them away from Hellorin's control. But they emerged from the Moldan's shattered peak in the mundane world, and the Magefolk, having never seen their like before, believed them to be responsible for the disaster.

'The Winged Folk, who dwelt closest to what is now known as Steelclaw, feared some kind of invasion from unknown beings from beneath the ground. They called on their allies the Wizards to use their powers of Earth to help them, and the Wizards cast a spell that would seal them beneath Steelclaw's remains. Unfortunately, Hellorin discovered their whereabouts and, since they were already confined by magic, they could not escape him. He broke the Wizards' spells and enslaved the Dwelven, taking them to the mountains to the north of Eliorand, to mine the gems that the Phaerie use so freely, for ornament and for trade.'

'You mean those mines were all excavated by the Dwelven?' Taine asked in surprise.

'He put the Sidrai to work cutting and polishing the gemstones. The greater part of the original mine network was excavated by the Oredai, though since Hellorin – disposed – of the Dwelven, he has used mortal slaves to continue the work, notwithstanding that they have no natural feel for tunnelling and for stone. To be underground was natural to the Dwelven, though the Sidrai spent a lot of time above ground, but not for mortals. Many of his human slaves die from overwork, lung diseases, accidents and cave-ins, but what is that to the Forest Lord, so long as he obtains his gems?'

'You seem to be very familiar with the mines and the conditions underground,' Taine commented.

'Indeed I am – and that brings me to the final, tragic part of my tale. You will see that I am Hemifae, like yourselves, but you do not realise that I am the same as Taine – part Phaerie and part Wizard.'

'The same as *me*?' Taine's mouth dropped open. 'But I – but how—' He put his hands up to his face, and when he took them away again, his eyes glistened. 'I thought I was the only one,' he said softly.

Kaldath smiled gently. 'Not many people can claim that. As soon as I saw you I recognised that you were the same as me. My father was one of the Phaerie diplomatic party sent to Tyrineld to negotiate the borders of the Wizards' realm and ours when he fell in love with my mother.'

He sighed. 'Their love was doomed. The year I was born a plague struck Tyrineld. Before a cure could be found, many perished. My mother was a Healer and, while treating the victims, she was infected, and died. My father brought me to Eliorand, along with a mortal slave who'd been bribed to say she was my mother.'

'That sounds not unlike my own background,' Taine said. 'But when Hellorin finally discovered my true identity he was livid, and I was forced to flee for my life.'

'That sounds like Hellorin – he never changes,' Kaldath said wryly. 'As far as we knew, my secret remained undiscovered, but I always believed that Hellorin could sense some fundamental difference. I'm sure that's why he sent me north, away from the city of Eliorand. I was Overseer of the mines and the Dwelven, and for many years I fulfilled my duties efficiently and well. But the more I came to know the Dwelven, the more I came to understand and care for them, and the more they came to trust me, I realised just how angry and unhappy they were, forcibly sundered from the Moldai, dragged unwillingly to a new and very different world, and enslaved. As time went on I felt increasing distaste for my role as Hellorin's slavemaster, and my sympathy with his slaves deepened until finally I could live with myself no longer. Though I could not return them to their original world, I joined with them in planning to overthrow the Forest Lord, so that they could be free forever from his tyranny.'

Kaldath was silent for a moment, the lines in his aged face deepening with sorrow, his eyes dark and clouded with the memory of old pain. 'We were not alone,' he said at last. 'Others joined us: human slaves and disaffected Hemifae, who were sick of all the privilege and ease going to the Purebloods, while they themselves were the ones who kept the Phaerie civilisation running. At first we were at a loss, unable to find a way to broach Hellorin's citadel, but finally an opportunity arose.

'The Forest Lord was desperately proud of his horses, caring far more about their welfare than that of his slaves. They were remarkable creatures, far superior to the ordinary beasts outside the Phaerie realms, though whence they came I do not know. Hellorin captured the original herd not long after we came here from the Elsewhere, but he was always tremendously secretive – almost suspiciously so – about their origins. As far as I know, he told only his son Arvain where he found them and how he subdued them.'

'I can help you there,' Aelwen said bitterly, unable to keep silent. Then she got hold of herself. 'But I beg pardon for interrupting again, Kaldath. Please finish your tale before I begin mine.'

Kaldath tilted an eyebrow, looking at her curiously. 'I am most interested in what you have to tell me, for I have often wondered about Hellorin's special horses. But as to my own tale: as I said, an opportunity finally presented itself, and it was all because of those very animals. The Forest Lord felt that he was too far from his horses, for they were quartered on the outskirts of the city, and so he ordered that the Dwelven should be brought down to Eliorand to construct a tunnel that would lead right through the hill itself beneath the city, linking the palace with the stables.'

Aelwen forgot her good intentions not to interrupt again. 'Why, I often wondered who constructed that tunnel,' she gasped. 'It's a work of incredible skill. I always believed that it must have been formed by some exceptionally clever magic, and I couldn't understand why its creator had not been honoured.'

'Hellorin honour the Dwelven?' Kaldath replied bitterly. 'That's the last thing he would have done, even if the situation had turned out differently, and his slaves had simply done their work and returned to the mines … But of course, they did not. Under cover of their legitimate work the Oredai dug a secret passage from the original excavation site, right up into the palace itself. It came out in the cellars. One night our forces flooded through the passage and the fight began.'

He paused, and rubbed a hand across his face. 'I blame myself. I should have known better than to let them go up against the Forest Lord – to even encourage them in such a mad notion. At first, however, all went well and we dared to hope. Though the Dwelven are small, they are formidable fighters. You had an example of that tonight. Through their skills and through sheer strength of numbers we overwhelmed the kitchen staff, then the guards and the courtiers without too much trouble – but we had failed to reckon with Hellorin's magic. If the Forest Lord had the might to defy the Moldai and bring his entire race through from the Elsewhere to this world, why would he find the Dwelven a threat? I knew that he had let part of his powers pass into the Fialan, and had calculated that, without it, he would be weakened, so that we might stand a chance – but oh, how wrong I was!'

A tear ran down his seamed old face and he wiped it away with a shaking hand.

'I should have known. I should have seen, but I did not, and after all this time I still can hardly bear to remember the consequences. With one spell – a single spell – Hellorin slaughtered the entire Dwelven race. And the legends are true. He deposited the bodies in this river on the edge of his borders and transformed them into an island. The other surviving rebels, human and Hemifae, were all captured and executed – all but me. I had helped the Dwelven and I was their Overseer, so he laid the ultimate blame at my door and decided that my punishment should be linked to their fate. Before all the Phaerie, he cast a spell that bound me here for ever with the ghosts of the race I had led to their deaths, and twisted my own magic so that I could age but never die. Here I have remained ever since, living through the

75

centuries in sorrow and remorse, surrounded by the unquiet spirits that are a testament to my failure to free the Dwelven or to keep them safe. And down through all those long and bitter years, no one has ever set foot here – until tonight. Until you came, apparently by accident, knowing of the Elsewhere and the Fialan. No wonder the ghosts are uneasy tonight. They know that you are the harbingers of change, and that one way or another, you will bring an ending.'

Kaldath looked from one to the other, his dark eyes searching their faces. 'The ghosts are not the only ones who are uneasy, however. You suddenly appear out of nowhere, talking of the Elsewhere, and I look at you with a mixture of hope and fear. I can see that you are weary, but please tell me your tale now. As I said before, I am certain that your coming here is more than mere accident, or coincidence.'

Ignoring a ferocious dig in the ribs from Taine, and overriding his protests in mindspeech, Aelwen took a deep breath and began to relate her tale to Kaldath. Her trust in the old man had remained steadfast throughout his tale, and all her instincts were telling her that he was, or would be, a friend. She began with a brief account of the ambush on the Phaerie, and saw his shock when she told of the fall of Hellorin, and how the Forest Lord had been taken out of time to preserve his life, and been trapped in the Elsewhere.

'And you say that Hellorin has a daughter now?' Kaldath gasped. 'And *she* is ruling the Phaerie?'

'Not any more,' Aelwen told him, 'but let me tell you the rest of it.' She tried to block out Taine's growing agitation as she recounted the tale, finally bringing events up to the present.

Kaldath, who had been hanging on to her every word, shook his head. 'I can only hope that the fates are kinder to you in your rash undertaking than they were to me, for if Hellorin should escape the Elsewhere, you may rue the day you decided to bring the Fialan to this mundane realm. The thought of its power let loose in this world chills me, and I hardly know whether to hope your friends will succeed or fail. I only wish that I could leave this place and help you, for something tells me that you'll need all the help you can get. But now you must rest. Tomorrow, with its burdens, will come soon enough.'

Much as they wanted to prolong the discussion with Kaldath, they could stay awake no longer. Curled in Taine's arms, Aelwen fell into the profound slumber of the utterly exhausted, but as time went by, she began to dream. Mounted on her black stallion Taryn, she was flying with the Wild Hunt. Their weapons, hands and shining raiment were all stained with blood, and the great, silver fellhounds, the hounds of terror, streamed ahead of them through the sky. As she rode, she felt the fierce exhilaration of their bloodlust and the savage joy of the kill – yet somewhere in the dark depths of her mind, a small, lone voice, like the frantic wingbeats of a trapped bird, kept repeating: 'This is wrong, this is wrong, this is wrong ...'

The Hunt flew into a bank of cloud that was tinged with the smoky blood-hues of a sullen sunset, and burst out of the other side into a scene of blood-freezing horror. The Forest Lord, vast, mighty, towering thousands of feet tall, bestrode the land like a colossus, with one giant, booted foot planted in Eliorand and the other in the Wizard city of Tyrineld. Below him, the forest was crushed and mangled, its trees strewn like splintered matchwood across the earth. The moors and farmland were a desert, a wasteland piled high with mangled corpses and gleaming shards of bone. In one huge hand, he held Aelwen's companions, Iriana and Corisand, Dael, Kelon and Taine, oh, Taine ...

Hellorin turned his head and looked directly at her. Their eyes met and locked across the crimson skies. Then slowly, with a feral grin, he closed his hand, and the screams of her friends tore into her heart with bloody claws.

The fist clenched tight.

The screaming ceased.

Blood dripped from the Forest Lord's hand, between his knotted fingers.

'No, no, no!' Aelwen woke up screaming, with Taine's arms clasped tightly around her, his face pale and taut with worry. 'Aelwen, wake up! Wake up, my love, it's only a dream. Just a dream. You're safe. I've got you.' His voice cut through the panic, bathing her in a calming flow of words, until her breathing eased, her frantic heartbeat slowed and the shaking had ebbed from her taut muscles. Forgetting all pride and dignity Aelwen clung to him, taking comfort in his warmth and nearness, until she felt steady and calm again, and only the bitter dregs of the dream remained, like a shadow on her heart. For the first time, then, she noticed that Kaldath was also kneeling beside her, his face grooved deeply with disquiet and concern.

'Do you want to tell me about it?' Taine said softly. 'Can you tell me?'

Aelwen looked from his worried face to that of Kaldath. 'I think I should,' she said.

It cost her a great amount of effort to recount her nightmare; to relive the horror and the fear. By the time she had finished, she was shaking again, and Taine held her close to him, stroking her hair. 'By the Light,' he said, his voice subdued, 'now I understand why you were screaming.'

Aelwen took a deep breath, determined to pull herself together, and eased herself out of Taine's comforting embrace. Rummaging around until she found her flask of water, she took a long swig, feeling it flood, cool and soothing, down her raw throat as she swallowed. 'I'm sorry, I didn't mean to be so feeble. I'm an idiot, getting all upset over nothing more than a bad dream.'

Kaldath looked graver than ever. 'Nothing more than a bad dream, you say? I view this as the gravest of portents. What if it is a warning? What if it foreshadows the Forest Lord's return?'

'But – but according to Corisand, Hellorin's trapped in the Elsewhere,' Aelwen protested, not wanting to think about the alternatives.

'Supposing he escapes?' Taine said. 'Supposing the Windeye and the Wizard have failed, and he has regained the Stone? We have no idea what's happening in the Elsewhere, and unless the Wizard and the Windeye return, we'll never know.'

'Unless Hellorin suddenly puts in an appearance.' Aelwen shuddered. 'Oh, we were fools not to wait at the tower until our friends came back.'

'We couldn't. Athina had no time left – she was forced to return to her own realm.'

'That would only have affected us,' Aelwen pointed out. 'Corisand and Iriana needed her help to send them where they were going, but we used Tiolani's flying spell. We could have done that any time.'

'So long as we had Tiolani's cooperation. But you know how emotional and uncertain she was. We had to strike while the iron was hot, Aelwen – if she'd been forced to wait, she might have had time to reconsider. Then the entire scheme would have failed.'

'And now, because I saved you and left her behind, she may well have changed her mind in any case. I wish we *knew*: about Tiolani, about Corisand and Iriana. How are we supposed to make a plan when we're floundering around in ignorance like this?'

'It was never like this in the legends we were told as children,' Taine said wryly. 'Real life is a lot more bloody complicated.'

Aelwen got to her feet. 'Then let's simplify it.' She began ticking points off on her fingers. 'One: we have to do something. We can't

78

just sit around here for ever. Two: my dream might just have been a nightmare, plain and simple, with no other significance at all. After the things Kaldath told us, I wouldn't be surprised. Corisand and Iriana might have succeeded, and if that's the case, they'll be headed for Eliorand.'

'And they must be warned that we've failed,' Taine finished for her. 'We must go straight to our meeting place in the cave. Maybe we can hide nearby and watch the approaches, just in case Tiolani decides to ambush us. And as for the matter of Hellorin's return ... Well, I have an idea about that.'

He turned to Kaldath, who had been watching their debate in silence. 'You want to free the spirits of the Dwelven, and be revenged on the Forest Lord, don't you?'

For an instant, the eyes of the Ancient One kindled. 'It is my greatest wish, and were it accomplished, I could finally lay down the burden of these weary years, and rest. But it is impossible. Hellorin holds us here on the island with his curse.'

'Ah, but if the Lord of the Phaerie is no longer in this world?' Taine asked slyly. 'Does his curse have power then? I suspect you can leave here, all of you, right now.'

Kaldath turned pale. 'Leave? Now? After all these centuries, could it really be so easy?'

'But surely, if that is the case, shouldn't Hellorin's spell be gone too?' Aelwen asked. 'Kaldath said that there was a curse and a spell, the curse to keep them on the island, and the spell to bind them in this ghostly form and stop them going to their rest.'

Taine shook his head. 'They can try, but I don't think it'll work. Those great Royal spells of the Forest Lord are like no other, to preserve the safety and continuity of the Phaerie realm. I suspect that this spell, like the flying magic, will have passed to Hellorin's heir while he is no longer in this world, but Tiolani never cursed the Dwelven. I may be wrong, but I suspect that Hellorin's power to maintain his curse passed from this world when he did.'

Kaldath straightened, suddenly looking old and fragile no longer, but fierce and strong. 'We will make some trials, Taine and Aelwen, while you complete your rest. If what you say is true, we will come with you to Eliorand, and wreak our long-overdue revenge upon the Phaerie. Then we will force Tiolani, last scion of Hellorin's house, to remove his accursed spell, and set us free at last.'

'That's fine,' Taine said, 'but before we do that we have to find our own missing companions, Iriana, Corisand and Dael. Once we've done that we'll all go to Eliorand together and pay Tiolani a little visit. Agreed?'

Kaldath nodded. 'Agreed.'

7
~

FROM ENDINGS TO BEGINNINGS

It felt like a new start. Though a thin veil of grey covered the sky, occasional glimpses of the sun could be seen beyond the clouds. The air was cool, with a sneaky breeze that tugged on hair, tweaked at clothing and slipped chilly fingers down the neck of Iriana's sheep-skin coat as she sat by the shore of the lake with Melik, using the cat's vision to look back at the island and its tower. Since the previous evening, when Iriana and her friend Corisand had returned from the Elsewhere to the Tower in the Forest, it felt as though her world, her life had been remade.

Everything seemed different now. In a scant handful of days, Iriana had grown up.

Some of her friends had taken years to do it, approaching the process day to day, step by step, gradually finding themselves with different challenges and concerns, changing relationships and new, seemingly ever-increasing, responsibilities as the reins of their life were transferred from the grip of their parents and teachers into their own, often unsteady hands. Iriana had observed them: Chathak leant heavily upon his effervescent sense of humour to cope with the changes; Ionor used his devastating intelligence and Yinze, her be-loved foster brother with the handsome face and flashing smile, had charmed his way effortlessly through any difficulties. Thara managed by being sturdy, practical and down-to-earth, helped along by her expansive belly laugh, sparkling eyes, and those lush curves that had men flocking from miles around. Melisanda, tall, fair and willowy, with her thoughtful grey eyes and her wry observations on life, had developed a fount of compassion, a boundless empathy with those in pain, and her mind and hands worked in tandem to create Healing magic of great power and exquisite skill.

Then there was Avithan.

In many ways, his climb to adulthood had been the most difficult of all. How could it not be? As the son of the Archwizard, his responsibilities – plus a heavy burden of expectation on the part of his parents – had descended upon him early. The pressure on him to conform to his father's wishes had been immense, yet somehow he had always managed to take his own path which, though it may have disappointed Cyran, had never put them into overt conflict.

Iriana had never felt that she'd matured in the same way as the rest of her friends. Though she had excelled in her studies and her magic was probably the most powerful in a group of very talented Wizards, it had seemed as though her foster mother Zybina and Cyran's soulmate Sharalind were determined to keep her a child for ever. Her struggle for independence had been hard fought and long. Out of the whole group, Iriana was the only one who had not travelled, or tested herself and her powers in any way, and that knowledge had eroded her spirits and gnawed at her confidence.

Now that had all changed.

Iriana had every reason to be proud of herself. She had passed beyond the boundaries of the world and the reality she had always known. She had found a new and wonderful friendship with Corisand, the astonishing Windeye of the shapeshifting Xandim, whom she had known now in both her human and equine forms. She had finally found the freedom, excitement and adventure she had always dreamed about.

Not bad for a blind Wizard girl who had been overprotected by well-meaning people all her life.

So why was she so sad?

Her victories had cost her dearly. She had lost three of the beloved animal companions who had acted as her eyes: Boreas, the great eagle, lost when he had taken a mate. Seyka, the beautiful white owl who had helped the Wizard guard the camp at night, slain by the Phaerie assassin who, not so many nights ago, had almost succeeded in wiping out Iriana and her companions. Dailika, the mare she had trained to carry a blind girl in safety and confidence, whose strange, peripheral equine vision she had shared on so many occasions; fled in terror and madness after Iriana had turned her into the weapon that had ended the cruel life of that same assassin. Was Dailika dead now, killed by her injuries or some wild beast? Did she wander the forest, lost in a nightmare of terror and madness? Or was she lying somewhere, injured and helpless, dying slowly, horribly by inches, waiting for Iriana to come and take care of her as the Wizard had always done?

It tortured her that she did not, could not, know.

Though Iriana did know the fate of her two lost Wizardly companions, it brought her no comfort. Esmon, Head of the Luen of Warriors, the kind, wise, amusing mentor who had taught her so much on this first expedition, was dead now, his throat slit, his heart pierced by the assassin's blade. She clenched her fists against the pain as she remembered having to perform his funeral rites, flashing his body into flame with her magic and scattering his ashes to the winds.

Lost also, but still foremost in her thoughts, was Avithan, son of the Archwizard Cyran. They had been the closest of friends for most of her life, and recently, on this ill-fated journey, had taken the first tentative step towards becoming lovers. Even Avithan, the stalwart rock of her existence upon whom she could always depend – though she would never admit that to him – was gone now. Though she had managed to save his life in the assassin's attack, he'd been so close to death that the powerful Cailleach, Lady of the Mists, had taken him back with her to her own mysterious, timeless realm Beyond the World, with the faintest of hopes that she might be able to heal him there. Even if she did succeed, however, the chances that he would be able to return were slim.

At least he has a chance, Iriana told herself firmly. She straightened her shoulders and lifted her chin. And without all the rest of it, the struggle and sadness and loss, she would have missed so much. She remembered the joy of buying provisions for their expedition in Tyrineld market, and the bubbling feeling of excitement that had come from knowing that she was about to escape the city and all her well-meaning but suffocating guardians at last, and have the freedom and adventure she had always longed for. She recalled the happy nights around the campfire, Esmon's jokes and all the valuable things he had taught her, the satisfaction of learning to use her special bond with her animals to safeguard the camp. The heady feeling of responsibility when Esmon had wanted her to take night watches just like the others.

She remembered the night when Avithan kissed her, and everything changed between them, becoming special and precious and new.

I wouldn't have missed any of it, she realised. And even though it all ended badly, with bloodshed and death and loss, I would pay that price, to have all the rest. Because of it I've changed and grown – and I'm strong enough to go on from here, and face the next adventure.

She got to her feet and called Melik, scooping the cat up in her arms to sit in his usual perch on her shoulders. She had better go and find Corisand and Dael. They still had a lot to do and a long way to go – and it was high time they got started.

Dael looked around the room and wondered where to begin. It was almost time to leave the tower that had been his home for the happiest months of his life, and he would have to choose which of his belongings to take with him, and pack them up ready to go. It was proving to be a difficult task. Before he had come here, the very idea of his own possessions had been so out of reach as to be laughable. All he had owned were the rags on his back and a blunt, rusty old belt knife that he had found one day beneath some bushes. Now he was surrounded by untold riches: an entire collection of warm clothing, a thick new cloak, boots for his feet and a new, keen blade that hung from his leather belt.

His new wealth consisted of more than just clothes. There, propped in a corner, was his fishing gear, the hooks and rods and other assorted paraphernalia that Athina had created for him, and on the table lay the books and scrolls that she had been using to teach him to read and write.

Dael sank down on the rocking chair by the hearth, his face in his hands. How he missed his beloved Athina, the Cailleach; builder of worlds and one of the most powerful beings in all Creation, who had taken him in on a stormy night when he'd been injured, starving and close to death. She had created this chamber for him, the first room that had ever belonged solely to him. Everything had been placed with a view to his comfort and pleasure, especially the cosy bed with its soft blankets and warm, down-filled quilt – again, the first real bed he had ever owned. Her thoughtful touch was everywhere, from the bright magical lamps that bloomed into radiance at his touch, to the soft cushions on the rocking chair, to the thick, tufted rugs on the floor with their bright and cheerful hues.

Up to the point where Athina had rescued him, he had existed in a world filled with insecurity, pain and fear. A lowly human slave in a world where magic and its wielders reigned supreme, he had been at the mercy of careless masters and his brutal, vile-tempered father who had dragged him into a mass escape of slaves, who had left him to starve in the forest, at the mercy of the Phaerie Hunt. He had been on the threshold of death when she had found him and taken him in.

She had healed him. She had saved him.

She had loved him, just as much as he had loved her.

She had left him – no, that wasn't true. She had been forced to leave by her fellow Creators; forced to quit this world that she had formed, incredibly, from her powers and imagination; a world that she loved so much she had almost sacrificed those powers in an attempt to save its denizens from their own folly. Dael would give all his new possessions, give the tower and all its comforts, give the entire world just to be with her again, but Athina's brethren would never permit her to return, and as a mere mortal, utterly devoid of magic, he could not follow where she had gone.

She had explained it all to him before she'd left, and they had clung to each other and wept. An arbitrary twist of fate had brought them together, but now they were being cruelly and permanently torn apart. Dael would live out the rest of his brief mortal life in a world which had made him little better than a beast of burden, and Athina would have all eternity to mourn his loss.

A great wave of fury at the unfairness of it all swept over Dael. A savage oath, howled in anguish, tore out of him as he leapt to his feet and overthrew the table, scattering pens and parchment. The ink hit the floor in a great dark splatter that obscured the brilliant colours of the rug. He stared in horror at the destruction. Without Athina, was he already reverting to the half-wild, hating, skulking creature that once he had been?

No. He set his jaw. It wouldn't happen. He would not permit it. He owed his benefactress far better than that. Slowly, carefully, he began to clean up the mess, and as he picked up the small collection of volumes that had taught him more about the nature and history of his world than he could ever have imagined, he vowed that somehow he would find room to take them with him. He wouldn't go back to the way he had lived before Athina had taken him in. She had given him his independence and his courage, and he was going to damn well fight to keep them.

'And I'll do more than that.' Dael stopped what he was doing and stood very still, a new fire of resolution burning in his heart.

'I escaped from the Phaerie. I survived against all odds. I found a wonderful home with the most extraordinary being who ever graced this sad little world. She saw someone, something within me that I never could have imagined in a million years. And now I'm going to be that person. I won't let her down. And if Athina can't come to me, then I'll find a way back to her. Somehow, somewhere, there *must* be a way, and I'll find it, even supposing it takes me the rest of my life.'

Corisand had very little to pack. Just a coat that had belonged to Athina, some clothing borrowed from Iriana and shrunk by magic to suit her shorter, more compact stature, a cloak and Dael's spare pair of boots that had been similarly altered to fit. She'd found a belt knife and eating utensils, which she was still learning to handle, in the tower kitchen, and blankets upstairs. She had come here with nothing but the beauty of her dappled grey hide and a burning desire in her heart to save her enslaved people, and she was aghast at all the paraphernalia she suddenly required. After all, until three days ago she had been a horse, or at least had taken the form of one, and her requirements had been comparatively few. Born of the shapeshifting Xandim, she had finally discovered her ability to change to human form, and with this new body had come all sorts of wants and needs. Clothing, blankets, eating utensils …

She gave a snort of disgust that sounded very like the horse from which she had so recently been transformed. All her life she had thought of these bipeds – in her own experience these were the Phaerie who had enslaved her people, though now she understood that they came in other kinds too, such as the Wizard and the mortal that made up the odd little group of which she was now a part – as being all-powerful. Who could have guessed that their bodies would be so feeble and frail? They couldn't run as fast as a horse, or jump as high and far, they couldn't travel long distances without a lot of rests involving all the fuss of camps and fires, blankets and tents to sleep in, pots with which to cook their food, cups, bowls and a bewildering array of implements with which to eat the stuff … Really, there was just no end to it.

Of course, she had one other possession. While she'd been thinking, Corisand's eyes had automatically come to rest, as they so often did, on the staff of dark, polished wood with its pair of twining serpents that no longer held the glowing green Fialan, the Stone of Fate. Now the Fialan lay glowing on the tabletop beside the staff, and from where she stood, six feet away beside the bed, she could feel its power beating against her skin.

She and Iriana had won the artefact in the otherworldly realms of the Elsewhere, having battled their way through dreadful obstacles and dangers, and brought it back to their own world in triumph. It was thanks to the extraordinary power of the Stone that Corisand could hold her human shape here, finally breaking the spell that the Phaerie Lord Hellorin had been using to enslave her race in their equine form. As a human, she could finally access the magic that was her birthright as the Windeye, or Shaman of the Xandim, and now she planned to use these hard-won powers to rescue her people from their long captivity.

In the meantime, however, Corisand had another challenge before her: one she could not put off any longer, though it made her afraid to the very depths of her soul. Since returning from the Elsewhere, she had stayed in her new human aspect, terrified that if she reverted to equine form she would once again be unable to access her magic. Unable to change back. All her life she had been trapped as a horse. Powerless, frustrated, unable to be all she could be; unable to help her people. She was the Windeye. She had inherited the burden on the death of her sire Valir, and in that hour her thoughts had changed from the drives and instincts of an animal. In a flash she had known the history of her race: their abilities, their potential, their betrayal and enslavement.

With the help of Taku and Aurora, two powerful elemental beings in the Elsewhere, and her newfound friend Iriana, Corisand had gained the Fialan and regained her human form in the mundane world. Her magic sang within her, the power and wonder and joy of it. How could she risk losing that again? How could she bear it, if she did?

There was no choice, however. The only way to get her people away, far and fast, from the clutches of the Forest Lord was to use his own magic against him: in this case, the spell, unique to the Phaerie royal line, that could make the Xandim fly. Hellorin's daughter Tiolani had agreed, albeit reluctantly, to help her with this, but in order to take advantage of it, Corisand needed to lead her people in her equine shape. She doubted that they would recognise or trust her in this new form, and she could not risk failure. In her heart she knew that this would be her only chance. If she wanted to save her people she must risk herself.

But not alone, since Iriana had come into her life. Corisand was still getting used to having a friend to lean on, and to support in her turn. Horses, herd animals who were never really comfortable alone, would group together. Sometimes they would form close bonds, but they did not make friends in the same way as these bipeds did. Since Corisand had become Windeye she had been increasingly isolated from her fellow Xandim, and she had felt that she would never regain that comfortable feeling of belonging that she had known in the old days of innocence and ignorance. Then Iriana had come along and she'd formed a new sort of friendship, unlike the former equine herd-bond: more specific and individual, both cerebral and emotional. The best part of it was that she never felt alone now. There was always someone to turn to. Somehow the burdens that attached to the role of Windeye seemed less insurmountable, now that she had a friend.

She and Iriana had discussed the matter long into the night, and had finally decided that she would stand the best chance of changing back from her equine shape if she had the Fialan with her. After several tries, concentrating so hard that she'd thought her brain would burst, Corisand persuaded the Stone to come loose from the staff. Then Dael had found a small leather pouch and attached a long braided leather thong, so that she could hang it round her neck and it would remain with her when she changed. It was no guarantee, but it was the best she could do.

Now it was high time she put their theories to the test, before she lost her nerve completely. Here in the mundane world, the Fialan's power was sufficiently contained for her to hold it in her hand, and she picked it up and dropped it in the pouch, which she hung around her neck. Knowing that Iriana had gone out for a walk by the lake, Corisand went to find her. The sooner she could get this over with, make the transformation and – hopefully – prove that she could change back again, the quicker she'd be done with this fear that lurked constantly at the back of her thoughts. As she came downstairs, the sound of curses came up to meet her, along with the delicious fragrance of frying bacon marred by the acrid smell of burning. Entering the kitchen she discovered Dael, hastily removing a sizzling, spitting pan from the stove. He poked at the bacon with a fork, turning it gingerly to see the damage. 'Could be worse,' he muttered, and turned to Corisand with a rueful grimace. 'I let my mind wander just for a minute, and see what happens. Life was a lot easier when Athina was here.'

Though he tried to speak brightly, Corisand could hear the tautness of pain in his voice, and see the shadows of sleeplessness beneath
his eyes, and though the instinct to comfort was beyond anything
she had known in her equine form, she reached out to touch his
shoulder. 'Never mind about breakfast. We'll scrounge something
in a little while. I'm going to find Iriana now. Want to come?' She
surprised herself with the invitation. She had meant to take this
frightening step with only the Wizard there to help her, yet how
could she exclude Dael, and why should she? As part of a race that
had been deprived of freedom, she found herself with a surprising
amount of fellow feeling for this young mortal slave, as had Iriana.
Though Wizards regarded humans as nothing more than intelligent
beasts of burden, Iriana's affinity with all creatures and her boundless
compassion had opened the door to thinking of Dael as something
more. She had accepted him, as had the Windeye, as an integral part
of their group.

'Does this mean you've finally decided?' he asked as they left the
tower. Corisand turned to him in surprise, and he shrugged. 'I've
heard you and Iriana talking. I know you have to risk turning back
into your other form.' This time it was his turn to pat her on the
arm. 'You'll do it, don't worry. Why, with a bit of practice you'll be
switching back and forth as though you'd been doing it all your life.
You'll see. Athina had every faith in you, so it must be all right.'

Yet Athina couldn't save herself, Corisand thought. She wasn't
infallible.

'I wish I could change myself the way that you can,' Dael said
suddenly.

'What would you turn into?'

Dael looked away across the lake, his eyes distant. 'Oh, a Wizard, a
Phaerie – somebody with magic. Then maybe I could follow Athina.
Maybe I could find her again.'

Corisand stopped walking for a moment, and turned to him. 'Dael,
I think we have a long, hard road ahead of us. But if there's any
justice in this world, you'll find Athina at the end of it. And I promise
that if there's any way to help you get back to her, Iriana and I will
help you find it. We three must make the oddest, most ill-assorted
group of companions the world has ever seen, but we are friends, and
we're all in this together.'

8
~

THE SECRETS IN THE STONE

The Windeye and Dael were led to Iriana's location by a series of loud bangs and crashes. The Wizard, with Melik at her side as always, was practising the use of magic as a weapon, remembering what Esmon had taught her and going through all the elements at her disposal: Earth, Water, Fire and Air. The sharp tang of woodsmoke filled the air, reminding Corisand of Dael's mishap with the bacon. It came from the smouldering remnants of a pile of flotsam at the side of the lake. Clearly, the Wizard had been working on the element of Fire already.

Dael gave a low whistle and turned to Corisand. 'I'm sorry we missed that,' he said softly. 'I'll wager it was worth seeing.' Not wanting to break her concentration, they waited where they were until she had finished.

Now Iriana had turned to Earth. She had placed a row of small rocks, about the size of her head, about twenty yards away from her on the narrow gravelly beach. As Corisand watched her, wide-eyed, she lifted her hand and the stone at the end of the row shattered with a crack, sending an explosion of shards spattering in the water and clattering across the gravel, hitting hard enough to gouge deep grooves. Melik put his ears back and yowled his disapproval, and the Wizard patted him briefly on the head before continuing down the row, detonating the rocks one by one – until she reached the last. This stone she levitated into the air, her taut expression clearly showing the strain. She whipped her hand back in a casting motion and sent the rock hurtling into the lake, where it hit the water with tremendous force, its impact throwing up a glittering plume of spray.

Iriana doubled up with her hands resting on her knees, clearly catching her breath before moving on to the next form of attack. Straightening, she gazed out across the lake with glowing eyes that were filled with a fierce purpose. Suddenly the surface began to churn and a jet of water rose up and shot with incredible velocity towards the shore, hitting a tree so hard that it rocked and shuddered, shaking loose a shower of leaves. With a sharp crack one of the lowest branches broke off, and Iriana swore. She went to the tree and fitted the injured limb back into place, and as she passed her hand over the joint, Corisand saw a faint blue glow. When she stepped back, the bough was part of the tree once more, as though nothing had ever happened to hurt it.

'Some warrior you're going to make,' Corisand called out jokingly to her friend. 'Every time you hurt one of the Phaerie, you'll be running up to apologise to them and heal them.'

Iriana shrugged. 'I don't think so. I don't have any quarrel with the poor tree, but I do have one with the accursed Phaerie – for Avithan, for Esmon and my poor animals.' She walked towards them, looking pale and tired, but very grim and determined.

I'm not the only one making sacrifices here, Corisand thought. 'Very impressive,' she said aloud, 'but I think you've done enough practising for now. What about letting me do some of the work instead?'

The Wizard hesitated, then nodded briefly. 'What do you want me to do?'

'Wait. Watch. Don't do anything unless I'm in desperate trouble and there's no way I can change back on my own. Then—'

'I'll do whatever it takes to get you back.' Iriana held out her hand. 'I promise.'

Corisand moved a little way apart from the others. She hoped her Windeye heritage, half instinct and half inherited memory, had been accurate in the matter of clothing – such a nuisance, but with only thin human skin to protect her instead of the lovely dappled hide of her equine aspect, it was essential. She knew that as long as all her garb derived from plant or animal sources, it should change with her. Inorganic materials such as metal fastenings would be discarded. Well, if that were true, she should be all right. All the gear she was wearing, kindly provided by Athina, was wool, cotton or leather, and any fastenings were made from bone or horn.

She put it out of her mind, and began to concentrate on making the change. For the first attempt, she had taken the accurate image of her equine form from Iriana's memory: now it would always be locked in her own mind when she needed it. Visualising the alternate shape standing before her, she moved her thoughts into the image.

All at once she felt the alterations taking place and, though everything was happening simultaneously, her mind registered each change so that time seemed to stretch for her as her bones and muscles lengthened, stretched and grew thick and strong. Her weight fell forward as her spine altered, and suddenly she was standing four-square on neat hooves that sank into the cool turf.

Her equine sense of smell, thousands of times stronger than that of a human, swamped her mind with information: the sweet water from the nearby lake, a fading drift of smoke from Iriana's Fire spells, the sharp anxiety of her friends, and the familiar, friendly curiosity of the other horses tethered nearby. Which plants were good to eat, which should be left alone, which small animals were hidden in the nearby trees and undergrowth. Her vision lost the intensity of its colour but became sweeping and panoramic as her head changed shape and her eyes moved to the sides. She shivered in delight as the cool breeze played across her dappled hide. You missed so much *sensation*, wearing clothes! Suddenly Corisand was filled with the urge to run. With a flick of her tail she was off, thundering along the smooth turf at the side of the lake, her mane and tail streaming behind her.

Oh, the blissful feeling of liberation! To lose herself in the movement, the sheer thrill of speed; the warming, stretching interplay of muscle and bone and the powerful drumming of her heart as the fierce blood raced through her body. For a brief, blissful time she cast herself loose from her worries, her responsibilities to her companions, her burdens as the Windeye, and became only horse; simple, elemental and free.

Then she slowed, and let the world flow back to her, and was Corisand again. With only a brief pang of regret, she turned and trotted back to her friends. Iriana was waiting, eyebrows raised. The Windeye ducked her head in embarrassment. 'I just needed to run,' she explained using mindspeech. 'It's – well, if you had ever been a horse, you would understand.'

Iriana grinned. 'It looked like fun. Are you ready to change back now?' she added more soberly.

Corisand took a deep breath. 'Yes. I'm ready.' Once more, she stepped away from the others, steadied herself, and reached within to make the transformation, forming a clear mental image of her two-legged self, just as she had visualised the horse a few moments before. She moved into the image and – nothing happened.

A chill went through her. It was as she had feared. She was power-less once more, her magic imprisoned behind what seemed to be a vast, dark wall.

For a moment of horrifying, paralysing doubt, Corisand's mind was blank. In her equine form, the instincts of flight were highly developed, and she felt the panic like a great, onrushing wave, poised to obliterate her rational thoughts. How could she transform without magic? Where could she start? How could she access her powers now? She was trapped again.

Trapped.

Once more the urge overcame her to run, to flee, ignoring re-sponsibilities, forgetting friends, returning to what she had been for most of her life: elemental Horse, all feeling and reaction, living in the here and now with no thought of the greater consequences.

The easy option.

The coward's way.

Suddenly Corisand was enraged that she could be so easily duped by her old instincts. Anger roared through her like a forest fire, dispelling her fears and doubts.

I am the Windeye, magical and powerful and I will be free.

Then she was herself again, could think again, could reason and act. Because of Hellorin's imprisoning spell, her powers were lost to her in her equine form, but she knew where she could find them. The Fialan was the key. When she and Iriana had returned to this world from the Elsewhere, she had used the Stone to maintain her human aspect and, true to the purpose for which it had been created, it had absorbed, stored and magnified her magic. All she had to do was find the way to reach that power, and set it free.

The Stone, in its leather bag, still hung around her neck. Now that she was calm and could think again, she felt its energy beating against her breast like a second heart; the heart of her magic. Pleased by the notion, the Windeye stretched out her thoughts to embrace the powerful artefact.

A tingling shock rushed through her, as though she had leapt into an icy mountain lake. Suddenly Corisand's mind was inside the Fialan, in a crystalline labyrinth that pulsed and sang, vibrating with a fierce intensity. Within this staggering emerald realm all aware-ness of the outside world and her external form vanished completely.

Once more she was her true self, the Windeye of the Xandim, and a heady elation rushed through her. With the help of the Stone of Fate, she could accomplish anything. Through the complex, crystalline structure that surrounded her, the path to her own magic stood out clearly from Iriana's powers like a luminous thread. All she had to do was follow. Easy. But even as she cast forth her awareness along that glowing pathway, something stopped her. Forces warped, complex and terrifying. Others had been here before her; had created the Stone for their own purposes and left their magic deep within.

There was Ghabal, before insanity had twisted his mind: ancient, cunning and inexorable. And there was Hellorin, brilliant, ruthless and utterly without compassion, so long as he achieved his own ends.

Corisand's first instinct was to recoil, as though those perilous beings were actually present, and could see her. Then she got hold of herself.

Don't be a fool! It's just their magic that they stored here and left behind for anyone to use.

For me to use.

It struck her like a bolt of lightning – the answer for which she had been searching so long and hard. The Forest Lord's power had forged the spell to enslave the Xandim, and what his magic had wrought, it could undo. The key lay right here. All she had to do was find it. And if that spell was stored in the Fialan, why not others? If she could only discover Hellorin's flying magic, could unlock and master it, then the possibilities were endless. Her heart sang as, at long last, she began to reach towards the tentative beginnings of a plan ...

Getting back into her human form would have to wait. There was no time to waste – no chance to think about the risks and the consequences. She had to do this now, for if she hesitated, she would never find the courage again.

Corisand closed her eyes. Carefully, she searched the depths of the Fialan with her mind until she found the place within the crystal lattice where Hellorin's magic was stored, seeming in her mind's eye like a strange, dark, convoluted snake. She recoiled, for its aura was repellent to her. This was the magic that had enslaved her people, and had chained her for so long, helpless and frustrated, in her powerless equine form. No wonder that its very touch was so abhorrent to her, and in its own way, the Phaerie magic seemed to find her own presence inimical, writhing away from her like an elusive serpent whenever she tried to capture it and use it for herself. But the Windeye had not come this far to be defeated now. She chased it down as it fled through the intricate interstices of the crystal, until, reaching out with her thoughts, she finally caught hold of it.

The magic writhed and coiled, twisting in her grasp, trying to escape and elude her, its touch burning like acid, but Corisand would not let go. She chained it with her will, holding it tightly with all her strength, seeking to understand it, trying to become one with it, until she mastered it at last. Suddenly, like a key turning in a lock, everything fell into place. Hellorin's spell of flight was hers. Harnessed side by side with her own powers, it waited obediently to do her bidding.

Now that the dreadful struggle was over, Corisand could open her eyes again and return to her the physical reality of her equine form in the external world. With a soaring sense of exhilaration, she cast the flying magic around herself like a glittering mantle, cloaking herself in a many-hued starfall of radiance. Iriana, knowing better than to interrupt with questions when magic was being worked, stepped back hastily, a worried look on her face. Dael, who had seen that Phaerie magic before and paid a bitter price for it, scrambled away from her with a cry of dismay.

The magic spread through Corisand like a gigantic wave, buoying her up so that her body grew suddenly light. With a joyful cry she bounded forward, stretched her limbs and leapt upwards – and suddenly the ground dropped away beneath her and she was up and running through the air, the wild wind flowing around her like a river, streaming cold and fierce through her mane and tail.

The broad skies beckoned, a road that could take her anywhere she wished, and a joyous feeling of power burst through her. As a simple horse, before she had become Windeye, the flying was what she had lived for – but oh, how different, how wonderful it felt to be flying free, running with the wind, uncontrolled and unconstrained, going where her own will and wishes might take her, instead of being subservient to the demands of the Forest Lord, her former rider.

A sudden glimpse of the treetops, flashing by far below her, brought her back to her senses with a jolt. She hadn't realised she'd come so high! For an instant, panic flashed through her, the magic faltered and she began to drop like a stone. Then shock drove back the terror, and the Windeye snatched once more at the reins of the spell, and held on tight. The terrible fall stopped abruptly, and she lurched to a bone-jarring halt in midair.

Corisand took a few moments to breathe deeply and calm her racing heartbeat. That was quite enough for a maiden flight, she decided. She ought to be returning to the others, for they must be wondering what had become of her. She turned to go back – and realised to her horror that she was utterly lost. In the excitement at getting the spell to work and the exhilaration of the flight, she had not been paying attention to her surroundings, and had come too far. Beneath her, the forest stretched in all directions, a cloak of green that obscured any landmarks. Of the tower, of her friends, there was no sign.

Too late, the Windeye realised her error. Before, when she had ridden with the Wild Hunt of the Phaerie, she'd had Hellorin to guide her, the huntsman and the other horses to follow. She had never flown alone before. This time it had been her responsibility to keep track of her location, to note the position of the sun and direction of the wind, and to keep checking below her for any landmarks.

Corisand cursed herself for a fool – but she would get nowhere by staying up in the air, stewing in self-recrimination. It was no good waiting around for anyone else to help her. Only she could get herself out of trouble. The lake would be a much bigger landmark from the air than the tower. Maybe if she flew higher, she could catch a glimpse of it.

As she ascended, the trees grew smaller and smaller beneath her. If she went any higher she would penetrate the thin, high layer of grey cloud cover – already she could feel the cold, damp mist of it chilling her body and catching in her throat as she breathed – and lose sight of the ground altogether. Now that the excitement had cooled from her blood, she felt a little clutch of alarm at how far away she was from the ground. Before it could grow into panic, she took herself sternly to task.

'What does it matter?' she told herself stoutly. 'If you fell from a quarter of this height you'd be killed anyway – but you're not going to fall and you're not going to die. You're going to find that lake and get back home.'

It was strange how quickly Athina's tower had come to feel like home, and horses did have an instinct for finding their way back to the stable. As best she could, Corisand attempted to calm the whirl of thoughts that had been in her head since she'd become the Windeye, and tried instead to tune in to the old, equine instincts of days gone by. She filled her mind with images of the tower and the lake, of

Iriana, Dael and even the blue-eyed cat Melik. In a little while she thought she felt it – a slight tugging sensation that came from further to her left than she had been expecting.

The Windeye set off steadily, following that faint tickle of awareness which insisted home lay *that* way. Then she saw it – a bright flash on the ground far away. Surely that must be light on water? And so it proved. As she drew closer she could see the lake, and then the tower, tall and graceful on its island.

The relief was like a deep breath of fresh air that swept away all her worries and doubts. Her heart singing, she swept down to the green sward on the border of the lake where her friends stood waiting, too stunned by what she had accomplished to speak – though that would not last long. As her feet touched the ground once more Corisand could hardly wait to tell them what had happened. In joy, in hope, in expectation, her link to her own magic blazed fierce and bright – and without warning she was back in her human form, sprawling on her face in the grass having once again made the abrupt, unexpected transformation from four legs to two.

The Windeye leapt to her feet, noting in passing, with some relief, that she'd been right and her clothing *had* transformed with her – but that was of little importance now. Her face alight with joy, she ran to embrace her friends. 'Iriana, Dael, I've found it. I've found the answer!'

9
~

A MOTHER'S VENGEANCE

At first, Sharalind wished that people would just leave her alone. That was the worst of being a Wizard. Everyone in the city had felt her son's passing. Everyone was shocked, stunned and grieving, and so they all believed that they shared in her own heartbreak, her own horror, her anger, despair and desperation – yet how could they?

Only she had lost a son.

Their well-meaning attempts to take care of her, to comfort and cheer her, were as nothing in the face of that bleak and agonising truth, and all Sharalind wanted was to be left alone – but that was not to be. In Cyran's absence she found she had inherited his mantle as Archwizard, and gained a spurious authority over the inhabitants of Tyrineld. People, anxious and uncertain, kept on coming to her, interrupting her grieving with an endless string of questions. 'What shall we do about ... ?' 'May we ... ?' 'Should we ... ?' She had tried in vain to refer them to the Heads of Luens; they just kept on arriving in an endless stream. Sanction this, forbid that, advise on the other, until she wanted to scream at them to go away.

Even the mortals wouldn't leave her in peace. The domestic staff who cared for the Archwizard and his soulmate, and the tower in which they lived, were usually an unobtrusive background fixture, going about their work quietly and efficiently without drawing much attention to themselves. Since yesterday – had this desolate eternity really only lasted such a short time? – they had rallied round Sharalind, showing a care and concern that was surprisingly sincere. Though they still said little – for above all, they knew their place – they had gone out of their way to make everything comfortable for her, trying to anticipate her every need with dogged persistence that defied every scolding and rebuff. Sharalind was very touched by their loyalty, but frankly, they were beginning to drive her crazy.

She pushed away the tray of food they had left for her, allowing the slices of roast chicken and perfectly cooked vegetables to grow cold on the plate. Even the bowl of freshly picked peaches failed to tempt her. She poured herself a cup of taillin and wandered restlessly across to the window, but there was no pleasure in the dazzling ocean and the golden sunlit day.

It didn't seem right. There should be gales, hailstones, thunder and lightning now that Avithan was gone, and she was all alone – for Sharalind did feel alone. Having sent one pathetic message to say that Avithan had been slain by the Phaerie, Cyran had remained away in the forest, desperately trying to find some kind of excuse, or scapegoat, for his own reckless folly in sending those inexperienced young people out into such peril, against the advice and wishes of their mothers. As far as Sharalind was concerned, he was wasting his time. There was not, nor ever could be, any form of mitigation for what he had done, and she would never forgive him as long as she lived.

Even her best friend Zybina was estranged from her now, though at first, when both Avithan and Iriana appeared to be dead, they had been united in their grief and a great support to one another. But yesterday evening Zybina's daughter had, by some miracle, been resurrected, and though Sharalind could tell herself until she was blue in the face that she was wrong to begrudge her friend's good fortune, it did not make her feel any less resentful. Her son, her true-born child, was dead while Zybina's girl, not even her own but some miserable little foundling brat from who knew where, had survived.

Why has her child, a mere foster child at that, been saved, and not mine?

She had found it impossible to forgive her friend's good fortune. Furthermore Yinze, Zybina's son, had returned from the lands of the Skyfolk, and was there to comfort her and grieve with her.

She still has a son, but mine is dead. It isn't fair!

Though Sharalind despised herself for such a mean-spirited at-titude, the jealousy snarled and gnawed within her like some trapped beast, and would not be denied, and her bitterness had driven an instant wedge between herself and her former friend.

She had often heard it said that there was no worse grief than to lose a child, that it left an indelible scar upon the heart that could never, ever be healed. She had sympathised with parents in such dreadful straits, had even thought she knew how they must be feeling, but oh, how little she had truly understood!

She had never expected the anger.

Sharalind was filled, consumed, ablaze with a fulminating wrath: a rage, a fury that wanted to strike out at the entire world. At every helpful idiot who told her that time was a great healer, all those well-meaning morons who insisted that everything happens for a reason. At Zybina, whose child had been saved, at Iriana, for being the survivor, at Cyran, who had sent her son out to die – but most of all, at the vile, filthy, evil Phaerie, who had taken Avithan's life.

They must be made to pay.

Until this point, the thought of revenge had never crossed Sharalind's mind. She had been too busy grieving, railing against fate, and trying to adjust to the vacancy that now existed where her beloved son had laughed and loved. Now, suddenly, her mind felt lucid and focused, with a purpose and a clear goal in its sights. She stood, gazing out of the tower window across the city, her eyes fixed on the distant walls of the Luen of Warriors, who'd been exiled and, whenever possible, ignored and slighted by her peace-loving soulmate. Weak Cyran. Stupid Cyran. Well, let him stumble around in the forest, groping desperately for some kind of absolution. What use was that?

For Sharalind, tears were no longer enough. She wanted to bathe in Phaerie blood. Would the specious authority, unwanted and unasked for, that she had gained in the Archwizard's absence be enough to get her the revenge she craved?

First of all, she needed the support of the Heads of the Luens. Though she knew for certain that not all of them would agree – Tinagen of the healers, for example, was bound to be a problem – she hoped to get enough of them on her side to sway the matter. For certain she could count on Omaira, Esmon's successor as Head of the Warriors, and probably Galiena, the new Head of the Spellweavers. Both of them were fiercely angered by the loss of their leaders, and must be longing for vengeance. Lanrion, Head of the Nurturers, Iriana's Luen, might be a little more difficult. Though he ought to feel the same as the other two, the wanton destruction of life was utterly abhorrent to his kind, and besides, Iriana had not been killed, though goodness only knew what *had* happened to her, and whether or not she would be the same after the experience remained to be seen.

As far as the rest were concerned: well, she would simply have to wait and see ... But she would be exerting all her considerable powers of persuasion.

Sharalind sat down by the window and began to send out messages in mindspeech to all the Heads of the Luens. That night, when the day's work was done and all was quiet, they would meet here in the tower. They all consented with alacrity; some, she knew, out of curiosity, but all of them out of willingness to be of service to the Archwizard's grieving soulmate. She took that as a good sign.

By the time everything was settled, the sun was setting and it was growing cool by the window. As she walked across to the fire, Sharalind's eye fell once again on the tray of discarded food on the table, and suddenly, for the first time since she had felt Avithan's death the previous morning, she was ravenously hungry. Though the gravy and vegetables had congealed into a greasy, soggy mass and the slices of chicken were stone cold and hardening around the edges, she sat down at the table and fell to, devouring every bite. She had a purpose now: a war to plan. If Cyran tried to put obstacles in her path, he must be dealt with.

No matter what it took, no matter what the cost, Sharalind wanted vengeance.

Unfortunately, as the meeting unfolded, it soon became clear that most of the Luen Heads did not agree.

'You must be completely out of your mind, and we'd be out of ours if we went along with this arrant folly.' Tinagen, never noted for his tact, had been the first to voice what the others were clearly thinking. Sharalind, seated at the head of the long council table, sighed wearily and pushed her hair back from her forehead. Persuading these hard-headed idiots had been every bit as difficult as she had expected. Even Galiena had proved to be a disappointment. 'All the Spellweavers mourn Avithan,' she had said. 'He was not only our leader but our friend, and we are grieved and angered by his death. We have discussed it among ourselves, however, and the majority of us cannot believe that he would choose this precipitate path of war. In the end he might fight, but he would not wish to risk our people without a great deal more information and planning than you require, Sharalind. It is with deep regret, therefore, that I must say no.'

Omaira, however, had come down firmly on her side and, to her surprise, Vaidel of the Bards, the youngest of the Luen Heads now that Avithan had gone. He had turned out to be more of a hothead than she had realised, his head filled with images of glory, heroism and victory from all the old tales and ballads he had studied.

But it's the victors who write the history and the songs.

Sharalind, as an archivist, knew that unfortunate truth all too well, and could not suppress the chill that ran through her at the thought. She was older than Vaidel, and supposedly wiser: should she really be pursuing this dangerous course? Firmly she pushed such uncomfortable notions away. Avithan must be avenged, and she would find a way to accomplish it with or without the aid of these snivelling cowards.

At length Aldyth, Head of the Academy and the Luen of Academics, her oldest friend – or so she had believed – whose support she'd been counting on, pushed his chair back with a sigh of regret and rose to his feet. 'Sharalind, I'm sorry, more sorry than I can say, but we must oppose this plan to make war upon the Phaerie. It simply cannot be. Just now you're grieving, with very good cause. You've lost your only child, and that's a crushing blow to any mother. No one knows better than I what it is to lose a loved one. It has been more than a century since my soulmate died, and I still miss her every single day. But I learned to endure, to live with, and finally to conquer my grief, and believe me, so will you. You are strong, Sharalind. Stronger than you know. You have the deepest sympathy of everyone in this room, and we would all go out of our way to help ease your pain and sorrow – but not through this. Not through war. Especially not a war without planning, preparation, information and forethought. You are acting impulsively now, and not thinking straight. Wait a while, my dear. A little while won't matter.'

He spoke gently, coaxingly, as if to a recalcitrant child – an image that was reinforced because he was standing and she was sitting down, so that he towered over her. Sharalind clenched her fists beneath the table and gritted her teeth, then stood up to face him. 'I think you have said enough,' she said coldly. 'More than enough to show me that you are not the friend I thought you were.'

'I am your friend, my dear, as I have always been,' Aldyth said gently, 'and that is why I do not wish you to embark on this reckless path. Give us all more time, I beg you. Even in a few days things may seem very different, but once you set this conflict in motion there will be no going back, not for anyone in the city. Would you really wish so many other mothers in Tyrineld to be grieving as you are now? All I ask is that you wait long enough to think, plan, send out scouts and spies, and gather intelligence. Then, if war still seems the wisest course to you – well, we can always reconsider.'

A rapid glance at the grim, closed faces around the table was enough to tell Sharalind that she would never persuade enough of them. Though they all sympathised with her in her loss, they dismissed her plans as nothing but a rash act stemming from her anger and grief.

Are they right? Would I know? Could I tell? Am I making a terrible mistake?

Resolutely, Sharalind shut off the treacherous, invasive inner voice. Could it be right to allow the Phaerie to kill Wizards without any repercussions? Could it be wrong to avenge her son?

Then she looked across the table and saw the furious glint in Omaira's eyes, and the bitter twist to Vaidel's mouth. She had support. There was still hope. She turned to the others with a semblance of regret. She did not have to feign the anger. 'Very well. If that is your decision, then so it must be. If you will not support me, I cannot proceed without your cooperation. You are all dismissed – but not with my thanks. No – say no more.' She lifted a forestalling hand as Aldyth was about to speak. 'I do not wish to hear more of your useless platitudes. Leave me now.'

As the others trailed from the room, she caught Omaira's eye, and nodded, almost imperceptibly, towards Vaidel, addressing them in the most private mode of mindspeech. 'Return at midnight. We have plans to make.'

In the blackest depths of the night, while the city slept, Sharalind worked out a different strategy with Omaira and Vaidel. By the next day, in the taverns, the marketplaces, the gathering halls and even the street corners, there were Bards singing songs of battle and glory, honour and revenge. By the day after that, Tyrineld was buzzing. When a race could communicate in mindspeech, news and conjecture could spread like wildfire. Since Esmon's death, thoughts of a possible conflict had been in everyone's mind and now, as rumours of impending hostilities spread, everyone was talking war.

Everywhere, opinions were polarising. Debate raged on all sides. The young, the rash and hot-headed; those whose pride had been bruised by the cowardly attack on the Wizardly emissaries and those who were afraid that this would only be the start of Phaerie depredations if they were not stopped now, all came down firmly on the side of Sharalind. Others, more thoughtful or studious, patient or cautious, looked back to the lessons of history. Battle between the wielders of magical power was always a terrible and destructive thing. But their arguments for patience, for diplomacy and for caution fell on deaf ears.

Conflict grew within the city. Luens were fracturing. Families were sundered and friendships lost or stretched to near-breaking. Soulmates quarrelled bitterly. Some folk, seeing which way the wind was blowing, began buying up quantities of supplies and commodities, and as panic spread, markets, the merchants and the artisans found themselves besieged. Increasing numbers of Wizards, no matter what their Luen affiliations, headed to the once-neglected Luen of Warriors, begging to be trained in offensive and defensive magic, and Omaira, with a fierce grin on her face and a triumphant gleam in her eye, was accepting them all.

The Heads of the Luens, all excepting Omaira and Vaidel, watched these developments in horror, and vainly tried to stem the groundswell of belligerence among their members, but they found dissenters on every side, even among their own ranks. When they tried to take their complaints and concerns to Sharalind, however, they discovered that she had made herself inaccessible. No one, it seemed, knew exactly where she was, she had blocked off all attempts at mindspeech, and there was no way of getting a message to her. The Luen Heads suspected that she might be hiding in the Warriors' fortresslike compound, but there was no way, short of the very violence they eschewed, of finding out.

Then, late that afternoon of the second day since the council, matters took a more sinister turn. Galiena of the Spellweavers and Callia of the Merchants suddenly found themselves voted out of office and replaced with new, pro-war Heads, which meant that now the Luens were equally divided; half of the eight supporting Sharalind and half against. Time was running out for the remaining objectors. How much longer could they last?

10

~

MASQUERADE

Chiannala loved the view from her window. Though the older Wizards and senior students at the Academy were given the largest rooms, with stunning views of the bays and ocean, she was more than satisfied with her own tiny cubicle that overlooked the city. Tyrineld, the focus of her dearest dreams and hopes, lay below her, gleaming like a pearl in the sunshine, and Chiannala loved to look out at the flower-decked balconies and the brightly robed Wizards – who could have guessed that there would be so many Wizards in the world? – striding or sauntering along the busy streets.

She had no wish to look at the cliffs and the ocean. She wanted no reminder of Brynne, the girl whose appearance she had stolen and whose life she had usurped. She did not want to think of the terrible deed she had done to make her most desperate wish, to train as a Wizard, come true.

Brynne was dead now. Drowned, or killed by the fall from the cliffs after Chiannala had pushed her. Dwelling on it wouldn't bring her back. Only in the darkness of her nightmares, night after night, did the ghost of the girl return to haunt her.

Chiannala turned away from the window and gazed around her cubicle, letting her lasting delight in the tiny room drive away her uncomfortable thoughts. The cramped space allotted to first-year students was spartan and workmanlike, crammed with a narrow bed, a desk with a hard wooden chair, and a chest for belongings. One wall had hooks for hanging robes and cloaks. One was lined with shelves to hold books, scrolls, writing materials, and any other paraphernalia, such as scrying crystals or healing herbs, that a spellcrafter might use in their work. And work they did, their teachers pushing them unmercifully to reach their fullest potential. Even in these first few days, while their tutors had been assessing the direction in which their talents lay and the range and depth of their abilities, the hours had been gruelling. The strain of stretching herself to extend the limit of her powers and work unfamiliar magic was exhausting, but Chiannala had never been so happy. She throve on the challenges, and loved every minute of her training, voraciously devouring every new scrap of knowledge, and practising every new skill far into the night.

It helped to distract her from the strange and unsettled atmosphere that pervaded the Academy, upsetting and puzzling the older students and the teachers, for the first-year class had come to Tyrineld at a very difficult time for its inhabitants. Several days after she first arrived, everyone had felt the death of Esmon followed, only yesterday, by the passing of Avithan and Iriana. Everyone save Chiannala. Even living in Nexis, there had been the occasional Wizard death, so she already knew that the ability to feel the passing of one of her own kind had not come down to her through her tainted blood. Here at the Academy, however, she had been forced to dissemble as she never had before, for such strong emotions were difficult to feign.

Grief and rage had pervaded the city. Chiannala had not known Avithan or Esmon, so she did not care much about them either way, but her heart had leapt when the others felt the passing of Iriana. So that bitch had come to a nasty end, and it served her right! She had been very careful to mimic everyone else's sorrow and hide her true feelings – but it was harder to conceal her dismay when Iriana had suddenly and mysteriously returned to the world. There seemed to be no getting rid of her, and the thought of her returning to Tyrineld made Chiannala feel tense and nervous all over again. *It won't matter*, she assured herself. *She'll never find out who I really am. How could she? And I'll have my revenge on her sooner or later – I swear I will.*

Though everyone at the Academy, students and tutors alike, had been miserable and distracted, life had to go on, and today would be a very important day for Chiannala, and for the rest of the young Wizards in her first-year group. They had been summoned to meet at sunset with the Heads of all the Luens, in the Hall of Light adjacent to the library. Over the last few days the tutors had pushed their students hard, to discover where their strengths and weaknesses lay, and had determined the areas in which they ought to specialise, at least for this first year. In the initial part of their training, particular attention would be paid to their strengths, because concentrating on what came naturally to them would help to build their confidence, an essential part of magic. Chiannala had no need to have her confidence bolstered, however – not where her magical abilities were concerned. She knew how good she was, and she was determined to be better. Like her fellows, she was wondering what the verdict of her superiors would be, but whatever it was, she was determined to excel. She had every intention of becoming the greatest Wizard of them all. And no one – *no one* – would ever know she carried the vile taint of mortal in her blood.

Chiannala turned her attention back to the window, in the hope of driving the thoughts of her parents from her mind: the Wizard father who had first taught her, had first given her hope that she might become more than a minor charm spinner in a backwoods settlement – and then had snatched that hope away; the mother who was nothing but a human slave who'd been given a chance to ape her masters. It was easier to hate them than to miss them; better to foster her resentment than to think how much she must be worrying and grieving them.

Chiannala had new parents now – proper, true, respectable Wizards. She'd had no chance to consider all the wider implications when she had changed places with Brynne. Everything had happened so quickly, she had simply seen her opportunity and seized it. Already, letters were arriving whenever her new family could find a messenger – and if her first days at the Academy were anything to go by, it would appear that potential messengers must pass by their blasted farm with distressing frequency – almost every day in fact. Already packages had begun to arrive for Brynne containing letters from Shelgan, her father, hoping she was being a good girl and working hard, and giving her detailed bulletins about all the tiresome creatures and crops on his wretched farm; and from her mother Larann, hoping that she was keeping warm enough – in this blissfully temperate city – and not working too hard, and were there any handsome boys – boys! – at the Academy. She was also desperately concerned that her little treasure was getting enough to eat, as if the great, fat lump needed to eat any more, and enclosing pies and cheeses, cakes and bread, sausages and ham, all carefully wrapped and protected with a time spell.

Chiannala gave it away or threw it into the sea. She had been forced to abandon the first, beautiful appearance she had crafted for herself with a transfiguration spell when she had run away from home, and she hated that she'd been forced to turn herself instead into this plump, apple-cheeked farm girl. Not that she cared a fig about boys – she was far too ambitious to burden herself with such distractions – but it positively sickened her to think that she'd performed such difficult and dangerous magic, twice now, only to go from sallow and bony to chubby and shiny-faced. Clearly, the advantages of beauty were closed to her now, but Chiannala was doing the best she could with the material to hand. She ate sparingly, keeping well away from the stodgier items supplied by the Academy's refectory, and sticking to a frugal diet of fruit and vegetables, and the odd bit of chicken or fish. As a result, Brynne's robes were already beginning to hang a little more loosely, and soon she would be forced to spend money on a seamstress to get them altered. Luckily, the farm girl's parents were generous in more than just food and good advice, and though Chiannala didn't have riches, the letters and parcels contained enough coin to ensure a comfortable life for a student.

Answering the fond missives from her stolen parents was one of the most difficult aspects of Chiannala's new life: far harder than any magic she'd been set so far. The first letter from Shelgan had left her utterly baffled until she had worked out that he had given many of his animals names – initially she'd thought he must be referring to other family members. Luckily, the real Brynne had mentioned that she was an only child, or all sorts of confusion might have ensued. Larann's letters were also full of these potential traps. Chiannala was forced to sweat over replies to the wretched things, wording her answers with extreme care and praying that she wouldn't reveal herself by slipping up over some petty detail. There was no alternative. Her journey with Brynne and Shelgan had been enough to show her the close bonds of love that knitted the other family together, and she knew that if she failed to write, they would be arriving in Tyrineld in no time to find out what was amiss with their precious chick.

The silvery chimes of the bell that summoned the students for breakfast broke into her thoughts and jerked her back to the present. Though the first-year students had a holiday today, while their tutors completed the deliberations that would decide their fate, punctuality at meals was still strictly enforced. Chiannala shook off the uncomfortable thoughts of family and, with a last, fond look around her sanctuary, left the room, eager to see what the new day might bring.

Whatever the difficulties, whatever the risks, her merciless act had been worthwhile.

The Academy's refectory was a large, airy room with floor-length windows which, in fine weather, opened onto a vine-decked colonnade and a courtyard in which small tables were set. This pleasant retreat, with its flowerbeds and central fountain, was reserved for teachers and privileged senior students, however. The first-year intake, along with the majority of the Academy's students, had their own long table inside. This year there were fifteen of them – seven girls including herself, and eight boys – and they were all there before her, for the time she had spent daydreaming and gazing out of the window had made her late.

Some of the sunlight went out of Chiannala's day. She hated being last. Though she knew she was being stupid, when she saw them all sitting there together she felt as if they were somehow ranged against her. Though she realised that this was nonsense, she couldn't seem to help herself. Since she had come to Tyrineld and the Academy, she had discovered a number of unpleasant home truths that had torn a ragged hole in her self-esteem. To her dismay she'd discovered that, though she had every confidence in her powers, she was desperately lacking in self-assurance when it came to interactions with her fellow Wizards. Growing up in Nexis, Chiannala had never mixed much with the other children. Her parents, Challan and Lannala, had refused to let her mix with either the barefoot brats of the human slaves that swarmed around the streets or the offspring of the other Wizards. They had always contrived to keep the truth from her – that a child with her background would have been unwelcome among the pure-bred Wizarding families, and only now, listening to the way her fellow students despised and disparaged half-breeds, did she realise just how much her mother and father had protected her.

These unpleasant revelations had only served to make Chiannala all the more determined to succeed, to beat the lot of them, to become so renowned for her power and skill that no one would ever *dare* to look down on her. Yet in her heart, the understanding that she was different could not be eradicated, and she very quickly became aware that Iriana's horrified and hostile attitude to her had not been unusual. If they ever discovered the truth, how her fellow students would revile her!

Well, they never would find out – not if Chiannala had her way. But the knowledge that she was fundamentally flawed put an invisible barrier between herself and the others. While the group weighed one another up and made friends or enemies, Chiannala tried wherever possible to stay aloof and apart from all the social manoeuvrings, rebuffing all attempts at friendship.

Stiffening her spine, she walked towards the table.

'Good morning, Brynne. Sleep well?' Haslen, as always, had a smile for her. Stocky and round-faced, with an untidy thatch of brown hair, he found the chubby Brynne less threatening than the other girls, and he was firmly set on making friends with her, while she was just as determined that he should not. Chiannala knew that because of her appearance he considered her an outsider like himself. He had already discovered that she was good at magic, and he hoped that she would help him with his spells. He was some four years older than his classmates, having come late to his powers, and even at this early stage he was finding the work at the Academy hard to manage.

Well, he could hope in vain for help from Chiannala! Despite the unprepossessing appearance of her borrowed (even in the privacy of her mind, she shrank away from the word *stolen*) form, she had her own fierce ambition, and she wasn't about to let a useless, talentless moron like Haslen hold her back. Barely acknowledging him, she went and sat down at the far end of the table.

Laurth was beside Haslen, his head a mass of blond curls. He was the class joker, always seeing the funny side and popular with every-one – at least among the students, for his teachers, who valued hard work and concentration, were less impressed with his light-hearted approach to life. To track him down, it was only ever necessary to follow the sounds of laughter and there he would be. He leant close to his neighbour, Haslen, whispering something into his ear, and Haslen, for once, instead of looking harried and anxious, threw back his head and laughed with abandon.

Chiannala's hands clenched into fists beneath the table. Were they laughing at her? To cover her embarrassment, she poured a cup of taillin and helped herself to some fruit, though she did not touch the figs or the succulent peach. Suspiciously, she looked around at the others. Were they laughing at her too?

Luckily, no one seemed to be taking much notice of her. At this end of the table. Gaernon was surrounded by the usual adoring crowd of girls. With his sleek mane of dark chestnut hair, clear green eyes and finely sculpted features, he had been especially blessed with good looks, and had a natural, easy-going arrogance that came from having been able to charm his way through life.

Chiannala scowled at him. If she'd been able to keep her old appearance, the first disguise she had created for herself from wishes and imagination, she might have been foremost among his coterie of girls – who knew, she might even have been *the* girl – but as it was, he could have little interest in the fat lump of a body in which she had been trapped. Rather than hurt herself with his rejection, she kept her distance.

Towards the centre sat the cleverest of the first-year boys, Briall and Rannart. To all appearances, they couldn't have been more different. Briall was very tall, even for a Wizard, not to mention skinny and gangling; all knees and elbows and bony wrists. His straight, dark brown hair was always flopping into his eyes. Rannart was broader, with a shock of wiry red-gold hair and a face that was peppered with freckles. Rannart was very practical, Briall more creative, yet the pair had befriended one another from the outset, and Chiannala was astonished at the lack of rivalry between them. She simply couldn't understand why they should help one another with suggestions and encourage each other to perform increasingly difficult spells. They ought to be the deadliest of rivals.

Didn't they want to be the best? Didn't they want to *win*?

Ferrin didn't. Chiannala didn't understand him, either. She had soon worked out that this narrow-faced, nondescript youth with his sandy hair and light, almost colourless blue eyes, was quite happy to disappear into the background and get away with doing as little as possible. She had heard him tell Briall that he hadn't wanted to attend the Academy, being content to inherit his merchant father's trade, which required very little magic. His parents had insisted he come, but they couldn't make him work – that was his boast. Of all the boys, Chiannala hated him most, and harboured bitter feelings against him. Having been forced to fight so hard, to commit such terrible acts to gain her place as a student at the Tyrineld Academy, she despised anyone who would throw away the honour through sheer – as far as she could see – laziness.

The dark-haired Ayron was a mystery. Like Chiannala, he kept to himself at all times, politely spurning any overtures of friendship from the others. His behaviour was so similar to her own that it made her uneasy. Did he also have a secret to hide? And if so, what was it? His eyes, dark and devoid of emotion, gave nothing away.

So far, though there had been a lot of the usual flirting and manoeuvring between the sexes, Nathon and Seirlin were the only ones to actually form a couple. Childhood sweethearts, they had been together before they had come to the Academy, having lived in the same street all their lives. Nathon was very tall, with clear grey eyes, and he wore his hair in a long, dark blond braid. Seirlin was slender and graceful, with long, straight copper-coloured hair. Her mother was a Spellcrafter of some renown, her father a Bard, and though they had decided to go their separate ways when their daughter was eight years old, they were still the best of friends. Seirlin seemed to be heading in an entirely different direction from her parents, for she was chiefly interested in the Luen of Nurturers, who studied the lore of all living things, both animals and plants. Nathon's parents, on the other hand, were still a devoted couple, who had been together for many years. Though both were Artisans, their son was hoping to follow the Bardic path.

The other close relationship in the class was that of the twins, Ursella and Orlene. They were big girls, sturdy and statuesque, their colouring vivid and dramatic with masses of bright red curls and sparkling emerald eyes. They were absolutely identical and in the short time the group had been together, no one had found a way to tell them apart. They were bold, outspoken and brimming with confidence, and even though they were pleasant, merry and rarely unkind, Chiannala found their brashness intimidating.

Valmai was completely the opposite, being pale and dark-haired, petite and shy, with a rare smile that lit up her face like sunshine. Like Chiannala, she had started out by being quiet and self-effacing, but that lovely smile had soon won her friends, who wanted to bring her out of her shell and see her blossom. Even Chiannala, very much against her will, found herself harbouring a sneaking liking for the girl.

The same could not be said for Mylosa. In her case, it was instant dislike on both sides. The girl was tall and imposing, with spun-silk pale blonde hair, silvery eyes, and hawkish, patrician features. She came from one of the oldest, most powerful Wizard families, one that had spawned a long line of Archwizards. Her mother, Galiena, Head of the Luen of Spellweavers now that Avithan had gone, had been Cyran's greatest rival for the Archwizard's post. Rich and haughty, Mylosa had little time for a homely looking farm girl like Brynne. Though Chiannala, realising how much trouble it would save in the long run, had tried to remain beneath her notice, unfortunately she had not succeeded. She was far too clever a student, and had no intention of pretending otherwise. Even in the short time the class had been together she had made the cardinal mistake of making Mylosa look stupid, but it couldn't be helped. Chiannala was not going to sell herself and her powers short just to placate an arrogant snob from a powerful family, even if it did result in an enmity that could make her life at the Academy very unpleasant.

Oddly, however, Mylosa wasn't her chief worry. The greatest danger, as far as Chiannala was concerned, came from Rhoslyn, a good-natured, friendly girl who had a smile and a pleasant word for everyone. If a delightful nature weren't enough, she was vivacious and pretty, with rippled waves of tawny hair and big brown eyes with sweeping dark lashes. Through the goodness of her heart she was always trying to befriend Brynne, having decided that the farm girl must be shy and lonely. Rhoslyn was always trying to draw her into groups and activities, until Chiannala wanted to throttle her.

The more she resisted, the more determined the other girl seemed to become, yet her chief threat lay not in her pushy friendliness, but in the fact that, like Chiannala, she came from Nexis. Things had been different then. Even the sunny Rhoslyn had not been friendly towards a half-blood. Worse than the hypocrisy, however, was the very real risk of exposure. Since the original Brynne had come from a farm on the coast, she would hardly be expected to know anything about Nexis, and Chiannala was constantly afraid that Rhoslyn would get something out of her that would expose her as an impostor. And the stupid bitch refused to be discouraged. No amount of cold, brusque, dismissive or downright rude behaviour would put her off. Here she was again this morning, smiling that sickly sweet smile, offering the ostensible Brynne more taillin, a sweet roll, butter ...

'I'm quite capable of getting my own breakfast,' Chiannala snubbed her.

Rhoslyn simply shrugged. 'I know that, Brynne, but kindness and good manners don't cost anything,' she said pointedly.

It was still a long way from losing her temper, but it was the closest Chiannala had ever seen her come. *Good*, she thought. *I'm finally getting to her.* Lurking in the back of her mind, however, was the uncomfortable thought that she always shied away from – that if circumstances had been otherwise, if she'd been a true, full-blooded Wizard, able to come here under her own identity, she would have appreciated and enjoyed Rhoslyn's friendship, and been on much easier, friendlier terms with the rest of the group. As it was, she felt as if an invisible wall closed her off from them, built of heritage, background, lies – and murder.

Chiannala shuddered. Sometimes, without any warning, the guilt would rise up and strike at her. She clenched her fingers tightly on the cup she was holding in a rigid, white-knuckled grip – and with a sudden crack the handle shattered in her hand, slicing into her fingers, and the cup fell, shattering on the floor and drenching her legs in hot taillin.

An abrupt silence fell in the refectory as all heads turned in her direction. 'Somebody shoot the juggler,' came a droll voice from somewhere across the room, and there was a ripple of laughter. Chiannala, her face burning with embarrassment, suddenly found herself the centre of attention.

Rhoslyn came to her rescue. 'Oh, you poor dear. How stupid of the kitchen staff to give someone a cracked cup like that. Why, you're bleeding! Let me see.'

'No, it's all right,' Chiannala snatched her hand away. 'I can do it.' She knew that *she* was good at healing, but she didn't have so much faith in Rhoslyn. Quickly she cast a spell to stem the blood that dripped from her lacerated fingers and, once that was done, cast another that began to seal the gashes with new tissue. Then she turned her attention to the burning areas on her legs where the taillin had hit her, and used a different spell to cool and heal the scalds. This therapeutic magic came to her effortlessly, and she knew that her hurts would need no further attention. *Not bad for a first-year student*, she thought with a little inward smirk.

Rhoslyn raised her eyebrows. 'Goodness, you did that really well.' There was frank and generous admiration in her voice. 'No wonder you didn't want me messing with it.' For once, Chiannala forgot to be irritated with the other girl, and was grateful for her kindness. Though the annoyance sparked again, when Rhoslyn said, 'I wouldn't be at all surprised, Brynne, if you were chosen to specialise with the Luen of Healers.'

'Just because I'm good at it, doesn't mean I'm particularly interested,' she replied. To join the Luen of Healers was the last thing she wanted. In her opinion you didn't get to be the most powerful Wizard in Tyrineld by messing about, healing stupid, whiny idiots who had got themselves hurt.

Rhoslyn passed her a clean handkerchief moistened with water from the jug on the table. 'Here, wipe all that blood off your fingers and I'll take care of your poor robe. You don't want to be trailing all the way back upstairs to change, and one thing I am good at is cleaning spells.' She turned her attention to the stained robe, and Chiannala felt the cold, clinging clamminess of the wet fabric fade away quickly, as did the brown marks of the taillin.

Apart from those on her own table, the other students in the refectory had lost interest in the clumsy first-year, and had turned back to their own conversations and concerns. Chiannala's classmates, luckily, had put the accident down to nerves about the forthcoming announcements. She was quite happy to let them think what they liked, just so long as no one ever suspected the truth.

That day seemed endless, with nothing to do but wait. Since today was a holiday for the first-year pupils, most of them sought to distract themselves by going into the town for the day. So far, their work had allowed them few opportunities for recreation, and those of them who had always lived in Tyrineld were glad to show off their city to those who had grown up in the farms or villages of the surrounding lands. Chiannala had rebuffed all their offers. As soon as breakfast was over she headed to the Academy's great library, to spend the day, as usual, in study. Let the others have their markets and shops, the busy harbour, swimming in the warm ocean and strolling in the flowering parks in the sunshine. She was going to be a better Wizard than all of them – that was all that counted.

Despite her fascination for her studies, however, the day seemed to crawl by so slowly that Chiannala actually began to wonder whether someone had been working with a time spell that had gone badly wrong. The library was hot and stifling, and more than once she found herself looking wistfully out of the window at the bright sun, and wondering if the others found the hours and minutes dragging in the same way. More than once she was tempted to go out and see if she could find them, but that thirst for knowledge, that compulsion to work the hardest and be the best, drove her on until finally the red sun dropped down towards the ocean until it was almost touching the horizon. Chiannala put away her books and papers and, slinging her heavy bag over her shoulder, hastened out of the library.

On her way across the courtyard, Chiannala noticed that a band of dark purple cloud was massing on the horizon, rapidly overtaking the setting sun, which shone on bravely, untroubled by the approaching storm. A cold breeze came snaking across the flagstones, making her shiver. Though she chided herself for being superstitions, she could not help but view it as a bad omen.

Having been closest to the Hall of Light, Chiannala was the first of the students to arrive. She halted in the doorway, overawed by the magnificence around her. She had only seen this chamber once before, on her first day as a student here, when all the newcomers had been given a tour of the Academy. Then it had been one of Tyrineld's rare cloudy days, and she had not seen the hall to its full advantage. Now, in the golden light of sunset, the vast chamber had exploded into jewelled splendour. The long hall was comprised almost entirely of stained-glass windows, or so it seemed to the wide-eyed Chiannala. Each glowing panel was held in place by what appeared to be the most delicate lacework of dark, carved stone. They were formed in a multitude of cunning geometric shapes, interspersed with tall, rectangular panels that reached from the smooth tiled floor right up to the soaring, vaulted ceiling. Some held beautiful, intricate patterns while others depicted glowing scenes from ancient legend, and from the noble history of Tyrineld.

Chiannala would have liked to have the time and solitude in which to wander through the hall, looking at all the images in turn, but that pleasure would have to wait for, though she was the first student to arrive, the Heads of the Luens were there before her. At the far end of the hall was a raised dais and there they sat in a semicircle, wearing their power and authority like royal mantles.

The venerable Aldyth, Head of the Academy and the Luen of Academics, sat in the centre next to blunt Omaira of the Warriors, Esmon's successor, a big, broad, imposing woman with short, sandy hair, a homely face and shrewd eyes that glinted with suppressed anger. According to gossip, she had found it difficult to restrain herself from riding out at once with her entire Luen to avenge Esmon's death. Surprisingly, Galiena, the new Head of the Spellweavers, was absent, as was thin, clever Callia, Head of the Merchants, and they had been replaced by strangers.

On the other side of Aldyth was Tinagen, Head of the Healers, tall and gangling with a profile like an eagle and a great shock of curling red hair, and Lanrion, Head of the Nurturers, who was not, by all accounts, as gloomy as his bony face and dark, saturnine looks implied, though today he looked grave indeed as he whispered to his neighbour Daina, Head of the Artisans, with her short, spiky grey hair and a stunningly beautiful young-old face which was marred by the ravages of sleeplessness and sorrow. Esmon, Iriana and Avithan had been loved and respected by more than the members of their own Luens. Vaidel of the Bards, young and dangerously handsome with his dark curls and his close-clipped beard, was fidgeting. It was all too plain that he found this ceremony a waste of time, and from the cold glint of anger in his eyes, it appeared that he would rather be out seeking his own vengeance on the killers.

Suddenly the hall grew dark as the threatening clouds finally covered the sun, and lost its vivid bejewelled beauty, its corners and recesses stalked by sinister shadows that crept out across the floor.

'Come on, Brynne, you're blocking the doorway.' While Chiannala had been observing the august Heads of the Luens and wondering which, after today, would become her own mentor, her fellow students had caught up with her and were jostling to enter. She let the flow of them carry her into the room and headed for the block of chairs, set out in three rows of five, in front of the dais. Her heart was beating quickly as she sat down in the front row. Which of the Luens had chosen her?

After a moment to let the students settle themselves, Aldyth stood and made a long speech about the origins of the Luens, their long and noble history, why the students were being selected, what an honour it was to be chosen and how he hoped that they would work hard and do their utmost to bring honour to their Luen ... Chiannala soon stopped listening to his droning voice. Which would it be? Which would it be? The question kept circling in her head. Though she had professed indifference earlier that day, even to herself, in her heart she wanted the Spellweavers, where she felt that there would be more opportunities to make a name for herself. And she most emphatically did *not* want to be attached to the Nurturers, Iriana's Luen. Her hand hidden in a fold of her robes, she crossed her fingers tightly as Aldyth's speech wound down and announced that the new students would now be told what they had waited so long to hear.

The students were placed in alphabetical order, and Chiannala fidgeted impatiently while Ayron was assigned to the Nurturers and Briall to the Spellweavers. Then, at long last, it was her turn.

Aldyth's voice rang out. 'Student Brynne will be attached to the Healers.'

Chiannala stiffened in disbelief. There was a buzzing in her ears that drowned out Aldyth's subsequent announcements. *Healers?* No, this couldn't be! What did she care about a bunch of people she didn't know, who didn't have the sense to keep themselves healthy? Aldyth had made a mistake. Someone had, that was for sure. She sprang to her feet, her mouth opening to scream, shout, tell them they had it all wrong, but Rhoslyn, who was sitting beside her, grabbed her arm and jerked her back down. 'What are you doing?' she hissed. 'Do you want to be thrown out of the Academy?'

Fear of losing everything made Chiannala duck her head and stay silent but, inside, her guts were roiling with anger. Would this be the end of all her dreams of greatness?

She vowed that it would not. She had murdered to win her place, this chance at the Academy. She wasn't about to waste it now.

11

~

SEA CHANGE

With the tide of opinion turning against them very quickly, the remaining pacifist Luen Heads – Aldyth of the Academics, Daina of the Artisans, Tinagen of the Healers and Lanrion of the Nurturers – planned a meeting with the two deposed leaders late that night. They were afraid of being spied on, even by their own members, so one by one they slipped out of the city by various routes and made their way around the headland of the southernmost bay. It was no night to be out and about. Before sunset, great banks of curdled-looking, sinister dark purple cloud had massed on the horizon, and now the storm had hit the city with a wild howling gale and torrential rain that penetrated cloaks and clothing in no time, making them cling, chill and clammy, to the skin.

Once they had rounded the southern promontory, nature took over from the city and the cliffs became high and rugged, their ledges packed with nesting seabirds. A set of narrow steps had been carved into the rock, barely wide enough for one person at a time to descend. The beleaguered Wizards picked their way down cautiously, their magelight illuminating each step and supplementing the natural night vision that was a talent of their kind. A rough-edged, guano-streaked rock face was on their left and a stomach-churning drop was on their right, to the rocks and crashing surf below.

As he followed Tinagen and Lanrion, Aldyth shivered violently, filled with misgivings.

I'm too old for this. I've outlived my time.

Almost five hundred years – where had all the time gone? As he picked his careful way down the cliff, he remembered the Tyrineld of his youth: smaller, less sprawling, the buildings simple, square and blocky, constructed from timber and mortared stone. It had been Wylnas of the Artisans who had discovered the spell to fabricate a flawless white material, like marble but impervious to the staining and depredations of the weather. One by one, the city's houses, towers and halls had been rebuilt in the new material, to new and beautiful designs. Chalisa, the Archwizard at that time, had an eye for beauty and a heartfelt instinct for harmony, and it had been her vision that had transformed Tyrineld into a jewel among cities. She had planned and schemed, cajoled, exhorted and browbeaten the Heads of Luens and the city's inhabitants, and somehow they had all found themselves working together with energy and determination until her vision was achieved, and Tyrineld was the wonder of the world.

Despite all his cares and worries, Aldyth found himself smiling in the darkness. Who knew better than he how stubborn Chalisa had been, how tireless, how proud? Who was better acquainted with her wiles and charms, her intelligence and fire, the tenacity that could sometimes cross the line into absolute pigheaded determination not to be beaten? One way or another, Chalisa always got what she wanted – including the tall, gangling redheaded Wizard with the ferocious intellect and the crippling shyness that drove him away from people and into his studies.

Again, Aldyth found himself smiling. To this day he'd never really understood what Chalisa had seen in him, but she had set out to win him as her soulmate and, as usual, what she wanted she had achieved. For more than three centuries they had been happy together, and would have been yet, had it not been for the devastating storm that had struck Tyrineld one terrible night, levelling half the city and leaving many of its inhabitants dead: killed outright or injured beyond the skills of the Healers to repair. Aldyth himself had been hurt, and the Healers were treating his broken arm and concussion when the worst moment of his life occurred, and he felt his beloved's death.

While Chalisa had been searching for survivors in some of the Academy buildings on the clifftop, the entire face of the precipice, battered relentlessly by savage gales and towering seas, had given way, taking with it the buildings, the search party, and Aldyth's lovely soulmate. Her body, buried beneath tons of rubble on the ocean floor, had never been found.

Aldyth, alone and wracked by grief, had decided to leave his own life; to die, as was the prerogative of the Wizardfolk when they had finally tired of the long, unreeling years and wished to rest. What was there to stay for? The city of Tyrineld had been devastated by the storm. The survivors, stunned and grieving the loss of so many of their fellows, including their beloved Archwizard, wandered the wreckage and huddled in the ruins, and no one seemed to know how to proceed. Many would choose death, as he himself was planning to do, Aldyth thought, as he surveyed the devastation from the ruins of Ariel's Tower. They would abandon lives that had suddenly become unendurable, and Tyrineld, once so proud and magnificent, would dwindle to a backwater fishing village. Gradually the ruined buildings would crumble, the survivors would scatter and disperse, and Chalisa's wonderful vision would become a thing of the past, lost from the world for ever.

'OVER MY DEAD BODY!'

Aldyth spun at the sound of those familiar, ringing tones – the beloved voice that he had never thought to hear again, except in memory. Chalisa stood behind him, though whether he saw her with his normal vision, or in his mind's eye, he could never, afterwards, be quite sure. All he knew was that she stood there: not wishful thinking or a trick of his grieving imagination, but truly in the room with him. With a cry he reached for her, but—

'Don't!' The authority in her voice stopped him in his tracks. 'Don't, my love,' she added more gently. 'You can't touch me now, for I have passed beyond this world. I should not be here at all: there should be no returning on the road that I have taken, but' – she smiled at him, that brilliant smile he had known and loved for so long – 'as you know, I can be very persuasive when I try. Even so, I am only allowed to come to you for a moment, but there is something I must say before I pass away through the Well of Souls.' She fixed him with a piercing look. 'My love, will you promise to do one thing for me?'

'Of course I will,' he said quickly. 'Anything.'

She grimaced; rueful, sympathetic, but when she spoke her voice was firm. 'The people need a leader now, Aldyth. They need unity and purpose. They need someone to guide them, to nurture them, to help them rebuild their city and their shattered lives. You must carry on where I left off. You must become Archwizard after me.'

Aldyth was thunderstruck. 'But I'm no Archwizard! I am nothing like you. I cannot lead our people.'

'Nonsense,' Chalisa said firmly. 'You are the best person I have ever known, and you are more than fit to be Archwizard. Believe in yourself, Aldyth, as I believe in you – then get out there and save our people.' Aldyth felt the faintest, phantom touch of a kiss on his lips, then Chalisa had faded away.

It had been her final request to him: how could he refuse? For love of her, he had found the courage and fortitude to take up the burden of this broken city and to help these desperate Wizards rebuild their homes and their lives. For almost a century he had ruled Tyrineld as Archwizard, before gratefully relinquishing the reins of authority to Cyran and retiring to his post as Head of the Academy. He had done his duty – more than his duty. Was there really any reason he should keep on lingering here?

While he had been lost in memories of the past, Aldyth had lagged a fair way behind the other two on the uncertain, slippery stairway. Pulling his attention back to the here and now, he followed them down, going as fast as he dared but resisting the temptation to hurry. One slip on these steps and Tinagen, Daina and Lanrion would be waiting for ever for him to join them, instead of a mere few minutes, not to mention Galiena and Callia, the two deposed Heads, who, since they no longer had their responsibilities to detain them, had been the first to slip down to the temple.

About two-thirds of the way down the escarpment a hanging turret had been carved by magic from the living rock. Round in shape with a rather fanciful, conical, pointed roof, it was just large enough for two small, compact rooms, one above the other. It had once been the home of Endarl, a legendary Wizard of long ago who had relinquished all communication with his fellows, in order to concentrate entirely, and without distractions, upon his magic. Anything he needed he apported down to his little haven, and as the years passed, the Wizards of Tyrineld finally began to forget that he was even there – until at last they felt his passing. He had left behind him a vast collection of writings that had heralded some remarkable advances in the practice of magic, including the invention of the spell to take a subject or an object out of time, and his more complex works were still being investigated by the Luen of Spellweavers to this very day.

The solitary door of the turret led directly from the bottom of the stairway into the upper chamber. Tinagen, Daina and Lanrion let themselves in, and Aldyth saw the blue globes of their magelight pause, then vanish inside as they ducked beneath the low lintel. He had just started to move again, and was still about two dozen steps up from the turret door when he realised that all was lost. The warning silver shimmer of magic flashed like a lighthouse beam through the open doorway and he froze, heart thudding in his chest. He shrank back against the cliff face like a hunted animal as the sound of voices came from below.

'Got them!'

'Some conspirators – they made it easy for us, coming to this lonely place.'

'Too true. It certainly came as a shock to Callia. Did you see her face when we arrested her?'

'And since we took her out of time so that she couldn't warn the others, that expression's going to be there for quite a while.' There was the sound of cruel laughter.

'Be quiet, the lot of you.' It was Omaira's voice, sharp with its customary snap of authority. 'Before you start getting too cocky, just remember that if Galiena hadn't decided to change sides and join us, we wouldn't have found out about this.'

'So that's how you knew.' Tinagen's voice was filled with venom. Aldyth had never heard him sound so furious. 'And what was Galiena's price? That Sharalind would reinstate her as head of the Luen – on condition, of course, that she becomes your puppet?'

'Something like that.' Aldyth knew Omaira very well, and knew that when she used that particular tone of voice it came accompanied by a wry expression and a shrug. 'As soon as Sharalind decides that she can truly be trusted.'

'In other words, you're holding it over her head as a kind of blackmail, or a bribe, to keep her under your control,' Tinagen said scornfully. 'I've known you all my life, Omaira. We haven't seen eye to eye on a number of matters over the years, but I never thought I'd see you turn traitor to you own kind.'

'What kind is that? You mean the Heads of the Luens? As far as I'm concerned, Tinagen, *all* the Wizardfolk are my own kind, and as head of the Warrior Luen, I'm pledged to protect them. You've got to face facts: if the Phaerie killed poor Avithan, it's going to mean war whether you like it or not. It's not unrealistic to be prepared—'

'Don't you *dare* use that poor young man's death as an excuse! You've been itching for something like this for years. It's not a defence that Sharalind is preparing, and well you know it. She plans to start a war over Avithan's death. She wants blood, nothing less will satisfy her, and she'll drag the whole realm of the Wizards down with her. It's one thing to defend oneself against an aggressor, but it's another thing to *be* that aggressor. That's something I won't be party to. And what's more, when the members of the other Luens hear about your ambush tonight, I think some of Sharalind's supporters will start to have doubts of their own. No matter how much you try to justify betraying your colleagues, people are going to start wondering when they'll be next.'

'Why, you sanctimonious old windbag!' It was the hot-headed Vaidel. 'Not everybody is as cowardly as you. How can you even live with yourself when—'

'Excuse me, Vaidel,' someone interrupted.

'What?' Aldyth could just imagine his anger swinging round to impale the speaker.

'Er – I thought Galiena said there were supposed to be four.'

'Shit!' Omaira's voice cut through the keening gale. 'Where's Aldyth? He can't be far away. We were definitely told that all of the dissenters were meeting here tonight. The old dodderer probably lagged behind the others. Get up that staircase quick and find him, because if we don't, and he carries word of what happened here back to the city, we'll lose the trust and support of the other Luens.'

'Not to mention that Sharalind will have our hides.' This time, it was Vaidel who spoke. Then several figures emerged, one by one, through the narrow doorway, and Aldyth realised that he had no hope of escape. There was no time to get back up the cliff before they caught him. He couldn't fight them all – he was a scholar, not a warrior, and he couldn't apport – he was too old now to manage the considerable expenditure of energy involved. Suddenly an image of Chalisa leapt into his mind. This time she did not urge him to stay, but smiled and beckoned, her face aglow with love. Was it a true vision, or his imagination reflecting the dearest wish of his heart? Aldyth did not care.

'There he is!' The cry went up from below him, all too close. 'Get him.'

Taking a last, deep breath, Aldyth opened his arms as if to embrace the dark, stormy night and the crashing waves, and took a mighty leap off the edge of the cliff, arcing out high and wide before arrowing down into the sea.

*

Ionor had his own special way of avoiding storms, both the weather sort and the gathering storm of conflict that was threatening to tear the city, the Wizardfolk and even his own lifelong friendships apart. He had never believed that such a chasm could open up in his own tight-knit group of companions. Melisanda was, like him, vehemently against the idea of war. Thara also, but he could sense, occasionally, that she was beginning to waver. Yinze and Chathak, both with loved ones to avenge, were openly welcoming the chance to strike back and were backing Sharalind wholeheartedly. They were already training with the Luen of Warriors, and were in no mood to hear talk of peace and moderation.

The Wizard was beginning to wish that he had remained with the Leviathan, and had never returned to Tyrineld. In a few short days the atmosphere had changed out of all recognition. This was no longer a gentle-paced city devoted to beauty, creativity and learning. Suddenly, everyone accepted war as a foregone conclusion, whether they were for or against. Fear and a kind of sick excitement stalked the streets; it was as though the conflict had already reached into every home and family. He felt increasingly isolated here; alienated from even his closest friends. For the first time in his life he was bitterly at odds with Chathak and Yinze. He was grieving for Avithan too – his friend's death had torn a deep and painful wound in his heart – but fighting the Phaerie and getting a whole multitude of other Wizards killed wouldn't bring him back and, Ionor was sure, it was the last thing that Avithan himself would have wanted. Thara and Melisanda, though they concurred with him, were both grimly busy now. The Healers were devising strategies and making preparations to cope with the carnage that must surely come, and Thara's cadre of the Nurturers, those concerned with growing things, were working themselves to exhaustion trying to accelerate the maturing of every harvestable crop, to feed Omaira's army and increase the city's stockpile of supplies.

Ionor had never felt so lonely, not even during his childhood. Except for his friends, he had never known a true family. His parents had conceived him in a starburst of passion that faded as quickly as it flared. His mother, Laranel, was a trading captain, highly placed in the Luen of Merchants. She commanded her own ship and was famed for her daring, both in the voyages she made and the ventures that sprang from them. His father, Nolior, was a Bard, well respected for his researches into ancient ballads and poems that cast light on some of the more obscure, barbaric and little-documented periods of the Wizards' ancient history.

This mismatched couple had met when Nolior took passage on Laranel's ship to the far-off Apiun Islands, to investigate some ancient inscriptions that had been found there. Their shipboard romance was a brief flowering of lust, never meant by either of them to last any longer than the voyage itself. Unfortunately it coincided with the passage through the Dead Zone, an area in the tropics where an undersea volcano had thrown up a strange, dull grey metallic ore that had an inhibiting effect on magic.

A Wizard called Zathbar, from the Luen of Artificers, had discovered much about the material, and had even gone so far as to fabricate a pair of bracelets from the vile stuff, but it was so unpleasant and dangerous to work with that no one else wanted to have anything to with it. Zathbar, horrified by what he had wrought, had buried the bracelets in the wild, hot, inhospitable lands of the Jewelled Desert, far to the south, and thankfully moved on to other things.

Only the Dead Zone remained – slap-bang in the middle of the north-south trade route. Mortal sailors were unaffected, but the Wizard captains got through the area as fast as they could, thanked their stars when they reached the other side, and did their best to forget about it. Only when Nolior and Laranel had gone their separate ways, and Laranel discovered, to her utter horror, that she was pregnant, did she realise that the Dead Zone had affected the spells with which Wizards controlled their fertility.

Laranel did what any Wizard did who didn't want their life's work to be hampered by a child. She had the baby and left him in the House of Children, where Wizard offspring were brought up communally by volunteers who came mainly from the Luens of Nurturers and Healers. Neither she nor Ionor's father had taken any further interest in him and he had grown up as a City Brat, as the occupants of the House of Children were colloquially known – as, indeed, had Melisanda. Her parents were both itinerant Healers who dedicated their lives to treating Wizards in far-flung, scattered communities. They, at least, had loved their daughter and always spent time with her on their occasional visits to Tyrineld, but the wilderness was no place to bring up a child, especially one whose father and mother were exposed to so much infection and disease. When Melisanda was a first-year student with the Luen of Healers, both her parents had perished when an epidemic decimated a backwoods settlement. Her grieving had brought her closer to her circle of friends; just one more bond to add to the many that they shared.

Now it seemed that those bonds were already fraying and breaking, leaving Ionor bereft. He had started the night sitting alone in the house he had shared for so long with Avithan and the others. Yinze and Chathak, grimly purposeful, were out training at the Luen of Warriors, and Thara and Melisanda were busy with their own concerns, for the Healers and Nurturers had many preparations to make for the conflict to come. Ionor belonged to the Academy, the Luen of Academics, who had nothing practical to do in preparation for war – nor, he suspected, would Aldyth allow his people to become involved in any of the planning, such was the strength of his opposition.

And what about me? Will my own opposition stand so firm, if put to the test? Will I join those who refuse to go to war, or will I swallow my scruples and go along, because Yinze and Chathak are going, and I want to be with them?

Ionor didn't want to abandon them. He felt sure that their chances of survival would be greater if he was with them, if all three of them were together.

But what of my own chances?

Was it cowardice not to become involved, or common sense?

He needed to escape all this: to step away for a while, and allow his thoughts to settle. Maybe even talk the matter over with a friend whose perspective was less trammelled by so many personal ties and conflicting loyalties. Luckily, such a friend existed. Lituya. Suddenly it seemed the most natural thing in the world to slip away from Tyrineld and all its worries, and head for the ocean to be with the Leviathan.

The streets were quiet that night, with the wild weather keeping everyone snug indoors. Ionor decided to enter the water in the harbour where, thanks to the protection of the long piers and breakwaters, the sea was relatively calm. The quays were deserted, with the boats moored snug in their haven, battened down against the storm. Shivering in the brutal blasts of wind and driving rain, the Wizard took off his outer clothes and hid them, wrapped into a bundle in his cloak, behind a pile of lobster pots in an open-fronted shed. As always, he put back his belt, which held a long knife in a sheath, and fastened it securely round his waist. Beneath the ocean, a tool or a weapon could mean his survival.

Ionor looked out at the ocean, wild and powerful in the storm, and his heart beat faster with excitement. Then, taking a deep breath, he sprinted through the downpour to the edge of the jetty, and made a clean dive into the water.

As he wrapped the undersea spell around him like an old, familiar mantle, Ionor no longer felt cold or wet. His wizardly night vision worked just as well underwater as it did on land, and he could see quite clearly where he was going. He left the shelter of the harbour, swimming strongly underwater and keeping near the bottom to escape the worst of the tumult on the surface, but here, so close to the land, it was impossible to avoid the violence of the great waves that came churning and crashing in. The chaotic currents hurled him this way and that, and the water was turbid with sand that had been stirred up from the sea bed.

Using all the strength and skill he had developed during his months with the Leviathan, Ionor fought his way through the turmoil, until he reached the place where the shelving coast dropped into the depths and he could swim down to a level where everything was calm and still. The Wizard felt his spirits grow lighter. It was such a relief not to have to fight the ocean any more, and such a joy to be back in this, his adopted element that was coming more and more to feel like home. All he needed to make things perfect was Lituya's company. Concentrating on the image of his friend, he sent out a call in mindspeech through the ocean depths.

Clearly Lituya was asleep, as the Wizard had to call for a moment or two before he got an answer. Eventually, however, he was rewarded with a reply. 'Ionor?' The mental tones were fuzzy with sleep. 'What is it?' The thought patterns sharpened with alarm. 'Is something wrong?'

'Lituya, don't worry,' Ionor cursed his own lack of consideration. Just because *he* couldn't sleep, it didn't give him the right to go round disturbing everyone else. 'I'm sorry I woke you. I was just feeling lonely and worried and I needed your company.'

'Well, why didn't you say so? I'll come at once.' There was a moment's pause, then he continued. 'It will be good to take some time just for ourselves but also – well, there's something I need to discuss with you.'

'What? What's wrong?' Now it was Ionor's turn to feel a stab of alarm, and the Leviathan's turn to comfort him. 'Don't you worry either. We'll talk about it when I see you. I'm sure it's not beyond the ingenuity of the Magefolk to solve.' Again, there was a slight hesitation. 'Ionor, I'm glad you came tonight. I've missed you.'

'Thank you, Lituya. You're a true friend. I've missed you too – I hadn't realised how much, until tonight. I'm heading into the southern bay now, so I'll meet you there.'

Ionor swam on, blessing the Wizards' night vision that allowed him to navigate these dark waters in safety. Through the spell that had been formulated for him to live among the Leviathan, he could glide along with little effort, his body protected from the changes in pressure and the profound chill of the depths.

In the southern bay, where the cliffs plunged straight down into the ocean, a kelp forest grew; a multitude of slender stems with long, elegant fronds growing all along their length that swayed and swirled like dancers in the shifting current. The strands of the giant seaweed stretched up and up, taller than trees, rooted on the sea bed and reaching right up to the warm water and bright light at the surface. It felt sheltered and comfortable among the waving ribbons, and the Wizard settled there to await his friend. Using an old sea-otter trick he took hold of one of the stems and twirled himself in the water so that it wrapped two or three times round his body, anchoring him in place. It felt so comfortable here, to be held gently without danger of drifting, to be cradled by the murmuring ocean that rocked him gently on its shifting tides.

Ionor had not realised how difficult life had become for him up on the surface in Tyrineld. Now that he had escaped, if only for a time, all the worry, grief and conflict that stalked the city, he realised that he was utterly worn out and weary. Gradually his knotted muscles relaxed and the tension seeped out of him, dissolving in the ocean currents that slid like silk around his body. Cradled in the kelp, he drifted, drowsed and finally fell asleep ...

Only to be awakened by a shattering splash and a clamour of voices, as something large and heavy hit the water and plummeted to the bottom. Shocked and shaken, the Wizard flailed among the kelp fronds, almost throttling himself as he tried to get free from the entangling stem he'd wrapped around himself. When he finally managed to get loose he swam towards the point of impact where the object had entered the water, which was still marked by a swirl of spreading foam. His common sense told him he was heading in the wrong direction, for surely the projectile could only have been a boulder – and judging by the size of the splash it must have been a large one – that had been dislodged from the cliff by the storm, and by heading in closer to the shoreline he ran the risk of being hit by any further falling rocks. Nevertheless his curiosity, that fatal flaw in the Wizardly character that had caused them so much trouble over the ages, nagged at him until it drove him forward. He followed the trail of bubbles downward, until there, floating in a tangle of kelp strands, he saw a dark shape below. Ionor's heart gave a lurch.

That's not a rock!

Unless his eyes were playing tricks on him, that could be a cloaked figure, down there among the seaweed fronds. In a frantic burst of speed, the Wizard swam down and reached for the mysterious object – and sure enough, his hand grasped a tangle of wet cloth.

'By the light!' Feverishly the Wizard worked to free the figure from the tangle of weed, hampered by the slippery fronds and the wet fabric of the cloak that wrapped itself around his arms and clung to his skin. After struggling for what seemed like an eternity, he remembered his knife.

Oh, you fool, Ionor!

Thanking providence for the sharp blade, he hacked at the slick, rubbery fronds of the kelp, and felt a surge of relief as the limp, cloth-swathed form came was freed at last.

Who was this? As Ionor dragged the limp form to the surface, he caught a glimpse of several gleams of magelight on the cliff path high above. Who was up there and why had they not tried to rescue the stranger? It looked to the young Wizard as though there was some sort of foul play afoot – and he had just rescued the victim. But was the poor soul alive or dead now? Well, as a Wizard he wouldn't have drowned, so everything depended on whether he'd survived the fall. Feverishly Ionor clawed the sodden fabric of the cloak away from the anonymous figure's face – and it was as though he'd been kicked in the stomach. 'Aldyth!'

From his very first days as a student at the Academy, Ionor had looked upon the old Wizard as his teacher, his mentor – and his friend. Having grown up with no real family to call his own he had formed a strong bond with the venerable scholar. Circumstances had prevented Aldyth from having a child with his beloved lifemate, but something in the gawky, intelligent boy had gone straight to his heart. From their very first meeting there had been a feeling that they belonged to one another. Ionor might not have sprung from Aldyth, but in their hearts they were father and son.

'Aldyth.' The Wizard's voice took on a greater urgency as he patted the slack grey face. Feverishly he felt along the old man's limbs, but he lacked the skill of a Healer to know whether anything had been damaged in the fall.

'Ionor?' The mental voice was thin and reedy, so that Ionor had to strain to catch his name, but then his heart leapt as Aldyth's eyelids fluttered open. 'Cold. So cold.'

Of course! He should have thought of that at once. Though the old man was a Wizard and could breathe underwater, he lacked the spell that Ionor employed to keep out the ocean's chill. It was a complex magic to perform, and though long practice had enabled Ionor to cast it on himself and maintain it with very little thought, it would be too difficult to work the spell upon another, not to mention having to maintain it for two people.

He would need some help.

'Lituya?' His mindspeech rang out through the depths. 'Lituya, come quick!'

'What is it? What's wrong?'

Because of their close attachment, Ionor could sense that the Leviathan had put on a huge burst of speed. 'My master Aldyth – I found him. He must have fallen off the cliffs. He needs our spell.'

'I come.' Already the Mage of the Oceans was entering the bay. Currents swirled around Ionor as the Leviathan pulled up beside him, his massive, streamlined form a darker shadow in the night. To Ionor's relief he wasted no time asking questions.

'Let us begin, my brother. Without our protection your friend the Elder cannot continue much longer.'

'I'm ready.' Ionor reached out with his mind to touch the consciousness of the Leviathan, then, conjoined, they sought the faltering life force of Aldyth, whose spirit was wan and flickering as a guttering candle. Together they wove the spell, fortifying him with their own strength and energy, forging a shield against the brutal power of the ocean, spinning and weaving their magic around the essence of the elderly Wizard. A golden glow flared and subsided around Aldyth's body as the spell took hold, permeating flesh and bone, and beating through his blood.

The two friends, Wizard and Leviathan, waited anxiously. Had they been in time? Or was Aldyth so near death that their intervention had been too little, too late? Then Aldyth stirred, stretched and opened his eyes. 'Ah, that's better,' he murmured drowsily. 'Warm blanket. Just the thing.' His heavy eyelids closed again, but just as Ionor and Lituya thought he'd drifted back into slumber, they snapped open. His body tensed with alarm and his fingers tightened around Ionor's hand like an iron vice. 'Sharalind! She has betrayed us.'

Ionor listened with growing horror as Aldyth gasped out his story of the meeting, the ambush, and the arrest of Tinagen, Daina and Lanrion. 'But what will Sharalind do with them?' he gasped. 'They're Heads of Luens, three of the most important people in the city. How could she justify arresting them like this? With what crime could she charge them?'

'Who knows?' Aldyth said bitterly. 'Her grief has robbed her of all reason; there's no predicting what she might do. But I suspect she'll just lock them away somewhere; render them incommunicado with the Time Spell and use them to hold the dissident Luens to ransom until they fall into line. In the meantime—'

'You can't go back,' Ionor said decisively. 'I can't have you disappearing into their clutches. I won't let them take you, Aldyth.'

'It won't be safe for you either, Ionor,' Lituya pointed out. 'Not unless you decide to join your friends and go to war with the others. Clearly Sharalind has decided to deal with all the dissenters, and your close association to Aldyth is well known.'

Ionor stared at him. In his concern over his mentor, his thoughts hadn't reached as far as his own involvement in this mess. With sinking dismay, he realised that the Leviathan was right. Unless he wanted to join in a war he felt was wrong, Tyrineld was not a good place for him to be at present. But how could he leave his friends? Though he had more sense than to believe he could protect Chathak and Yinze in a battle, he knew that if anything should happen to them, and he wasn't there, he would blame himself to the end of his days. And could he ever be certain, deep in his heart, that it had truly been his own moral compass that had steered him away from the conflict – or simply sheer craven cowardice?

Already sturdy Thara was talking about joining the fight: the fact that her Luen, headed by the dissenting Lanrion, had found so much work for its members in providing the city with enough stored provisions to withstand the dark days to come was the only thing that had kept her away so far. And though he knew that Melisanda was in complete agreement with his own abhorrence of war, her intense dedication to her vocation would drive her to go too, joining the cadre of brave Healers on the outskirts of the battle who risked their own lives to deal with the wounds, the maiming and insane destruction of life that would be the inevitable result of the hostilities. Apart from Aldyth, Ionor's cherished circle of companions were the only family he had. For Iriana's sake, and for Avithan, they would join the conflict. How in all conscience could he do any less?

Torn unbearably, the Wizard vacillated, while precious moments slipped away. Once she had got her captives to safety, the thorough Omaira must send people back to search for Aldyth. As a Wizard, she would realise that he was not dead or she would have felt his passing, and it wouldn't be like her to leave such a dangerous thread dangling loose.

'Ionor, come away with me,' Lituya said urgently, and Ionor realised that they were so closely attuned that that his friend had heard his thoughts quite clearly. 'Aldyth cannot stay here – that much is plain,' the Leviathan went on. 'We should take him to my people. We are only a few days behind them in their northern migration, and they were not hurrying. We should be able to catch them up. They will take care of your mentor, in honour and in safety. They will maintain the spells that keep him safe and comfortable beneath the sea.'

The Wizard knew that he was right, but ... 'But you could take him,' he began doubtfully. 'I don't have to go.'

'No, I cannot. He is old and weak and shaken. He does not know the spell, so I would have to maintain it myself, without sleep, without rest, all the way to the north. I need your help, my friend. *He* needs your help. Even Sharalind cannot go to war all in a day. Once Aldyth is safe you can always some back to join your friends, if that is what you decide to do.'

It was a way out of the dilemma, and Ionor seized upon it gratefully. 'You're right. Why didn't I see it before? It's the only thing to do. Come on, we'll go at once. I've delayed here too long already.'

Due to the spell keeping him warm, Aldyth no longer needed his cloak, so Ionor used it to bind the old man to his back. His mentor had lapsed into a stupor once more, which saved a lot of time in explanations, though it was also a cause for some concern, and made it more urgent than ever that they should start on their journey as soon as possible. Clumsily, because of the unaccustomed burden, the Wizard swam to Lituya and caught hold of the forward edge of his long, elegant fluke, at the place where it joined his body. That way he could rest on the great flipper and be pulled along, tucked safely into the Leviathan's slipstream as they sped through the water.

'I'm ready, Lituya. Let's go. It's time we were moving. If I'm to get to your people then return in time to help my friends, there's not a minute to waste.'

Without another word the Leviathan arrowed out of the bay and into the ocean, heading north. For once he kept his thoughts beneath a careful shield, so that Ionor could not hear him.

It's time we were moving indeed, my dear friend. But you won't be coming back here to risk yourself in this insane conflict – not if I can help it. My people desperately need some help with the creation of their own artefact – one of healing, not destruction. Our talents will be much more useful there than in war-torn Tyrineld.

By the time the sun rose over the ocean, they were far away.

12

~

THE STRANGER

The girl drifted awake to see a primitive ceiling, completely strange to her, of planks laid over roughly hewn beams.

What is this place?

Frowning, she turned her head. She was in a small room with chinked wooden walls and a window with curtains that had clearly started their lives as sacks for carrying some merchandise or other. A dazzling streak of sunlight shone through the narrow gap between them, and she screwed up her eyes and turned to look the other way. The opposite wall was festooned with the assorted paraphernalia of the fisherman, all neatly hung on nails: nets draped like giant, shadowy cobwebs; net floats which were beautiful glass spheres coloured amber, blue or various shades of green ranging from dark to light; neatly coiled longlines, bristling with silvery hooks, hung up safely high in the rafters where the wicked barbs could not tear at clothing or vulnerable flesh. In the corner was a tottering stack of crab pots, handmade with wooden bottoms and bentwood frames enclosed in a sturdy netting of tarred string.

The chamber was filled with the wild, salt tang of the sea, with a faint, but not unpleasant, odour of fish in the background. In the distance she could hear the hiss and sigh of waves washing against the shore, and the wild, high cries of the gulls. Though her bed was slightly on the hard side, she was warm and cosy beneath soft, clean, woollen blankets, and she felt comfortable and safe – but she had never seen this place before, and she had absolutely no idea where she was, how she had come to be there, or indeed, any memories of herself at all.

What's happening to me?

Like a bolt of lightning that came out of nowhere, fear flashed through her as the door creaked open. A big woman entered, statuesque and broad of beam, with a weathered face. She had dark brown hair, streaked with silver and twisted up into a practical knot, and piercing blue eyes. She was also a total stranger.

Who are you?

Who am I?

Brynne. The name came into her mind and stuck there.

Is that who I am?

Again, the girl fought vertiginous terror. Looking into these ghastly blanks in her mind was like staring into an endless abyss ... The image made her insides clench. To steady herself, she focused on the woman's kindly smile, holding on to it like a lifeline. 'And there you are, my lovely,' she was saying. 'It's good to see you properly awake at last. You've been drifting in and out of consciousness for days, and burning up with fever.'

'I – don't remember,' Brynne said.

'I'm not at all surprised,' the woman answered. 'You've given us some anxious times, let me tell you. My brother nearly died of fright himself when he pulled you out of the sea. He thought you must be drowned for sure.' She patted the girl's hand. 'But what do men know, eh? We women are a lot stronger than they give us credit for. Now, what you need is some good hot soup and a nice cup of taillin with plenty of honey.'

After the woman had, at her urgent request, helped her to the outhouse – at the bottom of the garden with a staggering view over cliffs and a rocky bay – she found herself tucked back into bed with the promised soup and tea, and a hunk of soft, new-baked bread. The only part of the house she had seen on her way through had been the kitchen, and she had barely noticed that: she had been in too much of a hurry on her way out, and too intent on getting back into bed before her legs collapsed completely on her return. She simply had an impression of dim and shabby cosiness. Besides, now that her most urgent need had been taken care of, she was conscious of a ravenous hunger, and was too busy concentrating on her food to think of anything else.

The soup was made from chunks of fish and vegetable in a strong stock. It was an unusual taste to her, but absolutely delicious. While she was attacking the steaming bowl, her new companion, who had left the room, returned with a basket that had wool and long needles sticking out of the top. She perched on the end of the bed, settling herself comfortably, and proceeded to knit away at a thick grey sock. 'And now, lovey,' she said, her eyes glancing up and down between the girl's face and her flashing needles, 'let's get acquainted. My name is Osella. Who might you be? And how came you to be floating around in the sea for my brother to pick up in his boat?'

The girl looked at her, anguished and afraid. 'I don't know,' she said. 'I think I might be called Brynne – that's the name that comes into my mind – but I've tried and tried, and I can't remember anything else. Who my family are, where I came from, what happened to me – it's all a horrible blank.' Before she could stop them, her eyes flooded with tears.

'There now, there, Brynne. If that's the name you remember then that's what we'll call you, at least for now.' Osella took the tilting bowl of soup out of her hands, and set it aside on the floor. Then she took the girl into her arms and held her while she wept. 'Don't fret, now,' she said. 'This loss of memory is probably just your mind protecting itself from what happened to you, until you feel better. I've seen it happen before, to fishermen who've been wrecked at sea. You'll start remembering soon, I'm sure of it, and in the meantime, we'll take good care of you right here. If you like, my brother or one of his crew can sail over to Tyrineld, and ask around to see if anyone's missing you.'

'No!' Fear jolted through her, and she clutched tightly at Osella. 'Don't tell anyone where I am. I'll be in danger.'

'In danger?' The woman frowned. 'What do you mean? How can you be in danger from people knowing where you are?'

'I don't know. I still don't remember. But when you talked about asking around, I just got this feeling, as if danger were near.'

'What are you saying? Surely you don't think someone tried to drown you deliberately?'

'I don't know. It's a feeling, nothing more. But it's a very strong one. Please don't ask anyone about me until my memory comes back, if it ever does.'

'Of course it will,' Osella soothed. 'You just give it time. What about finishing your soup and taillin, then you can have a nice sleep?'

'But I've only just woken up,' Brynne protested. Then she considered. 'But I think I could sleep a bit more.'

The next time she awoke it was evening. The darkening sky was a deep, rich, luminous blue, with a single bright star looking down through her window like a sentinel. Brynne blinked and stretched. There was less stiffness in her muscles and she had fewer aches and pains, though the catch in her breathing and the tightness in her chest still remained. In her mind, however … Brynne shuddered. There it was still, that blank, impenetrable barrier between her future and her past that, try as she would, she could not push her way through. Behind that wall terror prowled. That was all she knew.

Best to stay here. Best not to risk what lay beyond. Best to remain on this side, where it was safe and warm and comfortable. She pulled the bedclothes over her head and tried to will herself back to sleep – only to find herself high on a clifftop. She wasn't alone. There was someone else, just a quick flash of a beautiful face, contorted by jealousy and resentment, then the face became her own and she was falling, falling …

'Wake up, my pet. Wake up now.'

Brynne fought against the entangling bedclothes, struck out at the arm that was shaking her shoulder.

'There, now. Steady now. That's a good girl. Wake up now, it's just a dream, a bad dream you were having.'

Gasping, wheezing, Brynne pushed her face clear of the covers and opened bleary eyes to see Osella. 'Why, there you are.' The woman's smile was strained and her brow was furrowed with concern. 'That surely was some nightmare you were having. But you're fine now, you're safe here. We'll take care of you.' She stacked up the pillows behind Brynne's back so that the girl could sit up comfortably. 'There. Better now?'

Brynne nodded, though she still couldn't take in quite enough air when she breathed.

'Here you are. You have a nice warm drink.' Osella pushed a mug into her hand. Brynne sipped gratefully. It was some kind of taillin, but with honey masking the bitterness of some strange and pungent herbs that had been added.

'Go on,' Osella prompted. 'Drink up, it'll help your breathing. I don't know how your lungs weren't full of water—' For an instant she hesitated, and Brynne thought she saw a flicker of speculation in her eyes, but then she continued breezily, as if nothing had happened. 'But your chest's still weak because of the fever you contracted from being chilled for so long. Don't worry. It'll pass.' She ran a rough, callused hand over the sweat-damp tangle of Brynne's hair. 'You were lucky to end up with an old fishing family. We know, none better, how to deal with near-drownings.' She hesitated for a breath. 'You still don't remember what happened to you?'

Brynne shuddered, trying to keep her thoughts away from that blank grey wall in her head, and the horror that stalked beyond. 'I can't recall anything, but I had a nightmare where I was on a high cliff. I saw this face, beautiful but nasty, then it turned into my own and I was falling ...' She put her hands over her face as if to blot out the disturbing images. 'It was just a dream, a horrible dream. It didn't make any sense.'

Seeing the girl's fear, Osella pushed away the frown that had been forming and changed it to a reassuring smile. 'Well, dreams often make no sense. Now, do you want to go to sleep again, or would you rather get up for a while, and sit with me by the fire?'

'It would be good to get up for a while.' Brynne didn't want to sleep again. Didn't want to dream.

Osella found some of her own clothes, a green shirt and black skirt, for Brynne. They were loose on her, and the skirt was far too long, but she rolled the waistband over a few times and held it all in place with a belt.

'And we'd better take care to keep you warm enough.' The kind woman tucked a thick woollen shawl around her shoulders and began to lead her down the narrow wooden staircase. 'Come along now, sit by the fire and I'll get you something to eat. You woke up at just the right time – I've got a lovely big meat pie keeping warm in the oven. My brother and the youngsters are due back at any minute—'

Before Brynne even had time to start feeling nervous at the thought of meeting new strangers, in they came. Osella had barely finished speaking when the cottage door banged open and a deep voice, like honey poured over gravel, bellowed out: 'Ho there! Where is everybody? Is supper ready?'

Brynne tried to draw back but Osella put an arm round her shoulders and swept her into the kitchen. There stood a big man; tall, broad and bearded. His hair, which was a shade or two darker than his sister's, was bound back into a rough braid, and his eyes were blue and powerful as the ocean itself. His shirt and britches were the tough, thick weave favoured by working men, a colourful red and blue bandana was knotted round his throat, and he wore a sturdy jerkin of stained black leather. On either side of him, and a little behind, stood a young man and woman; by the look of them, only a year or two older than Brynne herself. They both were tall

– clearly a family trait – and the woman's rangy body held more than a hint of whipcord strength. Her hair, cut short and businesslike, had a coppery tint among the brown, and her eyes were large and green in a bony face. The man's hair was dark, almost black, and again clipped short, as was his beard.

'Brynne, this is my brother Valior, his son Derwyn and my daughter Seema,' Osella said. 'They were the ones who picked you up out of the ocean.'

When Valior smiled his weatherbeaten face lit up, and his tough, uncompromising mien was softened. 'Prettiest fish I ever caught. I hope you're feeling better.'

'Come along, Brynne, sit here at the table,' Osella prompted, pulling out a chair. 'You still haven't much strength for standing about.'

The fisherman kept looking at her as she settled herself, his vivid blue eyes fixed steadily on her face. 'So how did it come about that I had to fish you out of the sea, my little mermaid?'

Brynne found her face growing hot with a blush. 'I can't remember. I can't even be sure that Brynne is my name. It just came into my head when Osella asked me. When I try to think about who I am, or about my past, or what happened to me, there's this wall in my head …' A quaver came into her voice, and her fingers knotted in the woollen shawl.

'All right, you don't have to think about it right now,' Valior said hastily. 'If you can't remember it's plain that asking you a lot of questions is going to do no good at all – in fact it's just upsetting you. So I suggest we sit down and have our supper. It'll be welcome, let me tell you.' He smiled again. 'We had a busy trip, which is all to the good, but we worked all through last night so we're cold, dead tired, and we're hungry as bears.'

The fisherman was right. Brynne felt much more comfortable sitting around the table and eating Osella's delicious meat pie and vegetables from the garden, followed by baked apples. Derwyn and Seema spoke of the fishing and the boat, with a great deal of good-natured chaffing of one another. They had nothing to say directly to Brynne, but they seemed friendly enough, and she felt so shy that she didn't mind.

Valior also talked of the recent fishing trip at first, then his expression grew more grave as he told them of the gossip he'd heard concerning the tensions in the city. 'We came up with the *Northstar*, on her way back out from dropping off a catch in Tyrineld port,' he explained, as he mopped up the gravy from the pie with a large chunk of bread. 'According to Captain Galgan there's a rumour of trouble brewing in the city – if you ask me, those damn idiot Wizards have lost their minds. Because the Archwizard's son was murdered, his soulmate has decided to go to war against the Phaerie.'

Osella gasped, and turned pale. 'War! But what will that mean to us?'

'Well in the short term, it could be good. Prices are sky-high at the docks. They need our fish to help feed the army Sharalind is raising. But in the long term …' He shook his head. 'It's insanity. They had better be damn sure they can win, because if they don't, and those mucking Phaerie come swarming down here, they won't tolerate free mortals like the fisherfolk. I tell you, if the Wizards lose, I'm loading us all into the boat and I'm going to keep right on sailing until we're far away from here.'

Brynne suddenly lost her appetite. All this talk meant nothing to her; she had no memory of Tyrineld and no idea who the Phaerie were. When Valior mentioned the Wizards she felt an odd nudge at the back of her mind, as if something was trying to break through the wall of forgetfulness, but the barrier remained firm and obdurate, and what might have been a recollection stayed on the other side. She shuddered, and tried to fight her rising fear. She knew from the demeanour of those around her that the situation was very grave. If Valior took his family and sailed away, what would happen to her? What would become of her anyway? These people were very kind, but they were not her family and they didn't know her. Why should they encumber themselves with a stranger?

She was so lost in her thoughts that she didn't realise that Valior was speaking to her until she registered the expectant silence, and glanced up from her food to see everyone looking at her. Valior grinned. 'You were a long way away, little love.'

Brynne flushed. 'I – I was trying to remember something. Anything. But I couldn't.' She sighed and put down her fork.

He reached over and put it back in her hand. 'You eat up your pie now. Don't let me put you off your supper. You've been through a hard time, and you need to get your strength back. Your memory will return in good time, I'm sure – and even if it doesn't, you'll soon make some new ones.' He patted her hand. 'Don't worry about a thing, little mermaid. You'll always have a home with us, I promise. We'll take good care of you and keep you safe, and whatever happened to you before, we'll do our best to make sure you only have good things to remember from now on.'

Brynne's feelings were such a potent mix of relief and gratitude that her voice shook as she replied. 'Oh, thank you. I'm so grateful, I just can't tell you – I mean, you don't even know me, and ...'

'You daft girl.' Osella, sitting beside her, put an arm around her shoulders. 'You never thought we'd just throw you out to starve, did you? We'll soon get to know one another, for you'll have a home with us, as long as you want it. Why, you seem to fit right in.'

That night things were a little different. Brynne had, she discovered, been sleeping in Seema's bed, and since its owner needed it back, she was moved into Osella's room to share with her.

Osella took a lamp and showed her into the room. 'Girl, you've got that worried look on your face again,' she said.

'But it's such an imposition.'

'Oh, nonsense. Since my lifemate Evarn drowned, I've slept in this big bed by myself, and who needs more than half of a bed that size? You're more than welcome – and don't you *dare* thank me again.' She held up a hand for silence just as Brynne was opening her mouth. 'Valior told you at supper and I'm telling you now: from tonight you're part of this family. And don't worry about coming aboard as a passenger. We all pull our weight around here and there'll be plenty for you to do. You can help me round the house, and there are always nets to mend and lines to bait. You'll fit in just fine.'

Brynne sank down on the edge of the bed. 'Why are you doing this for a total stranger?'

'Because I have a daughter and Valior has a son.' Osella sat down beside her. 'And we would like to think that if some sort of mishap befell them, and they were lost and afraid, then someone would take care of them. Now, you get into your nightgown and go to sleep. I'll try not to wake you when I come in.'

Once all the younger members of the household had settled down, Valior and Osella sat, sipping taillin, on either side of the fire, which had now burned down to a bed of glowing embers. They were content in one another's company, as they had been for many years, since Osella's lifemate had drowned and Valior's wife had died of a winter fever. Now that were alone, they finally had the opportunity to discuss the newest member of the household.

'Poor mite,' Osella said. 'I can't imagine how frightening it must be, not being able to remember anything.'

Valior frowned into his cup. 'You know she isn't one of us, don't you? She doesn't exactly look like a typical Wizard, but I'm sure that's what she is. There can be no other reason why she didn't drown. Maybe we'd better start asking around and see if we can find her real family.'

Osella shook her head. 'That might not be a good idea. I'm bothered by that nightmare she had, Valior, the one I told you about. If that was some kind of memory trying to force its way out, then she didn't fall off the cliff – somebody pushed her.'

'Surely that can't be true!'

'Do you really want to take the risk? Because if it is true, and whoever tried to kill her finds out where she is, then that child could be in very real danger.'

Valior frowned. 'So we can't go round asking questions about her, or telling people we've found her.' He straightened up in his chair. 'Well, that's no problem. We'll keep her here with us where she's safe, poor little thing, and in the meantime I'll keep my ear to the ground. Maybe we'll find some answers. Surely somebody must have lost her and be looking for her.'

'Somebody will be looking for her, you can be sure,' Osella said. 'But if someone's asking around for her, how will we know if they're the ones who want to save her, or the ones who want to kill her?'

13
~

THE RELUCTANT HEALER

The Healers' compound stood a little way apart from the main complex of Academy buildings. That way, any contagion could be isolated, and those who were injured or sick in body or spirit could have the peace and quiet they needed to recover, away from the bustle and noise of the city. It was a pleasant place, a complex of four smaller buildings rather than a single large one, all surrounded by white walls enclosing sunny, sheltered gardens rich with herbs, beautiful trees and colourful flowers – none of which Chiannala noticed as she walked through the high arched gateway with her shoulders hunched and a scowl on her face.

This was the first morning of her placement in the Luen of Healers. Though she had tried to fight the decision with everything at her disposal: reasoning, argument, begging and even tears, her tutors had remained obdurate, and the atmosphere among the Luens at this time was so strained with the imminence of war that no one had much time to listen to the carping of a first-year student who thought she knew better than the most skilled and powerful Wizards in the city.

Chiannala was furious at having her ambitions thwarted in this way. In her daydreams and secret plans she had always been a Spellweaver, a powerful and innovative manipulator of magic. She simply could not fathom why those idiots had imagined she'd be any use at healing, which demanded both patience and compassion, neither of which, she was honest enough to admit, were among her strong points. Had she realised that this was exactly why she had been sent to the Healers in her first year – to correct this lack and make a more balanced and rounded Wizard of her – she still would have been angry and uncomprehending. She didn't care about being rounded or balanced; she wanted to be respected, deferred to and, above all else, powerful. To perdition with everything else.

What made it worse was that the only other first-year who'd been chosen for Healing was the stocky, moon-faced Haslen. Haslen the Hopeless, Chiannala called him in the privacy of her own mind. It was the final straw, being stuck with this buffoon. Not only would he be expecting her to carry him, because of his weak magic, but he had a crush on her besides. As if he had a chance! She shuddered.

Looking like Brynne might put me under a disadvantage, but I'll never be that desperate.

When she came to the door of what looked like the main building she almost kicked it open, but instead pushed it violently and marched inside, with Haslen hurrying to keep up with her. She found herself in a vestibule with tall, pointed, stained-glass windows that caught the sun and cast patterns of dappled colour across the polished wooden floor. On the walls to her right and to her left, two corridors led off in opposite directions. The rear wall had a broad staircase that started in the middle of the chamber and swept up grandly to the floor above. On its left was an informal seating area with groupings of little tables and padded chairs; clearly a waiting area. On the right of the stairs was a desk of dark, polished wood with a young man seated behind it, his hair a tumbled mass of vibrant red curls tied back into long tail. He was writing when they entered, working with intense concentration, but as Chiannala and Haslen approached he looked up. There was a frown on his face, and when he spoke his manner was anything but welcoming.

'Oh. You'd be the new student intake, right?'

'That's us,' Haslen said cheerfully. 'I'm Haslen and this is Brynne.'

Chiannala scowled, saying nothing, but the young man simply shrugged and turned slightly away from her, addressing his remarks chiefly to her more congenial companion. 'Just a moment – I'll call for someone to come and meet you. You'll start with a quick tour of the place, to get your bearings and see what a variety of work we do here.' After a brief pause when he was clearly communicating with someone in mindspeech, he was back with them.

'My name is Lameron. I'm a final-year student specialising in Healing magic. We – my contemporaries and I, that is – take turns to look after the entrance hall here, keeping records, directing people to the proper areas and so on. This frees the experienced Healers to get on with more important work.' He grimaced. 'Everybody hates this job. We'd all rather be getting on with practical healing, the stuff we came here to do, so we keep a very strict rota. We—'

At that moment a tall, slender blonde woman with stunning silver-grey eyes came through the right-hand doorway. 'Ah, our newest students. Welcome indeed to our haven of healing,' she said. Though her smile was bright and friendly, it was clear that she was worried and exhausted. Her eyes were hollowed and darkly shadowed in a pale, drawn face, and her shoulders had a weary droop.

'Melisanda, are you still here?' Lameron interrupted, frowning with concern. 'I thought you were supposed to go and rest hours ago.'

Chiannala stiffened. Melisanda? She had heard that name. This was one of that foul Iriana's closest friends! For an instant she felt vulnerable, in danger, as if the Healer's close association with Iriana could somehow expose her own charade. A shiver went through her – then with an effort she pulled herself together. What nonsense! Melisanda would be as oblivious as anyone else to Brynne's change of identity. How could it be otherwise? Unless she herself were to panic and start acting like an idiot, she'd be fine. Firmly, she turned her attention back to the conversation.

'Rest? I seem to remember that, from the dim and distant past,' Melisanda said. 'I simply can't be spared just now.' There was a pause while they held each other's eyes. Clearly they were communicating in very private mindspeech, and Chiannala thought it abominably rude of them. She watched with interest as Melisanda's worried expression became mirrored on Lameron's face, then the woman turned to herself and Haslen. 'I'm Melisanda, Tinagen's second-in-command. I'm afraid he's too busy to speak to you himself, but he sent me to show you around instead.'

She's a rotten liar.

Chiannala, so accomplished in the arts of deception, shook her head. Melisanda should stick to the truth, or learn to meet people's eyes frankly when she told them an untruth. Some people just didn't have a clue. Idly, she wondered where Tinagen really was. He was probably just too grand and important to be bothered with a couple of lowly first-year students.

Melisanda had gone back to conversing with Lameron. 'That new patient – what a mess! It's taking all we've got to keep him alive, let alone mend all the damage.'

'It's just not right,' Lameron protested. 'All for some stupid foreign stranger. According to Yinze he's a real bad—'

Melisanda cut him off with a sharp look and an upraised hand. Clearly, this was not something to be discussed in front of new students. 'Our job is to heal,' she rebuked him, 'not to make arbitrary distinctions between the people we should be helping. He was sent to us because we're the best; the only ones who have a chance of saving him. And if in the end we can't – well, it won't be for the lack of trying.'

Having quelled Lameron, she turned back to Haslen and Chiannala. 'I'm sorry we're all too busy to give you a proper welcome, but we have an emergency on our hands. I'll show you around, however, and let you find your feet. After that – well, the way things stand at present, you might just end up being thrown in at the deep end, but don't worry. We might stretch you a little, but we won't ask you to do anything beyond your capabilities.'

Chiannala smiled inwardly at Haslen's sudden worried look.

Melisanda was attempting to smile too, though it did little to penetrate the strain and worry on her face. 'Brynne and Haslen, isn't it?' she said. 'Well, follow me and we'll get started.' With her two students at her heels, she went outside.

There was a lot more to the Healers' complex than Chiannala had expected. Within the oval of the tall, enclosing walls were four long buildings, each with two storeys, set in a diamond-shaped configuration around a flagged courtyard. In the centre a fountain made a soothing background murmur as it cascaded into its pool in delicate arches of jewelled spray. Two of the buildings, including the one they had just left, were given over to housing and treatment of the sick and infirm. Behind them was a sunny garden with smooth lawns, bright and cheerful flowerbeds, sheltering trees and comfortable benches set at frequent intervals.

'I'll show you those areas later,' Melisanda said. 'First, I'll take you round the other two, which are dedicated to the study and refinement of our Healing magic.'

She gestured to the building on her left, and held the door open for them to enter. 'This is where we work in conjunction with those members of the Luen of Spellweavers who have an inclination towards our work. They consult with our own people to improve our Healing spells.' She opened the first of a row of doors in a long corridor, and Chiannala saw a number of tables in the spacious room beyond.

There was a pair of Wizards at each of them, working with crystals of different sizes, colours and types, which were all glowing brightly as magic was poured into them. The air crackled and hummed with the build-up of energy, and Chiannala could feel the waves of power coursing through her from all the way across the room.

'Here, for instance,' Melisanda spoke softly so as not to interrupt the workers' concentration, 'we have teams consisting of a Healer and a Spellweaver, investigating the use of crystals to amplify our healing powers. It's beginning to look as though certain crystals are most beneficial for particular conditions.' Closing the door, she opened another further down the hallway, taking them down the centre of a long room divided on either side into open-fronted cubicles. Each one held a patient in a bed, and each was bathed in a different coloured light: blue, gold, green, purple, pink and red. Again, there was a Healer and Spellweaver pair in each cubicle, generating the radiant energy.

'In this room we're investigating the healing properties, if any, of different colours,' Melisanda explained. 'We're working with volunteers from the infirmary, and getting some very interesting results.' She showed them through several more rooms, some with Wizards working on various samples of blood and tissue, others with various combinations of Healers working in concert to intensify their powers.

When Haslen and Chiannala had seen all there was to see, Melisanda led them to the next building, which had rows of glass-houses leading back from the central section, and an extensive herb garden behind. Here the rooms contained Wizards brewing, infusing, distilling and concocting various combinations of herbs, or working on individual plants to isolate and strengthen their healing powers. 'We work here alongside the Luen of Nurturers,' Melisanda explained. 'Earth magic and Healing powers have always had a very strong link, and nowhere is that more evident than here.'

When they had seen all there was to see, she took them into the third building. 'This is where we keep our own library of records, though obviously a copy of each is also sent to the Academy archives. We also have the studies of Tinagen and his four senior Healers, and the day infirmary, where people bring any minor problems they can't handle at home with basic healing spells. There is also a rest area and a refectory for the Healers who are working in the complex.'

Quickly she whisked them from room to room, and then indicated a covered walkway. 'This leads back to the main infirmary building where we started, but before I show you our main infirmary areas, we'll stop here for our midday meal in the refectory.'

'Already?' Haslen said.

'Take a look at the sun,' Melisanda said. 'It's well past midday. Time has a way of rushing by when you're preoccupied.'

'And when you're enjoying yourself,' the young man said shyly. 'It's been a really fascinating morning; there's been so much to see. I never realised just how much there was to being a Healer.'

Melisanda favoured him with a dazzling smile. 'Oh, I think you'll do just fine, Haslen. I can see you fitting right in here.'

She didn't say that about Chiannala.

Soon they were in the busy refectory and settled at a table with plates of food. Thick hot soup with lentils and vegetables was followed by a choice of roast meats and vegetables, with fruit and little cakes and taillin to fill in any spaces. Melisanda herself ate like a starving wolf, putting away an amazing amount for one so slender and delicate of build. When she finally pushed her plate aside and reached for her taillin and a cake, she happened to look up and notice the astonished expressions that they tried and failed to hide. 'Sorry,' she said with a shrug. 'I don't usually make such a pig of myself, but I've been working all night without a break. This is my first food since yesterday evening. You'll have noticed that we eat well in here. That's because Healing spells sap a great deal of energy from the practitioner, and it's important that we replenish it regularly, or we risk burning out. This is one of most important things you must learn here. The greatest danger a Healer faces is burnout. It happens when you throw so much of your energy into the patient that you don't have enough left to sustain your own life. And if you're unwary, unwise, or sometimes just too emotionally committed, it can happen more easily than you think ...'

Chiannala was barely listening. Throughout her tour of the Luen, she had been aware of an uneasy atmosphere. Healers not immediately occupied were whispering to one another in corners or standing around in murmuring groups, some with worry, some with anger and frustration, and in some cases even fear, on their faces. Something was wrong here – that much was plain. Something that was being kept from lowly students. She wondered how she could find out. She had a nose for secrets – there was no telling when it might come in handy to have information that someone didn't want her to know.

Melisanda sat back and sipped her taillin. 'Now, before we continue, do either of you have any questions about what you've seen so far?'

Chiannala was desperate to ask outright what was bothering everyone, but didn't dare; not on her first day. In any case, she knew she wouldn't get a straight answer.

Haslen pushed back his untidy hair and nervously raised his hand. 'What will we be expected to do here? At first, I mean.'

'For the first few days you'll mostly be observing the rest of us work.' Melisanda gave him a tired smile. 'Don't worry – unless there's a desperate emergency we'll ease you in gently, and you'll be super-vised and helped at all times. We'll put you with a mentor and you'll accompany them on their daily work, fetching and carrying for them and lending them an extra little boost of power when needed. They'll introduce you to the simpler, hands-on magic as they work, and of course you'll also have lectures on the theory from the senior—'

'I thought you said we would be thrown in at the deep end,' Chiannala interrupted sharply.

Melisanda gave her a hard, appraising look. 'I said if an emergency should arise you might be thrown at the deep end, and in this place there is always that possibility. If we have a serious crisis we may need all hands to help out – even if only temporarily. But had you been listening, Brynne, you would have heard me say that *unless* there is such an emergency, you'll be eased in gently.'

Her voice was winter-cold as she continued. 'One of the most im-portant things you must learn while training in Healing magic – any sort of magic really, but this discipline in particular, since it deals so directly with life and death – is to listen carefully. We can't spare the time to keep repeating ourselves to lazy or careless students. Remember, any sloppiness or mistakes on your part could easily cause the death of another Wizard.'

With that she pushed her chair back and walked out of the refec-tory, heading to the covered walkway that led to the main building and leaving Chiannala, whose face was burning in mortification, fuming in her wake.

Melisanda has no right to speak to me like that. Who does she think she is, the arrogant cow! I have a right to ask questions and voice my opinions, don't I? It's not even as if I wanted to be here in the first place, studying her stupid Healing magic.

She didn't realise how loudly she was thinking, until they reached the main infirmary building and Melisanda, with one hand on the door latch, swung back to face her. 'You know, Brynne, I just can't understand you. Only a few months ago, when you came to the Academy for your pre-training assessments, you professed a tremendous interest in Healing and said you couldn't wait to study it further, yet now you don't want anything to do with it. What has happened between then and now? You seem to have done a complete about-turn on your earlier wishes.'

She took a deep breath, controlling her annoyance. 'Be that as it may, I know you don't want to be here now. You've been making that perfectly clear ever since the assignments were given out. But at this stage of your life you need to be broadening your horizons and learning that magic, at the bottom of it, is all one and the same, and though we've broken it up into Luens for our own convenience there are numerous crossover points. I've shown you today, for instance, how we work closely with other disciplines – in this case the Nurturers and the Spellweavers – and we sometimes work with others too. It's all knowledge, it's all magic, and at this point in your life it's all adding to your experience and your skills. You have years and years ahead of you to specialise, and narrow your focus, but it's just too early for you to do that now.'

Unexpectedly she smiled, and it was like the sun coming out from behind a cloud. 'Don't think I can't remember what it's like. When you first come here it's all so exciting. You want pursue your particular interests, to devour them all in one gulp. Don't worry – you'll get your chance to do exactly that as you grow older, but initially we can show you other interests, other options; skills that you didn't know you were good at, or hadn't even considered before. It's our job here at the Academy to open your eyes to all the amazing possibilities of magic, and teach you the basics of each. Only then can you make an informed choice of which aspects you want to pursue. Only then can you call yourself a proper Wizard. Don't close yourself off to all those possibilities, all that potential, Brynne. You'll be missing so much.' Without waiting for a reply, she turned and went into the infirmary, leaving Chiannala, for once, without anything to say.

As they toured the main infirmary area, with its airy white rooms and comfortable beds, Chiannala could not help but be aware of the air of subdued activity around the place. Despite the fact that everything they could see was calm and under control, there was a muted bustle in the background, with people rushing back and forth. Was this something to do with the uneasy atmosphere she had sensed?

Somehow, she got the feeling that it was not. These people were busy and purposeful; more concerned and preoccupied than afraid and frustrated. It seemed to Chiannala that this must be one of the emergencies Melisanda had talked about; probably the mystery patient that Lameron had mentioned earlier. Her curiosity burned hot and bright, and she longed to be given a chance to participate, to prove herself to these Healers; all the more so because whatever the secret was, she wanted to be in on it. Knowledge was power, and she wanted all the power she could get.

While the Healer was showing them around the infirmary Chiannala kept a careful eye on all the comings and goings, and noticed that most of the activity centred around a door at the far end of the right-hand wing. Whenever she tried to casually drift in that direction, however, the eagle-eyed Melisanda deflected her with a seemingly casual comment or question and steered her away – until suddenly the door burst open, and a harried-looking Healer came out. 'Melisanda, can you come at once? He's fading on us again – and without Tinagen—'

'I'll be right there.' Melisanda turned to Haslen and Chiannala. 'I'm sorry, but you see how it is. You can go early today, but be back in good time tomorrow morning, ready to start your proper training.' She hurried away from them without a backward glance. Clearly, she had already dismissed them from her mind.

Chiannala didn't care. After Melisanda's lecture, she thought it might be wise to stay out of the way for a while, and not be seen hanging about trying to pry into matters that were clearly (according to the Healers) none of her business. There would be time enough to find out what she wanted to know, and right now, her only wish was to get out of this place and back to her room, where she could be alone. Melisanda's lecture to her had stung, of that there was no doubt, but it had also contained a lot of things to ponder and brood upon. Haslen wanted to linger with her and talk about their day, but she brushed him off as quickly as she could, abandoning all pretence at tact or good manners, and ignoring the hurt looks he was sending after her as she hurried away to her own little sanctuary. Not that that there seemed to be much peace there at present. Normally she would have put the unexpected free time to good use in the library, or practising spells in her room, but today she found herself oddly distracted, unable to settle to anything while the Healer's words were still echoing in her head.

'At this stage of your life you need to be broadening your horizons and learning that magic, at the bottom of it, is all one and the same.'

'It's all adding to your experience and your skills.'

'It's our job here at the Academy to open your eyes to all the amazing possibilities of magic, and teach you the basics of each.'

'Don't close yourself off to all those possibilities, all that potential.'

'You have years and years ahead of you to specialise, and narrow your focus.'

After pacing for a time she went to lean on her windowsill, and stood there looking out over the city. Nightfall found her there still, staring out unseeing as the lamps were kindled, glittering in the twilight all over Tyrineld.

She was chilled to the core by the thought of how close she'd come to having her deception discovered. How could she possibly have known that Brynne had professed such an ardent interest in becoming a Healer? That the wretch had spent her assessment at the Academy choosing the absolutely last thing that Chiannala would want to do? It was the farm girl's revenge from beyond her watery grave.

It was all very well for Melisanda to talk about years, she thought. Though she had to admit that there was good sense in the Healer's advice, she finally admitted to herself the fear, deep in her most secret heart, that she wouldn't have time to waste broadening her horizons and exploring her options. She had to learn all she could as quickly as possible; to make the most of every opportunity, every precious moment, just in case—

Her thoughts pulled up short. The truth hit her as though she had slammed into a brick wall.

Just in case this was all taken away from her.

Just in case they penetrated her deception and discovered who and what she was.

A despised half-breed with the taint of mortal blood.

A murderer.

An impostor who had no right to be at the Academy.

She tossed and turned all night, unable to sleep, finding no respite from her fears, and was back at the Healers' complex the next morning before Haslen had even finished breakfast. At some point during the night she had come to a decision: if Healing was the only magic she could learn right now, then by all Creation she *would* learn it. She realised now that by kicking so hard against the choices her mentors had made for her, she had only made them suspicious, and brought herself to their attention. And of course, stupid Brynne wanting to be a Healer hadn't helped. Well, she thought, she would just see about that. Once she had spent some time with the Healers, it should be easy enough to invent reasons why it just wasn't for her after all.

The idea of pretending to be no good at it never even crossed her mind. Chiannala was determined to excel at whatever she tried. Her pride would permit no less.

14
~

TURN AGAIN

The high tower room, tucked away in the most isolated, least used part of Hellorin's sprawling palace, was a far cry from Tiolani's spacious, luxurious chambers. The walls were stone, cold, stark and unadorned, and a single mat of fraying woven straw was all that protected her bare feet from the chilly flagstone floor. The bed was hard and narrow, and a flimsy wooden chair and table were the only furnishings. Across every surface, floor, walls, ceiling and even the window glass and the door, she could faintly discern the silver shimmer of spells set in place against the use of magic. There would be no apporting in or out of this chamber, Cordain had made absolutely sure of that.

Tiolani, with nothing else to do, paced endlessly from door to window and back, savage and frustrated as a caged wild beast. From a physical point of view it was the means of exercising herself in her cramped prison; emotionally it was a way to vent the savage turmoil of anger and hate that had consumed her since she'd been incarcerated by that treacherous snake Cordain, her ailing father's chief and most trusted counsellor.

Since she had been imprisoned, Tiolani had viewed the world through a haze of fulminating rage. Everyone had betrayed her. First, and worst of all, her lover Ferimon, aided by his sister Varna, had been using her as his stepping stone to power. Over and over, she shuddered at the memory of the way she had listened to him, believed him, and confided her deepest secrets while she lay trustingly in his arms.

He had persuaded her to rely on him, isolating her from the other courtiers who might have helped her, but she had desperately needed all the comfort he could provide after the murder of her brother and the near-death of her father in the same ambush – which, she had subsequently discovered, he had caused. It had been Ferimon who roused the feral humans of the forest to ambush the Wild Hunt. He had caused her brother's slaughter and bribed certain so-called healers to keep the Forest Lord hovering on the brink of death while he used his twisted charms to seduce Hellorin's daughter, now suddenly the heir apparent. And she, gullible, stupid innocent that she'd been, had walked open-eyed into every one of his honeyed traps, and let him do as he would with her person and her realm.

No one was there to comfort Tiolani as she paced away the torment of her captivity. No one was there to tell her that she'd been young, alone, felled by terrible grief, and easy prey for the slick and handsome schemer. Aelwen, her mother's half-sister and Hellorin's former Horsemistress, might have supported her in this blackest of times – but Aelwen had betrayed her too.

Aelwen and her head groom Kelon had fled the city, taking with them several of the precious Xandim, including Hellorin's mount Corisand. When Tiolani, Ferimon and the Wild Hunt had pursued them, Ferimon met his death at Kelon's hand, but not before the terrible extent of his treachery had been revealed. Tiolani's eyes had been opened to the truth and reluctantly she had joined the Horsemistress's new companions, one of whom – she still could scarcely believe it – had been Corisand herself, now revealed as the Windeye, or Shaman, of the race of shapeshifters who'd been enslaved and trapped in their equine forms by the Forest Lord.

She had returned to Eliorand with Aelwen and Taine as part of the plan to free the Xandim, but when they were arrested by that traitor Cordain, the Horsemistress had apported her lover out of danger, leaving Tiolani behind to shift for herself.

I don't owe her anything.

In her father's absence it had been her responsibility to rule the Phaerie, and she had failed miserably, thanks to those she had mistakenly relied upon. They were all false and treacherous. Not one of them could be trusted. She must save herself.

Now the pacing had purpose, allowing her to focus, helping her to think. Cordain, Varna, Aelwen and her friends were all her enemies now. If she could only find a way to turn them against one another, she could be free of them all.

At sunset she sent for Cordain.

He took his time in responding to the request she had made so meekly and politely, but the delay had not troubled her – in fact it made her smile, as she imagined him wavering, his curiosity at war with his pride. Oh, he would not come to her immediately, not he. He saw himself as the master of Eliorand now, in the Forest Lord's absence, and he would have to prove it – most of all to himself. On the other hand, he must be wondering why Tiolani had returned in the company of Hellorin's thieving Horsemistress and a dangerous wanted fugitive. What was she up to? Where had she been since he had coldly abandoned her to die in the forest? Ultimately, he would not be able to stay away, and in the meantime the delay would give her more time to refine her plans.

It was long after nightfall when Cordain finally arrived. Tiolani welcomed him into her chamber with gracious words, every inch the great lady, and gestured to him to be seated on the single flimsy chair. Though she was still clad in the ragged, filthy travel clothes she had arrived in, from her bearing she might have been wearing a coronet, a velvet cloak and gold-embroidered brocade. The Counsellor could not completely conceal the flicker of annoyance that crossed his face. She was, after all, *his* prisoner, not the other way around. But she could also discern a slight hesitancy in his manner; a hint of puzzlement. She knew he had expected the tantrums and tears of a spoiled young girl who'd been thwarted. This controlled, self-possessed young woman, every inch the daughter of a ruler – where had she sprung from?

She was at his mercy. Why was she not afraid?

For the lack of another chair, Tiolani sat down on the bed facing the Counsellor. 'Cordain,' she said, 'I asked to see you tonight because I owe you an apology. Since I stepped into my father's shoes, I have not behaved well by you, or any of my subjects. I have made many errors, the extent and gravity of which I have only lately discovered, and I have returned to set things right if I can.'

Cordain's eyebrows went up. 'Yet you return in the company of traitors and outlaws?' His voice was scathing and filled with disbelief.

'I returned in the only way I could,' Tiolani replied. 'If I had not pretended to cooperate with Aelwen and her friends, I would have remained their prisoner. I wanted to deliver the traitors to you and I did. It's hardly my fault that you made a mess of things and let them escape. Also, it was imperative that I get back to warn you of their plans – and to tell you that you were right about Ferimon.'

'Go on.' The Counsellor fixed her intently with his gaze.

Tiolani bit her lip. Even now she found it difficult and humiliating to speak of her folly. 'When I succeeded to power I was desperately lonely; grieving my brother's death and the loss of my father, and overwhelmed by the responsibilities of my new office. I let Ferimon seduce me, taking advantage of my every weakness.' She felt her face burning with shame. 'I was blinded by love for him. I trusted him absolutely. I failed to see that he was persuading me to turn my back on my father's trusted advisers, who might, had I only listened, have dissuaded me from the mistakes I was making. But it was far worse than a simple bid for power on his part, Cordain. Ferimon orchestrated the ambush that did so much hurt to my family, and threw our realm into turmoil and peril, then he used his own so-called healers to undo the work of those who were trying to bring my father back to health.'

'WHAT?' Cordain leapt to his feet, all his air of urbane self-possession vanished. In his anger he grabbed Tiolani by the shoulders, shaking her so hard that her head felt as if it was being jolted loose on her neck. 'You're lying, curse you. I would never have missed such a plot being hatched right under my nose.'

'Stop!' Tiolani shouted, loud enough to make him hesitate. 'Take your hands *off* me,' she hissed in a voice of icy venom. 'I may be your prisoner here, rightly or wrongly, but I am still Hellorin's daughter, scion of the royal line, and you may *not* handle me like some common felon.'

The Counsellor dropped his hands and stepped away, his eyes cold and hard as steel. 'Are you absolutely sure of Ferimon's treachery?' He did not beg her pardon.

'Absolutely.' Tiolani matched his coldness.

'Tell me. Tell me everything.'

Resuming her seat on the bed, Tiolani recounted what had happened after she'd been unseated from her horse by Corisand and been lost in the forest during the Hunt: her capture by the feral mortals, her discovery of the truth about her lover, and Ferimon's death at Kelon's hands.

Cordain dropped his face into his hands. 'Why did I never see it?' he whispered. 'It was my task to discover such treachery, and to warn my Lord Hellorin, but I failed him.'

'No blame attaches to you, Counsellor. Ferimon was very plausible. He deceived us both with consummate skill.' With those few well-chosen words, Tiolani put them both on the same side.

'But – but my lady, if you were captured by the ferals, how did you escape? And what brought Aelwen back here?' Though a little more respect had crept into his voice, he was still suspicious.

Tiolani had thought long and hard about what her story would be. She had decided that there was no point whatsoever in telling him about Athina, or the secret of the Xandim. If she came to him with a tale of how her father's horse had changed into human form, she would lose all the credibility she had gained so far, and she would never get him to trust her. Instead, she had come up with what she hoped was an acceptable alternative.

'By this time, the ferals had worked out that Ferimon had used them,' she told him. 'By killing him, Kelon won their friendship. They did not recognise me: they thought I was only a member of the Hunt, and so he persuaded them to let me go. Though we had all been split up by the storm, we finally managed to find Aelwen.'

'And how does Aelwen fit into this? Why did she flee, taking those horses? I would never have believed it of her. Why did she return, and why did you perform the flying spell that allowed it?'

'You saw Taine.' Tiolani shrugged her shoulders. 'Though I am too young to remember him, you must recall how they were lovers before he was exiled. It turns out that all these years since he disappeared, Taine has been spying for the Wizards.'

Cordain spat out a vicious curse. 'I might have guessed it,' he growled.

'Truly, you might, my Lord Counsellor,' Tiolani goaded him. The more angry he was, the more likely he would be to take her story at face value. 'Given that their blood runs in his veins, it hardly comes as a surprise. I overheard them, though they did not realise that I had – or my life would have ended then and there. Apparently Aelwen has been secretly in contact with him. She stole the horses to give to the Wizards, in the hope that they can work out some variation of their own on the flying spell, and have a tactical advantage over the Phaerie.'

'I don't believe it,' Cordain gasped. 'Aelwen, of all people, guilty of such duplicity? Surely this cannot be.'

'Love can affect a person in the strangest of ways. When the heart is entangled, it is all too easy to lose perspective on right and wrong – as I know to my cost.' Tiolani didn't bother to disguise the bitterness in her voice. 'Once Aelwen and her friends rescued me from the ferals, they decided to include me in their plan, for with the flying spell they could come back to Eliorand for many more of our mounts. To get me on her side, Aelwen told me that she had fled the city because she was afraid for her life, for, under Ferimon's influence, I had treated her very badly. She told me that her meeting Taine had been pure accident, and assured me that now my eyes had been opened, she was happy to come back with me, if I would only pardon him.'

Tiolani turned to Cordain in wide-eyed innocence and spread her hands. 'What could I do? I could not let them discover that I knew their true plan. In fear of my life, I pretended to be on their side, and promised to help them in every way.' She grimaced. 'I had incentive to be *very* convincing. But Aelwen didn't expect the reception we received from you and your guards.' Once again, Tiolani could not hide the bitterness in her voice. 'She thought, as I did, you would be glad I was safe, and would welcome me back with open arms as the Phaerie ruler. Then she and Taine would get the credit for saving my life. I could pardon them both, she would be reinstated and they would be left free to assemble the horses they wanted – at which point they would send messages to their Wizard allies who are hiding in the forest, make off with the stolen mounts and flee to Tyrineld.'

Cordain turned white. 'The villainy! This must be stopped!'

'In a way you already did stop it,' Tiolani said. 'Thanks to your little reception when we arrived, Aelwen and Taine must have given up any idea of returning to Eliorand in a legitimate way. But make no mistake, they want those horses. One way or another, I doubt you've seen the last of them.'

Cordain walked to the window and stood in silence for a long moment, staring out past the shimmer of the imprisoning spell to the city beyond. Then he turned back to Tiolani. 'Why did you tell me all this?' he said quietly.

'Because I want to make amends,' Tiolani replied without hesitation. 'I am deeply ashamed of the way I acted under Ferimon's influence, and I want to put things right, if I can. I am hoping that you will give me another chance, for my father's sake. I hope you can see your way clear to forgiving me, that you will guide me with your sage advice, as you have always guided Hellorin.' She looked up at the Counsellor, wide-eyed, innocent, sincere. 'Please, Cordain. Please give me another chance. Now that we have unmasked Ferimon's traitorous healers, surely my father will recover soon. I – I would hope to make him proud of me.'

'And how do I know you are sincere? Maybe you have other companions hidden away. Maybe Aelwen and Taine will return with reinforcements. Maybe this is all a trick.'

'Oh, rest assured that there will be a trick, Cordain – but not at your expense. I want to turn the tables on Aelwen and her conspirators, and I need your help to do it. I am going to give you a crucial piece of information freely, and if you find that I am speaking the truth, I am depending on you to keep faith with me, and reinstate me.' She smiled grimly. 'Taine and Aelwen have fixed upon a secret rendezvous point with their Wizardly associate. I'll take you there, and we will lie in wait and ambush them when they arrive. Is that enough to make you trust me?'

Cordain looked at her thoughtfully, for a long, long moment. At last he spoke. 'For your father's sake, I will trust you. Your own quarters and possessions will be restored to you at once, though until this ambush takes place, you will forgive me if I set guards to keep you there and curtail your freedom a little longer.' He smiled, then. 'You can tell my soldiers where this meeting will take place. If all goes well, and Aelwen and her companions are captured, you will regain everything: throne and birthright, and you will have gone a long way to atoning for your former mistakes. Is that agreeable to you, my lady?'

Tiolani had to bite her lip to force back the tears of relief and gratitude that wanted to spring into her eyes. 'That is more than agreeable. I thank you, Cordain, for giving me another chance. But ...'

'But?' He tilted an eyebrow.

'I have one request, my lord. Please ... Please may I see my father?'

Cordain took told of her hands. 'Of course you can, my little Tiolani. And be comforted. Now that we know the truth, we will root out these false healers. Hopefully, we will soon have him back on the road to health.'

'That is my dearest wish,' Tiolani assured him, but even as she spoke, she wondered: was it really? Or did she greet the prospect of Hellorin's return with mixed feelings?

Tiolani's were not the only mixed feelings in the northern forest that night. Kelon had been fighting with Danel again; in fact, these days, they seemed to spend most of their time and energy in a fruitless exchange of insults and accusations, instead of accomplishing anything useful. It usually ended in one or the other of them storming off, and this time it was Danel's turn. With a scowl on his face, Kelon threw himself down by the dying embers of the campfire (no one had bothered to organise the collection of any firewood, as usual) and wondered for the thousandth time what he was doing here.

The more time he spent in the company of Danel's group of ferals, the more convinced Kelon became that he had made a terrible mistake. He might be Hemifae, and share half his blood with these escapees, but he could never submerge the Phaerie heritage in the human, and in his travels with these former slaves he had discovered a fundamental truth: you might sympathise with the people at the bottom of the heap, but it did no good to anyone to join them there. Save for Danel – and her liking for him only went so far, and seemed to be diminishing on a daily basis – they didn't trust him, and he certainly didn't trust them. There wasn't anything noble or heroic about them; they were ignorant, brutish, filthy, unkempt, uncouth, and they were thieves.

Kelon was sick of the grime and the fleas, the continual whining and complaining and the endless fights. He was tired of being cold, exhausted and desperately hungry. He was worn down by having to keep a constant watch on his few scanty possessions. With a desperate, consuming ache he missed his old life, his home and the horses.

He missed Aelwen.

He should never have left her.

At the time it had seemed the only possible choice. His heart had been broken, his pride had been trampled in the dirt. Since Taine's unlooked-for return, the thought of staying around Aelwen and her lover, having to watch them together, had been beyond all bearing. But now that time and distance had blunted the edge of that hurt a little, Kelon had begun to harbour doubts. Though he certainly couldn't have remained around them for ever, maybe not even for long, he might have given himself time to settle, to think, to make a better, more reasoned choice.

He shook his head and sighed. Who was he trying to fool? What other choices did he have? He couldn't have gone back to Eliorand after being involved in stealing some of the Forest Lord's precious horses; he'd burned his bridges there. And Tyrineld was out of the question. The Wizards might have taken Aelwen in for Taine's sake, but they wouldn't want another Hemifae. Why should they? Besides, he would still be around Taine and Aelwen if he made his home in the Wizard city, so he would be no better off.

Kelon remembered what Athina had said, at that momentous gathering in the Cailleach's tower, when Danel had refused to be part of the plans to free the Xandim.

'The world is entering a time of upheaval and change ... This new era will be your opportunity, Danel. You cannot conquer the magic-using races, but you can influence their attitude towards you by helping them in their time of crisis. In other words, this is the perfect opportunity to make yourself some powerful allies ... The decision must be yours, whether the humans will be part of our company or not. If you think it better to return to grubbing for survival like wild beast in the forest, constantly looking over your shoulder for the Wild Hunt, you can leave immediately.'

Danel, the fool, had said she would rather die than ally herself with magic users, and had left, throwing away, as far as Kelon could see, the only chance the ferals had of building some kind of future for themselves. Now, Athina's reply echoed over and over again in his mind as he looked around the wretched campsite.

'Then die – if that is your choice.'

Danel should have listened to the Cailleach's words, for they had not been a threat but a warning. If the band of outcasts were doing this badly in the summer, what would happen when autumn came, and winter? There would be no hope for them at all, and deep down inside, every one of them knew it.

Kelon stared into the fading embers of the campfire. Would that be his future? A short, nasty brutish life, followed by a squalid, painful death? But thinking of Athina and that ill-starred meeting nudged another thought into his mind. The Wizard Iriana had spoken of the fisherfolk, a settlement of free humans that lived along the coast near Tyrineld. What if the ferals could throw in their lot with them? It could mean proper care for the babies, the sick and the infirm, who otherwise would never live to see another spring. It could mean hope, a future, a chance to make something meaningful of their lives.

The Wizards had no Wild Hunt. If they had permitted the free settlement of fisherfolk to exist, then surely they must have a more lenient attitude towards humans than the Phaerie had? And the only Wizard he had ever met, the young woman Iriana, had seemed a very decent sort of person.

And living so close to Tyrineld, I would be close to Aelwen, and maybe have a chance to see her now and again ...

No! Kelon reined in that runaway thought as soon as he realised where it was heading. He must forget Aelwen. She must have no influence over his decisions, must not be allowed to cloud his thinking. He must face, once and for all, that she was no longer part of his life. Even without her in the picture, however, surely the fisherfolk were the best possible hope for these hard-pressed refugees? Surely even Danel must agree with that? Feeling hopeful for the first time in many days, he got to his feet and went to find her.

She was standing beneath a tree a little way beyond the camp's perimeter, her dirty, smudged skin and filthy clothing blending into the background so that she was effectively camouflaged. Save that her odour came to him on the breeze – and he was horrified to realise that by now he must smell just as bad – he would never have known she was there. Then a muttered curse gave her exact position away, and Kelon realised that she was also pondering the ferals' options, and not finding any answers. As he approached her, she said, 'There's no point in sneaking up like that. I know you're there.'

'I was not sneaking.' Immediately, Kelon felt himself go on the defensive. What was it about this wretched woman that could put his back up so easily? 'I just had some thoughts about our future that might—'

'*Our* future?' She spat out the words as she spun to face him. In the darkness the expression on her face was difficult to read, but he could hear the venom in her voice. 'You talk as if you belong with us, Kelon; well, you don't. Evnas was right. I should never have let you stay with us. You've brought us nothing but bad luck from the minute we set eyes on you and—'

'Oh, really?' Kelon said coldly. 'I wasn't unlucky for *you*. It was very convenient that I came along at just the right time to take the blame for your poor leadership.'

He was expecting the blow that came at him out of the darkness, and stepped aside just in time to avoid the fist that went skinning past his face. 'If it wasn't for my leadership we would never have survived all this time,' Danel snarled.

'You've been lucky, that's all, and if you don't recognise that your luck has run out, then there's no hope for any of us.' His voice grew louder as his frustration increased. 'The fact is, Danel, when you walked out of Athina's meeting, you threw away our only hope of a future.'

'You walked out of it too!'

'Because I thought you had a plan! But ever since then we've done nothing but wander aimlessly around the forest, and what's the point of that? Maybe you can tell me, because I just don't know any more. Yesterday we lost Hilya and her baby, and no wonder neither of them survived the birth—'

'And that's my fault, is it?'

'You're the leader, so the final responsibility rests with you.' Kelon knew this bitter quarrel wasn't helping anyone, but now that he had started he couldn't seem to stop. 'We have people sick and injured. Now that Athina's supplies have run out we're starving again, and this is summer, the best time of year for surviving in the woods. What's going to happen to us when winter comes?'

'What would have happened anyway. Do you really think that Athina and her companions were in the least bit interested in what happened to us? It would have been Ferimon all over again. They would have used us while it suited them and then left us to our fate, so we're better off without them.'

'I don't see how.' Kelon started to pace, his movements jerky with anger.

'And I don't know why you are putting all the blame on *me*.' Now Danel's voice was rising too. '*You* wouldn't have stayed with Athina's lot in any case – you said so at the time. You made it quite clear to us all that you wanted nothing more to do with that lover of yours.' A sneer curled through her voice. 'Oh no, I forgot – she wasn't your lover, was she? She wasn't interested in you at all, and I'm not surprised.'

The image of ploughing his fist into her face rose up in him so vividly that it shocked Kelon into taking a step back from her. What sort of monster was he turning into? Soon he'd be no better than the others. 'You're not even worth my anger,' he snarled. 'The Phaerie always said that mortals were no better than animals, and the more time I spend with you and your followers, the more you prove me right.'

He turned on his heel and walked away through the trees, back to the ashes of the campfire and all the slumbering, blanket-draped forms that lay around it. Seemingly most of the weary ferals had slept through his fight with Danel, though in the end the pair had been too furious with one another to keep their voices down. Some of the sentries must have heard them, however, and Kelon had no doubt that the entire tale, with a number of embellishments, would be all around the camp before tomorrow morning's sun had cleared the treetops.

The fire was almost dead now. Kelon looked at the sleepers all around him and felt a weight of responsibility settle on his shoulders. It wasn't their fault they were ignorant. They had been raised as beasts and treated like beasts by the Phaerie. Was it any wonder that they seemed incapable of thinking for themselves?

Ignorance is one thing, but there's no excuse for stupidity. Surely it must be obvious that we need to keep the fire going, both for warmth and protection from wild beasts.

Kelon answered his own critical thought. *Is it, though? Would it be obvious to an animal? To a cow, say, or a sheep? Of course it wouldn't.*

But mortals aren't the same as cows or sheep. They have a language and communicate with one another. They are capable of carrying out quite complex tasks if someone tells them how. They can cooperate with one another if the circumstances demand it.

They bury their dead.

They grieve.

So what were they, these mortals? Not the same as the more evolved beings in the magic-using races, but different from the lower beasts. Where did they fit into the scheme of things? What would be their ultimate fate? Was this the only group in which the seeds of rebellion were growing, or was it all part of a general trend?

Kelon shook his head. This was not the time for such abstract speculation. Right now, there was the practical matter of the fire to be attended to, and it looked as though that was up to him. It was hard to find wood in the shadowy darkness of the midnight forest, and more than once he found himself wishing that the Phaerie night vision was as good as that of the Wizards. Nevertheless, he could see better in the dark than the humans, and managed to collect a good armful of the precious fuel before making his way back to the campsite. By the time he had nursed the fire back to life, he felt leaden with weariness, and more than ready to join the sleepers that surrounded him. Pulling his cloak around himself tightly, he curled up and closed his eyes, longing to escape in sleep from the turmoil of anger and worry in his mind.

He awoke with a jolt from a nightmare of running endlessly through the forest, to find that the sky was beginning to lighten with the approach of dawn, and he was no longer alone. Danel had emerged from the forest and sat down beside him. He cast a sidelong glance at her. Her posture was tense and changing expressions flashed across her face; her anger at war with sorrow, weariness and frustration. Her shoulders were hunched, as though the burdens of leadership were a physical weight crushing down upon her, and Kelon realised how much it must be costing her, and how utterly desolate and desperate she must be feeling, to have taken that first step towards a tentative reconciliation.

Somehow they had come to need one another in the days since they'd been thrown together. Inept though they were, Kelon depended on the ferals for his survival now, yet he had no illusions about how long he would last among them without Danel's support and protection. She needed him because the position of leader was such a lonely one. She dared not let herself become too friendly with any of the other ferals because it would weaken her position. In that way, the Phaerie had been right about the mortals being no more than mere beasts, he mused. Left to their own devices, the ferals had devolved into little more than a pack of wild animals, and, like any pack leader, Danel could have her authority challenged at any time. In Kelon she had found someone who was no danger to her, yet was far better educated and more knowledgeable about the wider world than herself; someone with whom she could discuss ideas and air her concerns and frustrations, someone with whom she could let her guard down, someone to ease the loneliness of command a little ...

When he wasn't attacking her himself, he thought, with a pang of shame.

Fate had thrown them together. They didn't even particularly like one another, yet they needed each other, and any schism between them endangered them both. Kelon sighed. He knew what he must do. In returning to the fire Danel had made the first move. Much as it rankled, it was his turn now.

He held out his hand. 'I'm sorry,' he said softly. 'It was just so dreadful – one of the hardest things I've ever done, burying that newborn child yesterday. It's been preying on my mind ever since, but I had no right to take it out on you. I know you're doing the best you can.'

'Am I?' Her tone was thick with bitterness. 'You were right, Kelon. I'm the leader, and every one of those deaths is on my conscience. I've done precious little for my people since I took over, and that weighs heavy; you've no idea how heavy. I was taking my frustrations out on you, too. The truth is, I don't know which way to turn now; what to do for the best.'

In the light of the fireglow, Kelon smiled. 'You know, I might be able to help you with that. I was thinking, earlier, and I had this idea ...'

15
~

DEPARTURE

It was well before sunrise on the day he was due to leave the tower, and the sky was just beginning to grow light, when Dael, carrying his pack and gear and still half-asleep, crept out into the magical pre-dawn stillness. He had come out alone to take a last look around, and say goodbye to the place that had been the only true home he'd ever known. The faint breeze was moist, cool and fragrant with scents of forest, water and grass, and a scattering of the brighter stars were still visible in a lilac-coloured sky.

Dael thought of Athina, saviour, friend, a mother to an orphan slave, and wondered where she was now, how she was faring, and whether she missed him as much as he missed her.

The Cailleach had impressed upon him that everyone must be out of the tower by sunrise on the third day after she'd left. 'In my absence, my concealment spells will become effective,' she had warned him. 'Essentially, there will no longer be a building there.'

'But what will become of it?' Dael had said. 'Won't it just become invisible?'

Athina had smiled. 'I think you would find it very difficult and in-convenient to live in an invisible tower. Besides, any curious Phaerie or Wizard might quite literally bump into it.' She shook her head. 'That would be a disaster. If either race discovered it, they would never rest until they had found a way to plunder all its secrets. No, we must do better than that, my Dael. I plan to enclose the whole edifice, garden and all, in a small bubble of time which I will shunt a little way out of the normal timestream – literally bend time around this location. Any intruder will only see the island as it was before the tower existed, or will be after it is gone. That's the way it must be, dear one, though I'm very sorry that you will lose your home. But if the Phaerie or Wizards should discover this place, do you think for one moment that they would let you stay here in peace? That is why I asked Iriana to take you with her, and protect you from being turned back into a slave again.'

Dael swallowed against a lump in his throat, but as well as sadness, there was also fear in his heart. For a little while he'd had a place to shelter him, and a beloved guardian who loved him, and protected him from the usual fate of his kind. To find this haven of comfort and happiness, only to have it snatched away from him, seemed too cruel to bear.

'Why don't you just destroy the tower?' he had asked, desperate to take his mind from his plight. 'What's the point of taking it out of time if neither of us can return?'

'Good question.' Athina nodded her approval. 'Let me see if I can explain in simple terms. If I were to destroy or obliterate the building, then this location would revert to what it was: an ordinary island on a lake. But if the tower is, in effect, still in place but simply displaced in time, a resonance will remain; a residual field of magic: the potentiality of a tower, if you will. Iriana or Corisand, or even their descendants, will be able to draw on that power, that potentiality – if they ever work out how to utilise it.' She sighed. 'Call it a parting gift from me to them, and to their world. Besides—' Suddenly she looked up at him and for an instant her eyes regained their defiant old fire. 'I may be forbidden to return here, but why burn all my bridges? You never know what may happen in the future, Dael. You never know.'

Which is all very well, Dael thought, as he returned to the lonely present of that bleak, chill dawn, and the continued ache of the Cailleach's absence. But unless Athina can return in my lifetime, it won't make a single bit of difference to me.

He looked around at the sound of voices to see Iriana and Corisand coming out of the tower carrying the last of their belongings, with Melik perched, as usual, on the Wizard's shoulder to act as her eyes. Neither of them looked cheerful. They'd only had a little time in which to recover from their last ordeal in the Elsewhere, and there was a wan fragility, almost a hint of transparency, about both of them that Dael did not like.

Dael didn't know a lot about magic, but even he could sense the power of the Stone, a strange pressure, like walking into a tingling gale. Now that Corisand had joined her own magic with that of the

Fialan in order to help her to change form, and perform the flying spell, it seemed as if a kind of merging had taken place between
them, and he could see that Corisand was having difficulty containing all the energy. A pulsing aureole of emerald light surrounded
her, shining through and around her form, and her struggle to keep
it damped and under control was written clearly in the lines of her
face. He wondered how long she could continue to bear such a burden. Knowing her strength of will, he would wager on it being long
enough – especially as she had himself and Iriana to help her. She
had certainly lost no time in learning to use the Stone. The first time
she'd used it to take to the skies, the feat had stolen his breath away,
though he didn't like to think about the implications.

Yesterday, following her triumphant flight, the Windeye had
rested for a while before repeating the spell, this time extending it
to the roan mare Rosina, the only other Xandim horse that was still
with them. Following the success of this second venture, she had
come to her companions with a new plan. Together they would fly
to the place where they had arranged to meet Aelwen and Taine;
Iriana riding Corisand, and Dael on Rosina. It would save them days
of dangerous travel through the forest, and give them an unexpected
and welcome edge when rescuing the Xandim. Furthermore, they
would no longer have to depend on Tiolani to perform the flying
magic to assist Corisand's people in their escape. Though she had
given her word, they all had doubts that Hellorin's daughter could
be trusted. Though it was certainly the best plan, Dael had his own
misgivings. Apart from a few quick lessons with Corisand and Iriana
over the last couple of days, when they had been able to spare the
time, he had never ridden a horse before. On the ground was one
thing – he thought he might be able to manage, with a bit of luck –
but flying all the way up in the air was an entirely different matter.
He only hoped that he would be able to stay on.

The Wizard and the Windeye greeted him, their voices hushed.
'It's almost sunrise,' Iriana said. Melik, draped around her shoulders
as usual, turned his head so that she could look at the tower. 'This
place is so big and solid. It's still hard to believe it can just vanish.'

'It's not vanishing exactly. Athina said she was removing it a
step beyond our normal flow of time, so it would be there, but it
wouldn't.' Dael tried his best to explain, but he wasn't sure if he
really understood it himself. Suddenly he resented them being there.
This place was *his* home. If he had to lose it, had to see it disappear,

then he wanted to be alone to grieve for all that he had lost. He turned away from Corisand and Iriana abruptly. 'I'll go and fetch the other horses.'

Corisand gave him a look filled with sympathy and understanding. 'Just remove the tethers from the Wizard mounts, and let them roam free. I've told them to stay here, in this clearing by the lake. They have plenty of water and grazing, and the trees will shelter them. Athina assured me that enough of her influence would linger in this place to protect them from thieves and predators – including those accursed ferals, with their taste for horseflesh.'

'I hope she was right,' Iriana said with a frown. 'I hate to leave them, but we can't take them with us when the flying spell will only work on the Xandim.'

'We'll come back for them,' Corisand assured her. 'Never fear.'

Their voices faded away to silence as Dael walked towards the trees. The sun was already rising, hidden by the leafy canopy that surrounded the clearing. When he had reached the forest's edge, he turned back and waited, his eyes fixed on the elegant tower that soared above its island on the lake. All at once, a finger of sunlight streaked down through the trees and fell upon the tower. For an instant the whole building glowed as bright as molten gold – then it shimmered, wavered as if it had been its own rippled reflection in the lake, and diffused into a cloud of golden mist. The haze obscured the entire isle for a moment, then drifted away to leave – nothing. No garden. No tower. Just a bare, rocky island dotted with a handful of bushes and stunted trees.

Dael hid his face in his hands, but just as sorrow rose up like a dark tide to overwhelm him, he had a sudden vision of Athina, seen in his mind's eye, yet as clear and vivid as if she was really standing there before him. Though she said nothing, the warm glow of her love reached out to envelop him, he felt the gentle touch of her hand upon his face, and he *knew*, knew for certain, that one day they would be together again. Though the vision vanished, that phantom caress remained with him, like a benison, like a promise, and he felt comforted and whole as he had not been since she left. It would be all right.

He had no idea how she'd done it, but with the tower's passing Athina had left a farewell for him, and an inestimable gift. Dael had stopped being afraid. He no longer saw himself as a victim, helpless in the hands of fate and those beings more powerful than he. He was not an inferior, but someone with an important part to play in the events to come. He would forge ahead, do his duty, and help the Wizard and the Windeye achieve their aims. Then, if they succeeded at last, they might think of a way to help him to find his own heart's desire.

There was no point in standing there looking at the dreadful vacancy where the tower had been. It was time to let it go into the past and the treasure chest of happy memories, and look to the future. Dael turned away from the lake, went to find the horses. He set the Wizards' mounts free with a farewell pat, and saddled the Xandim mare. She was reluctant to leave her new companions, but he took a firm hold of her bridle and led her out of the woodland and across to where the Wizard and the Windeye waited. When he came within earshot, he realised that he had not been the only one who had been reminded of their losses when the tower vanished.

'It's as if another link with him had been broken,' Iriana was saying, 'but I refuse to believe that Avithan has gone for good.'

'Athina did say that she'd do everything in her power to get him back to you – and she has a lot of power at her disposal.' Corisand laid a hand on her friend's arm in a gesture that Dael found essentially female. It was hard, seeing her now, to remember that she had spent most of her life as a horse.

'There's one thing: Avithan won't let her stop trying. Not for a single instant. When he really wants something, he just refuses to be shaken. He grits his teeth and digs his heels in, until finally the opposition – whether it be flesh and blood or merely adverse circumstances – crumbles away in the face of his stubbornness.' Iriana's fond smile included Dael as he came up to them. 'Neither Avithan nor Athina are the sort to give up – and neither are the three of us. One step at a time, we'll all get where we're going.'

'Then let's take that first step,' said Corisand decisively. 'Dael, we'll get you settled on Rosina first, before I make the change.'

They tied blankets for all three of them, rolled together in a single bundle, behind Rosina's saddle, and packed her saddlebags with provisions, balancing her load carefully. When all was ready, Corisand took herself off a little way apart from the others and stood very still for a moment, a frown of rapt concentration on her face. Around her neck pulsed the emerald radiance of the Stone of Fate, so vivid and bright that it penetrated the small leather bag that held it, as though the hide had suddenly become transparent, revealing the beauty and power of the gem within.

But Dael had seen the Fialan before. What was happening to Corisand was far more interesting. Wide-eyed, he watched as her outline began to shift, to blur, to grow. Her limbs thickened and elongated as she dropped to all fours, on fingers that had suddenly fused into hooves. The clothes she wore, linen, wool and leather, became smooth grey dappled hide. As for her neck and head ... Dael swallowed hard. He could take what was happening to her body in his stride, but so much of her character, her individuality, *herself* was concentrated in her face that his stomach churned to see her features alter, her head elongate and her human expression vanish. Her ears, black-tipped and elegantly tapered, moved up to the top of her head, and her eyes, now large, round and lustrous, shifted round to the sides. Finally, the unsettling transformation was over and, where a small, wiry, dark-haired human had stood, there was now a large grey horse with clean, strong limbs, a powerful arched neck and a long black, flowing mane and tail.

Dael shivered. At some point in the transition, he had unconsciously taken Iriana's hand, or she had taken his, he had no idea which. Now he looked across at her and saw the same disturbing thought that was in his mind reflected on her face.

It was as though the human Corisand had never existed at all.

Then the great grey horse trotted over, poked Iriana with its nose, and broke the spell. The Wizard laughed. 'Corisand says that while she was shifting we were gaping like a pair of baby birds. She wants to know whether we plan to stand here all day, and suggests we finish loading her and get on our way, before we all die of old age.'

Dael grinned and bowed to the Windeye. 'I beg your pardon for staring, Corisand. In both your human and horse forms you're extremely beautiful – but the bit in between? I'm not so sure.'

Corisand regarded him solemnly for a moment – then put out a long, wet tongue and swiped it up and over his face from chin to eyebrows.

'Ugh!' Dael spluttered and hastily wiped his face on his sleeve. Corisand let out a long, low whinny that sounded like a snicker, and Iriana sat down on the grass beside Melik and simply rocked with laughter.

After a short time they collected themselves, and completed their preparations. Though she had did not have a saddle, Corisand had a bag of rations and spare warm clothing to carry as well as a rider, and even Melik had not been forgotten in the preparations. Though he rode quite happily, perched in front of Iriana while they were riding normally, with their feet on the ground, he didn't have far to jump if he lost his balance. She was worried about him falling off when they were in midair, however. If there should be some sort of mishap, the results would be unthinkable. Iriana had put him into Seyka's old carrying basket with the lid fastened firmly in place with a leather strap, and hung it on one side of Corisand's withers, balancing it with the food bag on the other side.

Finally they were ready; there were no more preparations to make. Iriana, sharing Corisand's vision now that Melik was safely shut in his basket, gave Dael a leg-up into Rosina's saddle and helped him to get settled. He did his best to relax, sitting and holding the reins as he had been taught. He could only hope to deceive the horse into think-ing that he was competent, for he certainly wasn't fooling himself.

Corisand positioned herself by a large rock on the lake shore, so that Iriana could clamber up and mount that way. As they returned to stand beside Rosina, the Wizard called out to Dael. 'Corisand says there'll be a lurch as you leave the ground, so hang on tightly to the saddle. Falling off is definitely not a good option after that point.'

'What about you, Iriana?' he replied. 'You don't even have a saddle.'

The Wizard grimaced. 'Don't remind me. I have the strap that's holding the baggage in place, I'll have to make do with that – and of course Corisand's solemn promise that she won't let me fall.' She took a deep breath. 'She says she's ready to start the spell now, so here we go.'

Dael felt the power blazing from Corisand as she cast the magic around herself and Iriana, like a radiant starfall which swirled and spiralled outwards to include Rosina. Dael gritted his teeth and knot-ted his fingers in the reins, fighting the urge to shrink away, or even run, as the spell engulfed him, pulsing in time with his heartbeat and setting a vibrant tingling throughout his body. All at once he felt lighter, almost as though he could float out of the saddle and take to the air of his own accord – an alarming sensation that made him snatch nervously at the front of the saddle and hold on tight.

Then suddenly Corisand sped forward and took a mighty leap into the sky, accompanied by a wild yell from Iriana that might have been either alarm or excitement. Rosina snatched at the bit and raced after her companion and, without warning, gave an almighty bound that never landed but took her into the air, leaving Dael's stomach on the ground behind her – or so it felt. He screwed his eyes tight shut as terror burst through him, but after a moment or two, when he felt more secure and it became clear that nothing terrible was going to happen, he opened them to find the world was suddenly at his feet.

Far below him the forest stretched, a vast ocean of trees that reached far ahead until it lapped around the skirts of the northern mountains. The air felt cold, crisp and clean against his face and its song, as it whistled past his ears, was the only sound he could hear. Though Dael still clutched the edge of the saddle with a white-knuckled grip, it was simply a reflex now, rather than the fear he'd felt when they had taken off. Filled with the exhilaration of the flight, he had forgotten to be afraid. To see the world spread out below him in all its immense grandeur made him feel as though he ruled it all, as though it was his own personal plaything.

For an instant his mind flashed back to the time before Athina had rescued him, when he had fallen from the nets of the Phaerie slavecatchers and been lost in the forest. He remembered struggling on stumbling feet through every treacherous, perilous mile; starving, injured, exhausted, lost, terrified and absolutely without hope.

And just look at me now, riding the skies in lordly splendour like the Wild Hunt themselves! Look at me, not a slave any longer, but a friend and companion to these marvellous, magical beings, the Wizard and the Windeye. I'm useful, I'm wanted. I belong. My life is better than I ever dreamed it could be. I can make a difference, and help to free another race of slaves. What more could I ask?

'Athina,' whispered a small, sad voice inside his mind, but Dael, for once, chose to ignore it. What was done was done. For a little while he would put away those thoughts of loss and sorrow, and simply enjoy the glory of this wild ride through the skies.

The sun had passed the zenith when they finally saw the broad, glinting line that was the Carnim river that marked the boundary of the Phaerie realm, and all of them were growing weary. They had landed once, briefly, to give Dael and Iriana a chance to get out of the saddle and stretch their legs, and permit Corisand to relax for a short while from the pressure of continual concentration on her flying spell. They wasted no time, however, and soon were on their way once more, sipping from their water flasks and chewing trail rations as they flew.

They followed the shining path of the Carnim for another hour or so, until finally, on the northern bank, the land reared up into a low range of craggy hills, their surfaces too rocky and steep for trees or anything other than weeds and small shrubs to gain a foothold. As the companions swooped down towards the rugged eminences, they saw the river change colour to mark the confluence of the Carnim and the Snowstream. For a few hundred yards, until they were churned together by the swirling currents, the conjoined torrents looked as though the two separate rivers ran side by side in the same bed, with the Snowstream's opalescent blue-green glacier melt running alongside the Carnim's turbid flow, stained brown with silt and tannins from the trees.

Following the oddly bicoloured river upstream, they saw the canyon slicing down through the hills to channel the northern river into its broader counterpart. The Snowstream poured, surging and foaming, through the constricting rocky gates of the gorge as the two horses swooped down and entered the narrow defile. The sun never reached the bottom of this gloomy crevice. Ferns grew in profusion in every cranny of the damp rock, and swags of bramble and ivy snaked down from the clifftops on either side to hang in tangled, thorny curtains that dripped with moisture. Looming like a threat, the echoing walls of rock reared up on either side of them, and the roar of the river reverberated in the enclosed space until their ears were ringing. A cold, dank wind blew into their faces, carrying the faintly metallic tang of wet stone.

Iriana shuddered. 'This is a horrible place.'

'You should try it with the hearing of a horse,' Corisand replied. 'I think my head is about to explode. Couldn't Taine have found a less unpleasant location for a hideout?'

Iriana shrugged. 'Maybe he could, but this place is safer, I suspect. Who would linger here long enough to find a cave, unless they were absolutely desperate?'

'Well, for safety's sake we can put up with a bit of unpleasantness, but I hope we won't have to stay here too long.'

The cave was indeed well hidden. Taine had described its location as being within a mile of the confluence, on the eastern side of the ravine, yet it took over an hour of flying up and down this part of the canyon, carefully examining every cranny and shadow, before the companions finally found the opening, several hundred yards from the mouth of the ravine and about two-thirds of the way up the cliff face.

Dael was the one who finally spotted it, tucked away in the shadowy niche behind a jutting projection, partially obscured by ferns and a

tangle of ropy, thorny bramble briers that cascaded down the precipice from the forest above. He was never sure what drew his gaze to
the spot – he had passed it a dozen or more times already – but this
time, approaching from a slightly different height and angle, his eye
was caught by a deeper patch of darkness amid the shadows.

'Hold on,' he yelled, straining his voice to be heard above the roar
of the river. 'I think I see it!' With Corisand's help he managed to
manoeuvre Rosina across to the right place, and pushed aside the
overhanging greenery. 'Ow! If this is the right place, we're going to
have to be careful of these brambles.'

'It must be the right place,' said Iriana, sharing Corisand's vision
as the tangled vines were thrust aside and a dark void was revealed
behind them. 'Well done, Dael. You have my eternal gratitude. I was
sick and tired of flying up and down this accursed canyon.'

In an awkward, lurching move which had him almost tumbling
out of the saddle, Dael managed to scramble across into the cave
mouth. They had come prepared with lanterns taken from Athina's
tower, and he lit one now. 'I'll take a look inside,' he said. 'If this is
the right cave, I'll come straight back and tell you.' As Dael stepped
into the dark opening, he was pleased to note how brave he sounded.

The cave, its dark stone walls glittering in the lamplight, turned
out to be little more than a narrow tunnel that went back into the
cliff for about thirty feet. It then split, with a branching cave on the
right-hand side, the remnants of another passageway that had been
blocked at its far end by a fall of rock, leaving a chamber about nine
or ten feet on a side. Although the walls near the entrance still carried
the dampness of the canyon, the further in Dael went the moisture
grew less and less until, by the time he reached the branching cavern,
the walls were perfectly dry. The ceiling began from a low place,
about six feet high, not far inside the entrance, then gained another
foot or two at the far end of the cavern. The floor was rock, fairly
uneven, but smooth enough for them to get Rosina inside without
much trouble.

Dael hurried out to the others with a grin on his face. 'Looks like
the place all right.' A brilliant smile broke out across the Wizard's
face, and even the Windeye lifted her weary drooping head and
pricked her ears.

With Corisand pushing and Dael tugging on her bridle, Rosina
was finally persuaded to enter, and Dael led her along to the far end of
the straight section, where he hobbled her so that she could not turn

round and go back to the entrance. Unfortunately, the ceiling was too low for Iriana to enter the cave while still mounted on Corisand, even if the Wizard tried to lie very flat along the Windeye's neck to avoid hitting her head on the roof. Instead, the Windeye brought Iriana right up to the very mouth of the cave and hovered there, as close as she could to the lip of rock at the entrance, while Dael put out a helping hand to steady Iriana as she scrambled across, using Corisand's vision to see where to put her feet. Once she was safely inside, Corisand followed. Dael removed her saddlebags and Melik's basket and, while Iriana freed her cat, the Windeye changed back into her human form.

She clapped Dael on the shoulder. 'Well done, Dael. Had it not been for your keen eyes, we might have been flying up and down that accursed canyon all day.' She grinned at him. 'Just for that, you win the prize.'

'What's the prize?'

Corisand chuckled. 'Iriana and I will make dinner tonight.'

'Is that a good thing?' Dael asked dubiously. It was becoming a standing joke among the three of them that he always ended up doing the cooking, mainly out of self-preservation, because the other two were woefully bad at it. Obviously, cooking had never been a skill that Corisand had needed – or indeed been able – to acquire in her life as a horse, and in Iriana's case, there were human servants in Tyrineld to deal with the Wizards' domestic chores. Only a handful of her people had any interest in the culinary arts.

'Take heart, Dael,' the Wizard said. 'Since Taine told us not to light any fires while we're here, we're only having cold rations tonight – and not even Corisand and I could muck that up.'

They unpacked their provisions and settled themselves in the inner chamber, with Dael on the left-hand side of the entrance, Iriana on the right, and Corisand at the back of the cave. It did not take long to make their cramped quarters as comfortable as possible, with blankets and cloaks as primitive beds, and their packs as pillows. Iriana replaced their lantern with a globe of magelight, which she sent up towards the ceiling to hover above them and illuminate the chamber with its soft glow.

The companions had been up before sunrise that morning, after a night of very little sleep. Dael, indeed, had not been to bed at all. He'd spent the night roaming round the tower and its environs, storing up memories of what had been the happiest time of his life. Iriana was still feeling the after-effects of that wild night when she'd lost Esmon, Avithan and her animals, and had come very close to being murdered herself. Both she and the Windeye were still recovering from their journey to the Elsewhere and the battle to regain the Stone of Fate, while Corisand was also fighting the fatigue of holding the flying spell in place all day.

It was a relief to be able to sit down and rest at last. They had found their haven and could finally be comfortable. They were so ravenous that even the cold trail rations of bread, cheese and dried meat, washed down with water, tasted delicious to them, but none of them got to finish their meal, for now that they had relaxed, all their exertions and lack of rest finally caught up with them. Heads drooped and food fell from fingers gone suddenly limp. Desultory attempts at conversation petered out into silence in mid-sentence.

Corisand was the first to go, slumping back against the wall, her head tilting to one side as her eyes closed, and the rest of her body following suit. Dael caught her by the shoulders as she began to slide, and as he lowered her gently to the cave floor, Iriana slipped her pack beneath her head.

She looked so comfortable that it seemed only natural to follow suit. 'Sorry,' Dael mumbled to Iriana. 'Close my eyes – just for a moment ...' He curled up on top of his cloak and was lost to the world. Iriana stayed awake for about two minutes longer, prompted by the guilty thought that someone, at least, ought to stay awake and alert, but her weariness got the better of her and she gave up the unequal struggle. She lay down on her cloak beside Melik. Taine had said this place was safe, after all. A little rest, and she'd be fine ...

As her eyes closed, an image of Esmon, shaking his head at her and frowning, came into her mind, but she was already drifting into slumber. Melik lay by her side as if on guard, his sapphire eyes reflecting the magelight that she had left floating by the ceiling. The sound of soft breathing filled the cave. Slowly, almost imperceptibly, the cat's eyelids drooped, and soon even he was fast asleep.

16

~

ON THE BRINK

The next morning Chiannala arrived at the infirmary bright and early, to find the atmosphere had changed completely; the fear and unease that had permeated the place on the previous day had vanished. At first she wondered what the problem had been, and how it had been solved, but then, as she approached the desk in the main reception area, she overheard Lameron (whom she had already tagged as a dreadful gossip) saying, 'The rumour was that Tinagen had been arrested, but today he's back, so surely it can't be—' Then he saw Chiannala approaching, and shut up like a clam.

So was that really what had happened to Tinagen? There had been all sorts of rumours flying round the student refectory at the Academy the previous night, of Luen Heads going missing and being replaced. Chiannala knew that the truth would all come out eventually, and meantime this new, positive ambience within the Luen of Healers suited her down to the ground, for she was filled with newfound determination to excel. To her frustration, however, she found that there was little for herself and Haslen to do.

Though one problem had seemingly been solved, the other – the mystery patient behind the forbidden door – was still very much in evidence. Judging from the tired, worried faces going in and out of the room, the foreigner's condition had deteriorated, and he was taking up everyone's time and energy. Chiannala and Haslen were simply told to continue to observe, looking at what they wished and asking questions where they would – but not about the firmly closed door and whoever lay beyond it.

Chiannala was sure that this benign neglect, under the disguise of orientation, was not for their benefit, but was because the Healers were simply too busy and preoccupied to bother with them. She was bored and frustrated. If she had to be stuck in this place she wanted to do, to learn, to participate in the activity. It ill suited her nature to be thrust to one side. Then suddenly, late in the morning, everything changed. She was loitering near the closed-off area when a great commotion came from behind the door.

'We're losing him,' she heard. 'All together everyone – quick! Tinagen's the focus.'

Even through the distance and the closed door, Chiannala felt her skin prickle as the build-up of powerful magic, the result of a number of skilled minds working in concert, swirled through her. Then the shouting came again. 'It's no good. He keeps slipping away from us. There aren't enough of us. We need more. Wesnian, drop out. Get everyone you can find in here right now!'

The door burst open and one of the Healers she'd noticed yesterday came rushing out, his hair askew, his skin beaded with perspiration and his features white and drained. His eye lit on Chiannala. 'Here, you! Get in there at once. We need all the help we can get.' Grabbing her arm he thrust her through the door and into the passageway beyond before running off to recruit more help.

Chiannala went with alacrity. At last, a chance to see the secret patient. At long last, a chance to prove herself. Through a doorway at the far end of the corridor she saw a blaze of light, the blue-violet radiance of powerful healing spells. Bursting into the chamber she discovered a number of Healers, all focusing their power on Tinagen himself, who stood looking grey-faced and spent near the head of the patient's bed.

The face on the pillow, though almost as white as the snowy linen on which it lay, was fine-featured and gloriously handsome, with a tumble of black curls falling about his shoulders. Chiannala was stunned to see a great pair of wings, supported in position by a scaffolding of slender canes, their shattered bones braced and splinted by a network of spells. She gasped. One of the legendary Skyfolk? *Here?*

A woman with short, dark hair seized her arm and pulled her into the throng. 'No time to lose,' she said. 'Feed all your powers into Tinagen.'

'Verelle, she can't,' Melisanda shouted. She was standing close to the Luen Head, her sweat-soaked hair hanging in ropes and her eyes ablaze with power. "She's just a first-year student. She can't—'

'Oh yes I can,' Chiannala said defiantly. 'I will.' Before anyone could stop her she gathered all her power and flung it at Tinagen, and as it was sucked into the vortex of magic she felt it blending with the powers of the others, becoming part of a vast and incredible whole.

'Good girl,' muttered Verelle. 'Well done. As soon as you feel yourself tiring, though, drop out. We can't risk losing a first-year to burnout.'

Burnout? Nonsense! Chiannala had never felt more powerful or alive. She felt more magical energies blending with her own as other Healers crammed themselves into the room. It was a thrilling feeling to be part of it – like flying, she thought, as she bent all her considerable will to the task, pouring her power in a steady stream into the still, glowing figure of Tinagen.

Then all at once, something strange happened. She began to feel the life force of the patient, fluttering feebly against some inner part of her mind like the flicker of a guttering flame.

It shook her to the core.

Never before had she felt such an intimate bond with another individual. Though the room was full of Healers, all more experienced, it suddenly felt as if she and only she could hold him to life and save him. Abruptly she severed her power-feed to Tinagen, ignoring the ripple of shock and consternation that went through the others as they fought to compensate for the sudden alteration. Instead, she turned her focus directly onto the still figure on the bed, pouring all her magic, all her energy, directly into him and willing him to hold on, to breathe, to live, even though she could feel him fading. In her mind's eye – a true vision, not her imagination – she saw him receding down a long tunnel of darkness, slipping further away from her with every passing moment.

Grimly, Chiannala fought with all her strength to hold on to him. He *wouldn't* die. She wouldn't let it happen. Taking a deep breath, she sent herself after him into that strange, dark void.

She wished that she could see him properly, but in her vision he seemed ephemeral, shrouded in shadow; already he was abandoning his ties to the world. Well, she would just see about that. Somehow she made herself go faster, pushing herself towards him though it cost her a considerable amount of effort. Soon she was gaining, she was just behind him, and—

She suddenly realised that she was as incorporeal as he. How could she talk to him, touch him, pull him back? Even as she hesitated, he drew away from her again, receding into the darkness. Some instinct in Chiannala told her that if he went much further, there would be no returning – for either of them. She cursed under her breath. 'Hey you! Come back,' she shouted in mindspeech. 'Come back right now, you stupid idiot. You're going the wrong way.'

Though his form was still indistinct, still shrouded in shadow, she sensed him half-turn towards her, felt that inexorable forward progress slow. 'Don't want to. Go away.' He meant to sound fierce, she knew, but he was so far gone that his voice only held a thin edge of defiance, like the whine of a tired child.

'Don't be stupid,' she told him. 'You don't know what's waiting for you down in the darkness. Do you really want to give up light and life and everything you have in this world for the unknown?'

The shadowy figure shrugged. 'Too much pain. Tired. Done.'

'You're *not* done,' Chiannala snarled at him. 'Don't be so damn feeble. With a little effort now you can have your life back. Do you really want to give up everything? Just like that? Do you want to *lose*?'

His sigh was long, hollow and despairing; a chill wind blowing over wasteland in the dead of night. 'Already lost. Broken. Don't *want* to come back.'

Chiannala wanted to prove to the Healers that she was as good as any of them, and if that meant pulling this whining fool back from the brink of death, then she would do it – supposing she had to drag him every inch of the way.

To make things worse, she was running out of time. While she wasted precious minutes wrangling with him he was slipping further away from life, and dragging her with him. It was easy to be pulled in this direction; it felt as though there was some sort of natural tide sweeping them onward, but to get back she sensed she would be fighting the same strong current all the way, hampered by the reluctant stranger. If she went much further, she might not have enough strength to get herself back, let alone this weak, despairing idiot. Panic clutched at her, but she fought it down. She *would* get back – and by all the magic in her, she was taking him with her.

An idea struck her. Quickly she envisioned the weaving of her will into a silver net. She poured her magic into the image, and when it was ready she cast it round the dying man. He fought and struggled, thrashing like a landed salmon. 'Leave me alone, curse you! I *won't* go back.'

By now, Chiannala was tiring. It took enormous energy and

strength of will to keep herself in place against the pull of death's current. Already she could feel the weariness beginning to gnaw at her, sapping her strength and will. Inch by inch, or so it seemed, she was losing ground; slipping away from life and the reality she knew. If the stranger continued to fight her like this, they would both lose their lives. Gambling everything on one last try, Chiannala relaxed and stopped tugging at him, though she left the net in place. Maybe reasoning would work, where force had failed. 'In the name of all Creation, *why*?' she demanded. 'Why don't you want to live?'

'Nothing to live for. Crippled. Broken.' His voice thickened with hatred. 'No more flight, no more sky. *He* broke me.'

Relief flooded through Chiannala. Here at last was the lever she'd been looking for. 'Who broke you?'

'Filthy Wizard. Yinze.' He spat out the words with venom.

Yinze. Iriana's foster brother. Giggling girls around the Academy did nothing but talk about him. Despite her predicament, Chiannala smiled to herself. Fate worked in mysterious ways. 'What about revenge?' she asked in insinuating tones. 'Do you want to run away like a coward, without making that bastard pay for what he did to you?'

'How can I?' Chiannala was heartened to hear the snap of anger. If he was angry he would fight. Then her hopes were dashed as his voice sank once more into defeat. 'Lost. Broken. Done.'

'You *can* do it,' she urged him. 'You will. I'll help you, I swear it. Don't give up yet. Come back and let our Healers work on you. They're the best in the world – if anyone can help you they can. Yinze took everything from you. Are you going to let him get away with it? Imagine how good your vengeance will feel ...'

She had him now. He was still shadowy, still indistinct, but as he turned to her she could feel a strength growing in him that had not been there before. The savage pull of death's tide lessened as he added his strength to hers, and slowly they began to inch their way back towards light and life.

Death, however, was not done with them yet. Though Chiannala had expected that it would be more difficult to return, she had not realised just how much the growing fatigue would slow her down. Even with the help of the one she had come to rescue, it was a desperate battle: it was like trying to climb a mountain with both feet tied together. All at once, Chiannala realised that she'd made a terrible misjudgement. In the struggle just to keep herself and the other in place, to avoid sliding any further into the abyss, she had used up too much energy; too much of her strength. Weariness coiled tightly round her like thick iron chains, weighing her down, pulling her back. Bit by bit she felt herself slipping, losing the hard-won ground she'd already gained, and the more she struggled and fought, the more she weakened herself.

Panic jolted through her like a lightning bolt. So this was what Melisanda had meant when she'd talked about burnout! Finally, she realised why the Healer had been so determined to hammer the warning home. At last, too late, she understood her peril. She was trapped here between life and death, between light and shadows, and minute by minute she was slipping further down towards the dark. When she got there, there would be no coming back.

Chiannala's companion was weakening too. Though on the face of things she had persuaded him to go back, his heart had never really been committed to returning. Sick, in pain, wounded both in body and spirit, he had neither the will nor the strength for this fight.

She should never have persisted. She should have let him go. Now everything, all her hopes and her schemes, her plans and her dreams lay in ruins. What a fool she had been! Up to this point it had never occurred to her to abandon him, to let him go, to try to save herself. Now she finally understood that there was no alternative. Tasting bitter failure, she began to cast loose the net of will in which she had ensnared him. Knowing that it was hopeless, that she was lost in any case, still she prepared to gamble everything on one last try—

When suddenly a searing blue light came arrowing into the imprisoning darkness, and as it drew closer she realised that it held the will and spirit, the power and presence of Melisanda. It touched her, and she felt a blaze of renewed energy and vigour.

'You little idiot.' She heard the Healer's voice clearly in her mind. 'This is exactly the sort of situation we were trying to avoid.'

Now it was Chiannala's turn to be enclosed in the shimmering blue net of Melisanda's will, just as she had captured the faltering spirit of the stranger, only this was far stronger, brighter, more elegantly spun than hers had been.

'All right, Lameron,' Melisanda said. 'We're ready.'

Only then did Chiannala realise that they were not alone. Further back towards the light she saw a green shimmer that she recognised as Lameron, who was supporting Melisanda in a net of his own will, and beyond him, holding him in the same way, was the vivid golden blaze that was Tinagen himself. Together, they were strong.

Chiannala felt the darkness receding behind her as she was pulled steadily towards the light, still trailing the stranger behind her, held fast to her by the last shreds of her web of will.

Exhausted as she was, it would have been a pleasure and relief just to let herself go, to let the others bring her safely home, yet she understood how much energy it was costing them and the risks they were taking, and her pride would not let her be a helpless passenger. She dug down deep and found a few last drops of strength and purpose, and poured them unstintingly into the linked Healers' chain of power.

Faster now and faster she was moving – until suddenly she burst back into the light, back into her body, and found herself lying on the floor with a circle of Healers around her, who sagged so wearily that it looked as though they had been pulling with their physical muscles as well as mental strength.

Then suddenly they were all looking at her, and Chiannala trembled.

How had it all gone wrong? She was supposed to be a hero. She was the one who had saved the patient, the only one who had been able to bring him back. She had risked her life – had nearly *died*.

Stupid Healers.

They should have been grateful – but were they? No. Instead she was surrounded, hemmed in like a beast of prey by a circle of steel-eyed Healers, and all of them tearing into her at once.

She was a fool, a moron, an irresponsible little idiot. Who did she think she was, a mere student of two days, to try such an insane thing? She had been warned by Melisanda about burnout. If she couldn't listen, couldn't follow instructions, couldn't obey orders, she would be no good as a Healer. How dare she try to meddle with the delicate spells of older, experienced Healers? Proper Healers? She was a fool, and idiot, a moron.

And so on.

Chiannala was shaking. Looking around at the circle at those angry, accusing faces, she didn't see how hollow-eyed they were, how grey-faced and drawn with fatigue. She didn't sense the fear that clawed them, because they had come so close to losing a student. She didn't understand the sorrow and frustration of having to watch a patient slipping away from them, inch by inch, moment by moment, until they lost him to death. She only knew, or cared, that just when they ought to be heaping her with praise for her daring and self-sacrifice, they were attacking her instead. Once again she was the outcast, the pariah, the one who was never good enough.

The half-breed.

That small, nasty inner voice shocked her back to her senses. She *was* good enough. They had no right to treat her like this. *They* were the ones who were stupid and ungrateful. She was every bit as good as them – better than them, in fact. Only she had been able to bring back the dying patient. They were only jealous, all those so-called experienced Healers, because she had done what they could not. And she was *damned* if she was going to let them frighten her, make her feel stupid, make her feel small.

Chiannala staggered to her feet and let her anger rise, hot and searing, to burn the fear away. 'You've no *right* to talk to me like that! I saved him. I helped him. He wanted to die and I was the only one brave enough to go inside him and persuade him to fight. I'm not the one who's stupid here. I never wanted to be a Healer in the first place, but you made me, and then when I tried to heal somebody you all attacked me. Well, you can take your Healing and your Academy and your stupid city, and you can stick them up your—'

Luckily, before her temper could take her down a road she never wanted to travel, her tirade was cut off by the sound of a moan coming from the bed, and urgent cries from the two Healers who were caring for him while the others dealt with their recalcitrant student. In an instant, Chiannala found herself alone and ignored as the Healers clustered around the patient. Though his face was contorted with pain, his eyes were open, and they were fixed on Chiannala. As she caught his gaze, the connection sizzled through the air between them like a lightning bolt, shaking her to the core. Somewhere in the shadowy realm between life and death, a bond had been forged between them. They were one. They were together. For the first time in her life, she didn't feel, deep down inside, that she was isolated from the rest of the world.

'Let her be.' His voice was a mere whisper, yet it still had an echo of authority and command. Though he was addressing the Healers, he never took his eyes from Chiannala. 'She saved me. You should thank her.'

Tinagen ignored this, putting his hands on either side of the patient's head to block any pain. 'We'll talk about her later, Incondor. Right now, we need to concentrate on you. Save your energy. Now that you're conscious, it will be easier help you, because you can work with us. First of all we'll get you something to drink, and make you more comfortable. Then some of our team will feed energy to you, while others work on repairing the damage. We'll soon have you feeling—'

'Wait.'

Tinagen's eyes flashed. No one interrupted a Luen Head – not in that imperious tone. 'What do you want?'

'Her.' Incondor lifted a shaky hand and pointed at Chiannala. 'I want her.'

'I'm afraid that isn't possible,' Tinagen told him flatly.

The young man's eyes sheened with tears. 'I need her,' he whispered.

'Right now, I'm the best judge of what you need.' Tinagen turned to Chiannala. 'Come along, Brynne.' His tone brooked no argument. Fuming, she let him usher her from the room.

'Go back to the student quarters and stay there.' Tinagen's voice was like ice, like steel. 'Do not return here until you're sent for.' Then he turned on his heel and went back into the sickroom.

At that point Chiannala hadn't cared. She was still riding high on anger – and something more.

Incondor. So his name was Incondor.

He had looked at her.

He had *seen* her.

He had wanted her.

His name rang in her heart, beat in her blood as she walked back to the student dwelling, ignoring the glory of the sunset, her feet finding their way through force of habit while her mind was elsewhere. It was only when she got back, and looked around her precious little room, that her mood shattered and the enormity of what she had done came rushing in. The rage, the euphoria all drained away, leaving her empty, afraid – and horrified at what she'd done.

Chiannala was devastated.

Over and over again she cursed her stupidity, cursed her temper. Why, oh *why*, had she struck back at the Healers like that? Why hadn't she just kept her head down and her mouth shut like a good little student, and meekly accepted their rebukes? It wouldn't have killed her to bury her pride for once. She had done worse to get here, to stay here at the Academy. And now she had ruined everything.

She sank down on the bed, put her face in her hands and

contemplated the wreck of her future, the ruin of all her hopes and plans. When Tinagen had ushered her from Incondor's chamber his face had been hard and cold as granite, but she had seen the smoulder of anger behind his eyes. He looked at her as if she were nothing. An insect.

Oh, how *could* she have blazed up like that? What had she been thinking? No student would ever be allowed to get away with such behaviour. They would send her away, that was certain. She would lose her place at the Academy, after everything she'd done to get here: running away, robbing her parents, stealing a horse.

Murder.

No, no – she wouldn't think of that. She wouldn't think of Brynne, the farm girl she'd pushed off a cliff in order to steal her face, her background, her place here at the Academy. It was done, in the past; there was no going back now.

And she'd just thrown it all away.

Stupid, stupid, *stupid*. If they sent her away from here who could she be? Where could she go? She couldn't remain as Brynne and go back to the farm; her subterfuge would never stand up to people who had known and loved Brynne all her life. She certainly couldn't resume her original appearance and go back to her parents – not after what she'd done.

She had nothing. She had no one. She had no future. She would never see Incondor again. Desolate, devastated, Chiannala lay down on the bed and wept and wept.

She was not the only one who had problems.

'What in the world are we going to do about that wretched girl?' Melisanda looked across the table at Tinagen with eyes that burned with fatigue. They had retreated to his study to talk things over, but she suspected it was a mistake on her part. She should never have sat down. At present she felt as if she lacked the strength to ever get up again.

'Right at the moment I would like to tie her in a sack and drop her into the ocean,' the Healer snapped. He must have seen Melisanda's stunned expression, because he sighed and rubbed a hand across his face. 'I'm sorry, my dear. I know that doesn't help. I just can't seem to get my balance since I sold myself to Sharalind.'

Melisanda reached out a hand to cover his own – a gesture which would normally have been too familiar for her to contemplate. 'Don't be so hard on yourself,' she said softly. 'You didn't sell yourself. Sharalind backed you right into a corner where you had no other choice.' Her hand clenched on his in anger. 'She had no right to do what she did, arresting Heads of Luens. No right at all.'

'She did it because she could. Because she had the backing of enough of the other Luen Heads to let her get away with it.' He sighed. 'I felt as if I had no choice, Melisanda. If I had refused to cooperate and back her in her dreadful plans for war she would have taken me out of time, as she did with Daina and Callia, and all this unholy mess would have come down on your head, as my second-in-command. I don't mind telling you, as I would tell no one else, that I've never felt so afraid or so alone. And I was sick at heart and grieving over the fate of my dear old friend Aldyth ...' He broke off, and swallowed hard.

'Aldyth didn't die, though,' Melisanda comforted him. 'You must hold on to that. We'd have known if he had died.'

'Yes, but where is he? What happened to him? Did they find him after all and did Sharalind take him out of time, as she threatened to do with the rest of us, if we didn't fall into line? And if not, what became of him? How could he have survived that cold and stormy ocean? I live in fear, Melisanda; terrified that at any minute I will feel his death pangs ...'

A moment passed while he fought for control, then he continued: 'And worst of all I am ashamed; ashamed and sickened by what I've done. I should have joined Aldyth, and leapt off that cliff. I should have been like Daina and refused to compromise. I should have defied Sharalind as she did, and let myself be taken out of time. But I didn't. I told myself that now, in these dreadful times, my Luen needed me most. That at least if I were here, and active, I could do my best to protect my Healers from the worst of the devastation.'

He had been looking down at the table as he spoke, but now he lifted shattered eyes to look at Melisanda. 'The thing is ... The thing is I'll never know, never *really* know if what I did was common sense or cowardice. Was it you and all your brethren I was protecting? Or just myself?'

'Well, for what it's worth, I think you were right,' Melisanda said firmly, 'and so did Lanrion, or he wouldn't have made the same choice as you. Daina's and Callia's sacrifices were brave, but what good has it done their Luens? The Artificers are in utter disarray; scared, demoralised, fighting over the leadership, and the merchants are no better. At least you're here, you can help, you can act. And it wasn't cowardice, Tinagen. Never believe that. It took a lot of courage to do what you did, to sacrifice your own values, your own wishes, for the greater good.' She smiled at him and squeezed his hand. 'I had a taste of what it was like while you were missing. There was panic, confusion; we all felt so lost.' She smiled wryly. 'As your second-in-command I, for one, am infinitely relieved that you're still here.'

Tinagen managed a smile for her. 'Thank you, my dear. That means a lot to me, coming from you, for I know all too well that you would never lie to me to spare my feelings.'

'You'd better believe it.' Melisanda rose, and went across to the little spirit stove that stood on the workbench beneath the window. 'Now, I'm going to make us some taillin and we can address the problem of what in the world we're going to do with that appalling Brynne.'

Tinagen sat back in his chair, stretched, and ran bony fingers through his red hair that suddenly, in the last few days, had started to show a lot more silver. 'My immediate response to her outburst, and to what she did, is to expel her immediately. It worries me to have her at the Academy; to be putting so much power into the hands of someone with such a hot and reckless temper. But it's not that simple.'

Melisanda put a dollop of honey into each steaming cup of taillin and brought them back to the table. 'You're right – it's not that simple, though the girl has been a thorn in our side from the outset with her sullen attitude. I don't know what happened in the interim, but she's not the same girl that we interviewed on her preparatory visit to the Academy. She was so bright and bubbly then, and she couldn't wait to become a Healer.' She shook her head. 'I don't know what could have changed.'

'No matter what has changed, she's still brilliant. She may have lost the vocation, but the talent is unmistakably there. She may have been rash, disobedient and stupid, and had we not been there to save her she would certainly have died along with her patient, but it took courage to do what she did, and there's no denying that she was the one who brought him back – something that we, with all our experience, couldn't do.'

'And Incondor wants her, which complicates matters considerably.' Melisanda took a sip of her taillin, and sighed with pleasure as it slid, hot and comforting, down a throat that was dry from talking. 'I suppose it's understandable. Bringing him back like that was bound to forge some kind of link between them; of gratitude if nothing else.'

'It may be understandable, even inevitable, but it's a bloody nuisance. Since we sent her away, Incondor has been angry and upset, and it's affecting his recovery. He's already slipping back downhill again.' Tinagen scowled at his taillin as if the blame lay in the bottom of the cup. 'It sticks in my throat, but I don't see that we have any choice. We have to have the little wretch back. A lot hinges on our relationship with the Skyfolk right now, with war brewing between ourselves and the Phaerie. He's Queen Pandion's nephew; it wouldn't do for us to lose him. Anyway, we swore an oath. From what I hear he's a nasty piece of work who brought his troubles on himself, but it's our duty to save him if there's any way we can.'

'So that's it, then. We take Brynne back – and the cartload of problems that come with her. I only hope we're not storing up more trouble for ourselves in the future.'

'Not much point hoping that, I'm afraid.' The Luen Head rubbed his tired eyes. 'That girl has got problems written all over her. But taking care of Incondor should keep her out for trouble for the present, and there's no doubt she'll learn a great deal, which is to everyone's benefit.'

'You never know, it may even be enough to rekindle her passion for Healing.'

'That's my Melisanda.' His smile for her held more than a hint of pride. 'Always finding the good in the bad.'

'In her case it's not so difficult. She's only a minor matter compared to the rest of our current situation.' For a moment, Melisanda let her mask of constructive competence drop to reveal the fear and frustration that hid beneath, gnawing ceaselessly at her heart, and Tinagen, seeing a glimmer of tears that she quickly blinked away, remembered with some shame that he was not the only one who grieved. Her losses were far greater. Iriana and Avithan had been like family to her, and now Ionor, whom she had loved so dearly, had gone missing just like Aldyth.

He knew what was in her heart. Ionor had been outspoken in his objections to Sharalind's war plans. Had she taken him too? He realised that his own arrest had shaken her deeply, and how upset she was that Chathak and Yinze – and possibly even her dear friend

Thara – were going off to fight. Would she lose them too? She must be fighting that fear for every minute of the day, yet she did not, could not, let it affect her work. She had remained capable, staunch and dedicated throughout a succession of crises, and he had no idea what he would have done without her. She had held everything together in his absence and, he was ashamed to admit, since his return. His own arrest and ensuing crisis of conscience had shaken him to the core. Since his return he had been distracted, and had not been giving his best to his Luen, his Healers or his work.

Well, that would have to change. He could no longer afford such self-indulgence. It was time to face up to his responsibilities once more – and the first of these was to take care of this brave young woman to whom he owed so much. 'Come along, Melisanda,' he said. 'You must put aside Brynne, and all the other troubles that beset us, for a time. When did you last eat a proper meal? When did you last sleep?'

She blinked, frowned, and then gave an embarrassed little shrug. 'I can't remember. The days have all blurred into one.'

'I thought so. And I, selfish fool that I am, have been letting you do your work and my own while I wallowed.'

'You weren't wallowing,' Melisanda protested. 'You were arrested, for goodness' sake.'

'True – but then I was released, and since I got back I've been wallowing, and letting you take up the slack. Well, it stops right now. You're to go home and rest—'

'I can't go home, I can't!' The fine thread by which she'd been holding herself under control was fraying. 'Don't make me go back there, Tinagen. So many of them are missing now, there are too many empty spaces, and now the others are preparing to go too.' She dropped her face into her hands. 'We always thought our happy little family would last for ever. We always thought that nothing could divide us. What innocents we were. What fools.'

In a flash Tinagen was on his feet, and went to put an arm around her shoulders. 'Don't despair, my dear. Maybe the war won't happen. Maybe Cyran will return in time to put a stop to all this nonsense.'

Melisanda shook her head. 'I haven't had a lot of luck with "maybe" lately.'

'Well, right now you're in no condition to deal with anything. I'm going to have a meal sent in here, and see that you eat it.'

'I will if you will.' She glanced up at him, and for a moment her old spark was back. He was so glad to see it that he gave in at once. 'Very well. We'll eat together, and then we'll find a bed for you here at the Luen, in a nice quiet room that's not being used right now. And once you're there, I don't want to see you for at least eight hours – all right?'

Stubborn to the last, she shook her head. 'I'll never sleep.'

'You'll sleep.'

And I'm going to put something into that food to make damn sure you do.

He patted her shoulder. 'Trust me, I'm a Healer.'

'What about Brynne?' Still she wouldn't let go of her duty.

'Don't worry about Brynne. I'll deal with her. Our hands may be tied on the issue of having her back, but I'll see that she doesn't get away with her behaviour. Now,' he added briskly, as he went to the door, 'I'm going to see about that food. It wouldn't reflect well on my Luen if I let my greatest asset collapse from overwork.'

17

~

UNLOOKED-FOR REUNION

Kea sat on top of Ariel's Tower at sunset, looking out across Tyrineld. She had taken to coming up here to be alone with her thoughts, for Sharalind was far too busy to use the flat roof terrace any more, and it was always deserted. It was a perfect place for thinking; private, secluded, and somehow above the cares and tribulations of the city. The winged girl was desperately missing the mountains of her home, and somehow being in the highest place for many miles around helped to clear her mind.

The terrace was a pleasant place, bounded by a wall that was just the right height to lean on. The view was spectacular in either direction: across the thriving city with its elegant buildings and blossoming gardens, or across the shimmering ocean and the ships plying to and fro. Within the parapet there were stone benches set into the curving wall, and the circular roof was tiled in a pretty mosaic. In the centre there were chairs and a table, and large pots of flowering plants brightened the area with their vibrant blooms.

It had only taken a few days for Kea to become familiar with the city. Because she could see everything from the air, it was easy to fix the layout in her mind, and the locations where her new friends could usually be found. From here she could look down at the places that had become important to her: the two adjacent houses in the pretty square, one of which was Yinze's, and the other where she was staying with Thara and Melisanda; Yinze's Luen of Artisans and the building down near the sea that housed the Dragon Atka. Unfortunately she'd also become familiar with the Luen of Warriors, where her Wizard companion could usually be found since his return with her from Aerillia.

Kea sighed. Had she been wrong to come here? She was beginning to think so. She should have stayed in Aerillia where she belonged and immersed herself in her work, until she had buried her growing feelings for this handsome Wizard with the charming smile. It was hopeless anyway. Had she not promised Queen Pandion that there would be nothing more than friendship between them? Mating between Skyfolk and Wizards wasn't natural. It had to be wrong.

But what of their friendship? Kea had become close to Yinze back in her own city, when they had worked together on his harp. She had been looking forward to continuing that companionship in Tyrineld yet, as soon as he'd returned, he had abandoned her for his old Wizard comrades without a backward look. Was she being selfish to expect more from him? After all, he had lost two of his dearest friends; one dead, one missing. War was brewing, his people were divided against one another and everything was in a state of flux. Nevertheless, surely she had a right to expect better from him – or had he just been using her in Aerillia, to assuage his loneliness? She felt hurt and betrayed. Maybe she had been nothing but a convenience to him in his own lonely exile, to be discarded now that he no longer needed her.

It could be no coincidence that a similar situation applied to poor Atka, Kea reflected. Since the Dragon had come here from Dhiammara, Chathak, immersed in his grief over his own losses, had simply ignored her, leaving her alone to worry about her unanticipated pregnancy and the near-impossibility of caring for a hatchling in this temperate, foreign clime. She would never have guessed that the Wizards could have proved so fickle.

Only Ionor, it seemed, had honoured his bond with his Mage partner, the Leviathan Lituya, but now they had both absconded, leaving the city at dead of night to return to Lituya's people in the north. The Mage of the oceans had sent out a call in mindspeech to herself and Atka the night he left, otherwise she would never have known what had become of him. Certainly Ionor's fellow Wizards, even his closest friends, had never mentioned it – at least not in front of her.

Had it not been for Atka, Kea would have emulated the Leviathan and returned to her own people. Chathak, still concerned with his own sorrows, had passed the problem of the impending Dragon's egg to the already overburdened Melisanda. Though the Healer had made time for a long talk with Atka, and promised that the Wizards would find a way to care for her offspring when it arrived, she'd simply had no time to help any further. Apparently, with war brewing, no one cared about the visiting Magefolk students. They had learned nothing since they had come here and indeed it seemed as if, having plundered the knowledge of the other Magefolk species, the Wizards were not prepared to honour their side of the bargain.

Queen Pandion was going to be furious when she found out – but should Kea be the one to tell her?

The winged girl had a way of sending messages back to her people. She had brought with her a basket of homing birds, trained to return to their roosts in Aerillia, in case she needed to communicate with her family or Master Crombec in an emergency. So far she had hesitated to send word of the recent happenings in Tyrineld, knowing that once Pandion had discovered the situation she would inform the Dragon and Leviathan leaders, and all three would be deeply – and rightly – concerned about the consequences of a war between Wizards and Phaerie. She knew that they should be told, and that as the only Skyfolk representative in Tyrineld she should pass on the information, but Cyran was still absent and she had heard the rumours of Sharalind's increasing instability, for when a person had wings it was easy, unavoidable in fact, to eavesdrop on private conversations. No one bothered to look up. Perched on rooftops, cornices and high walls, she had been privy to the uneasy gossip that spread from mouth to ear to mouth, all over the city.

What concerned her most was the talk of some of the Luen Heads being arrested, and certainly there had been some sudden changes of leadership. It seemed that Sharalind would stop at nothing to get her own way over this war, and surely it was Kea's responsibility, indeed her duty, to warn her own people? Yet if she passed information to Pandion, would she not risk being detained as a spy? It was nerve-wracking to be all alone; a foreigner in a city where the situation was so unstable. Though she despised herself for being a coward, Kea couldn't help it. She was afraid and, she suspected, not without good reason.

Of course, there was an alternative. She could go home, and take her information back to Pandion in person.

Once the idea was in her head, Kea couldn't let it go, and the more she thought about it, the more sense it made. What was the point of staying here? She wasn't learning anything. Yinze didn't seem to want or need her. The journey back to Aerillia would be long and lonely, and it would be a lot more dangerous to travel alone than in a group, but she could make it, she was sure. Without winged bearers to accompany her she would be forced to leave most of her possessions in Tyrineld and travel very light, but ...

What about Atka? Lituya has already abandoned us. How can I leave her all alone here in her condition? She can't get home the way I can – she's trapped. If I'm lonely and afraid right now, imagine what she must be feeling.

She wrestled with her conscience. On the one hand, she was neither comfortable, nor happy, nor safe here in the Wizard city. She was homesick, pining for her mountains, her mentor, her family and friends. But on the other hand there was Atka, now a good friend too, who was equally alone, equally homesick and desperately vulnerable. How could Kea just pack up and leave the Dragon now?

How could she live with herself if she did?

Kea pondered all these problems, her thoughts circling round and round as the sun began to sink into the western ocean, turning the waves into a blaze of molten gold. The sight was breathtakingly beautiful, but so dazzling that she was soon forced to turn her back on it, blinking away the glare, to look down at the promontory below the tower and the city that spread out beyond, its white buildings turned to amber in the honeyed evening light. The air smelled of dust and herbs and sunlight, all overlaid with the fresh, salty tang of the ocean. Throughout Tyrineld, Wizards were gathering outside, in gardens, on balconies and rooftops; eating, drinking and enjoying this peaceful and lovely time of the day.

It was a magical moment, suspended in perfection. From up on the tower roof everything seemed so tranquil, it was impossible to believe that this was a city torn apart by turmoil and conflict, and on the brink of war.

Below her, the door of the tower opened. She ducked behind the parapet, afraid of being accused of spying, then did just that, edging up to peer over the sill. Two figures stood on the path below her. One was Sharalind and the other ...

First of all Kea saw the wings, and all the breath left her body in a shocked gasp. It was one of the Skyfolk! One of her people was here in Tyrineld. Then she recognised the wings, their shape and colour, and the face of the person below, and her heart soared with joy. It was Master Crombec, her beloved teacher and mentor.

Kea sank down and sat with her back to the parapet, her emotions all in a whirl. First there was a spurt of annoyance – *does he think I'm so useless that I need to be supervised?* – followed by an overwhelming flood of relief. Now she wouldn't have to worry about whether to report to Pandion; someone older, wiser and senior to her was there to make that decision. Crombec would decide whether she should stay here or return to Aerillia. Maybe he'd be able to help Atka, if only with some good advice. And he was sure to have brought an escort with him; both bearers and guards. If he did decide that she should leave, she would no longer have to go alone with little more than the clothes on her back.

All these thoughts flashed through Kea's mind following that first, startled moment of recognition. Then she collected herself and peered cautiously over the parapet again to focus on the dialogue below, which was clearly the continuation of a conversation that had been going on inside the tower.

'And of course we'll be delighted to offer to offer our assistance to our friends the Winged Folk in any way we can.' Sharalind sounded anything but delighted. 'I fear that Queen Pandion will find me remiss in my arrangements for her representative here, but I'm sure you understand that—'

'Not at all, not at all. Do not trouble yourself.' Crombec's voice was soothing. 'Given the tragedy that has beset your people, especially yourself and the Archwizard, how could things be otherwise? I'm sure it has done Kea no harm to take time to settle in. And what of Yinze? How does he fare? He must be frantic over his missing sister, and the passing of such a close friend as your son must have been a terrible blow to him.'

'Indeed.' Sharalind's voice took on a hard edge. 'And like the rest of the Wizardfolk, his thoughts at the moment are fixed on revenge against the Phaerie. He is currently training with the Luen of Warriors.'

'It's understandable, of course.' Crombec replied in that same calming tone. 'He is bound to be shocked and angry. Feelings would naturally run high in one so young, but since his beloved sister is involved, it can only exacerbate matters.' He sighed. 'Poor Yinze. He talked of Iriana constantly when he was with us in Aerillia. Though she was not of his blood, I know how much he loved her.'

'At least *she* survived,' Sharalind snapped.

Well, you needn't sound as though you wish she hadn't.

Kea couldn't stop the resentful thought. It was just as well that *she* wasn't having this conversation, she realised, and indeed it seemed that even Crombec was anxious to shift onto safer ground.

'Given the strength of Yinze's feelings, do you think there will be a problem taking him away from the fight to help Kea and myself?'

Sharalind shrugged. 'Our alliance with the Skyfolk is of paramount importance to Cyran and myself. Yinze's personal considerations must not outweigh his duty.'

Crombec opened his mouth as if to say something, then shut it again, clearly reorganising his thoughts. He inclined his head in a bow to Sharalind. 'My thanks, madam. Your duties must weigh heavily on you at present – I will not keep you from them any longer. With your permission I will go and speak to Kea. I'm sure she will be most surprised to see her old teacher again so soon.' He flicked a glance up towards the parapet, and Kea ducked back down with a curse. She'd forgotten that, unlike the Wizards, the Winged Folk *were* accustomed to looking up.

After a moment or two she dared another quick glance, but the path below was empty, and she heard a loud click as Sharalind closed the tower door behind her. Crombec, with outstretched wings, was already gliding towards the centre of the city, and the house that Kea shared with Yinze's female friends. Plague on it! There was no way she could get back before him. With another muttered oath she spread her wings and launched herself from the top of the tower, following her mentor home.

Hot and out of breath, Kea landed in Thara's garden, only to find Crombec, as cool and unflurried as if he'd been there all day, sitting by the fountain and accepting a glass of cool elderflower cordial from Melisanda. She was shocked to see how pale and haggard the Healer looked, and remembered with a flash of guilt that she was not the only one who had troubles. Then Crombec was calling to her and standing up with his arms outstretched, and for a few moments Kea forgot everything else in the joy of their reunion.

Melisanda, in the meantime, had been fetching another glass for Kea, and now she settled them both down at the round wooden table with glasses and a bottle of the cordial – Thara's own delicious recipe, Kea knew – between them. 'I must get back to the Luen now,' she apologised. 'Tinagen chased me out to have a break, so I came back to check on the cub that Yinze brought back for Iriana. Ludea – she's the mortal servant who looks after our house,' she added in an aside to Crombec, 'is making you some supper, so you'll be fine even if none of the rest of us make it back this evening. Are your bearers settled, sir?'

'Yes, indeed. Lady Sharalind arranged quarters for them, and I will be staying next door with Yinze and his friends, so that I can be close to my old pupils.'

'I'm sorry we've afforded you such a poor welcome, but the way things are at present ...'

'Don't concern yourself, my dear.' Crombec smiled at Melisanda. 'I understand the situation, and you have given me a delightful welcome. I will be quite happy here with Kea to keep me company.'

When the Healer had taken her leave, he turned to his pupil with a twinkle in his eye. 'Well met, my favourite pupil. Now – just how much did you overhear back at Ariel's tower?'

Kea blushed. 'I'm sorry about that. I know you taught me better than to eavesdrop. But with the situation as it stands, I've been desperate for any information I could get —' She broke off and reached across to grasp her mentor's hand. 'Oh, Crombec, I'm so glad to see you! I've been so lonely and afraid. Lady Sharalind has been arresting the Luen Heads who disagreed with her and I was afraid she'd take steps to silence the visiting Magefolk too, in case we reported back to our rulers.'

'There there, my dear.' Crombec patted her arm with his free hand. 'You're not alone any longer. Sharalind is aware that I must report this business to Queen Pandion, but she won't interfere with me, not in Cyran's absence and certainly not when I came armed with a personal request from the Queen. If she has been listening to her soulmate at all in the last few months, she will realise just how important it is, not just to the Wizards but to all the Magefolk, that I am allowed to complete my work.'

'What work?' Kea interrupted. When Crombec raised his eyebrows she added, 'I didn't overhear all that much; only what the two of you were saying after you had left the tower. So I don't know why you're here – or why it involves myself and Yinze.'

'Since I need your assistance, I have Queen Pandion's permission to tell you everything, but what you are about to hear must be kept in the very strictest confidence ...' With that he went on to tell her about the visions of war and disaster experienced by the four Magefolk leaders, resulting in the very knowledge-sharing project which had brought Yinze to Aerillia and Kea to Tyrineld. As he went on to tell her of the decision to build an artefact to amplify the power of each race, for use in times of desperate need, her eyes grew wide. 'And this is why you're here?'

'Exactly.' Crombec took a sip of his drink. 'A group of us have been working on the project in secret, but so far with very little success. It was only when our young Wizard friend came up with his harp that we began to wonder: could we do something similar? But we need Yinze's knowledge and expertise, just as we need yours, for I know that you were also very much involved in the crafting of his harp.'

'And because that trouble with Incondor forced Yinze back to Tyrineld, and me with him, you had to follow us all the way back here.'

Crombec grimaced. 'Not the sort of journey I would have chosen. I'm getting too old now for such long-distance flights. However, since events here seem to be racing towards exactly the sort of catastrophe that Queen Pandion and the others foresaw, it's as well that I came when I did. We must get to work without delay, Kea. Our only problem is that we need Yinze to cooperate, and Lady Sharalind thinks that might present a certain amount of difficulty.'

'Difficulty?' Kea frowned. 'The way Yinze is feeling at present, I'd say it would be impossible. Lady Sharalind told you about the loss of his friend and his sister. He's determined to avenge them, Crombec. I never see him any more. He spends his whole time training with the Luen of Warriors, and plans to go with Sharalind's forces when they leave. You'll never persuade him to stay tamely behind and help us.'

Crombec raised an eyebrow, and she caught a sudden glint of iron in his gaze. 'Will I not, my dear? Well, we will see.'

Blazing with rage, Yinze stormed into the house, slamming the door behind him with an ear-splitting crash. His temper was not improved by finding Kea and his old teacher Crombec waiting in Thara's garden, drinking Thara's cordial as if they hadn't a care in the world. With a sweep of his arm he sent the bottle and glasses flying, to hit the flagstones in a burst of shattered glass.

'What in the name of perdition do you think you're playing at?' he shouted at Crombec. 'What gives you the *right* to come marching in here as if you own the place, telling me what I should do and where I should go? You've got a nerve to carry on as if you own my life. I don't have time for this nonsense. I have business of my own to take care of.' As he spoke he strode back and forth with shards of the glassware crunching under his boots, spitting out a furious tirade that included not only Crombec but Kea besides, calling her stupid, thoughtless, treacherous and selfish.

She opened her mouth – whether to protest or explain she wasn't really sure – but Crombec lifted a hand and motioned her to silence. He simply sat there, in a ring of splintered glass that glittered like diamonds in the moonlight, and waited until the young Wizard had shouted himself into silence. Then he got to his feet, spreading his great wings out behind him like a mantle of shadow. 'Fie,' he said softly. 'For shame, Yinze. Oh, not for attacking me – I have heard more than my fair share of youthful rages in my time, and they bother me not one whit – but how dare you, how *can* you say such cruel things to Kea when she has never been anything other than your friend? She had no part and no say in any of these decisions, yet you've abused her thoughtlessly and indiscriminately. She deserves better of you. Though she isn't dead or missing, she still deserves your care and compassion.'

Kea saw the Wizard's face whiten again with anger. *What in the name of all Creation is Crombec doing? Yinze has just calmed down. What good will come of setting him off again?*

This time, however, Yinze's furious tirade was appreciably shorter, and ended abruptly on a choking sob. He turned on his heel and walked away from the Skyfolk, flinging himself down on a bench beneath the downswept branches of a willow tree. Though he had turned away from herself and Crombec, Kea saw his shoulders heaving and knew that he wept.

At last she understood. Instead of letting himself mourn, Yinze had been using his grief to fuel his need for vengeance and bloodshed. Crombec had been drawing that violence out of him like poison from a wound. Though every fibre of Kea's being strained to go to him, to comfort him, she understood that this was not the time. It was better to let him grieve.

She and Crombec sat in silence for a time, watching the moon shimmer on the ocean and the bats darting low over Thara's flowers, hunting insects. After some time had passed, Crombec raised his finger in a circling motion, and Kea felt the tingle of magic at work. As she watched, the splinters and shards of glass rose up and gathered together in a miniature whirlwind to spin in the air above the table, revolving in a spiralling dance that glittered like frost in the moonlight. Gradually the jewelled vortex began to coalesce, and sank back down towards the tabletop where it settled into a cloud that gradually reformed itself into the cordial bottle and two glasses, intact and unscathed as they had been before.

Kea had never seen anything like it. 'That was amazing,' she said softly.

Crombec gave her a sad little smile. 'But I can't put the cordial back into the bottle. Even magic has its limitations. It cannot mend a broken heart.' He looked up and Kea, following his gaze, saw Yinze standing by the table and regarding them with ravaged eyes. 'Nothing ever truly will,' the old Skymage went on, clearly addressing his remarks to the Wizard this time, 'though time, and work, and the love of your friends will help to ease the pain. I cannot even begin to imagine how you must be grieving now, how torn and desperate and hurting you must be, but please know that Kea and I care for you very deeply. If there is any way we can help you through these darkest of times, you have my word that we will.'

He pulled out another chair and gestured, but when the young Wizard remained standing he went on: 'I understand, truly, that you feel the need to join the army and take action – but please, Yinze, consider this: your harp of Air magic is unique. You are the only one who has crafted such an implement. Though I helped you with the physical structure and the details, as did Kea, you are the one who imbued it with magic, and the only one who knows how that is done. If you go off with Sharalind's forces and are killed, that priceless knowledge will be lost for ever. My people's only chance to make an artefact that can help us in the troubled times that have been foreseen will be gone.'

Yinze leant forward, and looked deep into Crombec's eyes. 'I. Don't. Care.'

Crombec sighed and sat back. 'What is hurting you most of all, Yinze?'

For a moment the Wizard looked taken aback. He stood in thought for a moment, then suddenly sat down. 'It's Iriana. Oh, I know she isn't dead like Avithan and Esmon, and that's something to be grateful for, but something happened to her – something devastating, and she's out there somewhere in the wilderness. I don't know where she is, what's happening to her, if she's lost, afraid, in danger or already hurt, and I can't help her while I'm stuck here in this accursed city. To go with the army is my only chance of finding her.'

'The army is no good to you,' Crombec said flatly. 'Wherever your sister is, it cannot bring you to her in time.'

Yinze leapt up, knocking his chair over with a clatter, and hammered both his fists down on the table. 'Don't you think I *know* that? But I've got to do something! If you think I'm just going to sit here in Tyrineld making an accursed harp for you while Iriana is out there somewhere—'

'What if there's a better way?' Crombec's quiet words had all the power of a thunderclap.

Kea stared at her mentor, open-mouthed. Yinze, as if in a daze, set his chair back upright and sank down into it, naked shock on his face. 'What do you mean, a better way?'

'I brought bearers with me, Yinze. I thought I might need to stay for some time, so I needed to bring a fair amount of clothing, a number of volumes and scrolls for research, and all my tools and equipment to craft a harp. In addition, Queen Pandion insisted on an escort for my protection in these troubled times.' He leant forward. 'If we fly, we can move many times faster than an army on the ground. We can take you to your sister, and, more importantly, bring her back with us.'

Hope blazed up in Yinze's eyes, so painfully bright that Kea could hardly bear to look. 'You would really do that? You'll help me bring Iriana home?'

Crombec nodded. 'I will help you with all my heart, as long as you can find a scryer who can give us at least a rough idea of her location. We have no time to comb hundreds of miles of forest, for every moment that we waste in futile searching, the risk to Iriana will increase.'

Yinze's face fell. 'Don't you think I've already asked our best scryers? I've been harassing them until they're sick of the sight of me, but none of them have any idea of where Iriana might be.'

'Why didn't you tell me?' Kea demanded.

'What difference would that have made?'

'I would have suggested you ask Atka.'

'What, the Dragon?' Yinze shrugged. 'Why should she be any better than our own scryers?

'Atka was telling me that the Dragon scryers have had great success using fire, and that she had done some training with them before she came here. You should ask her to search for Iriana, Yinze. It couldn't hurt to try.'

The Wizard leapt to his feet. 'Thank you, Kea. I'll go at once.'

'Wait.' Crombec held up a hand. 'If I help you, there is one condition, Yinze. If and when we find Iriana, I'm asking you to forget about avenging your friend Avithan. To put aside your thoughts of vengeance, come back to Tyrineld, and work with us. Are you prepared to do that?'

Yinze didn't hesitate. 'For Iriana? I'd do anything.'

18

MORE THAN ONE SURPRISE

Though it was evening, those who lurked upon the clifftop, op- posite the cave, were very much awake. This small troop were the most accomplished of the Phaerie warriors, led by Nychan, who was tall, dark-haired and fair of face; renowned for his prowess with sword and bow and a skilled tactician in the games and contests of war which Hellorin held on a regular basis to keep his fighters sharp. They had been sent by Cordain to watch the cavern mouth, and had been camped out among the trees for the last two days, waiting for the intruders to arrive. While they waited in ambush here, the Chief Counsellor was gathering together all of the Phaerie steeds so that they could be guarded from any further depredations.

According to intelligence provided by the Lady Tiolani, there should be two groups of thieves and traitors: firstly, the Wizard who had been assigned to steal the Phaerie steeds, accompanied by a human slave, and secondly, the former Horsemistress and her lover, who had arrived at Eliorand with Tiolani, but escaped Cordain's clutches by means of an incredibly daring apport.

The first pair, the Wizard and her human companion, had arrived at the cavern earlier that day riding two of the Wild Hunt's stolen steeds, and Nychan and his warriors had been absolutely stunned to see them come flying – flying! – down the canyon. How had they done it? It looked as though the Wizardfolk had already managed to master a version of Hellorin's flying spell. If they succeeded in their vile plan to steal the Phaerie horses, the threat to the Forest Lord's subjects would be incalculable.

Also astounding was the fact that their stolen mounts had included – the sheer temerity of it! – Hellorin's own prized and precious grey mare. Since the creature was purported to be unrideable by anyone save the Forest Lord, the Wizard must be either an extremely skilled horsewoman, or capable of some very advanced magic. Nychan could see why she had been chosen by the Archwizard to be the thief. Watching the way she handled herself and her horse, he found it impossible to believe Tiolani's tale that she was blind. What other unknown powers could she wield?

Without being aware of what he was doing, he gripped the hilt of his sword. He must make sure of the Wizard first. Though he had no idea of the extent of her abilities, he could tell from what he had already seen that she'd be a force to be reckoned with. He must disable her and take her out of the fight as soon as possible, though he needed to fall short of killing her. Cordain's orders had been specific – she must be kept alive at all costs and brought back for questioning. The extent of the Archwizard Cyran's plots must be discovered. What else might he be planning?

It did not matter so much to Nychan whether the other conspirators lived or died, but he would prefer to take them prisoner if possible. That way he could take them back to Eliorand, where Cordain would make them all pay a thousandfold for their plots against the Phaerie.

Cordain had ordered him to hold fast until both groups had arrived, and all the rats could be caught together in one trap but, as Nychan waited with scant patience while the sun sank towards the horizon and vanished behind the trees, he began to doubt the wisdom of that plan. He already had the Archwizard Cyran's agent exactly where he wanted her, and though his orders had been clear, he preferred to trust his experience as a warrior over that of Cordain who, when all was said and done, was nothing but a politician.

Here was the Wizard, an unknown quantity but certainly very powerful, all alone with only a human slave to help her. It made far more sense to attack her at once, to overwhelm her with numbers before her fellow conspirators could get there to help her. Once she had been taken prisoner and rendered helpless, Nychan could conceal warriors inside the cave itself to await the arrival of the others, for the warrior mistrusted Aelwen's extraordinary apport skills, though these freak abilities did turn up in Hemifae from time to time. Though it would be exceptionally difficult and dangerous to make a blind jump into a small cave, who could say for sure that such a thing would be beyond her, or that she wouldn't try it?

Even at this moment, he and his men could be out here sitting on their hands like a bunch of idiots, while the conspirators were meeting in the cave across the gorge. And if Aelwen could apport herself and her lover in there, it would be a lot easier for her to jump everyone out, one at a time, to some other location. Why, they might already have come and gone without anyone being any the wiser!

Though the odds against such a scenario were, admittedly, long, Nychan wasn't about to risk letting a couple of lowborn half-breed Hemifae and a meddling Wizard make a fool out of him. Beneath the dappled shadows of the leaves, the warrior smiled grimly to himself. There was no way his plan could fail. When Aelwen and Taine arrived they would walk – or apport – right into his hands.

He used mindspeech to give his troops their orders. It was essential, at this point, to be as stealthy as possible. Quietly, they fetched their mounts from the horse lines hidden deep beneath the trees, and at his command they mounted the well-trained animals, who glimmered faintly in the sunlight from the flying spell, the most powerful that Tiolani had been able to lay on them before they left the city. There were twenty of them in all: a large number to capture such a small group of fugitives, but Cordain had decided to take no chances.

Silently, in small troops of five, they drifted across the ravine on their airborne steeds. Landing one group at a time on the narrow ledge in front of the cavern, four riders dismounted and moved into the cave while the fifth took all the reins and led the horses back across to the camp to make room for the next troop, until they were all across except for one horse keeper who waited on the far side of the gorge. Issuing orders in the most private form of mindspeech, Nychan led his troops into the cave, surprised to find no one on guard to raise the alarm. How could they be so careless? Well, their negligence would cost them dearly. The Wizard and her slave were about to receive an unwelcome surprise.

Dael found himself in the most astonishing place. 'How did I get here?' flashed into his mind, then was gone just as quickly. It didn't seem important – his surroundings were just too incredible. He was in the midst of a forest carved from stone. The leaves of the trees seemed carved from thin, translucent jade, so real that it felt as if they should flutter as he passed. Stone birds could be seen amid the branches, some poised as if to flutter away in the next heartbeat;

others with their heads raised and their throats swelling in a song that seemed just beyond the range of human hearing. Tiny jewelled insects fed from exquisite blossoms with petals of translucent quartz, so real that again and again he just had to lower his face to them, in hope of catching some faint scent.

How long Dael wandered he did not know, enthralled as he was by the marvels around him, but presently he came to the edge of the magical woodland and looked out across the floor of a cavern to the biggest tree he had ever seen. Was it formed of some wood and bark so ancient that they seemed petrified, or was it made of stone like the forest he had just left? Dael had no idea, but he felt no sense of danger: more a feeling of gladness and homecoming. The great tree seemed to draw him towards it, and he walked across the glittering sandy floor of the cave like a sleepwalker, his eyes fixed on his goal. As he drew closer, he noticed a staircase curving around the trunk that led to a door, about halfway up the vast shaft and high above the cavern floor.

Standing in the doorway, looking out, stood the dearest, most familiar figure ...

'Athina!' Suddenly Dael was charging towards the tree and the Lady was hurtling down the steps at breakneck speed. They met at the bottom, hugging rapturously, lost in the miracle of a reunion that neither of them had ever hoped to see.

It couldn't possibly be real. After a time, Dael pulled back from the embrace a little. 'I'm dreaming, aren't I? This has got to be a dream. A lovely, wonderful dream, but in a little while I'll wake up back in my world, and you'll still be exiled here.'

Slowly, Athina shook her head. 'It seems perfectly real to me. Tell me, Dael, do you usually *know* when you're dreaming?'

He thought about it. 'I can't say I do – not usually. And if I do suddenly realise that I'm dreaming, it makes me wake up.'

'So you're not dreaming, then, but having no magic you can't be here in actuality. Yet somehow, a part of you has managed to find a way through ... Tell me, Dael, are you sleeping very close to the Fialan right now?'

He nodded. 'I'm with Corisand and Iriana, resting in that small cave that Taine told us about, on the borders of the Phaerie realm.'

'That explains it, then. I don't know how, but your proximity to the stone in such a confined space has somehow created some sort of doorway that your mind, or spirit, has passed through while you sleep. And in order for the Stone to be free to work like that, I suspect that Corisand must be sleeping too.'

'A doorway? There's a way through?' The voice, taut with excitement, came from above them, and Dael looked up to see the young Wizard Avithan standing on the staircase above them. The last time Dael had seen him, he had been pale and still as a corpse, his features partly obscured by the eldritch glimmer of the tangled time spell that Taine and Iriana had produced in haste in order to save his life, but this was certainly Iriana's beloved, whom the Lady had brought with her into her timeless realm in the hope of saving his life.

Clearly, she had succeeded. Now he was bounding down the staircase, his face alight with a terrible, yearning hope. 'If he can get through, then maybe—'

'No.' Athina held up a hand, her eyes so flat and implacable that Avithan came to a dead stop at the bottom of the staircase. 'I am sorry to destroy your hopes, Avithan, but it just doesn't work like that. The Stone of Fate is in the other world, on Dael's side of the barrier that separates that reality from this. There is no way that we can access it from this side. I'm sorry, but that's the truth. As it is, Dael will only remain here until Corisand awakens. Then the portal will be gone.'

Avithan shook his head and held up his hands as though to push her unwelcome words away. 'But if a portal exists, surely there must be some way—'

Dael flinched as a horrible, banshee wail stabbed into his hearing. He awakened abruptly, with a naked blade at his throat. In the blue radiance of Iriana's magelight, which was now flickering wildly like a fearfully beating heart, he saw a tall warrior standing over him with menace in his cold grey eyes. The Phaerie had come!

It was Melik who gave the alarm. The senses of the small predator were far more finely honed than those of his clumsy, two-legged companions. The sounds, the smells of the alien Phaerie, the *feel* of their magic, assaulted all his senses the moment they entered, jolting him out of sleep. His piercing wail of alarm woke the others as the intruders rushed into the cavern. One of the Phaerie struck at the cat with his sword, but his aim was hampered in the cramped and crowded area. Melik streaked across the cave towards the exit, found it blocked, and dodged behind Dael instead, where a narrow crevice in the rock provided him with a sanctuary, out of harm's way.

Iriana, roused by his cry and the flash of bright panic from his mind, leapt to her feet but could see nothing but a forest of legs and booted feet, poised to kick and trample, followed by a glimpse of the small fissure, then darkness as the cat squeezed inside. Blinded, she hesitated to loose her magic lest she injure her companions. In that instant's pause, she felt the sharp pain of a stunning blow to the side of her head, and crumpled into oblivion.

As Corisand woke, all the instincts of her other, equine shape overwhelmed her human body, bringing her to her feet almost before her eyes had opened and poising her to flee – or fight. The first thing she saw, amid the crowd of stinking, fierce-eyed Phaerie, was the fist, holding the hilt of a sword, that clubbed Iriana to the ground. The second was the sword at Dael's throat. Then the intruders' attention turned upon her. Corisand could sense their puzzlement; even pick up some of the muttering between them.

'Who's *that*?'

'But we counted them in – just the Wizard and her human slave.'

'Where did *she* come from?'

'What's that glowing thing around her neck?'

'Can you *feel* that power?'

Their confusion gave her a single instant in which to act. Her assailants shrank back in alarm as she engaged the Othersight that was so necessary to her magic, and her eyes blazed with molten silver. Now, with her arcane vision, she could see that the air in the cavern was tinged red with hate and anger, laced with the vivid purple flashes, still superimposed, of fear and panic. Fuelled by so many people and emotions, the atmosphere throbbed and roiled, twisting and coiling like a living entity.

Perfect.

Corisand extended her powers, pulling the highly charged air towards her, intending to form a shield – but before she could do so one of the Phaerie, bolder than the rest, darted forward and snatched at the glowing Fialan. The thong broke with the violence of his tug, but he did not hold on to his prize, for the power of the Stone smote this stranger, and he cried out in agony and dropped it as though it were a red-hot ember. Dael, who had suddenly found himself ignored as all eyes had turned to Corisand, reached out his hand without thinking and caught it. He flinched, expecting to be burned like the Phaerie, but to his surprise the Stone seemed to accept him as a companion to Iriana, who had borne it briefly, and Corisand, its current bearer. Its power surged through him like an unfamiliar tide, and as its welcome sang in his mind, he knew for the first time that incredible feeling of euphoric power familiar to the wielders of magic.

At the same moment, Corisand got her shield into place at last. Honing the silvery barrier so that its boundaries burned like fire and bit like blades, she pushed it outwards, thrusting against the intruders; trying to force them out of the cave. For a moment, it seemed to be working. There was only room for four Phaerie in the inner chamber itself, though she had glimpsed a crowd of them in the passage outside, and so she concentrated upon the immediate threat. Taken utterly by surprise, the shocked Phaerie staggered backwards, shrinking away from this alien power, and Corisand's heart leapt with glee as she struck her first blow against the ancient enemy of her people.

There was only one problem. Iriana lay outside the boundaries of her shield. Frantically the Windeye tried to push harder, to extend her barrier far enough and fast enough to protect her friend.

But the leader of the Phaerie, curse him, rallied his men. 'Don't touch the shield,' he shouted. 'Drive it back with our own magic. And get that Wizard out of here.'

Quickly forming his warriors into a phalanx, with himself at the apex to focus their conjoined powers, he pitted himself against her, his will like a dark wall of adamant, pushing, grinding at her bright barrier. Corisand tried to drive it back with all her might, until she could feel sweat breaking out on her brow and running down her face. Desperately she tried to push against the Phaerie, trying to extend her shield far enough to protect Iriana, but it was no good. From where she was standing she could reach Dael, but to her horror, the intruders had already laid hold of the unconscious Wizard, and were dragging her out into the passage. Corisand could not save her. Without the Fialan to draw on, she had to rely on her own power, and strong though that was, she was badly outnumbered. Her legs were trembling, and she could feel herself beginning to tire.

The shield inched back towards her a little way. Grimly, she gritted her teeth and summoned the last shreds of her strength to stretch it out again – but she could not hold out for long. Once more, her circle of defence began to shrink, creeping slowly but inexorably back towards her, and she had nothing left to stop it. All she could do was try to hold on for as long as possible; to postpone the inevitable a little longer. Maybe Iriana would regain consciousness in time to come to her aid ...

In her heart, Corisand knew the Wizard could not. The Phaerie leader flashed her a feral, triumphant grin. He was enjoying the contest now. He might not know who or what she was, but he knew he had her.

From his prone position on the floor of the cave, Dael could feel the tides of power swinging back and forth between the Windeye and her protagonists. The two conflicting waves of arcane energy, Xandim and Phaerie, each held a wealth of differing sensations: Corisand's spell was cool, vibrant, tingling; open and expansive as the sky and the mountains; singing like the wind in the treetops and tasting of the fresh dawn air. The Phaerie magic, on the other hand, was dark and ancient, feeling like caves and secrets hidden long within the earth, as crushing and grinding as the slow, inexorable movement of continents. It growled and muttered like some primeval monster lurking deep within its lair, and tasted of earth and the sour, metallic tang of damp stone.

Dael realised that the Fialan, clutched tightly to his breast, was connecting him with these impressions. Somehow he was experiencing the magical battle in the same way as the Stone itself. Though he could hear no actual voice it was communing with him somehow, letting him feel what it felt. He suddenly realised that it was doing more than just attuning itself to the waves of power: it was absorbing them, adding them to all the energies it already held.

Then he saw the Windeye stagger and sway, and all at once his consciousness returned to the here and now: to his own dire plight, and that of his friends. The tide was pouring through him the wrong way now. Corisand was losing. Panic writhed within him. If the Phaerie should capture them ... 'Help me,' he begged the Stone. 'Please, help me.'

The Fialan's response sang through him as its power flared, and suddenly it was in his mind, and he knew, without being told in words, exactly what he needed to do. He could not risk breaking the Windeye's concentration by giving her the Stone. That left only one option. Dael inched his way across the floor, keeping low, not drawing attention to himself, until he reached Corisand. Then reaching up he took her hand, acting as a living conduit between her magic and the power of the Stone.

Exquisite agony flared throughout his body as the magic consumed him, a vast, inexorable torrent that threatened to overwhelm the fragile vessel that channelled it. He felt as if he was on fire, entombed in ice, pierced over and over by a million knives. It flayed his frail human flesh until his spirit stood exposed: terrified, desperate, resolute – and invincible.

Dael could feel Corisand beginning to rally as the fresh energy poured into her. Slowly, step by step, the Phaerie were being driven back, and the gloating grin vanished from the face of their leader as his spell began to crumble beneath the onslaught of the Fialan's power. Her face ablaze with triumph, Corisand drove her brightening shield at her enemies and began to push them slowly back out of the cavern, crowding them into the tunnel beyond. Their horses were on the other side of the ravine. There was an almost sheer drop from the cave mouth to the river and rocks below. They had nowhere left to go.

Dael's spirits rose. Outnumbered though they were, it looked as though they might win after all. He'd begun to hope too soon. Suddenly the leader of the Phaerie reappeared in the cavern entrance, the cocky, feral grin back in place. 'You think you have us?'

'It looks that way to me.' Corisand replied evenly.

'And what of your friend, the Wizard? *We* have her – or had you forgotten? Lower your shield now and surrender to us, or we will cut her throat.'

19
~

GUARDIAN OF THE PORTAL

The Phaerie's words pierced the Windeye's shield as no magic could. She thought of Iriana, alone, blind and terrified, at the mercy of the enemy, and with a sick, sinking feeling in her stomach, realised that there was no hope for her friend. Even if she dropped her shield, the enemy would not release the Wizard. They would simply have three captives instead of one, and the Stone of Fate besides. Surrendering now, for Iriana's sake, would get everyone killed. But how could she live the rest of her life with the knowledge that she'd abandoned the closest of friends, the best of companions? Iriana had given the Windeye the Fialan. Without her, Corisand would never have won the Stone, and all would have been lost.

At that moment, the dreadful truth hit her. She could not think of friendship now, for guardianship of the Fialan had conferred a far greater responsibility upon her. All *would* be lost if the Phaerie took the Fialan and used it to bring Hellorin back – not only for the Xandim, but for the Magefolk too, and even the lowly mortal race. Wielding the power of the Stone of Fate, the Forest Lord could bestride the entire world.

She could not help Iriana.

She glanced away from the Phaerie, and down at Dael. 'I can't do it,' she said softly. 'Dael, I can't drop the shield, no matter what they do.'

She saw her own horror and dismay reflected in his face. 'No, Corisand! You can't just let them kill her.'

'How can I let them have the Stone of Fate? You know I dare not give it over into Phaerie hands – not without a fight.'

Corisand felt the Fialan's energy waver as Dael shrank from taking responsibility for the Wizard's death. 'Stop that!' she hissed. 'Stand firm, or you'll get us all killed.'

'I will not wait here all day,' the Phaerie snarled. 'Capitulate now – or your friend's blood will be on your hands.'

Corisand clenched her teeth, determined to prevent her emotions from showing on her face. 'I will not.'

'So be it then.' He shrugged, then suddenly that smug grin – oh, how Corisand was beginning to hate it – was back on his face. 'I lied about your friend, of course. Already she is being taken back to Eliorand where she will be questioned until every detail of this evil Wizardly plot is wrenched from her. Then—'

'Plot? What Wizardly plot?' the Windeye demanded in astonishment.

'Did you think we were unaware of your plans? The Lady Tiolani has told us everything.'

So that accursed Tiolani *had* betrayed them! Corisand threw all the power of her anger into her shields, desperate to drive these Phaerie out. She must escape, and try to get help to Iriana. But her anxiety gnawed at her concentration, and it seemed harder than ever to force her shield against the Phaerie defences and push them back. This was no good! She must think of another spell, a killing spell, one that she could perform in the eyeblink between dropping her shield and the inevitable attack by the enemy as soon as she did.

She had never used her magic to kill before.

'Help me, Dael,' she hissed. 'You heard him. Now our only chance of saving Iriana is to escape from here and get rid of as many of the enemy as possible. Don't falter now! Everything depends on you.'

He tried: she could feel the effort he was making, and see it on his face when she dared glance away from her foe. Nevertheless, Corisand could feel Dael weakening. The strains of carrying such a burden of powerful magic were far too great for a fragile mortal frame. His body had taken on a strange aura of energy, a form of translucence, as though he were drifting out of the world. His eyes seemed unfocused, fixed on some far-away vision, and the hand that held the Fialan had begun to tremble. 'What's happening, Dael? What are you seeing? Please, hold on a little longer – for all our sakes.'

Dael gasped for breath as his heart raced and laboured in his chest. The power of the Stone was consuming him now, taking him over, sending spasms of pain, pulses of heat, shocks of searing cold through-out his body. Corisand, the cavern, the enemy, all faded away as his vision was obscured by a blinding emerald light. There was no way, now, that he could let go of the Fialan. It had consumed him; taken him over. He could feel it hollowing him out: soon there would be nothing left but a crumbling shell with a core of incandescent magic.

Am I dying?

Is this what it's like?

Dael forgot his companions, forgot his peril. If he were truly dying he wished, oh how he wished, that he could look upon his beloved Athina once more, so that her kindly, lovely, otherworldly face would be the last thing he saw.

All at once the blazing radiance of the Fialan dimmed and Dael's vision grew dark. He felt the Stone roll from his limp fingers, and a further wave of weakness swept over him, coupled with a terrible, wrenching sense of loss. He seemed to lose all hold upon himself: his memory, his identity, his emotions vanished, and his last thought, as consciousness left him, was baffled anger that the Stone, which had been helping to save him and his friends, had killed him instead. Then he was falling away from the world – or the world was falling away from him …

With no idea how he had come to be there, Dael found himself standing in front of a massive, carven door so silvered and weathered by time that it was impossible to tell whether it was formed from wood or some ancient stone. He blinked, shaking his head. What in all Creation had happened to him? Last thing he remembered, he'd been in the cave, with Corisand, dying … Curious, he put out a hand, and as he touched the door it swung open, away from him, inviting him to enter the shadowy space beyond. All around him was a dim and formless void. There was nowhere else to go. Moving like a sleepwalker, compelled by *something* – he knew not what – Dael stepped through the eternal doorway, and the door swung slowly shut behind him.

For a moment he was in utter darkness but, strangely, he found himself devoid of fear – in fact, cleansed of all emotions save a faint, stirring curiosity to find out what lay beyond. He took a single step forward and, as if triggered by his movement, a faint light grew around him. Looking round, he found himself in a narrow cutting, with steep, rocky banks overgrown with moss and fern rising up past head height on either side. Overhead the sky was black and starless;

the only light came from a glimmering, silvery mist that swirled and flowed along the ground, hiding his feet and the path on which he stood. The air was chill and heavy, laden with fine droplets of water that prickled against his shivering skin.

Dael took a tentative step forward: had he imagined it, or had the faint gleam of the mist brightened, just a little? He took another, experimental stride, and the radiance responded, growing slightly stronger once more. Intrigued now, he tried a backward step – and the light went out completely, plunging him into utter blackness.

All right then: something in this place wanted him to go onward, and unless he wanted to stay here for ever, he had better do just that.

He had the oddest conviction that time had ceased to exist for him as soon as he'd walked through those mysterious doors. With a flash of panic he realised that he was no longer breathing, and the absence of his heartbeat seemed an echoing void, for he had been accustomed to hearing it since he had lain in his mother's womb. Strangely, the fear vanished very quickly, as though it had been nothing but a reflex left over from his former existence, an old habit that had outlived its use. A fatalistic calm seeped through him: he ceased to worry about his companions' problems and perils, about the fate of the Fialan, about any danger to himself. The only thing he could still feel, the one overwhelming emotion that he refused to let go, no matter what, was the everlasting love he felt for the Cailleach. 'Athina, help me,' he whispered, though he knew full well that she had been trapped in her own realm and could not come to him. Her very name, however, seemed to warm his heart, and drive him onward to meet his fate.

As he went on, he found that the levels of the high rock walls on either side were gradually dropping and the path was opening out, until finally he found himself standing in a landscape of gently roll-ing hills. In the distance he saw a bright and twinkling spark of light, which came closer and closer to reveal itself at last as a lantern held in the hand of a strange, bearded figure, stooped as if with age and leaning on a tall, gnarled staff as he walked along. He was shrouded in a dark grey cloak, and his features were hidden in the shadows of a deep, cowled hood. The mysterious apparition stopped in front of Dael. He did not speak, but simply gestured for the young man to follow, then turned and began to walk back the way he had come.

There was no choice but to obey: Dael found his feet beginning to move of their own accord, and reluctantly he stumbled after the sinister being, drawn on by some unbreakable compulsion to an unknown destiny.

The hooded one led the way into the hills, and as they went, Dael noticed that the sky was now glittering with unfamiliar stars. Gradually the silvery, silken mist vanished from around his feet, and he found himself walking on short, springy turf, in the midst of a silence so profound that it set up a hollow roaring in his ears. As he trudged on he found that the memories of his past, of his friends and the danger they were in, were slipping away from him. He tried to recall the exhilaration of his first, wild, airborne ride courtesy of Corisand's flying spell, the delicate, chiselled bone structure of Iriana's proud and rather serious face, the vivid blue of Melik's eyes, but they eluded him, as though he were trying to hold on to mist. Even his physical body seemed less substantial. When he lifted his hands his flesh seemed to have a shimmering translucency, and he could discern the faint outlines of the horizon through the trans-figured flesh. Nothing was as it should be, and the strangeness twisted in his guts like a knife.

Dael felt as if his old life was being sloughed away – save for one solitary anchor to reality. Athina did not leave him. Even as his other memories became more vague and evanescent, her face stood out with greater clarity in his mind, her glorious eyes kind and loving, her voice low and musical, her arms outstretched to hold him tightly and prevent him from slipping away. Whatever this place was, it seemed to have no power over his benefactress, and as he clung to every remembrance of their life together like a talisman, the images of his other companions became clear and bright once more.

Somehow, Dael knew that he mustn't let his strange guide know that he'd been able to hold on to his old life despite all compulsion to forget. He continued to stumble along like a sleepwalker, keeping his eyes unfocused and his expression as slack and blank as he could possibly make it.

After some indefinable time, his eyes latched on to something new in the unchanging, monotonous landscape of curving hillsides and shadowy vales. On the brow of the nearest swelling rise was a darker shadow which, as he drew closer, resolved itself into a small copse of gnarled and ancient trees, their knotted, tangled boughs forming a seemingly impenetrable barrier. As the hooded figure approached, however, he lifted his staff on high, and the trees straightened, standing proud and tall, lifting their branches high in an arch to form a path into the unseen mysteries of the centre.

Dael did not want to enter, but that uncanny compulsion that had dominated him for all of this strange journey still held him in thrall. It drove him on, following in the footprints of his guide as they passed between the ranks of trees. Finally they came to the heart of the grove. Here the land dropped into a slight hollow, which cupped a pool of dark and shining water, with the trees thronging close all around its mossy banks, as though standing guard and protecting it with their overhanging boughs. Though Dael no longer held the Fialan, enough of its power remained coursing through his mind and body to tell him that this place was alive with an unearthly magic: an oddly alien force, unlike anything that either Corisand or Iriana could conjure. It hummed in his ears, tingled on his skin and surged like a tide in his blood, reminding him of Athina: it felt like, and yet unlike, her power, but the similarity was sufficient to let him cling to that slender thread of familiarity like a drowning man clutching tightly to a rope.

Dael was so caught up in the mystery of this place that he had almost forgotten his guide – until a sudden movement in the corner of his eye made him start, and take an involuntary step backward. The hooded stranger had turned towards him, and now raised the silvery lantern high. For a frozen moment the two of them stood in tableau and, though he could see nothing but darkness within the shadows of the cowl, the young man was aware of an intense scrutiny by the unseen eyes whose stare seemed to brand his flesh as though someone had held a candle flame to his skin.

Suddenly, Dael felt a stab of annoyance. Why, this – this *being* was nothing but a coward to stare so hard at him, while hiding its own face within that hood. Boldly he glared back, and had the unpleasant sensation that he had locked eyes with the shrouded figure. He refused to give in, however, but held his ground, unwilling to turn his eyes away. He was no longer the beaten, lowly, terrified human slave he had once been: he was Athina's protégé now, and the friend of Wizard and Windeye. He had held in his hand the Stone of Fate itself, and known more power than any of his race had ever experienced before ... Gritting his teeth, he maintained the deadly tension of the two linked stares, and stoutly refused to give in.

Abruptly the tension broke, and Dael felt a surge of triumph as the other looked away. Though he could hardly believe he had beaten this mysterious, powerful being, his elation turned to dread as a chilling hiss came from the depths of the cowl. The figure gestured towards the pool and, for the first time, spoke. Its voice was like a blade that flayed Dael's flesh, like spiders crawling in his blood, like the raw, chill darkness of the cruellest winter's night.

'So brave for a mortal. Bold indeed – but that will avail you nothing in this place, between the worlds, at the Well of Souls. Brave or craven, soon or late, all must pass this way in the end – yes, even one who has known power far beyond the wildest imaginings of your pitiful kind.'

He gestured once more towards the pool, and spoke again. 'All the magic of the Fialan cannot help you now, little mortal. All that is past and gone, a part of the lifetime that is over. You have passed into my realm now, the realm of Death. You must abandon your old existence, your old memories, your old loves and ties, much as a serpent sheds its skin. You must forget them all for ever, and enter the Well of Souls, that you might be reborn into a new and different life.'

Dael stood frozen in horror. Abandon his friends? Lose even his recollections of them, for ever? Even the precious memory of Athina?

'Never!' he shouted. 'I won't desert my friends. I won't forget Athina – not ever! And I won't go into your accursed pool – suppose we stay here till the end of time!'

Death gave a sinister chuckle. 'Oh, will you not?' he said softly. 'Well, you are the most amusing mortal to have passed this way in many a long age – but enough is enough. What makes you think you have a choice, you lowly little human? Beings far greater and more powerful than you have been forced to pass this way, and none have bested me yet, or escaped their fate. I tire of this nonsense. You *will* go into the Well.'

Without warning he advanced on Dael, suddenly grown taller; towering, menacing, looming above the quaking mortal. Dael took a hasty step backwards, and turned to flee – but there was no escape. He ran head first into some kind of invisible barrier and fell to the ground, half-dazed. It was as if a wall had been constructed around the Well of Souls, leaving him with nowhere to go but into those sinister dark depths.

Unable to reach the trees, and with nothing else to hold on to, Dael dropped to his knees and dug his hands as hard as he could into the soft, yielding moss around the pool. 'I – won't – go,' he shouted. 'I *won't*!'

The spectre let out a snarl, and dropped his staff and lantern. He swooped down on the desperate young man, arms outstretched to grasp and hold. His long, bony fingers dug into Dael's flesh like iron talons, hauling him bodily from the ground with terrifying strength and lifting him high in the air. Dael writhed and twisted in a last, hopeless attempt to escape his fate, but his efforts only made his tormentor hold on tighter and intensified the pain. Death swung him backwards, preparing to throw him down into the Well of Souls ...

'Athina, help!' Dael cried. 'Help me, please!'

'I am here.' Her beautiful voice came out of nowhere; strong, calm, kind. Dael opened his eyes to see her standing on the brink of the pool, between Death and the water. She had grown tall as the towering spectre, but her form was less solid: she appeared shimmering, wraithlike and translucent – but at least she was there, and Dael dared to hope at last.

'Put him down, my brother,' she said firmly. 'This one is mine.'

'Step aside, Cailleach,' the spectre snarled, but he lowered the young man and set him on the ground between them. Dael wanted to run to Athina, but he found he could not move. To his frustration he was forced to remain rooted to the spot, though she was almost near enough to touch.

'All mortals in this place belong to me,' he went on. 'You have no power here, and you may not intervene.'

'This mortal is special, Siris. He has lived under my protection—'

'Oh, so this is your little pet,' Death sneered.

A flash of anger, glimpsed then gone, lit Athina's eyes. 'So Uriel has been here. I might have guessed.'

'He has. And he told me he had exiled you into your own realm, beneath the Timeless Lake.'

'Exiled? I may be prevented from entering the living worlds that my other siblings wrought – for the present, at least.' From the grim tone of her voice, Dael suspected that she did not intend to tolerate that obstacle for ever. 'However, this place is different, is it not?' she continued. 'Here there is neither life nor death, it is betwixt and between. Your realm is a gateway, Siris, and you are its keeper – and such portals hold a special power all their own.'

'And who knows that better than I?' Siris snapped. 'You may have been able to come here, Athina, and it is glad I am to see you – but it changes nothing. The mortal has come into my realm now, and is no longer yours but mine.'

'Not quite, my brother. No mortal has passed as Dael has passed, filled with the extraordinary magic of the Stone of Fate. Though its power proved too much for his frail mortal frame he is still linked to it, bound to it. He must return.'

Dael felt a sickening wrench of disappointment, as though someone had punched him hard in the gut. For a wonderful moment he had hoped, oh how he'd hoped, that Athina had come for him, that she might take him with her. But it was clearly not to be.

'This cannot be true.' For the first time, Death sounded unsure.

'Can it not?' Athina smiled grimly. 'Would you care to put it to the test, my brother? Do you dare? For if Dael is catapulted into another world, still linked to the power of the Fialan, there will be such an explosion of energy as will destroy the Well of Souls for ever. And then what will happen to the dead, whose fates are in your keeping?' Her voice became softer, more cajoling. 'Those beings who must pass from one life to another, leaving all they have come to know and love, may see you as evil, Siris, but you are not. On the contrary, you are their guardian, and your role is vital to their continuance. When the rest of us were busy fashioning our worlds and populating them with life, only you gave thought to what would happen to the living essences of our creations once their mortal shells had perished, or had been destroyed by some sort of misadventure. You realised that we could not carry on indefinitely, creating living souls from the very energy of the Cosmos, and you were also the first to realise that life, once created, can never be destroyed.'

She smiled at him, her eyes soft with memories. 'How you were mocked by your siblings, for not creating worlds as the rest of us did. You were derided as lazy, as stupid, incompetent – particularly by Uriel, as I recall – yet none of them ever saw that what you were creating here was a vital foundation of all that they achieved.'

'You never mocked me.' For the first time, Dael was sure he had heard a softening in the spectre's voice. 'You always understood what I was about.'

'And because I *do* understand, you must realise that I do not make this request of you lightly. It is not only that I came to love this mortal above all others – it is for the sakes of all his kind, and all those other beings who use the Well of Souls. What will become of them all if the Well is destroyed? This is not a situation that any of us could have foreseen, my brother. Dael is tied to his world by a power not of our creating. He *must* return there, and remain until that power sets him free.'

Though the spectre's face still remained hidden, once more Dael became aware of his intense scrutiny. Long moments passed, and them Death sighed, and shrank down to normal size. 'Very well, Athina. It shall be as you say. I dare not risk the destruction of the Well of Souls. When your mortal enters the waters, I will return him to his own world forthwith.'

A great tension seemed to go out of Athina, and she too let herself return to the same height as the others. 'Thank you, Siris. Thank you for believing me.' Her mouth twisted wryly. 'You were always a better listener than Uriel.'

'I always loved you better, my sister.' There was such sudden, unexpected warmth in that dry and dusty voice that Dael stared at him in wide-eyed astonishment. 'And I was never jealous of you, as he was,' Siris continued. 'For what it is worth, I informed him that he was wrong and presumptuous to exile you as he did, that he had no right to do so, and that he should mind his own affairs instead of interfering in yours.'

He shrugged. 'Uriel always did take entirely too much upon himself, and we have never seen eye to eye on anything, that I can remember. He hates that you have always been a better Creator than he. Oh, he is good with structure: rock and stone he knows, the foundations and the bones of worlds – but you, with your innate compassion and sympathy, always understood the interlinking web of life, in all its diverse and amazing complexity. Uriel's attempts to emulate what you do were never quite adequate.' He shrugged again. 'Consider the Moldai, for example. Are they mountains? Giants? Do they really belong in the Elsewhere, or in the mundane realms? Consider the Dwelven, or their servants of old the Gaeorn, those monstrous rock eaters with the mandibles of diamond. All exist apart from the plants and forest, birds, beasts and the higher, more complex forms of life that you created. He could never achieve a fraction of the wonders you have wrought. He lacks the skill, the patience – and, most importantly, the heart. You pour your love into all of your creations, Athina. You hold back nothing, and it shows. Even this insignificant mortal ...'

'This one is far from insignificant.' Athina went to Dael, and suddenly her form became less ethereal. As she put her arms around him, he could feel the living, vibrant warmth of her, just as he had of old.

'He looks the same as all the rest to me,' Siris said.

Athina hugged Dael again. 'Some things were simply meant to be,' she said. As they embraced, he felt her slip something into his pocket, and spoke directly into his mind, something she had never done before. 'When you enter the Well, fill this vial with the water. Keep it secret. Keep it safe. These waters have many strange powers. Who knows, they may bring you back to me one day.'

Dael gasped, his hope blossoming anew – then he saw warning in her eyes and the barely perceptible shake of her head.

'Don't count on it,' she was telling him, as clearly as if, once again, she had put the words into his mind. 'Don't hope too much.'

His heart sank again, yet now, at least, he had a faint spark of hope to sustain him through the sorrow of another parting.

Siris, looking at them, sighed. 'Enough,' he said gruffly. 'Finish saying goodbye to your pet, Athina. I will send him back, and perhaps we can put this unfortunate business behind us.'

Athina nodded and stepped back. 'Farewell, brave Dael,' she said softly. 'Do not lose heart. All will be well.'

'Farewell,' Dael answered. If she believed him to be brave, then brave he would be, and if she told him all would be well, he would trust her. Taking a deep breath, he approached the dark and silent pool – and stopped abruptly, as searing beams of light fountained up from its surface. But all would be well. Athina had promised him. Shielding his eyes from the brilliant light with his hand, he stepped to the brink, knelt, looked down into the Well of Souls – and gasped.

Beneath the unruffled surface of those deceptive waters was a dizzying vortex, a spinning whirlpool of stars that swirled endlessly down into infinity. He tried to draw back, but the Well had caught him. The whirling took hold of him, drawing him downward until suddenly he toppled into the water, which closed over his head. The vortex was pulling him downward, and Dael know he only had an instant in which to act. He snatched Athina's little vial from his pocket and pulled out the stopper, replacing it quickly and hoping that the vial had time to fill. Then all at once he was slamming back into his body with a shattering force that sucked a huge, wheezing gulp of air into his lungs, like the first breath of a newborn. His eyes flew open in shock – and there he was, back in the cave.

20

~

MIXED FEELINGS

As she struggled to maintain her shields against the Phaerie, Corisand felt everything slipping away from her. 'How does it feel to lose?' the Phaerie leader taunted. 'For you've lost already. How else do you think we found you here? Lady Tiolani exposed your little nest of plotters and gave us the location of your secret lurking place, and once we've taken *you*, we'll have you all. You're weakening, you're beaten, and you know it. Soon you'll find out what it means to cross the Phaerie!'

Corisand gasped. He had to be speaking the truth. Tiolani had betrayed them all! And what of Taine and Aelwen? Imprisoned? Tortured? Dead? What of Iriana? Gone, captured, at the mercy of a pitiless enemy. Dael ... Grief and guilt wrenched at her heart. Destroyed by the power of the Fialan, Dael was gone too, on a darker and more lonely road. She need not glance down at the crumpled form that lay grey-faced and still at her feet to know that he was dead. She had asked him to hold on to the Stone for longer than he could bear, and she had killed him. And for what?

She had lost the Stone of Fate when Dael succumbed, and could no longer use its power to help her. It had rolled away somewhere when it fell from his hand: into some hole or crevice, probably, since she could no longer see its glow. Forced to give all her concentration to her shield, she was unable to search for it – but the Phaerie had seen it now, and had sensed its power. Once she was vanquished, they would have all the time in the world to find it, for without the Stone, she was losing the battle. The Phaerie were too many for her. They could just keep on wearing away at her, until she faded through hunger or thirst, or they finally sapped her strength.

228

The end came without warning. Suddenly her shield burst apart, the enemy came streaming through, and she was overwhelmed.

Less than a month ago, Aelwen had believed that she'd never see Taine again. Their reunion, beyond all hope and expectation, had transformed her life, and the joy that filled her, the jolt of pure, bright pleasure that she experienced every time she saw him, were the most wonderful feelings she had ever known. So she had never expected that, after such a short time, she would be cursing his name.

Aelwen was a horsewoman. She had worked in the Forest Lord's stables since she was a girl. She had the strong legs of a rider, the strong arms, back and shoulders that came from years of controlling powerful horses, but it took an entirely different set of muscles to slog on foot through miles and miles of endless forest, to wade chest deep, or even worse, to swim across freezing cold rivers, to plough through stretches of mosquito-infested, glutinous muskeg and to hack a route through tangled undergrowth with briars tangling in her hair and tearing at her skin, and branches whipping across her face ...

Right at this minute, Aelwen thought, glaring at Taine as he slipped through the trees as effortlessly as a shadow, she would have gladly traded her lover for her horse.

It was all very well for him. In his years as a fugitive and a spy, he had grown accustomed to this form of rough travel, and become a very skilled woodsman. But they had been on the march for the best part of two days now, following the river staying on the Wizards' side to avoid detection, with the spectral forms of the Dwelven thronging around them, producing wave after wave of anger and hate that beat against Taine and Aelwen remorselessly, draining their flagging spirits even as the forest was wearing down their bodies.

It had begun to feel as if they would never reach the ravine in which the others should be hiding out. At first, Aelwen had been able to apport herself and Taine over the rougher sections of the terrain, but the effort had proved to be increasingly exhausting for her, requiring longer and longer rests afterwards, until they had decided that they would ultimately make better time on their own aching feet. (Aelwen was wearing riding boots, and the pain of her blistered toes and heels was growing worse by the hour.)

Kaldath, despite all the years he carried, fared better. Somehow, his close connection with the Dwelven spirits allowed them to carry him along, and his body, neither truly alive nor dead, but caught by Hellorin in a strange, magical limbo of immortality, did not feel the strain of all the hard travel. He also was immune to the oppressive miasma of emotion that emanated from the ghosts, which was sapping so much of Taine and Aelwen's energy.

'We're almost there,' Taine had said that morning, when they had risen before sunrise to resume their grim march. 'It's shouldn't be all that much further.' He had led them to a reasonably safe place to cross the border between the Wizard and Phaerie realms, where the Carnim river spread out in a series of riffles interspersed with rocks and gravel bars. The water had still been waist deep in places, however, and had contained a number of hidden dips and crevices where a false step could result in a soaking. Despite using a drying spell on herself when she reached the far side, Aelwen still felt slightly damp, with her hair hanging in rat-tails, and her clothing stiff with silt and mud.

Hours had passed since then, and now the sun had sunk down behind the treetops once more. Stealthily, they crept along, with even greater caution than ever, now that they were on the northern, Phaerie side of the river. Suddenly Taine, walking ahead, stopped and raised his hand. 'Almost there,' he whispered. 'Look.'

Aelwen followed his pointing hand towards the river, and saw the extraordinary, bicoloured waters, the light and dark streams running alongside one another.

'We're finally near the confluence of the Carnim and the Snowstream,' Taine whispered. 'The gorge is just ahead.' He turned to the ancient guardian of the Dwelven ghosts. 'Kaldath, can you send some of the spirits into the ravine to scout for us? Have them check the woods along the top of the cliffs, too, on either side. I want to make sure we're not walking into a trap.'

'Of course.' Kaldath walked a little way apart, and Aelwen saw the air roil and shimmer as the Dwelven spirits clustered around him in response to his mental call. Then suddenly they were gone, and the feelings of oppression, of sorrow and anger in the air all vanished. Kaldath came walking back to the Hemifae. 'It should not take them long to find out what you need to know.'

'In that case, I'm going to make the most of what time we have.' With a sigh of relief, Aelwen sank down onto the soft leaf litter, propped her aching back against a tree trunk, and stretched out her legs. She took her water flask and a strip of jerky out of the pouch at her belt, took a swig, then began to chew her way through the leathery strip of dried meat.

Taine sat down beside her and put an arm around her shoulders. 'You've done well,' he told her. 'It's a tough journey through deep forest for someone who isn't used to travelling for long distances on foot. Hopefully, once we join the others, you'll be back in your element, astride a horse.'

Aelwen grimaced. 'I wouldn't count on it. Tiolani was captured, remember, and we were forced to leave her behind. Without her flying magic we won't be going anywhere in a hurry. Of course,' she added in brighter tones, 'Iriana and the others – if they made it – should have brought their mounts with them, so at least we won't have to slog the entire way to Eliorand on foot.' Then her expression relapsed into gloom. 'That is, if they succeeded in winning the Fialan and getting back from the Elsewhere, and if they managed to get here, and if the Phaerie haven't caught them already.'

'Well, we'll soon find out.' Taine was looking across at Kaldath who had risen to his feet as the air around him grew turbulent once more. The ancient one stood for a moment, listening intently, then he rejoined Taine and Aelwen, looking grim. 'The Phaerie are here,' he said gravely, 'and so are your friends, as far as I can ascertain from what I have been told. According to the Dwelven there seems to be some sort of fight going on inside the cave. We had better get up there quickly.'

Taine looked at Aelwen. 'Have you strength enough for one last apport?'

'Into a *cave*? Somewhere I've never been before? We could be entombed in solid rock!'

'I've been there before, many times,' Taine replied. 'You can take the placement from my mind.'

'But if the place is full of people, both the Phaerie and our friends, how can we know where there'll be a clear space?'

'Wait a little while,' Kaldath said flatly. 'The Dwelven will take care of the Phaerie.'

Hands seized Corisand roughly, holding her tight enough to bruise. She struggled at first in the grip of her captors, but when her efforts earned her nothing but blows, she finally desisted and hung limp in their grasp, her face, ribs and stomach throbbing fiercely. Her mind, however, was still working with the rapidity of terror.

I'll act cowed and scared – that won't be difficult. Surely they'll drop their guard at some point, and there'll be a chance to escape. I just need to buy myself some time to work out a way—

The Phaerie captain – Nychan, she recognised him from her days with the Wild Hunt – might as well have been reading her mind. 'Bind her tightly, and someone signal across the gorge for the horses to be brought, and another net. I don't know who, or what this one is, but the sooner we get her safely back to Eliorand, the sooner Cordain will be able to start finding out what she knows.'

He was just turning away from her when it happened.

Out of nowhere, Corisand was struck by an oppressive, gut-freezing sense of dread. Waves of rage and hatred seemed to come at her out of the empty air, striking fear into her heart as even the Phaerie had failed to do. Then suddenly strange, spectral creatures poured into the cavern, dropping from the ceiling, oozing from the walls, erupting out of the floor. An odd shivering in the air, like the heat rising from a courtyard on a summer day, made the apparitions visible against the surroundings and in these roiling shadows, flashing out like lightning through storm clouds, was the deadly glitter of fangs and claws, and eyes that burned with a white-hot rage.

The Phaerie started screaming as the invaders swarmed over them. Blood sprayed and spattered as great rents and gashes appeared in their bodies, their limbs and faces. The discordant, high-pitched, screeching shrieks of triumph that came from the attackers ripped the air, mingling with the Phaerie cries of agony as eyes were gouged, flesh was torn and bones were snapped.

Her captors let go of Corisand, who dropped to the ground and curled up into a ball. The creatures seemed to be concentrating on the Phaerie and leaving herself and the still form of Dael unscathed, but she wasn't about to risk attracting their attention. Besides, this way she didn't have to see the hideous carnage that was taking place all around.

Hours seemed to stretch by while she lay there, but in reality, it could only have been a matter of minutes before the screaming stopped, the shrieks of triumph died away and the sickening waves of rage and hatred dissipated from the atmosphere. All that remained was the stench of ordure and blood, and the silence of the Phaerie dead.

After a while, the Windeye finally plucked up the courage to open her eyes and look around, and what she saw in the pale remains of

Iriana's dying magelight brought nausea flooding into her throat. Mangled corpses lay on the floor, limbs missing or badly askew, as if the bodies had been tossed carelessly aside. Only she and Dael had been left untouched, and Dael was— Her mouth fell open. 'You're *alive!*'

Dael, though spattered with Phaerie blood, was sitting up and looking around in horror at the scene of carnage. Then he turned his gaze to her. 'What in perdition happened here?' he demanded, his eyes huge and round. 'What did you *do?*'

Corisand began to deny doing anything, but was interrupted by the sound of voices coming from the outer part of the cave, frantically calling her name, and those of Dael and Iriana. Relief swept over her. It was Taine and Aelwen! 'We're in here,' she called.

They appeared in the entrance to the smaller cave, Aelwen looking pale and shaken at the sight of all the dead. 'Corisand, Dael. Thank providence you're safe. Are you all right?' As quickly as the slippery floor would allow she picked her way through the corpses and knelt down beside the Windeye. 'Have you been hurt?'

'I'm all right.' Corisand grabbed Aelwen in a bone-crushing hug. 'I thought you'd been captured,' she said. 'Tiolani—'

'So she did betray us.' Aelwen's expression tightened with pain. 'Are you sure you're not hurt? You look terrible.'

Corisand realised she must be as gore-spattered as Dael, and hastened to reassure the Horsemistress. 'I'm just so tired – I couldn't hold the Phaerie off any more. Then those dreadful, dreadful – *things* – attacked out of nowhere, but they only hurt the Phaerie, and left us alone.' She paused, looking narrowly at Aelwen. 'You don't seem at all surprised by any of this. Do you know what they were, those beings?'

'Never mind all that – did you get it? Do you have the Fialan?'

Taine, in the meantime, had been helping Dael to his feet. 'They didn't hurt me,' the young man was explaining, 'but only because they thought I was already dead, and—'

'Where's Iriana?' Taine interrupted.

'They took her,' Corisand said. 'She was outside my shield, and I couldn't keep them away from her. They took her away, back to Eliorand.'

Taine spat out a violent curse. 'We're going after them,' he snapped, already turning to leave the cave. 'How much start do they have?'

Aelwen leapt to her feet. 'Plague take Tiolani! Without her fly-ing spell, we'll never catch them. Quick – we'll explain everything else later. We have to get across the ravine. Maybe there's probably enough of the spell remaining on the Phaerie horses to get us to Eliorand.'

'I can do better than that,' Corisand said. 'I do have the Fialan and – the Fialan! Where is it? It rolled away somewhere.' She looked wildly around the cave, daunted by the idea of scrabbling among the mangled Phaerie corpses in search of the stone.

Taine had no such compunction. 'Where did it fall?'

'Around here, near the wall somewhere, I think,' Dael replied.

Taine squatted down. 'There's a natural opening down here, just a small crevice – ouch!' He snatched his hand back with an oath and looked in astonishment at the bleeding scratches. 'There's something in there.'

'Melik,' Dael cried. He knelt down by the aperture and called to the cat, his voice low and coaxing.

'We don't have time for this.' Taine pulled a pair of leather gloves from his belt and thrust his arm back down the hole, pulling a snarl-ing, spitting, very frightened feline out by the scruff. 'Here.' He dumped Melik into Dael's arms, where the cat fought and struggled to be free. Dael bore the scratches without complaint, and in a little while Melik calmed and lay trembling in his arms.

Corisand, in the meantime, had spotted the Stone of Fate, which had been dislodged from the same hole when Taine had pulled the animal out. 'I've found it!' she cried. As her fingers closed around the pulsing green gem she felt the power flooding back into her, along with a euphoria so intense that it brought tears to her eyes. Then at the edge of her vision there was a movement, and she swung around to see a strange old man standing in the entrance to the cave. Without thinking, she raised the Fialan and summoned its powers to strike.

'Corisand, no!' Aelwen shouted, grabbing her arm. 'This is Kaldath. We met him in the forest. He's a friend.'

'As I said, we'll explain everything, but we've got to get after Iriana right now,' Taine said urgently. 'Those accursed Phaerie have a head start on us, there's no time to waste. What if the flying spell wears off?'

'I was trying to tell you,' the Windeye said. 'After you left I dis-covered how to cast my own flying spell, using the Fialan. As far as that's concerned, we're no longer dependent on Tiolani.'

Aelwen let out a whoop, and hugged her. 'Corisand, you are truly amazing.'

'Indeed you are,' said Taine. 'Kaldath, can you ride?'

'I can. And wherever I go, the Dwelven will follow.'

'Then let's get moving,' Aelwen said. 'The Phaerie have left their horses on the other side of the ravine, so if you can perform the flying spell, Corisand, I'll take Rosina across and bring back mounts for everyone.'

'No, it'll be easier if I transform back into a horse and fly you across the gorge in relays. We have Rosina too, so it won't take very long. We'll have more room to get organised on the other side, and when we're ready, it will be far easier to take off from there.'

In only took a very short time to get everyone across the gorge, and select horses for those who had none. The remainder of the steeds would follow their Windeye, obeying her call, and Corisand suddenly realised that she had made a start on freeing her people – albeit only a handful. The rest must wait. For now, the most urgent consideration was saving Iriana's life. Dael rode Rosina once more, with Melik in his basket strapped securely to the saddle. Taine, Aelwen and the mysterious Kaldath had the best of the Phaerie mounts including, in Aelwen's case, an enormous flame-red chestnut stallion that had belonged to Nychan. Corisand, who had changed back into her equine form, had the Fialan fastened securely around her neck once more, in a makeshift bag fashioned from fabric torn from the tail of Aelwen's shirt, and a length of spare thong from one of the packs. They had decided to head back to Eliorand in the straightest line possible and as fast as they could. Though there was little hope that they could catch the Wizard before she reached the city, they were determined to try.

Taine raised an arm. 'Let's go,' he cried, and urging their horses forward, they bounded into the air, and headed north in search of Iriana.

21

~

RETRIBUTION

Iriana's stomach lurched as she swung giddily in the air, and the meshes of the net bit into her skin. Her head throbbed, and she felt sick and sore all over. She had no idea what had become of her friends, or of Melik, her eyes. Had they survived? The odds had not looked good when she'd been taken. For certain, they could do nothing to come to her aid.

She was alone, blind, helpless. Terrified.

This was exactly what Sharalind and Zybina had been trying to protect her from all her life. The nightmare. The disaster that could happen if she lost all the animals who let her utilise their gift of sight. But if she could only survive to see her foster mother and Sharalind again, she could put up with having them say 'I told you so.' Iriana knew better than to give up, however. She had been in a similar position when the Phaerie assassin had attacked in the forest, and she had found a way to survive then.

She would now.

She wracked her brains for a way to escape her predicament, but all she had were questions.

How long had she been unconscious?

They were probably taking her to Eliorand, but how long would it take to get there?

Had the others been taken captive too – or were they dead?

No, she would not think of that. She had to believe her friends were still alive, that they had managed to escape somehow. That was the only way she could hold on to her own hope.

How many of her captors were carrying the net? Dael had told her of his own capture during the Wild Hunt, and she suspected that the scenario would be similar, with four of the Phaerie, on their flying steeds, carrying the net aloft. Were the others with them? It seemed very quiet, with few noises of harnesses creaking and horses breathing. She could not be sure, but she suspected that the rest of the enemy were elsewhere.

Suddenly, it dawned on her that the Phaerie *were* flying, and that could only mean one thing. Iriana bit back a curse. Tiolani had turned out to be a traitor after all.

Iriana knew her only hope was to think hard and act fast. Very well, then, her first priority must be sight. If she could only see, she might stand a chance of defending herself, and if, better still, she could manage to gain control over one or more of the beasts, she might even cause enough chaos to drive her captors out of the sky; for until she reached the ground, she would be helpless.

Though it was hard to concentrate between her anger at Tiolani, her fear of what the Phaerie would do to her, her aching head and the nauseating swing and sway of the net, she began to extend her consciousness outward then still further out, trying to make contact with the minds of the Phaerie flying steeds. As she encountered their thoughts, she had a sense that there were four of them, flying in a diamond-shaped formation, with one in the lead, one on either side and one behind.

Initially, Iriana tried to impose her will upon the mind of the leading horse, but it proved very resistant to such outside influence, plunging in the air and shaking its head furiously, as if trying to dislodge the unwelcome intruder. The rider cursed, tightening the reins cruelly, and Iriana hastily switched to the animal on her left-hand side.

Ah, this was better; a mare, more gentle and amenable than her initial choice. Having gained a foothold, the Wizard waited a little, letting the horse get used to her presence, then gently took control of its vision. Oh, what relief to be able to see again – though her heart sank at what she saw. Though Eliorand was not yet in sight, the northern mountains had grown a great deal closer, and the snow-capped peaks now dominated the sky.

It was high time she acted.

Holding tightly to the meshes of the net, Iriana took a firm grip with her mind on the mare's consciousness. She wanted to keep her vision steady in what was to come. Controlling a horse was entirely different from influencing a cat, a dog or a bird of prey, all of which were predators. It was much easier, however, to plant a suggestion that was completely in tune with an animal's nature. Horses were prey animals, their key motivation was fear. Because the equine spent its entire life primed to run, to escape, it was a simple matter for the Wizard to trigger panic in the leading mount's mind.

Danger! Run! Flee!

The net gave a lurch and started swinging as the horse tried to bolt. The animal continued to plunge and shake its head wildly, desperate to get away from the fear with which Iriana had infected it, but with a great effort, the rider wrenched it back under control and kept it in position.

At that point, the Wizard realised, with a sinking heart, that it was no good. She couldn't control the mare she was using for vision as well as the leading mount whose mind she was filling with fear. She would never manage to subvert all four animals at once – at least, not enough to overcome the riders' control. Though she frantically tried to think of another plan, terror and panic clouded her racing thoughts, and she could discover no way out. Through the horse's eyes she could see that the mountains were drawing nearer. She had very little time left in which to act, for once they had her in Eliorand, with no animals around that she could use for vision, escape would be impossible. Though she knew that there could not be any friends within range of her call, she sent out a cry for aid in mindspeech, hurling the thought out as far as she could into the void.

Her captors laughed, cruelly. 'That's right, little Wizard, cry for help,' one jeered.

'And much good may it do you,' laughed another. 'I should save my strength if I were you. Once we get you to the city you'll be—'

His words were cut off by a scream, wild, savage and shrill, from above. The shadow of mighty wings obscured the sun as a sleek, dark shape came plummeting out of the void, striking with wicked talons at the face of Iriana's tormentor. The Phaerie shrieked and let go of his reins, clutching at his eyes as blood spurted out from between his fingers. Suddenly, a new source of vision burst into Iriana's mind, and she was viewing the scene through wonderfully familiar eyes.

Boreas had not forgotten her.

Iriana's heart soared with joy and hope as the great eagle wheeled upward and stooped again, hitting the blinded rider hard and almost knocking him out of the saddle. Then another shrill cry cut through the air; another deadly winged shape came hurtling down. The eagle had brought his mate and both birds were working together, swooping at Iriana's captors and trying to drive them out of the sky.

Cries of anger and dismay came from the Phaerie. Two were wildly firing spells at the eagles while the third tried to draw a bow and steady his panicked mount at the same time. The fourth, blinded, was crouching low over his horse's neck, the blood still streaming from his face. He had given up all attempts at controlling the animal. It was fighting desperately to free itself from the net which was tethering it to the other three beasts, all of which were rearing and plunging wildly, pulling this way and that, terrified of the attacking birds.

Iriana was now in very real danger of being tossed out of the pitching net. She clung to the meshes with all her strength and swore at the Phaerie with every curse she could think of. Why didn't the stupid fools land, instead of trying to carry on an aerial battle with foes too fast and too fierce for them? The female eagle struck the Phaerie marksman from the side, knocking the bow from his hand then swooping away to avoid the spells being fired at her by his two companions. She then joined Boreas, who kept circling then darting in at the riders, using his beak and talons to devastating effect. Already their clothes were in tatters and blood was flowing from their backs and shoulders.

At last the Phaerie capitulated. 'Head down,' their leader yelled. 'We'll get a better shot at them from the ground.' The words were scarcely out of his mouth when Boreas struck him from behind. He lurched, lost a stirrup and hung over one side of his mount's neck, clinging desperately to keep from falling – until the female eagle, following her mate, struck him again. With a wail he fell, vanishing into the trees below, where his cry was suddenly cut short. Now the situation was perilous indeed, with the net swinging between four uncontrolled horses that were maddened with terror, and three mounted Phaerie who struggled desperately, with only two of them able to defend themselves and keep control of the situation. Fortunately, when they urged their mounts towards the ground, the animals were desperate to comply.

They hurtled down into the trees at a perilously steep angle and breakneck speed. Iriana curled up in the net, protecting her head. Using all her power, she wrought a shield around herself – and only just in time. Branches splintered as the net smashed into them and despite her shield Iriana was banged around until, bruised and dizzy, she hit the ground, with churning hooves and splattering mud all around her.

As the eagles followed her down, she found that her vision was no longer hampered by the trees. The blinded rider had apparently been knocked from the saddle during the descent and was nowhere to be seen, but there were still two others to contend with, so there was no time to lose. She was still tangled in the net; she needed to buy herself enough time to get herself free. 'Get the birds,' one of the Phaerie shouted, and she realised with a chill that now the enemy were on the ground, Boreas and his mate were sitting targets.

In a single flash of Fire magic she burned through the meshes of the net, then, scarcely taking time for a breath, she began to pelt her enemies with the last thing they would expect from a Wizard's Earth magic: a fusillade of fireballs that would stick to clothing and sear into flesh, while Boreas and his mate continued their onslaught from above. One of the Phaerie dodged behind her, out of the line of fire, but she hit the other with one of her flaming missiles. He fled into the trees screaming, his clothes and hair on fire, then suddenly the screams ceased and an ominous silence fell.

It was Boreas's eyesight that saved Iriana. Her own instinct would have been to look in the direction the Phaerie had fled, but the eagle's perspective from above took in the whole area, and in a flash of horror she saw the last foe charge her from behind, sword upraised. Even as she spun he was almost on top of her. Instinctively she hurled a fireball, catching him squarely in the middle of the chest. He reeled back, but his sword struck her on the shoulder, slicing a deep, slanting cut into the top of her arm. Though his clothes were on fire and he must have been in agony, he drew a dagger from his belt and came at her again. Sick and dizzy with pain, blood spurting from her arm, Iriana switched to her other hand and launched another ball of searing flame straight into his face. With a shriek he staggered forwards, his hair on fire and his face obscured by flame, and she leapt back from his flailing arms, sickened by the agony and torment she had wrought. He dropped to the ground and rolled, trying to douse the flames, but it was too late. His thrashing subsided and he went limp, his features a blackened ruin glimpsed through a barrier of fire.

The dreadful stench of burning flesh filled the air. Almost too late, the Wizard realised that she was in danger of setting the entire forest ablaze, and immolating herself in the process. Frantically, she doused her flames, using Air magic to deprive the fire of the vital air it needed in order to burn. The fire died away, leaving only the revolting stink of burned flesh drifting through the trees. Swamped by exhaustion, Iriana sank to the ground, weak and dizzy. She knew she should act quickly to staunch the blood that was pulsing from her arm, but right now she simply lacked the strength ...

I'll just rest here for a minute or two. Then I'll deal with it.

Guarded by the eagles, she lay down on the carpet of moss and leaves, her life blood pumping out onto the forest floor. Though a voice somewhere at the back of her mind seemed to be protesting, her thoughts were too hazy and confused to heed the warning. Her mind began to wander over the recent events. Today felt different to the terrible night when Esmon and Avithan had been lost, and she had driven her horse to trample and kill the Phaerie assassin. This time she had been attacked by enemies, and had done what she needed to survive.

A vision of Esmon came into her mind. It was just as if he was standing before her, real and solid, and he was smiling at her with approval. 'You did extremely well today, girl,' he said. 'I'm glad you were listening to all the lessons I tried to teach you when we were travelling, and I'm proud of you.' He held out a hand. 'I think you deserve to rest now, Iriana. Come with me, and I'll take you where nothing will harm you, ever again.'

The forest seemed to have faded around her, leaving only the figure of the warrior Wizard in the midst of a grey haze.

I'd like to rest for a while.

She took his hand, and suddenly they seemed to be floating, flying, as the world was left behind.

The remaining companions were speeding through the sky with Corisand, riderless this time, in the lead, Dael riding the familiar Rosina again, and Aelwen, Taine and Kaldath mounted on Phaerie steeds whose former owners were now dead. Though Corisand was controlling the flying spell, she had to push to keep up with the other horses, who were stretching out at full speed, desperate to escape the sinister presence of the Dwelven ghosts who swarmed through the air, following Kaldath in a shadowy swarm that roiled like smoke.

'How can we ever hope to find Iriana?' Dael looked around at all the endless miles of empty sky through which they sped. 'I can't bear to think how she must be feeling right now. Without Melik she's blind and helpless – it must be terrifying for her.'

'We go north,' Corisand replied grimly. 'We head back to Eliorand by the straightest and fastest route. That's what the Phaerie will have done. We keep looking around, ahead, to either side. The sky is clear; there's no cloud cover for them to hide behind. Sooner or later we'll see them. We'll find them. We'll find Iriana. We won't rest until we do.'

'At the rate we're moving we stand every chance of catching up with them,' Aelwen added. 'You're all right, Corisand, but Rosina and these other horses are terrified of the Dwelven spirits that follow us.'

At the mention of the ghosts, Dael shuddered as a chill ran down his spine. The horrifying memory of the way they had ripped the Phaerie apart in the cave was branded into his mind. Though they had saved his life, and for that he owed them his gratitude, it was still hard not to fear them. He kept his eyes fixed resolutely forward, not wanting to look back at the sinister followers that crowded on his heels. 'I don't blame the horses.' He stroked Rosina's sweat-damp neck. 'I'm not very keen on those – *things* – myself.'

'The Dwelven are not *things*, Dael,' Kaldath rebuked him gently. 'Once they were people just like you and me. They may have looked very different, it's true, but they were people nonetheless. They loved and worked, they laughed and cried and danced and feared.' He looked back at the Dwelven spirits, his face creased with the memory of ancient pain. 'They strove for freedom, just like you, and they bled and died. They are as much Hellorin's victims as you are – and now, at long last, they will have their revenge.'

Dael thought about that for a moment, then took a deep breath. 'You're right, Kaldath. It's easy to be afraid of them because, well, they're ghosts, and we've seen how dangerous they can be, but also because they look so very different from the way we do. Yet from what you say, they are just as much victims as any of us, and if they can help us strike back at those accursed Phaerie, I welcome them with open arms.'

Kaldath smiled, that gentle, wise smile. 'In a way, Dael, you should understand them better than anyone else, for they were slaves as you were a slave. Unlike you, however, it took death to give them their freedom and power. You accomplished that while you were still alive.'

'This is all very well,' Corisand interrupted, her voice terse with impatience, 'but what about Iriana?' She was less sure of this strange alliance with Kaldath and his horde of spirits than the others seemed to be. Her people had also been enslaved by the Phaerie, but she felt no kinship with the Dwelven. Horses had always been able to see and sense ghosts much more easily than humans did, but that didn't mean she had to like them – or trust them.

'I'm not sure that what Dael said about Iriana being helpless is true,' Taine said. 'She'll be afraid of course – she'd be a fool if she wasn't – but in the short time I knew her, she struck me as a real fighter. I will never forget that first night I met her, when she'd been attacked by the Phaerie assassin, and had lost almost all her companions, both human and animal. She was blind and terrified then too, but she had the grit and courage to fight back, and against all odds she won. She was worn out, beaten up and grieving, but from somewhere she still found the strength and generosity to heal me after I'd been mauled by that bear. Today she can use the steeds of our enemy for vision, and if there's any way in which she can strike at the Phaerie you can guarantee she'll find it. We shouldn't discount that.'

'You're right, Taine,' Corisand said. 'You should have seen her when we went to the Elsewhere to find the Fialan. We met with some very strange and dangerous situations, but Iriana was adaptive, inventive and brave, and she always found a way to get us through. I remember this one time, when she got me to fashion a boat out of air. Well, I had never even *heard* of boats, let alone seen one, but Iriana …'

As Aelwen listened to them praising this foreign Wizard, this traditional enemy of her people, she felt unease prickling though her once again. She barely knew Iriana; there had been so little time when they were briefly together at Athina's tower, and everyone had been preoccupied with so many things. When she'd been reunited with Taine he had already met the Wizard – had spent a night with her – and the two of them had clearly developed a bond of affection. Though she'd told herself over and over that it was nothing, that she was being stupid, she couldn't help feeling a nasty little nip of jealousy. Now, hearing Taine and Corisand praising Iriana to the skies, she couldn't help but feel a little left out.

Though she was becoming increasingly fond of Kaldath, he had walked hand in hand with death for too many years to be a truly comfortable companion. And she couldn't see why Iriana and Corisand made so much fuss of Dael. As for Corisand, Aelwen was dreadfully unhappy with these revelations about the true identity of Xandim. She loved the amazing Phaerie steeds, had built her life around caring for them. Much as Hellorin looked upon himself as their owner, in her heart she had always felt they were hers. Now they belonged to her no longer. They weren't even horses – and the idea of *people* trapped inside them made her desperately uncomfortable. She didn't want to lose them, it would be like losing part of herself, yet if she betrayed Corisand and somehow found a way to prevent her from freeing her tribe, that would make her a slavemaster, no better than Hellorin himself. Riding had been as natural to Aelwen as breathing, yet now, riding this borrowed Phaerie mount, she felt herself second-guessing her every move. Worse still, the horse sensed her uncertainty, and was playing her up in a way that she would never normally have allowed, and she hesitated to restrain it, knowing what she knew.

Right now Aelwen was feeling lonely, and very much adrift. She had loved her old life in Eliorand: her horses, her stables, her grooms and all the little details of her daily, yearly routines. Now it was all in tatters. She missed Kelon, always by her side, always sturdy and steady, predictable, dependable and utterly loyal. She looked across at Taine, still deep in conversation with Corisand, and felt a stir of unease.

Had she been wrong? It was the first time she had admitted her doubts to herself, but once she had let them emerge, they would not subside. Had she acted too rashly? Made a mistake in leaving, in running away from the security and contentment of her position as Hellorin's Mistress of Horse? Had she failed in her responsibility to Tiolani, her sister's daughter? Shouldn't she have stayed, have kept her mouth shut, maintained her position and done everything in her power to steer Hellorin's headstrong child to a more temperate, reasonable course? Had she thrown it all away in pursuit of a memory, a dream, a stranger who was no longer her love from years ago?

It was her decision, her flight, her theft of the Xandim horses that had precipitated Tiolani's pursuit of her, Kelon running off to join a bunch of vicious mortal outlaws, Ferimon's bloody death – but this last gave Aelwen the jolt she needed to rein in her runaway thoughts. Ferimon's death had been a blessing; he was a traitor whose evil acts had almost slain the Forest Lord. His unsavoury influence had sub-verted Tiolani, had robbed her of her innocence, leading the naive young girl down a path of bloodshed and destruction. In bringing about Ferimon's demise at Kelon's hands, Aelwen had saved the Phaerie from a dire fate indeed. Tiolani's folly was on his head, and her own, and had nothing – or little, at least – to do with Aelwen's decision to flee. Kelon's choice in following the outlaw leader Danel and her ragged band had been his own decision.

As for herself, Aelwen had not left Eliorand to search for Taine. She had fled in fear of her life as Tiolani became increasingly unstable and started killing Hemifae because they carried mortal blood as well as Phaerie. Now, the only question that remained was whether she had made the right choice in cleaving to Taine rather than Kelon. Had she abandoned the one who loved her unreservedly, even though she could never quite return his feelings in the same way, to pursue a stranger, a dream, an illusion – or a joyous reality? She looked across at Taine, so steady, so focused, all his concentration bent to the task in hand, his keen eyes endlessly scanning the skies and the forest all around to find a frightened young girl and save her from an unspeakable fate. She looked at him – and in that moment she thought she knew the answer.

'Look! What's that? Over there.' Taine had risen in his stirrups and was pointing towards the north-west, where a thin, dark, oily-looking thread of smoke was rising above the trees. It was most likely just another band of feral mortals making camp, but as one they turned towards the sinister beacon, praying that they had found the Wizard.

It wasn't really a clearing; just a narrow slot where a great tree had fallen, bringing down two or three others with it. The ground was a leg-breaking tangle of dead and rotting boughs, weeds, brambles and scrawny saplings that had taken advantage of the extra light and seeded themselves among the bones of the recumbent giants. Trails of crushed and splintered vegetation indicated where the Phaerie steeds had fled and there was a larger churned and trampled patch which was surrounded by a number of charred and blackened areas. The acrid smell of smoke and the sickening stench of burned flesh dimmed the air with a choking haze, though there was now no sign of any flames.

There were two Phaerie corpses in the devastated area, one at the edge of the trees and the other nearer the centre of the open space.

Both were hideously burned and disfigured, their bodies contorted by the agony of their deaths. A tangle of smouldering rope was all that remained of the net.

In the centre of all the ruin lay Iriana, not far from the hollow where the roots of the mighty tree had been torn out of the ground. Her skin was sheet-white beneath the smudges of charcoal and smoke, and her life blood pumped slowly out from a long, deep gash in her arm, and soaked into the ground beneath. She was guarded by two of the biggest eagles that Corisand had ever seen. One stood over her body, its wings mantled protectively, while the other, more cautious, perched in a tree nearby.

The Windeye, transfixed with horror, made a stumbling, clumsy landing, and staggered to regain her balance. She was already shifting back into her human form when the others came down beside her and crowded forward – only to halt as the eagle opened its wings and gave a harsh, threatening cry.

The lid of Melik's basket had sprung open. 'No – it'll get him!' Dael shouted in dismay as the cat leapt out and rushed towards the eagle. Corisand spun a spear of air to knock the bird away, but even as she did it the eagle lowered its head with that lethal, curving beak – and rubbed it along Melik's flank. The cat arched his back against the caress, raised his tail, and purred like thunder, then moved aside to nose at Iriana.

'Wait, wait, it must be Boreas,' Corisand shouted. 'It's Iriana's eagle, that left her to find a mate.'

Taine, who'd had his bow poised to shoot, paused, though his arm still strained against the string. 'Well, we've got to get it away from her,' he said urgently. 'She's bleeding to death down there.'

To his surprise, Dael found himself stepping forward. He called to Melik and the cat left Iriana's still form and ran back to him, leaping up into his arms. Carrying Melik he approached the eagle cautiously, but since the cat clearly trusted him, Boreas seemed content to let him pass.

As he dropped to his knees beside the Wizard the others crowded in as quickly as they dared, still wary of the fierce guardian, but the bird drew back a little and took to the air, landing on one of the upthrust roots from the fallen tree, which placed him uncomfortably above the heads of Iriana's kneeling companions. Corisand could feel his fierce golden eyes burning into her, and knew that if Boreas sensed any threat towards Iriana, he was ready to strike.

Everyone clustered around Iriana, kneeling on the ground that was wet and sticky with her blood. Taine put a hand to her throat, feeling for a pulse. 'It's faint but it's there. She's still alive, but for how long? From my Wizard heritage I know enough to slow the bleeding a little, but I'm no Healer ...'

'I am.' Kaldath, who did not know Iriana, had been standing back to give her friends room, but now he came forward and the others pressed closer together to make a space for him.

'Can you help her, Kaldath?' Corisand asked urgently. 'Can you?'

The ancient one laid his hands on Iriana's wounded arm. He drew in a deep breath and grew very still. Even Dael could feel the prickling build-up of magic radiating from the old man.

'As some of you already know, I am like Taine,' Kaldath said, and though he spoke aloud his eyes remained distant in concentration, 'a Hemifae with Wizard blood, from my mother. According to my father she had a singular Healing gift, and passed it on to me.'

While he spoke, the lethal gush of blood from Iriana's arm died away to a trickle, then an ooze, then stopped completely. 'Though I had no formal training, my father had all the old Healing journals my mother had kept while she was at the Academy, and afterwards. Even when I was young I loved to read them. It seemed to bring me closer to her; as though I could hear her voice speaking to me from the past.'

A shimmering blue-violet glow suffused the Wizard's torn flesh, and before the eyes of the astonished observers, the ugly gash began to close. 'My father made me keep my skill a secret, lest the other Phaerie discover my Wizard heritage, so I practised on animals, and it was only when I was sent as Overseer to the mines that my skills finally came into play. Even to the Dwelven, those tunnels were a desperately dangerous place, but Hellorin never cared if his slaves were injured or died. There were always plenty of replacements. As time went on I saved many lives, and gradually the Dwelven came to trust me, and became like a family to me, despite their alien forms.'

Kaldath breathed in deeply once more. The wound was completely closed now, a long red scar the only sign that it had ever been there. 'Now,' the ancient one said, 'I will use Healing magic to accelerate the production of new blood in Iriana's body. Anyone who wants to help can feed their power into me, so that I can help Iriana replenish her life force and her energy.'

Eagerly, Corisand reached out a hand, but he drew back. 'Take off the Fialan, my dear. The Stone of Fate contains too much raw power for such a delicate operation. You run the risk of burning out Iriana – or myself, as the conduit.' He smiled at her as she hastily pulled the thong over her head and tucked the leather pouch safely away in her pack. 'Your own not inconsiderable magic will more than suffice, O Windeye of the Xandim.'

'Take some of mine, too,' said Aelwen, stretching out her hand.

'And mine,' Taine added. 'We all want to be part of this. We all want to help.'

'If only I had some magic,' Dael said disconsolately. 'I feel so useless.'

'You? Useless? Never.' Corisand spoke briskly. 'You too are filled with the force of life, Dael, just as much as any of us. Your love will be the conduit. Hold Iriana's hand, and send love flowing into her as we work. Lend her your strength. It will help, I promise.'

Dael, his face brightening, reached out and grasped the Wizard's cold hand. He sent his love and strength into her; imagined it filling her with energy as the others fed their power into Kaldath, who had laid his hands over Iriana's stumbling heart. For the space of a few heartbeats time seemed to stand still as they were all united, as one, a single glorious entity linked by purpose, selflessness and love.

After a time, Iriana began to breathe more easily. The colour crept back into her face, and the ghastly transparency of impending death ebbed away from her skin. Suddenly her eyes flew open. Melik pushed between Taine and Dael, and as his eyes went round them all, looking from one face to the next, it was clear that the Wizard was borrowing his sight once more. 'You came,' she whispered hoarsely. 'Thank providence you came. You saved me.' She tried to move, and winced. 'Oh, festering bloody bat turds. I feel terrible.'

With his free hand, Taine stroked her tangled hair. 'You saved yourself, little sister,' he told her. 'We only finished the job off for you.'

But Iriana did not hear him. Already she had slipped back into unconsciousness. Kaldath looked grave. 'She's far from out of danger yet,' he said. 'This poor girl is still fighting bravely, but she has lost so much blood, she barely has enough to sustain her life. To have any hope of saving her, we need somewhere sheltered and safe to tend her. Does anyone know of such a hiding place?'

Taine nodded. 'I always know where there's a hiding place.'

22

GOOD INTENTIONS

Back in Tyrineld, Tinagen let Brynne have the night to suffer. To wait, to reflect, to consider the enormity of what she'd done and wonder if she'd be expelled from the Academy. And she *would* be wondering, now that there had been time for her temper to subside. Furthermore, the gossip mills must be grinding overtime by now – in an enclosed community such as the Academy it was inevitable. Her fellow students would have heard the rumours, would be curious, would be asking questions.

Tinagen smiled. She was prideful, was Brynne. He would make sure she had plenty of time and opportunities to feel humiliated.

He looked out of his study window; saw the peaceful courtyard with its fountain glittering in the early morning light, and watched his Healers going back and forth about their business. Productive, busy, organised. He shuddered to think of the damage Brynne might do if he allowed her back. She had it in her to shatter this ordered little world in which he took such pride.

For a moment he felt a prickle at the back of his neck; a shiver of prescience. He shouldn't do this, shouldn't let her come back. He just *knew*, in his bones, that it would be a terrible mistake. But war was brewing. A woman out of her mind with grief and thirsting for revenge, a woman who would stop at nothing to achieve it, was running the city. He had been arrested; had known fear and shame, had felt loss and grief. His world had been rocked on its foundations, and he was at his lowest ebb.

So he let it slide.

He would allow that little wretch to come back, and take care of Incondor. After all, what could it hurt? There would be plenty of opportunity to bring the girl into line, and he would have her watched constantly. With an effort he shook off the unease that dogged him when he thought of her. It was ridiculous, having an attack of the vapours because of a temperamental young girl. It was probably just a reaction to all the difficulties he had faced in the last few days. After all she was just a student, when all was said and done.

Turning away from the window and its peaceful scene, he went to find Tameron, and arrange for someone to go and fetch Brynne.

It had been the worst night of Chiannala's life. She hadn't slept, but had spent the hours weeping and pacing, worrying and fretting; berating herself for her stupidity and temper and staring, terrified, into the black abyss that was her future. The morning had proved even worse, as one by one her fellow students had come knocking at her door, all oozing what appeared to be sincere concern, but unable to hide the undertones of avid curiosity and relief that it was someone else in so much trouble, and not themselves.

Chiannala hated the lot of them. Why should they have every-thing when she had nothing? She was a better Wizard than every last one of them, yet tomorrow they would still be here while she would be – where would she be? Her future gaped before her, a terrifying void, and she tasted bitterness down to the very dregs of her soul. By the time Tinagen's summons came she had worked herself into such a state that it was almost a relief to be getting the dreaded interview over. Judging by the expressionless face and carefully hidden thoughts of the young Healer who'd been sent to fetch her, the rumours of her transgressions and her outburst had been winging round the Luen too, and the thought of them all discussing her behind her back made her writhe with shame.

It felt like the longest walk she had ever taken. Before she faced Tinagen she tried to claw back some of her anger and defiance. Even in this extremity, her pride wouldn't let her give in without a struggle. But Chiannala just didn't have it in her. She was too exhausted, wretched and terrified to summon her usual fighting spirit, and before she reached the Luen she was forced to face the mortifying fact that she'd do *anything* – beg, plead, grovel, apologise, whatever it took – just to be allowed to stay.

When she was shown into his room Tinagen was standing, staring out of the window, looking distant, cold and stern. He dismissed the messenger who'd brought her without even looking round, and when the young Healer had gone, closing the door behind him, the Luen Head remained where he was; silent, aloof and unwilling to acknowledge her with as much as a single glance.

Chiannala waited, torn between dread of what she would hear when he finally spoke, and the need to have this torture end; to hear her fate and be done with the terrible uncertainty. But Tinagen remained distant and unspeaking, refusing to turn and acknowledge her. The minutes crawled by in an agony of suspense and Chiannala's nerves stretched tighter and tighter. And still she waited, trembling now, dry-mouthed and with a hammering heart, until finally she could bear it no longer.

Tears flooded her eyes as her self-control snapped at last. Her courage failed her, and the final shreds of her pride dissolved. 'Oh sir,' she cried, 'I'm sorry. I'm truly, deeply sorry. Please don't send me away.'

Tinagen swung round to face her, his gaze flat and uncompromising. Again, he did not speak, but merely waited until the chasm of silence grew so deep that Chiannala felt compelled to rush in and fill it. She did not realise that she was doing exactly what he'd planned she should; she had no idea that before he dealt with her he needed to know exactly how repentant she really was, and that this was his way of accomplishing that goal. She only knew that her future at the Academy hung by the most slender of threads, and that this was her last and only chance to convince him to let her stay.

'It was very, very wrong of me to speak to you, and to the other Healers, as I did yesterday – especially after you had just saved my life. You had every right to be angry. I acted foolishly, on impulse, going into Incondor's mind like that, unprepared, untrained and—'

'Why did you?' Tinagen's cold voice cut across her outpourings like a knife. 'Such techniques are only ever attempted by our most skilled and experienced Healers. What possessed you, a new student with no training whatsoever, to even try such a thing?'

'I don't know, sir.' Chiannala hung her head. 'It just – felt – right. I looked at him and there was a kind of connection ... I can't explain.' She clasped her hands, twisting her fingers nervously. 'I acted on impulse: I knew he was slipping away and there wasn't much time.'

'How did you know what to do?'

'I can't say, sir,' she replied miserably. With every passing moment, it seemed more likely that he would cast her out. 'As I said, I acted on impulse. I just seemed to know what to do, and where to go.'

Tinagen left the window and sat down at his desk. 'Sit.' He gestured to the chair on the opposite side. She finally dared to lift her face and saw that, for the first time during their conversation, the hard, flat look had left his eyes. Now he seemed irritated and oddly resigned, and she wondered what it meant. Did she dare to hope? Chiannala held her breath.

The Luen Head put his elbows on the desk and steepled his fingers. 'Brynne, one thing has been puzzling me, and also Melisanda, who conducted your initial interview and assessment for the Academy. At that time you were filled with enthusiasm. You said you couldn't wait to become a Healer. Yet when you eventually came here as a student, you seemed aghast at being assigned to this Luen, and did everything in your power to resist the placement.' His eyes drilled into her; piercing, penetrating, refusing to be denied. 'Before we go any further I will have the truth from you. Why the sudden turnabout? What happened to bring about such an extreme change of heart?'

Oh, curse that stupid Brynne!

It was fortunate that Melisanda had already asked this, but had been distracted before receiving an answer. That had given Chiannala time to think of a response. She looked up at him, wide-eyed, innocent, then lowered her eyes as if ashamed. 'I was afraid.'

'Afraid?' Tinagen barked, making her jump. 'What do you mean, girl, afraid?'

Deliberately, she bit her lip. 'Well, sir, when I was growing up I always dreamed of becoming a Healer. I'd practise by taking care of the animals on the farm. I wanted to cure people, to help them.' She looked up at him and forced a shimmer of tears into her eyes. 'But when I came for that interview and actually saw the work you were doing, I suddenly realised what a terrifying responsibility a Healer carries, and what a heavy burden it must be to hold people's lives in your hands, day after day. And I started thinking. What if I get it wrong; make mistakes? People would die and it would be my fault. I couldn't get it out of my mind. The more I thought about it, the more afraid I became until I just couldn't bear it any more, and it seemed that the only way to escape the fear was to run away from it; to do something else, to *be* something else. I told myself there would be other ways to help people, without putting their lives at stake.' She blinked, let the tears roll down her cheeks and lowered her eyes again. 'I'm sorry,' she whispered.

For a long moment Tinagen paused and simply sat there, pinning her down with that penetrating stare, until she had to use every scrap of willpower she possessed to keep herself from writhing and fidgeting beneath his gaze. Finally he spoke again. 'And how do you feel about Healing now, after what happened yesterday?'

The tiny spark of hope that had been smouldering within her suddenly blazed up bright and strong. 'I – I feel different. Oh, sir, I know I made a mess of things. I know I acted stupidly and rashly, but that feeling of being able to bring someone back from the brink – it felt so wonderful, so *right*. I don't think I'm afraid any more. I *do* want to be a Healer, sir, more than anything. Please, please let me stay. I'll work so hard, and I promise I'll never be rude and insubordinate again ...'

'Don't make promises unless you're sure you can keep them.' Tinagen frowned. 'Because frankly, Brynne, your attitude has been regrettable from the outset. What came over you yesterday, to act so appallingly towards senior members of this Luen? And in front of a patient? I warn you, girl; such behaviour will not be tolerated here.'

'Sir, I'm so ashamed of that outburst.' Chiannala was beginning to be sickened by this humble, penitent role that she was playing, but she was determined to stick it out, to see it through in the hope that he would let her stay. Everything, her whole future, depended on it; furthermore she was desperate to explore that powerful, strange connection between herself and the mysterious Incondor.

'That still doesn't explain why,' Tinagen said impatiently. 'Is there any possible way you can justify such behaviour?'

Oh for goodness' sake just tell me whether I'm to stay or go, and be done with it.

It was getting harder for Chiannala to curb her thoughts, but she was careful not to let even a flicker of her impatience show on her face. 'You see, when you and the other Healers brought me back, I was just so shaken by what had happened.' She'd had all night to work out this part of her story. 'I had almost died, Incondor had almost died but he'd been saved. But you were all so angry, and I was angry with myself, and so embarrassed because I'd done such a foolish thing that it just – exploded out of me.'

She tried the lowered eyes again. 'I'm so dreadfully ashamed. My parents brought me up better than to act that way. It's not like me, sir, I swear.'

Again that strange expression, part irritation, part resignation, passed across Tinagen's face. He sat back in his chair. 'Very well, Brynne. It appears that you're truly penitent, and you certainly show some potential as a Healer, so this is what we're going to do. You can stay at the Academy and remain with the Luen of Healers, but you must consider yourself on probation. Any more irresponsible acts, any further outbursts of temper like the one we suffered yesterday, and you will be out – of both Luen and Academy – before you can blink. From now on you will be respectful to your seniors, and that means every single Healer in this place. You will be obedient, and you will work harder than you could ever have dreamed possible. Is this all quite clear to you?'

'Yes, sir – oh, yes! Oh, thank you, sir.'

You old blowhard.

'I'm so grateful for this chance. I'll work hard and be respectful, truly I will. I promise I won't give you any cause to regret letting me stay.'

'See that you don't.' For an instant that stony look was back in his eyes, but Chiannala didn't care. She was so glad to be free of that dreadful suspense, so relieved that her future was secure after all, that it left her weak and shaking. But Tinagen had not yet done with dispensing good news. 'Now, Brynne,' he went on, 'one of the chief reasons I'm letting you stay is that yesterday you really did help our patient. So for the next few weeks I'm suspending your usual student schedule and placing you with Incondor's team of Healers – in a very junior, minor capacity, of course. He is not yet out of danger, and will need a considerable amount of complex, difficult work to piece his damaged body back together, so you should learn a great deal in the days to come. If, after that, you still want to be a Healer, and if your superiors are pleased with you, then you may remain with us. It will be up to you.'

'Oh, thank—' Chiannala began, but he silenced her with a brusque wave of his hand. 'Frankly, it's more than you deserve. See that you prove yourself worthy.' He got to his feet. 'That will be all. Report to Tameron in Incondor's chamber. You may as well begin at once.'

Chiannala fled, her heart singing. Once she was safely out of the room she found herself alone in the empty corridor, and just for an instant, she let the gloating triumph show in her face. Safe! Against all the odds she had had fooled that horrible old misery Tinagen, who thought he was so clever. She had another chance and she wasn't going to waste it. Not she. She sped off down the corridor on flying feet, heading for Incondor's chamber.

23
~

PARIAHS

Valior's fishing boat *Venturer* bounded through the choppy waves with her white sails straining and her bows plunging into the blue-green water, sending up plumes of white spray on either side. Brynne stood in the bows, balancing on the slanting deck and holding tightly to the rail.

'One hand for the ship and one for yourself; that's what they say,' Valior had told her, 'but fishermen usually need both hands for the ship. In your case though, Brynne, you'd better stick to both hands for yourself just now.'

She would soon learn, Brynne assured herself. With a little practice she'd be able to balance on the shifting deck as well as Derwyn and Seema. Then she would be a sailor too. The notion filled her with delight. She would be able to work and help, making a real contribution to this family who had been so kind as to shelter a mysterious, destitute girl who had lost her memory.

As always, her mind shied away from the great blank obstacle in her mind, and the fear that snarled and scrabbled behind it. Increasingly, she was pushing away all thoughts of her past as she throve and blossomed in the present.

Oh, how she loved the sea! The vast open spaces and glorious skies: sunset, sunrise and the star-scattered velvet darkness. The shadowy green depths and the lively sparkles of sunlight on the surface. The white gulls flashing overhead, the shrill song of the wind in the rigging and the rhythmic surge of the waves, like the beating of a giant heart. The giddy, joyous swoop and lift of the deck beneath her feet, the air moving like cool silk against her skin, and the fresh, salt tang in the air. This was where she belonged now. After only a few short days, she couldn't imagine living anywhere else.

Brynne glanced back at Valior, standing in his usual place at the helm, so steady, solid and kind; at dark-haired Derwyn and tall, rangy Seema, who were already teasing her as if she were their little sister, as they trimmed the sails. The motherly, comforting Osella would be waiting when the vessel pulled alongside the little wooden dock at home; waving, smiling, looking forward to hearing what the catch had been like, and how Brynne's first fishing trip had gone.

Sure enough, after the *Venturer* had dropped off her catch and they had made their way back to Freedom Cove and the fishing settlement called Independence, Osella was standing on the small wooden dock that was Valior's home mooring, at the very edge of the village. She was waving, her dark green cloak flapping in the gusting wind that had tugged floating strands of her hair loose from its untidy knot, but she was not smiling. As the *Venturer* swung alongside the jetty and Derwyn and Seema leapt ashore with the bow and stern warps to moor the boat, Brynne looked at Osella's grave expression and felt a clutch of alarm.

What had happened? Had Brynne's real family been found? Had some mishap befallen them? The girl whose hostile face still haunted her nightmares, the one who, Brynne was sure, must have pushed her off the cliff – had she turned up to finish what she had started? But as Valior jumped across to meet his sister, and the wind blew snatches of Osella's words across into the boat, Brynne blushed to realise that this problem, whatever it might be, had absolutely nothing to with her.

'... a whole bunch of them ...'

'... filthy, dressed in rags ...'

'... out of the north ...'

'... stuff going missing all through the village ...'

'... Captains' meeting ...'

By this time, Valior was frowning too. 'I'll go up right away.' With that he was off, striding up the winding lane edged by the cottages made of local stone, and heading for the inn. Osella, still with that worried expression, climbed aboard the *Venturer* and began to help the others get everything squared away; coiling ropes, stowing sails and swabbing fish scales and slime from the deck. As they worked, she finally satisfied their curiosity and told them what had been hap-pening in their absence.

It seemed that a sizeable gang of feral humans, escaped Phaerie slaves from out of the forest, had come down from the north and descended upon the settlement. They had asked for shelter, food, a place to stay where they too could share the freedom that the fisher-folk enjoyed.

No one had been pleased to see them.

'I'd like to get my hands on whichever idiot told them about this place; putting ideas into their heads,' Osella said angrily. 'Just how are we expected to absorb so many? And why should we?'

'But you absorbed me,' Brynne said.

Osella made a sound that was somewhere between a huff and a snort. '*You* were one young girl in trouble. This was a great stinking mob that descended on us. Though there were quite a few of them who needed help, people who were hurt or sick or had small children, a lot of the others were simply spoiling for trouble. *And* they're a pack of thieves. Within ten minutes of their arrival, people were missing clothes from washing lines, vegetables out of the garden, not to mention rabbits and chickens – but worst of all, one or two folk lost gutting knives and other blades that could be used as weapons. I promise you that these aren't the sort of neighbours that any of us would want, even if we could take them in.'

'Which we can't,' Derwyn said. 'If we start harbouring fugitive slaves, we'll ruin our own arrangement with the Wizards. Our own freedom was too hard won to start risking it for a horde of armed thieves.'

Up the hill, in the village tavern, the Captains were saying much the same thing. Though the fisherfolk had no formal system of governance – they were a fiercely independent lot who, due to their race's history of enslavement, objected in no uncertain terms to being told what to do – in practice it was the Captains of the five biggest vessels that fished the deep ocean who were the leaders of the community. Though there were many other fishermen and women in the settlement, these plied the coast in the little boats called cobles, catching mackerel and salmon in their season, and setting out their little home-crafted pots made of wood and tarred string to trap lobsters and crabs. There were also the foyboatmen, who made their living ferrying passengers to various points around the Tyrineld bays, and a number of artisans such as boat builders, the glassblower who made the glass floats for the fishing nets, and the makers of ropes and sails. Those who stayed at home, because they had young children to care for, or because they were elderly or infirm, or simply weren't suited to the rigours of a life at sea, made and repaired nets, cultivated gardens packed with vegetables and laden bushes of soft fruits, or cared for rabbits, chickens, pigs or goats.

There were six leading Captains in all who dealt with the major decisions for the community, for one of the five deep-sea vessels, the *Radiant Dawn*, was co-captained by a brother and sister, Abran and Loellin, who took turns, season and season about, at being the one in authority. There was another woman Captain, Shaena, whose ship was the *Intrepid*; a tall, leathery woman with short-cropped, greying hair; her brawny arms knotted with muscle from years of keeping up with the men at trimming sails, hauling nets and holding the tiller steady in the teeth of the blasting winter storms.

The other three Captains were men: Valior of the *Venturer*, Mordal, the youngest of the Captains, master of the *Intrepid*, a man of medium height with a long, smooth fall of blond hair braided back into a pigtail, a jutting jaw that bespoke his obdurate character, and a badly crooked nose that had been broken in a fight some years before when weatherbeaten Galgan, the oldest and most respected of the Captains, had put the young upstart firmly in his place. Galgan, with his steely eyes, his white hair and short, silver beard, was still forging determinedly on when most other skippers would have been content to pass their vessel, the *Northstar*, to their sons and spend their last years on land, taking a well-earned rest from the rigours of a life at sea. His crew were out of the same mould: a quartet of grizzled veterans who, though their physical prowess was not what it once had been, could still outfish, outcurse, outyarn, outdrink and outfight any sailor in Independence.

Today, no one was yarning or fighting, though at the Captains' table in the back room of the tavern the six leaders sat with drinks in front of them and grave expressions on their faces. 'So there you have it,' Abran was saying to Valior and Galgan, who'd been the last to dock. 'They just turned up out of nowhere, the whole damned crowd of them, and demanded that we take them in.'

'What do you mean by a crowd? How many, exactly, are we talking about here?' Galgan, the undisputed leader of the group, demanded.

'About forty to fifty, I should say, but some are women with young children, and some are injured or sick.'

'Anything contagious?' Galgan's expression darkened.

'We couldn't be sure, so I sent Douala the Herbwife to examine them,' Shaena said. 'She'll be able to tell us. We didn't like the look of them, Galgan, to tell you the truth; the leader, a woman called Danel, spoke politely and begged for our help, but a lot of her followers looked mean and desperate enough to take what they needed. Then the stealing started, so we put some food in Shennon the boatbuilder's big shed to trick them in there, and locked them up with guards on the doors until you came back.' She grinned. 'I think you could safely say that they're not very pleased.'

Valior shrugged. 'Beggars can't be choosers. Once they started stealing, they forfeited any rights they might have thought they had to our help. When I'm at sea Osella is in the house on her own, and I don't want to spend every minute worrying about her safety.'

'Well, with the best will in the world, they'll certainly be no use to us here,' Abran said. 'This was the first time that any of them had even seen the sea, let alone had any experience with boats. To be honest, they seem a pretty clueless bunch – I'm amazed that they managed to survive in the forest for so long.'

'To be fair, Abran, they've really suffered,' Loellin said. 'Some of the things they told us would make your blood run cold – about the Phaerie with their flying horses hunting them down like animals, just for sport. That's why they came down here, once they'd heard of us. They decided that, no matter what happened to them, anything had to be better than Hellorin's Wild Hunt.'

Galgan sighed. 'And I'm sorry for them, Loellin, truly I am, but we can't sustain the burden of them for long. When I passed Shennon on the way up here his face was like a thundercloud, and he let me know in no uncertain terms that he needs his shed back. Then there's the matter of food and water, and arranging for them to get their slops out of there ...'

'And if you keep them cooped up together in those conditions for much longer, you'll have an epidemic on your hands that could spread through our whole community. And then where will we be?' Douala, a stick-thin woman with grey-streaked hair and dark eyes couched in a fan of wrinkles, stood in the doorway with a frown on her face.

'Come in, Douala, and join us,' Galgan said. Mordal brought her a chair from another table, and the Captains moved closer together to make a space.

Douala sat down, and refused the offer of ale or spirits in favour of a glass of water. 'Those folk have certainly been through some hard times,' she said. 'I don't think we can save a couple of the smallest babies, they're too starved and weak, but we might, with luck, do something for the other small children. One man has a leg that's so badly infected that I'll have to take off the entire limb, but I doubt we'll save him, even then.' She spread out her hands in defeat. 'Every single one of them has been weakened by cold, hunger, and long travel. The fact that they're as filthy as pigs in a wallow – and that's being insulting to the pigs – doesn't help, and several of their injuries are beyond my skill to treat. We really need the Wizard Healers, but why should they bestir themselves for a bunch of runaway Phaerie slaves? Besides, we'd have to use our annual trading concessions to pay for their treatment—'

'And we certainly can't sanction that,' Galgan said decisively. He looked around at the other Captains. 'These people are in desperate straits, and I pity them, but we have a responsibility to our own community. We have to take care of them first.'

Valior sighed. 'You're right, I know. It cuts deep to abandon those fellow humans, who've already suffered so much, but we just don't have the resources to take care of them.'

'It's not just a lack of resources, Valior,' Galgan said. 'These strangers are a light-fingered bunch, and I won't tolerate that. Even in the short time it took to speak to their leader, the others were pilfering stuff all over the place. Even though people were willing to take in the women with small children, and were coming out of their houses with food for the rest, it didn't make any difference. I don't care what they've been through; we don't have room for thieves in our community, and that's the end of it.'

Shaena frowned. 'I agree with you both, as a matter of fact, but we haven't even mentioned the most important concern of all.' She took a sip from her glass and looked around the assembled faces. 'It took us a long time and endless hard work and sacrifice to reach our unique arrangement with the Wizards. As far as I know we're the only community of free humans, and we're still tied to them by trade agreements. But if we start taking in others – especially escaped slaves – the Archwizard will have us back in bondage before you even blink. I'm telling you, these newcomers are a deadly threat to all the fisherfolk of Independence. Though it goes against the grain, the only possible thing we can do, and the sooner the better, is to take this to Sharalind.'

Valior sighed. 'You're right, Shaena, and though we're mostly men at this table, only you had the balls to say it. For the survival of our own families we've got to turn those poor bastards over to the Wizards – and somehow find a way to live with ourselves afterwards.'

'Though it goes against my grain to involve the Wizards in this, when you get right down to it, that's the only thing we can do,' Galgan said. 'Does everyone agree?'

One by one, the Captains nodded.

'Then we'll all go across together and see Sharalind.' Galgan got to his feet. 'We'll do it right now. The sooner we get this over with, the better.'

It felt wonderful to be under a roof again. Kelon, footsore, aching and exhausted after walking all the way from the forest, was just so glad to have food and shelter once more that he didn't particularly care, at this point, that he couldn't go any further whether he wanted to or not. The fisherfolk seemed to be decent people. Though their welcome had been constrained, to say the least, with more grumbling and consternation than pleasure, surely that was only to be expected. Kelon had seen the size of their community. A group such as the ferals, ragged mendicants with nothing to their name, was bound to put a strain on local resources. But they had worked hard at concealing their dismay and had done their best to provide food and shelter for their unexpected guests, even sending their Herbwife to treat the sick and injured.

Even if the accommodation in this boatshed was spartan, the ferals had warmth, shelter and food in their bellies, and to Kelon's mind the indignation of Danel and the others was premature at best, and downright unreasonable at worst. So what if the door was guarded, to prevent the strangers from wandering around at will? The ferals had brought that upon themselves. His face burned as he recalled the spate of petty thefts and pilfering that had taken place within the first half-hour of the ferals' arrival, and his own embarrassment and shame when the missing items were discovered. To have stolen from people who'd been nothing but kind and hospitable! Not for the first time, Kelon looked on his companions with a jaundiced eye. Instead of giving them shelter, the fisherfolk had every reason to drive them away with sticks and stones.

The interior of the boatshed was a great, echoing space with sturdy wooden walls; its roof beams almost lost in the shadows high above. It was big enough to construct one of the large ocean-going fishing boats, yet since the ferals had moved in its dimensions seemed reduced by the thronging crowd of mortals, and the echoes rang with the din of crying babies, people arguing, people laughing or weeping, people in conversation. There was the clatter of spoon against plate as the ferals stuffed themselves with the fish stew so generously provided by the fisherfolk, and the resounding snores of someone who was so exhausted that they could sleep through all the racket.

A stove in the corner provided welcome warmth and a reason for any number of squabbles, as individuals juggled for position, vying for who could get closest. Danel had finally been forced to step in and give the prime territory closest to the heat source to the sick, the infirm, and the handful of families with small children. Oil lamps hung on brackets along the walls, providing a soft golden glow and lending a cosy air to the scene.

Kelon looked around appreciatively. This was infinitely better than camping out in the forest, at the mercy of weather, wild beasts and, worst of all, the Wild Hunt of the Phaerie. Though the fisherfolk had not been overjoyed to see the refugees they seemed like a decent, kind community. Despite the thefts, he hoped they would do their best for their unwelcome guests. Why *some* people had to complain about the situation ...

His eyes tracked across the chamber to Danel, who was prowling around the shed like a trapped animal, with a thunderous scowl on her face. The refugees kept distracting her with a complaint here, a question there, a quarrel to be settled further on, but he knew that she was looking for him and spoiling for a fight because it had been his idea to come here. Well, as far as he was concerned, she could stuff it. It was the ferals' own fault that they'd been locked up and he was damned if he was going to take the blame.

Kelon's eye fell on the cluster of long, straight planks, no doubt used in boat construction, that had been propped upright against the wall in the far corner, away from the stove. Taking his blanket – another fisherfolk gift – he made his way across to them while Danel was preoccupied with handling a dispute over sleeping space, and wormed his way behind them, where he found a pile of sawdust and curled, fresh wood shavings that must have been swept hastily out of sight when the shed was cleared for the visitors. He scooped out a nest, wrapped the blanket around himself and settled down, breathing in the fragrance of the freshly planed wood with delight.

Peace settled around him, more warming than the blanket, as

gentle and comforting as an embrace. A wave of relaxation spread through him as the tension drained from his muscles, and he simply let himself drift in the flow. This was the first time since his escape from Eliorand that he'd had a chance to be alone, and he'd had no idea until this moment what a strain that had been.

For once Kelon wasn't thinking about Aelwen, or Danel, or the future. For a brief, charmed interlude he simply lived in the present, accepted its gifts with gratitude, and fell asleep, happier than he'd been in many a long day.

24

~

LIE DOWN WITH DOGS . . .

Sharalind was surprised by how much she enjoyed the short journey on Captain Galgan's boat from Tyrineld port to Freedom Cove. It seemed like for ever since she'd been out in the fresh air, and though the bright sunlight could not lighten her grief for her son, at least it bolstered her spirits enough to give her the strength to carry on.

She would need that strength, for there were so many burdens on her at present. Her days were all filled with plans and meetings, closeted in her chambers with the Luen Heads and others, ironing out the thousands of tedious logistical details involved in putting an army together. She had to keep constant vigilance against dissenters who might ruin her plans, and now the fisherfolk had dumped this mess into her hands.

If she had been surprised when the Captains had visited her in a deputation the previous evening, she had been absolutely stunned to hear what they had to tell her. She had been aware, of course, of the bands of feral humans who dwelt in the forest, but the Wizards had tended to leave it to the Wild Hunt to keep their numbers under control, and it was generally agreed in Tyrineld that at least the accursed Phaerie were good for *something*.

She had never expected to find a bunch of them turning up on her own doorstep, and with the utter temerity to ask for sanctuary and protection.

Her first impulse had been to round up the lot of them and have the Luen of Warriors dispose of them quietly, but there was no rush. The fisherfolk had them contained and surely the morning would do. Besides, she couldn't pretend not to be curious. Why had the mortals come here? True, they had not thrown themselves on her mercy but had gone to the independent fishers – but did they expect that they could simply become absorbed into the little seaside community without anyone noticing?

Sharalind needed answers. If these ferals were slaves who had escaped from Eliorand, she might be able to gain information that would be of benefit when she moved against the Phaerie. But what could she offer them? Captain Galgan had already warned her that they were a pack of thieves with no idea how to behave in a civilised community. They could never be permitted to roam at large in the Wizard realm. Well, she would just have to talk to them, and take things from there. Perhaps there was a way of involving the fisherfolk ...

'We'll soon be there, Lady Sharalind.' Galgan came up beside her and broke into her thoughts. 'On behalf of the community of Independence, I would like to thank you for taking this problem off our hands.'

Plague take it! The fishers have no intention of being involved.

However, Sharalind hid her chagrin behind a smile. 'I'm grateful to you for bringing the matter to my attention. I understand that it may have been difficult for you to report your fellow mortals to the authorities.'

'Because we're the same species?' Galgan's friendly mien darkened. 'These are no people of mine, Lady. To the Wizards we humans may all seem as alike as a flock of sheep, but just like you Wizards, we're all different.' He spat over the side. 'And some of us are more different than others.'

Really, talking to these free mortals was like trying to pick a way through a forest filled with bear traps! 'I had no intention of offending you,' Sharalind said stiffly. If he wanted an expression of regret from her, that was all he'd get. She, soulmate to the Archwizard, was certainly not going to lower herself to *apologise* to one of these creatures. Still, the fisherfolk were helping to feed her army. She needed them at present. Maybe pretending to ask the Captain's advice would smooth things over – and in truth she had no idea what she was going to do with those wretched ferals. She had a feeling that they would make very bad slaves, and she wasn't for a single moment going to allow them into the city to carry intelligence of Tyrineld back to their former masters. The Phaerie were notorious for being cunning and devious, and it had just struck her that these so-called escapees might not be what they seemed.

She turned to Galgan. 'Captain, would you and the other fisher-folk be prepared to help these people and teach them to support themselves from the sea as you have done?'

'No, I wouldn't.'

The abruptness of the flat refusal shocked her, but before she could ask him why, he anticipated her. 'Why should we teach this bunch of foreigners to take the bread out of our own families' mouths? That – and I don't apologise for saying it – would be a downright stupid idea.'

Undaunted by the shocked gasps and ominous mutterings from the Warrior escort she had brought with her, he continued. 'Lady, I'm going to be frank with you. If you give this lot precedence over your own humans who've been born and bred in Tyrineld and have served the Wizards all their lives, you'll have an uprising on your hands – and deservedly so. If you're handing out freedom then they should have it, not a crowd of filthy, thieving outsiders who've done nothing to deserve it.'

He faced her eye to eye, without a trace of deference or fear. 'Why don't you send these ferals out with your army? Of all people *they* should want to get their own back on the bastard Phaerie.'

Why, the man is brilliant!

Sharalind was too delighted with Galgan's suggestion to be an-noyed at his temerity – but she didn't have to tell him so. 'Thank you, Captain, for your frankness, and for your most interesting sug-gestion,' she said frigidly. 'I will certainly take it under consideration.'

He shrugged. 'Better consider fast, because we're here. I'll need to go and bring us into the dock now.' With that he walked away.

Sharalind felt uneasy in the fisherfolk village. This was the first time she'd ever been here, and the cluster of neat little houses that snuggled into the curve of the bay surprised her with their cleanli-ness and the skill with which they had been constructed. Who would have thought that mere humans could accomplish so much, without being instructed and supervised by a Wizard master? Though in principle she had been in favour of Cyran's plan to grant the fishers their autonomy, she had never really thought that the former slaves would amount to much, but seeing this place, its neat gardens with their colourful flowers, thriving rows of vegetables and washing flap-ping on the lines, she was forced to make some rapid readjustments to her thinking.

The trouble was, she really had no idea how to treat these fishers.

What she could see here was a community filled with people, just like Tyrineld but on a much smaller scale. She simply wasn't accustomed to viewing mortals as people. Until now, she'd considered them to be little more than animals – but these were certainly more than that, as was so clearly demonstrated by the forthright Galgan.

Is it the same for the entire human species, I wonder? Or is there something special about the fisherfolk that makes them different? But I've no time for that sort of conjecture at the moment. Right now I have a sizeable problem on my hands.

'Here we are, Lady Sharalind.' Captain Galgan drew her attention away from her thoughts. 'As I told you, we shut them safely in the boatshed for the present.'

Sharalind nodded. 'Very well, Captain. Let us go and deal with your unwelcome guests.'

Kelon's interlude of peace couldn't last, of course. When he awoke, stiff and hungry, he saw narrow strips of daylight glimmering through the gaps between the stacked planks. Another day had dawned – and by the sound of the raised voices that had awakened him, it had already brought trouble. As soon as he emerged from his den behind the timber, Danel was ready to pounce. '*There* you are.' She seized his arm. To his dismay, she didn't look any more friendly than she had done the previous night. 'While you've been skulking in your hiding place, I don't suppose you've thought of a way to get us out of this mess you've put us in?'

'Maybe if your people hadn't started out by stealing from the fisherfolk, they might have received us more kindly,' Kelon retorted, 'and if you had taken my advice about sending in a small deputation to speak to their leaders and explain the situation, instead of turning up in one great mass, then we wouldn't be in this situation. It might make you feel better to shift all the blame onto me, but if you were any sort of leader you'd—' He broke off and shrugged. 'We've already had this argument over and over, and I've better things to do with my time than dig up the same old grievances again. Just leave me out of it, Danel, and deal with your own problems. I'm done with it all.'

He started to turn away from her, but suddenly her fist slammed into his gut. Kelon doubled over, gasping for breath, pain exploding through him.

'I should have killed you at the start,' Danel snarled. 'I should have sliced you open and splattered that Phaerie blood of yours all over the forest. I'd do it now, save that it would ruin the one slim chance we have of these smug, arrogant pricks ever taking us in. But I *am* the leader here, and I'll get my people out of this somehow, even if it means we have to fight our way out with our bare hands. And when we do escape you'd better run, Kelon. Run fast and far, because if I ever see you again I promise you that I'll take you apart piece by piece.'

Wheezing, Kelon straightened up to find himself surrounded by a hostile ring of ferals, all with murder in their eyes. Even as his mind raced to find something – anything – he could say to diffuse the situation, he was saved by the tortured squeal of the great door sliding back on its runners. The ferals blinked, their eyes watering in the bright daylight, and Kelon was no longer the focus of attention as everyone looked towards the entrance of the shed.

A knot of people stood there. Kelon recognised the fisherfolk Captains – and with them, flanked by a half-dozen warriors who were grim of countenance and armed to the teeth, was a tall, stately woman with silver-threaded dark hair braided into a coronet on top of her head.

Wizards. Kelon felt his heart thump hard against his ribs. The fisherfolk had betrayed the ferals, and sold them back into slavery to a different set of masters. He closed his eyes, as if by erasing the sight of the ancient foes of the Phaerie he could also blot out all the implications. Danel had been right after all, and he'd been wrong. By bringing them here, he, Kelon, had betrayed her people. For a moment his mind went utterly blank, and when he got hold of himself again the tall woman was speaking.

'I am Sharalind, soulmate of the Archwizard Cyran. As you may be aware, your former masters are no friends of my people, which is why you still have your lives, at least for the present.' Her eyes swept across the crowd of mortals, cool and calculating, then she surprised them with a smile. 'It may be, however, that you will find us more reasonable and compassionate than your previous owners, and you will have the chance of making a good future for yourselves and your families, even as these good fisherfolk have done.'

Again, there was that sweeping look, as though she were trying to search out their very thoughts. 'Of course, there are conditions. But if you earn that precious freedom, I promise that it will be yours. I need everything you can tell me about the Phaerie; information about Eliorand, its defences, the Phaerie numbers and weapons, the speed and scope and secrets of their renowned flying steeds. Have any of you been in Eliorand recently? Can any of you tell me what I need to know?'

Almost light-headed with relief, barely able to believe his good fortune, Kelon took a deep breath and shouldered his way through the enclosing ring of ferals. 'I can help you, Lady. Not only have I recently escaped from Eliorand, but I was formerly the head stable-man to the Forest Lord's fabled steeds.'

Sharalind's eyes narrowed. 'You're no mortal,' she said. 'You're Hemifae. How came you to be here, with these ferals?'

'You are most perspicacious, my Lady.' Kelon inclined his head in a respectful half-bow. 'I am Hemifae indeed, and recent events in Eliorand have given those of us who carry mortal blood an uncertain future, to say the least. I escaped when the chance arose and fate threw me in the path of these ferals, who sheltered and helped me as well as they were able, though to them I was tainted with the blood of the Phaerie. I owe them a debt of gratitude, Lady. If you're willing to help them as you have said, then I can tell you everything you need to know – and a great deal more besides.'

'That remains to be seen,' said Sharalind, but she could not hide the gleam of satisfaction in her eyes. 'You will come with me now. The rest will remain here, for the present.'

'Wait!' Danel thrust her way forward, though Sharalind's brows drew together at the human's peremptory tone. 'I lead these people. If he goes with you, I should be there too. Besides,' she added with a sidelong look at Kelon, 'the Hemifae is not the only one with information. It's thanks to us that Hellorin is fighting for his life in Eliorand, with his son and heir dead and only his daughter Tiolani, naive and inexperienced, left to rule. Surely that must deserve some consideration, not to mention gratitude, from you.'

Sharalind's eyes narrowed. 'It certainly deserves some considera-tion. If you attacked one ruler, then why not another?'

'Why would we attack a ruler who is offering us our freedom? Such a one would deserve nothing but gratitude and loyalty from my people.'

For a long moment the two women locked eyes, and a shiver of unease went through Kelon. The very lives of the ferals lay in Sharalind's hands. Did Danel not realise what risks she was courting, addressing such a powerful user of magic with so little respect?

Then Sharalind shrugged. 'Very well, I will hear what you have to say.' Turning away dismissively from Danel, she spoke to Galgan. 'Captain, will you transport me back to the city with these two?' Though it was phrased as a question, her tone said otherwise.

'Take them and welcome, Lady. And the sooner we can get the rest of them off our hands, the better I'll be pleased.' The Captain cast a jaundiced eye across the ferals.

'Bring the Hemifae and that other girl and put them on board the boat,' Sharalind ordered her escort. 'Use the time spell – they must be kept under control at all times, and I don't want them conferring with one another until I've had a chance to question them. When we get back to Tyrineld bring them to me – but for pity's sake have them cleaned up first. They stink worse than a midden.'

With one last, disdainful glance for the ferals she swept out of the shed, accompanied by the Captains of the fisherfolk. Her troops marshalled Danel and Kelon out at swordpoint, marching them down the hill to the dock. Kelon took grateful gulps of fresh air and looked around the neat, well-built village on its beautiful stretch of coast. It looked like such a pleasant place to live; he found himself hoping desperately that he would be allowed to stay here. Before he had time to see much they were put aboard one of the waiting boats, herded into the bows and told to sit down – then the leader of the guards made a strange gesture, and Kelon knew no more.

In what seemed like an eyeblink, Kelon found himself standing in a chamber with walls painted pale blue, and a floor covered in a mosaic of small blue and white tiles. In the centre, like a vision of paradise, was a sunken pool of steaming water, deep enough for him to immerse himself and long enough to stretch out in. The window was curtained with white muslin drapes that drifted gently in the breeze, and shelves of dark wood on the wall opposite the door that held an array of soaps, sponges, long-handled brushes with soft bristles and a selection of perfumed oils in cut-glass bottles. Beneath them, a table in the same dark wood held a pair of large, soft, white towels, neatly folded, and hanging on a hook behind the door was a set of clean clothing; not unlike his own ragged tunic and pants, but in a soft cotton fabric that was probably more suited to this warmer clime.

There was no one in the room apart from himself, but the message was plain, and though his heart lifted at the thought of being clean again, his face burned with shame. Though there had been many worse aspects to living rough in the forest – hunger, cold, disease and danger from any number of predators, not to mention the Phaerie Hunt – he had still been inordinately distressed at having to live in such grime and squalor. Even if he'd had the chance to wash his only set of clothing, there would have been little possibility of drying it, and if an opportunity arose to swill himself down in some icy cold stream, running the risk of chills that might to lead to more serious illness, there was nothing clean on which to dry himself, and the ferals had no soap, or the means of making any. Everyone was filthy and they stank, and Kelon's loathing of their stench turned in upon himself when he realised that he must smell the same.

Now, looking at the pool of clean, sparkling clear water with curls of steam rising up from its surface, he felt that he would do anything, risk anything, for Sharalind, so intense was his gratitude – even though he realised that she was doing this for her own benefit rather than his. Out of curiosity, he opened the door a crack and peeked out, though he knew what he would find; and sure enough, a pair of guards were stationed outside.

'Be quick and get cleaned up, you filthy animal,' one of them growled. 'You're not coming out until you do.'

Unable to endure the contempt he saw on their faces, he shut the door quickly and hastened to do as they said. Stripping off the verminous rags he wore and kicking them into a corner, he sniffed at the bottles of oil until he found one that was sharp and spicy rather than sweet and floral. Pouring it liberally into the water, he took the soap and plunged into the pool. It took Kelon a long time to get himself thoroughly free from all the grime, and he enjoyed every minute. At last, dressed in the unfamiliar Wizard clothing and feeling clean for the first time since he'd left Athina's tower, he opened the door again.

'Well, that's better,' one of the guards said. Though Kelon's position here was dubious to say the least, he was astonished at how much his confidence had risen through being clean and presentable once more. He gave the sour-faced warrior a jaunty grin. 'You'll never know how much better it is – and I hope you'll never have to find out.'

On hearing such a frank reply from someone of tainted mortal blood, the guard's brows drew together ominously, and Kelon felt a clutch of unease.

Will these Wizards be any better than the Phaerie under Tiolani's rule?

He realised that his best chance of surviving and forging a future for himself here in Tyrineld was to make himself as useful as possible to Sharalind, and as the guards marched him off, he began to work out his strategy for doing just that.

As he was taken through a bewildering series of corridors, Kelon couldn't help noticing that all the Wizards they encountered were garbed as warriors, and all had that grim, flat-eyed look of individuals who had been trained to kill. A shiver passed through Kelon. Just what was he getting himself into? His escort, still unspeaking, took him up a spiral of steps that clearly led up into some kind of tower, and ushered him into a large, sunlit room at the top. It had two windows, one overlooking a high-walled courtyard where Wizards were performing drills using both conventional weapons and magic. The other casement showed the pastures and fertile orchards and vineyards beyond the city, with rolling moorland, stained with the great, magenta swathes of heather, sloping upwards in the distance.

Between the windows the pale yellow walls were covered in numerous maps, charts, lists and diagrams, and opposite the door was a broad, sturdy wooden desk with Sharalind seated in state behind it, in a high-backed chair of heavily carved wood. At her right shoulder stood a steel-eyed woman with a harsh, uncompromising look about her. Before the desk stood Danel, already, to Kelon's utter dismay, complaining in a loud, shrill voice. He knew that she was so desperate to save her people, and unfortunately, as the leader of the ferals, having spent a great deal of her life in the harsh environment of the forest camp, aggression was all she knew. Her reaction now, all snapping and snarling, was similar to that of any wild beast that had been captured.

'We came here in good faith, seeking sanctuary from the cruel Phaerie,' Danel said. 'We first escaped into the forest, then came to the fisherfolk, because we don't *want* to be slaves any more. Would *you* deny of your Wizards a chance to better themselves; to improve the lives of their families? We deserve those things too, and one way or another, we mean to have them.' She put her hands on the desk and leant forward in an aggressive move that had Kelon wincing inwardly. The warrior Wizard beside Sharalind said nothing, but took a step forward, her cold, mean eyes fixed on Danel's face. The feral leader took her hand from the desk and stepped back hastily.

For the first time, Cyran's soulmate spoke. 'Does a pig deserve a chance to better itself?' she asked contemptuously. 'Does a cow, or my horse? You forget yourself, human. It may be true that you are one step above the lowly beasts, but you are not on a par with the magical races of this world, and it would pay you to remember that. If you wish to live as the fisherfolk do, you must first prove your worth to the Wizardfolk. With the fish they provide, the humans of Freedom Cove make an important contribution, not only to their own well-being, but that of Tyrineld as a whole. It requires a tremendous amount of experience and skill to learn to read the wind, waves and weather; to anticipate where all the different species of fish will be, each in its proper season. The fisherfolk work punishing hours and risk their lives daily in brutal conditions at sea. Their work is highly dangerous. Many have given their lives in order to preserve the freedom of their compatriots. They have earned their privileged position among us many times over.'

She got to her feet, and looked Danel straight in the eye. 'Is there any way in which your ferals can prove themselves as the fisherfolk did?'

Danel hesitated for a moment, clearly nonplussed, but she rallied well. 'Lady, what would you have us do? I suspect that you had something in mind even before you brought me here.'

'Your instincts do you credit.' From her dismissive tone, Sharalind certainly didn't credit Danel with much intelligence. 'You have already told me what you know about the attempt on the Forest Lord's life ...'

Had she? That was news to Kelon. Clearly Danel had been a lot less fastidious about taking a bath than he had, if she'd had enough time to tell the whole tale.

'But,' the Wizard continued, 'you have no real inside knowledge of the current conditions in Eliorand, therefore you are of no further use to me as informants. There is one way, however, in which you can redeem yourselves. I want you to join my army—'

'Why? So that we can get killed doing your dirty work, acting as bait, going in unprotected against magic users?' Danel's eyes blazed with anger. 'That would solve your problem of what to do with us, wouldn't it?'

Sharalind shrugged. 'If I wanted an easy solution for what to do with you, I would have you all killed right now.' Against Danel's fire she was as cold as ice, but her eyes and voice held such an intensity that the feral leader took another step or two backwards.

'As it is,' Sharalind went on, 'I see a way for us to benefit one another. You need not fear, we will protect your people from the Phaerie magic in battle as far as we possibly can, and when your able-bodied companions join my force, I give you my word that the others – the young, the sick and the infirm – will be given the best of care here in Tyrineld. I won't lie to you – I don't expect all of you to come back from this confrontation, even as I know that not all of my Wizards will be returning. That is a heavy responsibility for me to bear. If we are victorious, however, to those of you who do return we will grant lands in the forest on our side of the border, and all the assistance you need to form a thriving settlement of your own.'

'And the alternative?' Danel grated.

Again came that cool shrug from Sharalind. 'You can always go back and ask the Wild Hunt if they have a better offer.'

Danel's eyes flashed and she opened her mouth to speak – then closed it abruptly and swung away from Sharalind to stare, scowling, out of the window at the warriors practising their fighting magic in the courtyard below. Sharalind, watching her intently, let the silence stretch out until Danel turned back.

'All right.' The leader of the ferals punctuated her words with a curt nod. 'It's true that nothing comes free in this world, especially in troubled times. We'll fight with you and gladly, if we can win our freedom and a place to call our own. I'm tired of running and hiding, struggling and starving. You may think of us as lowly creatures, but we deserve better than that. I only have one question, Lady Sharalind. When all this is over, what guarantee will I have that you'll keep your word?'

'Before you take your next breath, I could make you and your people slaves once more.'

Danel faced her squarely. 'And if you turned us back into slaves, could you trust us to fight for you?'

Sharalind got to her feet and gave the feral leader a long, measuring look. 'This is Omaira, Head of the Luen of Warriors and leader of my army.' She gestured towards the steel-eyed Wizard at her side. 'She will be my witness. And your companion is—?'

'Kelon, my Lady,' he supplied.

'And Kelon will bear witness for you and your people, Danel.' She held out her hand. 'Take my hand, leader of the feral humans, and together we will swear allegiance to one another. Give me your word that you will fight for the Wizards with your hearts, your blood, your lives if necessary. I will give my solemn oath to you that your vulnerable ones will be given the best of care, and when the fighting is over, and the Phaerie are defeated, I will grant you lands of your choosing in the forest beyond Nexis, and provide help in clearing, planting and making those lands fruitful; not to mention assistance in building a settlement where your descendants can dwell in safety and freedom for all time.'

'Done!' Danel clasped the Wizard's hand, then blushed, realising her response might not be sufficient for the gravity of the occasion. 'I mean – I swear we'll support you in every way you ask, and you'll have the gratitude and allegiance of my people for all time.'

'That is, supposing you defeat the Phaerie, of course,' Kelon said.

Both women swung round with identical scowls. 'Be quiet. Your turn will come,' Sharalind told him, then turned her attention back to Danel. 'I can see why you find this individual so annoying, yet he has information that I must hear, so if you would like to return to your people and tell them the good news, I will make arrangements for comfortable housing for them. But—' She lifted a warning finger. 'There will be no more theft, do you understand me? I will see that your companions have all they need, and anyone caught stealing from this moment on will know no mercy. Make it very clear to them, leader of feral humans. If you wish to build a future in the realm of the Wizards, there are certain standards of behaviour that are expected – and will be enforced.'

Danel nodded. 'That's fair enough. I'll tell them all right, don't you worry. There'll be no more trouble of that kind.' With that she left, escorted by one of the guards who had been waiting outside the door.

Sharalind turned to Kelon. 'Now, Hemifae. What tidings do you have for me that are so important?'

Kelon bowed to her. 'First, Lady, let me thank you from the bottom of my heart for the chance to be clean again. It was neither in my upbringing nor my nature to live like an animal in the forest, and you have my profound gratitude for restoring my dignity to me once more – but I will waste no more of your time with thanks,' he added hastily, seeing signs of impatience in the tightening of Sharalind's mouth.

'Lady, I fled Eliorand very recently, so I can tell you a great deal about current conditions in the city. But I have other tidings of far greater import to bring you. Not long ago, I saw the Wizard Iriana, and sat in the same room with her—'

'*What?*' Sharalind sprang to her feet, knocking over her chair. 'Where—'

'I know what happened to your son.' Kelon forestalled the question he knew she was about to ask.

Sharalind went absolutely white, and sank back into the chair that Omaira had set upright for her. 'Tell me.'

Kelon took a deep breath and prayed that he would survive the next few minutes. If she did not believe him, the consequences would be unthinkable. 'Though Avithan has left this world and is lost to you, he did not die, and maybe there is even the faintest shadow of a hope that one day he may be returned to you.'

'This cannot be true.' Her expression darkened, and the look in her eyes turned Kelon cold. 'I warn you, Hemifae, you toy with my grief at your peril.'

'Lady Sharalind, I would never toy with a mother's grief. I swear on my life that I know why and how Avithan was taken from this world, and far more besides: matters of grave importance to the future of our entire world. Danel knows some of this information also, and can corroborate my story.'

'Then why did she never mention it?'

'Because she is a mere feral human, Lady; uneducated and unconcerned about any matters save those that impact on her immediate survival, and those of her people. I truly believe she did not understand the significance of the meeting we attended with Iriana and a number of others, including a being of tremendous power who took Avithan beyond the boundaries of our world, in the hope that he could be healed of wounds that were so grievous he must otherwise have perished. Much was discussed at that meeting, and many matters were made clear. You should understand their significance, and particularly in the absence of the Archwizard, it is a matter of gravest urgency that you be informed.'

'Bring the Hemifae a chair,' Sharalind ordered Omaira. When he was seated, she leant forward, her eyes fastened hungrily on his face. 'Tell me everything, Kelon, every single detail – but first, tell me about my son.'

'Now tell me about your life,' Incondor urged Chiannala. 'I've told you about mine.'

In the time she had been looking after Incondor, the long hours spent in one another's company had brought them very close, and it seemed natural to share one another's secrets. In was as if their encounter right at the very gates of death had formed a special bond of trust between them.

Incondor had told her of his hatred for Yinze and his fear that the Wizard had revealed to the Queen his plans to smuggle forbidden intoxicating spirits into Aerillia. He had gone on to relate how he had taken the harp and almost destroyed himself. Now they were co-conspirators, Chiannala felt a bond with this alien, foreign Mage that she had never known with anyone else in her life. 'You won't find mine so interesting,' she replied. 'Oh how I wish I could fly like you.'

'Once I'm better you will,' Incondor promised. 'I'll have you taken up with me in a net. I still have my bearers here, though they chose to stay outside the city. They're from my own household staff and they are very loyal – after what Yinze did to me, they have no greater liking for Wizards than I do.' Incondor gave her a charming smile. 'Present company excepted, of course.'

They were talking privately in mindspeech, for other Healers were constantly in the room, one at all times suppressing the Skyman's pain while the others worked to piece together and repair the remnants of his wings. Though his general health was improving rapidly due to the advanced Wizardly Healing skills, the structural damage to his wings was taking much longer to mend. The twisted, shattered travesties of the beautiful feathered pinions still needed to be held together by a framework of bracing struts and splints, and even Tinagen was beginning to look concerned.

Fear was making Incondor impatient and ill-tempered, and his explosions of anger were getting worse and more frequent every day. The Healers had discovered that the only one who seemed able to calm and distract him was Chiannala, so she was encouraged to spend as much time with him as possible – and it seemed that this was the opportunity that she had so wanted, to get close to him. During their merging when she had fought to hold him to life, Incondor had discovered that she was not who she claimed to be, but he had not revealed her secret. The longer they had spent together the closer they'd grown, and now she felt that she could trust him.

In their bonding, and in subsequent conversations, she had already detected a broad streak of ruthlessness in his make-up, and she had a feeling that he would understand her motivation in doing the terrible thing she had done. She had already made some tentative allusions to half-breeds, not knowing how the Winged Folk reacted to such aberrations, but had discovered that, no matter what the official position might be, Incondor himself had no objections – in fact, she had a sneaking suspicion that more than once, he'd availed himself of the humans his people kept to cultivate the lower terraces of their mountains – not something she wanted to dwell on, but at least it helped her own position now.

Oh, it would be such a relief to unburden herself! The strain of keeping up another person's identity was immense, and she hoped that it would be eased if she had someone to confide in. So, making certain that their mindspeech was shielded from the other Healers, she took the plunge and told him who she really was, and how she had come to be here.

She had to hand it to him – as her tale of the audacious substitution of herself for Brynne unfolded, not once did his face betray any of his surprise, admiration or even amusement. But his replies said otherwise. 'Incredible! Ingenious! And what cool courage it took, to see your opportunity and seize it as you did. Never have I seen such ingenuity and nerve in the females of my own kind!'

Now Chiannala had to struggle to keep her emotions from showing on her face. 'Nevertheless, you can't imagine what a relief it is to be able to confide in someone at last. It's been very lonely, Incondor, living another person's life, and I'm in constant fear of being caught out.' She lifted her chin. 'Yet if I had to do it all again, I would. Living as a true Wizard, being able to develop my powers as they do – anything is worth that.'

'And now you have a friend.' Incondor took her hand and grasped it tightly. 'I owe you my life, Chiannala, and if things go wrong for you here, I promise you will always have a place in Aerillia with me.'

Was he promising her this from love, or just gratitude? Just at that moment, it was enough to Chiannala to know that he wanted her with him, and cared for her enough to help her, though she wondered what would happen when he was finally healed, and ready to return home. All her life she had wanted to be here in Tyrineld – so much that she had killed to achieve her aims. No matter what she felt for Incondor, was she really prepared to uproot herself and lose everything she'd won here?

Well, he wouldn't be going anywhere yet. At present, she had time enough to wait and see how things developed. If war with the Phaerie was really brewing, who knew what the future might bring? It was good to know she had an escape route if she needed one.

25
~

RESTORATION

T iolani was glad, not to mention profoundly relieved, to be restored to her proper position of honour and respect within the Phaerie court. She was back in her comfortable old rooms, and though Cordain had stationed a guard at the door, it was such an improvement on the cold, bare chamber where he'd kept her imprisoned that she didn't care. It was such a relief to be able to bathe again, and eat whenever she wanted. And what luxury it was, to be clad in a shimmering gown of silver, black and gold brocade, with the glitter of diamonds at her neck and ears. Her life had improved immensely – but it had not brought her peace of mind.

Now that Ferimon's treacherous Healers had been rooted out and removed, the damage they had done was being corrected and the Forest Lord's condition was slowly beginning to improve at last. Tiolani was glad of it – of course she was – but what would her father say when he recovered and saw what a mess she'd made of things? She had nightmares about it every time she closed her eyes.

Though she had convinced herself that she owed nothing to her former companions; especially Aelwen, her mother's own sister, who had abandoned her so callously to whatever fate might bring, she still suffered inconvenient pangs of guilt at betraying them to Cordain. But what choice did she have? They had left her alone to survive as best she could, so they could hardly complain about the methods she used. Or so she kept telling herself.

The fate of Varna was also gnawing at her. Her former lady in waiting, Ferimon's sister and her best friend all throughout her life – or so Tiolani had thought, until she'd discovered that Varna had been part of the plot to seduce and betray her. The girl had been imprisoned, waiting for her former friend to decide her fate, but before she did so, Tiolani wanted to confront her, to face her and ask why. How could she have done this terrible thing? She wanted to, needed to ask those questions, but somehow she kept putting it off. She didn't want to admit to herself that she was afraid of the answers.

The plan to capture her former allies wasn't going well, either. Nychan and his warriors had not come back; neither with their prisoners nor, if the traitors had not yet arrived at the cave, to have the flying magic renewed before going back to resume their vigil. The spell must have worn off by now, so they were stranded between Eliorand and the borders of the realm. She had been scrying for hours to try and find them, in the hope that the spell could be renewed over such a long distance, but so far she had found no sign of them.

Tiolani's eyes were stinging from gazing for so long, with such intent concentration, on the silvered scrying glass that was propped on the windowsill. No matter how hard she looked, or how far she sent her mind winging across the forest south of Eliorand, the image in the mirror was clouded and unfocused, and she could see no sign of what had happened, either to her former allies or the warriors she had sent to capture them.

'Well?' Cordain's brusque, impatient demand slashed like a knife across her focus, and the vague amorphous forms – the only images she had managed to grasp – shattered into pieces.

Ablaze with anger, she whirled round from the high tower window with a snarl. 'Curse you, Cordain! How in perdition do you expect me to accomplish anything when you keep on interrupting? I can't renew the flying magic without some kind of image to work on – not at this distance.'

'Hellorin could always renew the flying spell no matter what the distance.' There was a nasty, accusing edge to Cordain's voice.

He had a nerve! There he sat, making himself at home in the most comfortable chair by the fireside, while she was wearing herself into exhaustion, trying to find his stupid warriors. Tiolani's hand itched to strike him. 'And Hellorin might have passed the knowledge on to my brother Arvain,' she snapped, 'but considering he never bothered to teach me the spell at all, because I was only a *girl*, and not his precious *heir*, you can count yourself bloody fortunate that I've ac-complished what I have.'

She picked up her gold-chased goblet of spiced wine from the windowsill and took a long drink to ease her parched throat. How many hours had she been here now, trying fruitlessly, both with her mind and her scrying mirror, to make contact with the missing warriors. Wearing herself out trying to put right this stupid old idiot's mistakes, and what thanks did he give her?

She turned back to Cordain with a fulminating glare. 'If this mess is anybody's fault it's yours, and you only have yourself to blame. I told you to let me go with them. You should have listened, but no – you knew best. You didn't trust me. Well, see where it got you. It's clear now that your precious Nychan has mucked up his mission, or why has he not returned, or at least sent us tidings?'

'Perhaps *you* should be answering that,' Cordain retorted, his eyes as hard as flint. Too angry to sit any longer he rose from his chair and paced away from her, only to turn back and point an accusatory finger. 'How do I know they didn't walk into a trap? How do I know that *you* didn't betray them? You and those fine friends you arrived with, Aelwen and Taine.'

'You bastard!' Tiolani shrieked, and flung the goblet at him, forcing him to dodge aside with an oath. It missed him by a hair's breadth and flew past his head, splattering him with sticky, blood-red wine as it hit the wall behind him. Cordain took an involuntary step towards the door. He'd forgotten that her rages could be every bit as incandescent as her father's.

'Are you going senile?' she shouted. 'Have you forgotten who tried to warn you that this was a stupid idea? Didn't I tell you the Wizard was dangerous? Didn't I warn you that she'd already slain Hellorin's spymaster Dhagon, the most lethal killer in Eliorand? Didn't I tell you, over and over, that you needed to send me with Nychan, to act as bait and lure Iriana into a trap? But no, you wouldn't listen. You didn't trust me. And just look where it got you! How *dare* you try to shift the blame for this mess onto me. When my father wakes up and finds out how you've treated me—'

Her words jolted Cordain to the core. She could have said nothing more likely to influence him. He let her continue to rant while he made a swift reassessment of his position. The Lord of the Phaerie definitely seemed to be improving now, thanks to Tiolani's revelations that had resulted in the removal of the spurious Healers brought in by Ferimon. What was he likely to say about his Chief Counsellor's actions while he'd been indisposed? Tiolani had been the worst sort of fool, it was true, but she had almost paid for her folly with her life. And on her miraculous return, what had

Cordain done? Actually imprisoned the Forest Lord's only surviving heir.

As for her deeds, Hellorin might regret the deaths of the key Hemifae traders and artificers that Tiolani had dispatched, but he would not view their murders in such a grave light as Cordain did. He had far too much blood on his own hands for that, and would view their loss as more of an inconvenience than an atrocity. Indeed, he might even be secretly delighted that his daughter had inherited his merciless nature. Though Tiolani had made mistakes, she had finally unmasked the traitor who had almost slain the Phaerie Lord and killed his son. And Hellorin was more likely to be pleased, rather than concerned, by the way she had pretended to make an alliance with her enemies then betrayed them at the first opportunity.

Cordain saw things differently, but he would no longer be in charge once Hellorin was restored. The tables would be turned then, and Tiolani would have power over *him*. Maybe it was time he started trusting her – or pretending to, at any rate. In fact, there was a certain amount of reason in what she was saying. It looked as though Nychan's ambush had failed. Unease crept up Cordain's spine like the touch of cold fingers. How powerful was this Wizard, if she could manage to overcome so many armed warriors? Just what was he up against here? For the thousandth time he wished that the Forest Lord was back to shoulder all the ruler's burdens, but what was the point of that? In the real world it was up to Cordain, but at least he could shift part of the responsibility onto Tiolani.

Furthermore, until Hellorin recovered, only she could cast the flying spell. Without her the Phaerie were grounded and helpless: not a good situation to be in with a powerful Wizard on the loose. It was imperative he send out another squad without delay to find out what had happened to Nychan and his men. Cordain needed to make his peace with Tiolani immediately. He was forced to trust her, to reveal his plans – and to hope that he'd made the right decision.

'Well?' Tiolani demanded, jerking his attention back to her.

Hastily Cordain gathered his wandering thoughts. 'My Lady Tiolani, you are absolutely right.' (There, that should cover whatever she'd been saying.) 'I owe you an apology,' he went on. 'You must understand that I was forced to be cautious at first, simply because you'd arrived in the company of thieves and traitors. I was simply trying to safeguard your father's realm for when he returned, but I am not accustomed to ruling, as Hellorin is. If I have made mistakes I apologise most profoundly.'

Tiolani regarded him with narrow-eyed suspicion. 'And what has brought about this sudden change of heart?'

Cordain forced a smile. 'You argue most eloquently, my dear. It's a wise man who is not afraid to admit that he was wrong. I needed to be sure that I could trust you, but you've convinced me now, and with that Wizard at large, we need to work together to safeguard the Phaerie realm.' He held out a hand to her. 'Come, child – please forgive me. We are more powerful together than we could be singly, and we have a great deal to do in very little time.'

Concealing her relief, Tiolani took his hand. In this game of shifting power between them, he must never know how much she needed him. She had betrayed both sides now. Until her father could recover and protect her, she was treading a very dangerous path.

She smiled fixedly again. 'Let us be friends once more, Cordain, and work together to protect our people. How may I assist you? I presume, to begin with, you will want to send out more warriors, to find out what happened to Nychan and his men.'

'Indeed I do,' said Cordain. 'I would also like you to come down to the stables with me, my lady. I have a surprise for you.'

Tiolani didn't like surprises. It was a long time since she'd had a pleasant one. Suspicious and uneasy, she followed Cordain through the palace, doing her best to ignore the curious looks she was receiving from all sides. She was cheered, however, when she emerged through the massive outer doors to find bright sunlight and a cool, lively breeze. Despite all her troubles, she felt her spirits lift a little. After her imprisonment in the palace, it was wonderful to be able to move about in the fresh air again. And there, waiting for her at the bottom of the steps was her dear Asharal, the horse that had been a gift from her brother.

'Asharal!' she exclaimed delightedly. 'Oh, how long it's been since I saw him last.'

Cordain smiled. 'Just to prove that I really do trust you, my lady, I thought you might like to fly across to the stables with me.'

'I would love to. I've missed my Asharal.' Her face grew clouded. 'If only I'd been riding him, instead of Corisand, on the night Aelwen and Kelon absconded, things might have turned out very differently.'

'Had that been so, you might never have discovered Ferimon's duplicity,' Cordain said. By this time she had told him a carefully edited version of what had transpired that night. 'Would you really have wanted that?'

'I suppose not.' She sighed. 'Though I do feel like such a fool for letting him deceive me so easily.' She shrugged. 'Anyway, what's done is done. There's no changing it now. Come on, Cordain. Let us deal with the problems of today.'

Tiolani was finding it easier to accomplish the flying spell, now that she'd had a little practice. In no time at all she and Cordain were airborne, rising above the palace and the city below, herself on Asharal and the counsellor riding his own Gial, whose shining coat was so dark that it verged on black. Knowing what she knew now, Hellorin's daughter found herself wondering what the horses, especially her own mount, would look like in their human form. The memory of the way she'd abused Asharal, riding him into lameness and total exhaustion with the Wild Hunt, in her frenzied pursuit of the feral mortals who'd ambushed Hellorin and killed her brother, was not a happy one, and she was all too glad to shrug it off.

It doesn't matter. What's done is done.

She seemed to be using that phrase all the time lately. It was the only way she could keep going – to put the past, with all its mistakes, behind her and look to the future.

In the present, things were looking up. To be riding on her precious Asharal in the sun and the wind was a joy. To be able to look down again at her city, its shining rooftops, its graceful trees, its markets and parks with all the Phaerie going about their daily business, was a miracle. To be safely back in Eliorand, restored to her former position – even if it *was* in an uneasy alliance with Cordain – was more than she could ever have hoped for. Ferimon was dead and gone, and Aelwen, with her inconvenient appeals to Tiolani's conscience, was out of the way, hopefully for good.

Hellorin would not die, and was apparently on the road to recovery – though that wasn't necessarily such a comfortable thought. She shuddered to think what he would say about all the mistakes she'd made since the future of the realm had been thrust into her unready hands. But he loved her, didn't he? He would understand, surely? Surely. Especially since she was saving his beloved horses for him. And she *would* save them. Now that she knew what Corisand and the others were planning she could be on her guard. The Xandim could be scattered, hidden ...

At that moment, they finally came in sight of the stables, the barns and buildings neat and tidy amid their patchwork of surrounding paddocks and meadows. But what was this? Why were there so many animals here? Tiolani's heart almost stopped beating. Everywhere she looked there were horses. Stallions, geldings, mares and foals; grey, black, chestnut, brown, roan and dun. All of the Xandim – surely it must be all of them – gathered together in one place. A lure, a temptation and a target. Easy pickings. Cordain had done half of Corisand's work for her already.

Furious, she rounded on the counsellor. 'What have you done, you fool? *What have you done?*'

He was still justifying his actions, defensive and more than a little annoyed, as they descended towards the stables and the crowded fields below. 'The animals were too vulnerable, scattered as they were between this place, the outlying meadows and the northern pastures where we rest them in the summer. Here, all together, they can be safeguarded. I have warriors hidden all around the perimeter ...' He droned on, smug and complacent, until Tiolani itched to slap him.

'Don't you see what you've done?' she interrupted. 'The way things were before, the Wizard's biggest problem was collecting the horses all together. She might have taken some of them, but it was virtually impossible to get them all.'

'The point is,' Cordain cut across her, 'we don't want the Wizard to get any of them. Even if she captured a few, she'd still have the start of a breeding herd, then the Phaerie would lose all of their airborne supremacy over our foes. The only way to guard against that happening is to keep the horses together.'

While they'd been speaking they had landed, and now that they'd dismounted, he reached across and patted her arm in a condescending way that had Tiolani grinding her teeth. 'Now don't you worry about it, my dear. You are young as yet, and untrained in strategy. Just leave these annoying details to me and everything will be fine. I promise I won't let anyone take your father's horses.'

She had trapped herself, of course. Cordain had based his strategy on the lie she'd told him: that Iriana wanted to steal the Phaerie horses as breeding stock to give the Wizards an advantage in warfare. He had no idea, because she couldn't tell him, about the true identity of the Xandim steeds, and the fact that Corisand planned to rescue her people – all of them. And thanks to Cordain, here they were. Tiolani thought quickly. 'But what if the Wizard comes,' she protested. 'You've put all our eggs in one basket, and crowded together like this, they make a perfect target.'

'Of course they do.' Cordain beamed at her. 'Too perfect. Irresistible, in fact.' He gave her a toothy smile. 'A target, a temptation – and bait for the perfect trap.'

Tiolani stared him, dismayed by such arrogance, such complacency. 'You're taking a dreadful risk,' she said. 'I hope you're right. For all our sakes, you'd better be.'

'The fool! The idiot! The thrice-cursed imbecile!' Hellorin stormed. With an oath he tore his attention away from the patch of clear ice on the floor of Aerillia's throne room, and got to his feet.

The Moldan sat on her throne at the far end of her immense hall of ice regarding him dispassionately. 'I don't know why you keep watching.' Her voice came to him echoingly across the great stretches of blue-white shining floor. 'It only makes you angry and frustrated. When I provided the ice-mirror so that you could scry into your own world, I didn't realise that you would become so obsessed.'

'Not so much obsessed as desperate,' Hellorin snarled. 'And can you blame me? While I am trapped here, my kingdom is falling into ruin. Tiolani and Cordain can't even make one good ruler between them, while I am forced to sit there and watch them make mistake after mistake.' He smote his fist into his palm. 'I must get back. I *have* to! Ten thousand curses on that Windeye for taking the Fialan and leaving me here to rot. She robbed me of the only chance I had.'

A gigantic figure on her throne of ice, Aerillia looked at him, considering. Despite their former alliance, it was unfortunate that Hellorin had ever been allowed to return to the Elsewhere. He no longer belonged here. He caused nothing but trouble, spreading ripples of unease and unrest throughout the sensitive atmosphere of this world where the Old Magic ruled, and the repercussions from the slightest action might set in motion a devastating chain of events.

At least the Fialan had been taken from the Elsewhere, much to Aerillia's relief. The Windeye and her Wizard friend had achieved the impossible. But that still left Hellorin and Ghabal, now recovered from the damage they had taken in the battle for the Stone of Fate, here in this world, with a mammoth grudge still festering between them. All too soon they would be back at one another's throats. It was inevitable.

She wanted them gone, with all the problems and danger that

came with them. Let the mundane world have them both and be damned to the consequences! She knew a way – risky, uncertain but a chance at least – to use the Fialan as a gateway one more time, and if she told Hellorin how to wrest such a portal open, then Ghabal would surely follow. Everyone here in the Elsewhere would be better off without them. She must take one final risk of helping the Forest Lord, and hope and pray that her idea worked.

Aerillia came out of her thoughts and looked across the vast expanse of her throne room, to where the Lord of the Phaerie was still muttering and cursing over the scrying mirror of ice. She took a deep breath and gambled all.

'Hellorin, listen to me. There may be a chance, just one slim chance, for you to get back to your own world and regain everything you've lost.'

Hellorin scrambled to his feet and charged towards her. 'You know a way?' he roared. 'Why in all perdition didn't you tell me sooner?'

She held up a hand and he stopped dead, as though he had run into a wall of stone. He was held there, helpless, raging soundlessly.

When Aerillia answered, the chill of a thousand winters was in her voice. 'You may have power, Lord of the Phaerie, but if you take that tone with me, here on my own ground, death will find you swiftly. There are few indeed with the power to end your life, but you had better believe that I am one of them. I did not tell you before because this possibility has only just occurred to me. I hesitate to tell you now, because it is only a slender hope, and depends on your enemy the Windeye making one mistake. Everything hinges on Corisand's use of the Fialan ...'

Hellorin forgot his rage and listened carefully as the Moldan of Aerillia outlined her idea. One chance, one opening, one mistake from the Windeye was all he'd need.

26

~

OLD FRIENDS

In the new hiding place that Taine had found for them, Iriana's companions were beginning to despair. The journey here had almost finished the Wizard, who'd been desperately weakened by blood loss from the wound she had taken.

They were now concealed in the centre of a dense thicket. Taine, with his part-Wizard heritage, had managed a spell to persuade the bushes to part, allowing access for the companions and their mounts. Once they were safe inside, the undergrowth had closed back into place and grown over the top of their campsite in a domelike covering that protected them from the worst of the weather, and also from being seen by any Phaerie flying over in search of them. Corisand, now back in her humanoid form, had made a roof for it; an invisible shield of solid air that kept out the rain and wind, while preventing the heat from their fire from dissipating. Aelwen, just to be on the safe side, had cloaked the area with a spell of glamourie, to prevent the light from their fire being seen from above. Here they did what they could for Iriana, applying what simple healing spells Taine and Kaldath knew between them, while Corisand worked her spells upon the air to keep it flowing in and out of the Wizard's lungs.

All two dreadful days, Corisand had watched over her friend, scarcely moving from her side and accompanied by Taine, Kaldath and Dael, who cradled a wretched-looking Melik in his lap, while Aelwen did her best to make the rough shelter as comfortable as possible and the Dwelven kept guard around the perimeter of the thicket in case any enemy should come near. Boreas and his mate kept watch from a tree nearby.

Corisand's only focus was her friend. As the sun went down and the shadows gathered she kept her ceaseless vigil over Iriana, pouring all her energy and will to live into that still, pale form. At some point during the night she must have dozed, for suddenly she opened her eyes and found that she was no longer in that dark, cramped little lair amid the thorny thicket. It was no longer dark but daylight. She seemed to float, suspended in the air above an ocean inlet that twisted and turned, with one gigantic precipice after another dropping into the water from the hills on either side. Small, tough evergreens, scrubby bushes, ferns and vivid green moss clung tenaciously to the steep crags, taking advantage of every tiny ledge and crevice to find a foothold, cloaking the tough old bones of the rock in a tattered patchwork of viridian and emerald. Long, slender waterfalls plunged endlessly down; gleaming threads of silver against the dark grey basalt cliffs. Beneath the Windeye the calm, rippling water murmured its ancient song, and all around her the air was shimmering with an opalescent mist interlaced with rainbows.

Corisand's heart warmed and glowed within her. Her spirits, weighed down by weariness and worry, soared like eagles. The land was alive; she could feel its energy, its massive, powerful life force that poured into her from all around. She was back in the Elsewhere – that much she knew. But where was this unfamiliar place?

Looking at the intricate, meandering coastline, she judged it to be somewhere near the tall, rocky pinnacle of the Moldan Basileus, but he was situated out in the open ocean, and she could not see him from where she was. In case he was somewhere close, she tried calling out to him in mindspeech, but he did not answer.

But someone did.

Above the Windeye, on her left as she faced towards the inner part of the fjord, was a massive eminence with a rounded summit. The crags and ledges nearest to her had a strange trick of structure, a combination of shadow, light and plant growth that resembled a face, but no human features were these. It reminded Corisand of no creature that she had ever seen – it was simply the visage of some strange, primeval being that was essentially and powerfully itself. Then a voice, deep and rumbling like the roar of a distant avalanche, with a power that shook the Windeye to her bones, came into her ears and mind.

'Welcome, Windeye. We've been expecting you. I have heard much about you from Taku and Aurora, and all to the good. I am Denali, the Great One, the Earth mother of the Evanesar.' Her voice softened with a little humour. 'I believe the others may have mentioned me.'

'Indeed they did, O Great One.' Corisand found her voice falling naturally into the formal cadences of the Evanesar speech. 'I should have realised where I was, for Taku once described your beautiful home to me. He called it the Labyrinth of the Mists, and hoped that one day I might be able to see it for myself.'

'And now that you have?'

'I can see that he did not exaggerate. In fact he described it perfectly, and with such wistful longing: *"Oh, the beauty! The calm, shining ocean; the miles upon miles of convoluted cliffs and islands twisting and twining back upon one another to form bays and deep inlets; the thousands of slender waterfalls cascading down the cliffs in sprays of silver, and the mists glowing softly with ever-changing rainbows."* I don't know why you have brought me here, but it is an honour and a joy that I will never forget.'

Corisand took a deep breath. 'But by your grace, O Great One, I cannot linger at this time. My friend Iriana, who was here with me before and helped me defeat Ghabal and Hellorin, is wounded in my own world, and may be dying—'

'Fear not, friend Windeye.' On hearing the new voice Corisand spun around and there, where there had previously been an inlet of shimmering water, was the great ice-serpent glacier form of Taku. 'Why do you think we brought you here this time? Iriana is also with us, and we will give her all the aid we can.'

'Well, you didn't actually think we would just leave the poor creature to perish, did you?' The sharper tones came from above, and there, stretching across the sky, its outspread wings made of ever-changing, scintillating colour, was the great eagle form of Aurora.

'Look,' Taku commanded. 'Look closely, Windeye. Look into my heart.'

And when Corisand peered down at the glacier, there lay Iriana, frozen into a cocoon of clear blue ice. Unable to stop herself, she gave a cry of distress.

'Oh, come now, Corisand,' Aurora said. 'You might have a little more faith in us. You should know we would never do anything to hurt your friend.'

'I do know that – of course I do. It's just that she looks so—'

'Dead? No, I have her safe.' Taku's voice was more sympathetic. 'Though when we brought her across she was hovering on the very boundary. But my Cold magic has kept her life suspended by a slender thread, and we are here because the Great Mother of the Evanesar has offered her gift of healing.'

'I will bestow it gladly,' Denali said. 'You did us a great service, far greater than you will ever know, in removing the Fialan from our world. We owe you this favour, and more.'

Corisand detected an odd note in the Great One's voice, and had an uncomfortable feeling that there was something she was not being told, but right now, Iriana was her only concern. Anything else could wait.

In her deep, rumbling voice, Denali began to chant; an ancient song with no discernible words, as old as the bones of the very earth itself. The shell of blazing cyan-blue ice that enclosed the Wizard began to pulse and glow, brighter and brighter as the energy built, until the radiance was blinding; piercing the soul and overwhelming the mind until Corisand was sure she could endure no more; that she must fly apart and explode into a thousand pieces.

Then suddenly it was over. Silence fell; so profound that it beat against Corisand's ears and she could hear the whisper of her own blood in her veins – and into that stillness, a small, wondering voice said: 'Oh.'

The Windeye blinked the last of the dazzle from her eyes to see Iriana, standing on the broad, rough surface of the glacier that was Taku and gazing up wide-eyed, with her own vision, at the extra-ordinary alien face of Denali in the cliffs above. Corisand, about to call out, longing to rush over and hug her friend, found herself halted by the expression of profound respect on the Wizard's face.

Iriana bowed deeply. 'Madam.' Her voice rang out across the gulf of air between herself and the ancient being. 'Like calls to like, and I know it was your elemental Earth powers that forged the link with my own Wizardly Earth magic and brought me back. I am honoured to be in your presence, and deeply grateful that you saved my life.'

'Child of the Wizardfolk, you are more than welcome,' came Denali's reply.

'Well, there's gratitude for you.' Aurora shattered the gravity of the moment. 'Don't mind *us*, will you? Taku and I – though we brought you here in the first place – didn't have a thing to do with it at all.'

Iriana laughed, and held up her arms outstretched towards the mighty shimmering figure in the sky. 'Aurora, I love you.'

'*What?*' For once the great Evanesar of the Air seemed at a loss for words. 'Now, let's not get carried away, Wizard.'

Iriana laughed once more, and knelt to lay a hand on the white, sharp-ridged surface of the ice serpent's back. 'And I love you too, dear Taku. I'm more than grateful that you brought me here and saved my life. I felt that I had gone away on a long, long journey, then I heard you calling me.'

Then she leapt across the intervening space between herself and Corisand, and hugged the Windeye tightly. 'Corisand, my best, my dearest friend. All the while I was slipping away I knew you were there, unmoving, unresting, holding me to the world with the sheer force of your will.' She laughed. 'You weren't about to let me go anywhere.'

'Not if I could help it.' Corisand laughed too. 'You promised to help me save my people, remember? I wasn't going to let you get out of that so easily.'

'You speak more truthfully than you know,' Taku said. 'It was your need, Windeye, that called to us, and though it would not normally be our policy to intervene in Death's realm, you and Iriana need one another, and we, here in the Elsewhere, need both of you.'

The great serpent's head, with its vivid blue eyes, reared above them, and Corisand could feel the concern in that steady gaze. 'You must beware, my friends. Hellorin has regained his strength and is plotting again. We know that he is seeking a gateway back into your world – and even worse, our own brother, Katmai, the Evanesar of Fire, has been moved to pity by the plight of the Ghabal. His quarrel with us, the rest of his Elemental family, has been long and bitter, for he always felt that we should have intervened in the matter of the Fialan, and found a way to take it for ourselves. Now he has allied himself with the Mad One. If the Lord of the Phaerie finds a way back to your world then Ghabal will surely follow, and with Katmai's power added to his own, there is no limit to the damage he could wreak.'

'But what can *we* do about it?' Corisand asked in dismay. 'How could we possibly fight a Moldan and an Evanesar together, not to mention Hellorin?'

'Katmai cannot follow you into the realm of the mundane. The presence of an Evanesar would be too much for the fragile fabric of your reality – it would be torn apart like a cobweb. Our brother has simply used his powers to increase those of Ghabal, which makes

292

the Moldan a formidable adversary indeed. We other Evanesar can, however, use you and Iriana as our emissaries in much the same way. We cannot give our additional powers to you directly, but if we could but pass part of our power into the Fialan—'

'The Fialan?' Iriana interrupted. 'But, madam, that's impossible. Think of the battle we had to get the Stone out of this realm. We dare not bring it back again.'

'As I was about to say,' replied Denali with some asperity, 'it would be impossible for us to use the Fialan. You and Corisand, however, would be our conduits – if you were prepared to take the risk.'

'Great One, no!' Taku protested. 'Their forms are too frail. They were never meant to endure such immeasurable energies.'

'Then we are lost, for unless we find some way to confine the magic for long enough to get them back to their own realm and drain it into the Fialan to make it safe, then Ghabal will be able to rampage unchecked through the mundane world.'

The silence stretched out as all of them tried to think of a way to put their plan into action. 'Surely there must be some way to shield them from these titanic powers,' Aurora said at last.

Shield – shield! The word suddenly set off an explosion of ideas in Corisand's mind. 'Wait,' she said excitedly. 'We know that I can make air into a solid shield to stop hostile spells from coming through, and so can Iriana. Could there be a way to make a shield that can hold magic in, instead of keeping it out?'

'It's certainly a possibility,' the cautious Taku said, 'but can the answer really be that simple, Corisand? And you, Iriana, are in a weakened state following the injuries you sustained in your own world. Do you think that between you, you would have the strength to hold in so much power for long enough?'

'Well, they'll never know until they try,' Aurora said impatiently. 'Besides, we can help them.' She turned her gaze on the massive Evanesar of Earth. 'What do you think, O Great One? Is Corisand's suggestion achievable?'

'Let me think,' Denali replied. 'It would be possible to keep an opening in your shielded receptacle to allow the magic to be put inside, but I doubt, Windeye, that you would be able to seal it in time, before the power escaped again.'

'We might be able to accomplish it,' Taku said, 'if all five of us contributed some of our power to making the shield and then sealing it. That way it would belong to both worlds, and should last long enough for Corisand and Iriana to take it back. Then the Windeye can act as the conduit to pass the magic into the Fialan.'

'Why can't I help with that?' Iriana asked indignantly.

'Because only one of you can wield the Stone at one time, and because you will need all your strength to complete your healing when you return,' Denali said firmly. 'Be patient, Wizard, and let Corisand take on this part of the burden. Your task will be to conserve your energy and your powers for the battles that will come, for that is where you will be most needed.'

Iriana sighed. 'It's hard to be patient when I want so much to help.'

'Your time will come, my friend,' Taku told her. 'Never fear.'

'All right – but I *will* have a part in creating this thing,' she added belligerently. 'I deserve that, and more to the point, you need me.'

'You certainly will,' Taku replied with a chuckle. 'For you are quite correct, we do need you.'

At that moment a new voice interrupted them. Corisand and Iriana looked around in astonishment to see Basileus. He had left his isolated rocky pillar in the midst of the ocean and come among them once more, but taking his preferred form when moving about in the Elsewhere, that of a gigantic bear.

'Basileus!' Denali sounded astonished. 'It has been aeons since you last left your sea-girt pinnacle. You are always most welcome among us – but what brings you here at this time?'

'I wished to speak to the Windeye,' the Moldan said in his low, booming, grinding voice.

'Me?'

'You indeed, O Shaman of the Xandim. Since you left me last, I have been giving much thought to your mission to save your people, and I wondered where, once you have freed them – for I have every confidence that you will – you plan to take them? Have you a home for them in mind?'

'No,' Corisand confessed, feeling more than a little chagrined. 'I've been concentrating so hard on simply rescuing them from Hellorin, I never really considered what would happen afterwards.'

'Then I may have a solution, if you find it acceptable. Some hundred leagues or more to the south of Tyrineld, between the realms of the Wizards and the Skyfolk, lies my own mountain, the form my consciousness inhabits when I am in the mundane world. It is called the Wyndveil, and the lands on its lower slopes and around its feet are fair and fertile. I would like to offer it to you and your people, to be your home too. Since the departure and death of the Dwelven I have been too lonely to return there, but who knows? If I have friends dwelling with me once more, I may just change my mind and come back to the mundane world to help you.'

He gave a deep, rumbling chuckle at the sight of Corisand's open-mouthed astonishment. 'Well, Windeye, what say you? Does my plan sound good to you?'

'Oh yes – oh please – I mean thank you!' Such unexpected good fortune had left Corisand reeling. Though she had not consciously been considering the future, her concerns must have been lurking, buried beneath more pressing problems, at the back of her mind, for suddenly she felt lighter than air, as if she might float away at any second. 'A real home of our own, under no one's sway. Basileus, I can never, never thank you enough for this. It will mean everything to me and my people. It will mean we have a real future.'

'You need not thank me, my friend,' Basileus replied. 'Indeed, if you succeed in your mission I will be in your debt. I have been watching your progress in the mundane world. I know how you and your friends are helping to release the Dwelven from their endless suffering. For that alone, my race will be deeply in your debt. It will be my pleasure and my honour to give you a home.'

'If she ever gets that far,' Aurora's acerbic voice interrupted. 'I hate to spoil this touching scene, but we need to give our attention to dealing with Ghabal, if the Xandim, the Wizards, or anyone else for that matter, are to be truly safe in the future.'

'You are right, and I beg forgiveness for my interruption.' Basileus sounded humble enough, but there was a twinkle in his eye as he looked up at the great eagle. 'I will detain you no longer, but Windeye, once you have returned to the normal world, and if you free your tribe, remember my promise and seek out the Wyndveil. It will be the home of your people for all time.'

Suddenly, soundlessly, he was gone, leaving Corisand with further thanks unspoken.

'Now,' Denali said into the silence that followed his departure. 'Let us continue. We were speaking of a vessel to contain our power so that the Wizard and Windeye can take it to the mundane world and transfer it to the Fialan. Corisand, can you begin?'

Corisand pulled together her whirling thoughts and nodded. She had a long way to go before she could think of taking her tribe to their new home. 'How big do you think it should be?'

'Perhaps about the size of your head,' the Great One replied. 'Something reasonably small will be much easier for you to control.'

'Will all that power fit into such a small space?'

Denali chuckled. 'Power can be compressed to fit into something as tiny as a drop of rain, if need be – though working at that scale *does* take considerable skill.'

'Well, I'll do my best.' Corisand tried to ignore the churning in her stomach. Her own life, and probably Iriana's too, depended on her getting this right, and everyone was depending on her. She took a deep breath and switched to her Othersight so that she could see all the silvery currents of air that moved around her. Stretching out her arms, she gathered the strands up in handfuls and began to spin them into her usual shield – except that instead of enclosing herself inside it, she made it much smaller, and left herself outside.

'Now, Iriana,' Denali said softly, and on her left, Corisand felt the Wizard adding her own Air magic to the construct – then combining it with her powers of Earth and Fire, rendering the shield as hard and durable as diamond, and in addition, making it visible to normal eyes. The result was a sphere of transcendent beauty about the size of the Windeye's head that turned and shimmered in the air, throwing off starbursts of glittering rainbow sparks as it caught the light.

'Now it is my turn,' Taku said. Lifting his head, he breathed gently on the sparkling globe. A small patch turned white and opaque, as if frosted over, then the ice appeared to melt, leaving an open space in the side of the sphere, into which the serpent blew the mist of his icy, magic-laden breath. Then with a flick of his nose he sent the orb spinning high into the air, to rest on a small ledge, high on the craggy face of Denali.

'This time it is up to me,' the Great One declared. It was difficult for Corisand to see the sphere, so high and far away on its cliff-face ledge, but it looked as though the tiny, shining mote gradually changed colour from pale iridescence to glimmering gold as it filled with Denali's power. Then, after a time, the Great One called to Aurora. 'It is done. The time has come for the vessel to be sealed.'

The mighty eagle swooped down swiftly and picked up the shining globe in her claws. It burst into an explosion of blue-white incandescence, and bolts of lightning shot into it, turning the receptacle so bright that it lit up the whole night sky. One final flare, brighter than the rest, sealed the magic within. 'Done,' Aurora's voice rang out. 'It is sealed. Now you can take it back, Corisand.'

'And as soon as you do,' Taku added, 'we must return you to your own world, for even the receptacle that we have made will not contain the power of the Evanesar for long.'

'What do we do with it when we get back?' the Windeye asked. 'How can this magic be transferred into the Fialan?'

'As we have previously agreed, you will be the conduit,' Denali said. 'Hold the globe in one hand and the Fialan in the other, and use all your will to command the Stone of Fate to absorb the power you are sending to it.'

'And don't linger,' Aurora added. 'What you are doing is extremely dangerous, Corisand. Get the energy through your body and into the Fialan as fast as possible, lest it burn you out.'

'I understand,' Corisand said. 'And thank you, O Great One. Thank you, my dear friends Taku and Aurora, for everything.'

'I also thank you,' Iriana added. 'Without you, I would have perished. When all this is over, I hope that we can still come back here and see you again.'

'We will see,' Denali said. 'You still have a long way to go before all this is over. Now, farewell to you both, and may fortune favour you.'

'Farewell, farewell,' echoed Taku and Aurora, as the Elsewhere faded around the Wizard and the Windeye, and they suddenly found themselves back by the campfire in the drab, everyday world.

Iriana shot up from her recumbent position. 'Quick, quick,' she shouted to Corisand. Taine, Aelwen, Dael and Kaldath, firing questions, tried to gather round their companions, but were driven back by the blazing globe of incandescence in the Windeye's hand. Quickly Corisand pulled the Fialan from its leather pouch and, with her entire will, commanded it to absorb the energy from the other-worldly sphere.

The energy flashed through her, and she cried out with pain. It felt as if her flesh was being seared from her bones, so intense was the magic. Then suddenly it was all over. The blazing orb vanished into nothingness; all its power drained and passed through Corisand into the Fialan. The Windeye slumped to the ground, shivering, and Iriana helped her sit up and placed a blanket round her shoulders. 'Is it done?' she asked softly.

'It's done,' Corisand confirmed. She threw her arms around the Wizard and hugged her. 'We did it. We actually did it.'

'*What in the name of thunder did you do?*' roared Taine. 'Will some-body please explain?'

'And what happened to you, Iriana?' Dael added. His voice shook a little. 'We thought you were dying.'

Windeye and Wizard looked at one another, and burst out laughing. 'Better make yourselves comfortable,' Corisand said. 'It's a long story ...'

'But while we're telling it, everyone had better start packing up the camp, because the Evanesar have healed me, and we're ready to go.' The Wizard looked at her friend.

'That's right,' the Windeye said. 'It's finally time to free my people.'

27
~

FLIGHT OF FREEDOM

Hovering below treetop level, the Windeye and her companions peered through a screen of boughs at the distant Phaerie city. For the last few miles they had crept through the forest, taking advantage of the thick cover that the trees provided and hidden by a shadow cloak that the Windeye, her powers buoyed by the Fialan, had spun large enough to cover them all. By now Tiolani must surely have found out what had happened to the warriors she had sent out after Corisand and her companions. She would have flying sentinels guarding her city, and she would be thirsting for revenge. Oddly, however, despite the lofty vision of Boreas, whom they had sent ahead so that Iriana could scout through his eyes, they had seen no airborne warriors – yet, as Taine said, that did not mean there was no one there. 'They can use spells of glamourie to conceal themselves from us, just as we mean to shield ourselves from them,' he said in mindspeech. 'And—'

'Wait!' Iriana interrupted sharply. 'Boreas is flying over the stables now. There's a *mass* of Xandim in the fields outside. Did Hellorin normally keep so many packed so close together?'

'No, he certainly didn't. What can Tiolani be up to? I want to see for myself what's going on.' Corisand landed between the trees, followed by the others and, once Iriana had dismounted, morphed to her human form. As her companions gathered around her to care for her body while she was absent from it, she quickly switched to her Othersight and, snatching up handfuls of the streaming air, spun them into the silvery disc of a mirror, just as the Evanesar had taught her. Pouring her consciousness into it, she rode the winds towards the complex of paddocks, barns and stables that had been her home for most of her life.

Shock ran through her. All the Xandim were there! She was their Windeye – she felt a sense of completeness she had not known when the herd were scattered between the city and the outlying meadows near the mountains, where they reared their foals, or rested after an arduous season of hunting, under the watchful eyes of a group of Aelwen's stablehands who stayed nearby in a small cabin. Relief and suspicion warred within the Windeye. On the one hand, this had solved her greatest problem – how to free all of the Xandim if they were scattered over a wide area. On the other, however, *why* were they all clustered here like this? It could only be a trap.

Tiolani must think I'm a fool.

From the body language of the herd, Corisand could see how uneasy they were. There were strangers hiding somewhere nearby, and the barn was the most likely place. She followed the flow of the night wind to the wooden building, slipped in through the open window at the top – and came face to face with a Phaerie warrior.

For one shocked instant she recoiled, forgetting that she was invisible to him, then she pulled herself together and slipped through the opening. Sure enough, in the glimmer of the flying spell she could see them. Tiolani and a number of warriors; so many that they were crowded into the barn. But unless Hellorin's daughter had seriously underestimated the Windeye and her companions, there were not enough to defend the entire herd of Xandim.

Corisand left the barn and rode the winds towards the city – and sure enough, there were the rest of the Phaerie forces, led by Cordain whom she recognised from former Wild Hunts, concealed behind the northern city walls. That was all she needed to know. Quickly, she returned to her friends and her own body, and told them what she had discovered.

'I thought it must be a trap when Boreas saw all those horses,' Iriana said.

Taine shrugged. 'It doesn't make that much difference to our plans – except that now we'll be able to turn the enemy's trap back on them. In fact, they've done us a favour. Not only have they collected all your people for you, Corisand, but they've also massed their forces for us. Tiolani has no idea of warfare, and Cordain is an administrator, not a strategist.'

'It will still pay us to be wary,' Kaldath warned. 'I don't want us to commit ourselves then find that they have an unpleasant surprise up their sleeve after all.'

'Well, there's not much we can do about it if there is,' Taine argued. 'Besides, whatever they may or may not have up their sleeves, *we* have the Fialan and your Dwelven up ours.'

'Then let's do it,' Corisand said, impatient with all this debate. 'We all know the plan. Aelwen will apport herself, Taine and Kaldath with their mounts to the skies above Eliorand along with the Dwelven forces, and—'

'Aelwen, are you *really* sure you can apport three people at once, and the horses too?' Taine was frowning. 'You couldn't do it when we escaped from Eliorand the last time.'

'I didn't believe I could – but I had precious little time to think at all when we were ambushed by Cordain,' Aelwen replied. 'This time it's only for a very short distance though, and the horses will be buoyed by Corisand's flying spell.'

'I hope you're right,' Taine said doubtfully.

'We all hope she's right – just as Corisand and I hope that we can handle Tiolani and her warriors, and free the Xandim while you're providing the distraction in Eliorand,' Iriana said. 'Our entire plan is balanced on a knife-edge, but it's the only one we've got. We're an awfully small army to free one race from the clutches of another, but we do have a number of things going in our favour, and all we can do is try.'

'Our original plan didn't count Tiolani and her forces in the barn. What if the two of you might need a little extra help?' Taine asked.

'If we do, we'll be sure and let you know,' Iriana said wryly. 'Now, are you ready, Corisand?'

'I'm ready.' Switching back to her equine shape and drawing on the power of the Fialan that still hung round her neck, the Windeye renewed the flying spell over herself and the mounts of her companions. As Taine gave Iriana a leg-up onto her back, she was happy to feel the Wizard's slight weight. It wouldn't hamper her, and now that they had come so far and her goal was almost within her grasp, it felt reassuring to know she had a friend so close to her who shared her hopes and concerns, and would give considerable help in the battle to come. In a quick flash of recollection it came back to her how lonely she'd been when she first became the shaman of the Xandim; how isolated and weighed down by a colossal burden of responsibility that had been hers and hers alone.

Well, she wasn't alone any more.

In the faint light of a new moon she looked ● gratefully at her companions. Kaldath's wise, lined old face that still held an echo of how handsome he must have been in his youth; Taine, looking grim and businesslike as he tested his bowstring; Aelwen, by his side as always, her mouth set in a purposeful line, but her eyes shadowy and troubled; Dael, hanging back out of harm's way, ready to duck into a hiding place among the bushes as he had been instructed, his task to stay out of danger and to keep Melik safe in his basket while the others joined battle, for Iriana would be sharing Corisand's vision during the fight. Though the Windeye couldn't see Iriana, she could feel the Wizard on her back, closest of all, linked by touch and thought and a bond of friendship that would never break.

'Be sure and hold on tightly once the fighting starts,' Corisand warned her. 'I don't want to lose you.'

'I will, don't worry,' the Wizard reassured her, gripping tighter with her knees and twining her left hand more tightly in Corisand's long mane. 'I'm not hurting you, am I?'

'Not a bit,' the Windeye assured her, then took a deep breath. There could be no putting it off any longer. 'All right – get your shield in place.'

The air thickened and tingled with magic as Iriana complied, surrounding them both in a shimmering globe of unyielding air. Though her Air magic differed from Corisand's own powers, she had been learning a trick or two from watching the Windeye at work, and the shield was the best she had ever conjured.

Corisand turned her concentration on the Fialan that hung around her neck, throbbing like a living heart, its power glowing through the leather pouch in which it was encased. She accessed her Othersight and saw the air moving fluidly around her like strands of silver silk. Since she was in her equine form this time, she was forced to use her mind, rather than her hands, but she manipulated the streaming, shimmering flow while reaching out at the same time to grasp the deep indigo shadows from beneath the trees. Spinning them together with the glistening streams of air, she formed her shadow cloak, as she'd been taught to do in the Elsewhere by the Evanesar, and made it big enough to cover both herself and the Wizard on her back.

When it was in place she heard the murmurs of amazement from the others, who had not seen the phenomenon before.

'You *are* still there, aren't you?' Taine asked, lightening the moment. 'You haven't decided to start without us?'

Corisand reached out with her thoughts to all her friends. 'No, I haven't, but I'm about to get going now. Everyone ready?'

They all gave her their affirmation, and she heard the battle-ready edge to Taine's voice, the hint of unease beneath Aelwen's, the longing that throbbed in Kaldath's tones and the fear, disguised beneath bravado, in Dael's reply. Her heart went out to him. He was the most helpless, the most vulnerable of them all, yet he was ready to stand by his companions and do whatever he could to help. In a way, he was the bravest of them all.

'And I'm ready too – but you already know that.' Iriana's mental tones broke into the Windeye's thoughts. 'Come on, Corisand, we're all in place, so hurry up and give the word, and let's get on with this. Your people have waited long enough. It's time they were free.'

'Then *go!*'

Before Aelwen, Taine and Kaldath had time to apport, the eager Windeye bore Iriana out of the trees and sped towards the stable complex.

For the second night in a row Tiolani, mounted on Asharal and desperate to see what was happening outside, fidgeted in the stuffy barn with warriors and their steeds crowded all around her. Only the faint glimmer of the flying spell that covered all of them lit the darkness and the only sound was quiet breathing and the occasional snort or fidget from a horse. She was beginning to wish that she had not persuaded Cordain that he should be the one lying in ambush with the larger force behind the city walls, and she should be the one who, with a smaller, select band of fighters, should conceal herself close to the massed herd of Xandim.

'Please reconsider,' he had urged her. 'You are the last one capable of performing the flying spell, the only one who can continue Hellorin's heritage and line. Surely you can see that we must keep you safe? I beg of you, Tiolani, stay in the city with the majority of our warriors. They will be better able to protect you there. I would prefer that you remained securely in the palace, but we may need your powers if there should be an attack. Whatever happened to our warriors back in that cave strikes fear into my heart. What could possibly have inflicted such terrible damage?'

The second squadron of warriors that they had sent to the cave had come back, deeply shaken, with tidings of the gruesome slaughter of their fellows. Though Cordain and Tiolani had done their best to see that the news went no further, they had been unable to prevent the horrific tales spreading from mouth to mouth, growing more grisly with each telling, until a pall of unease hung over the city.

Tiolani had no idea how her former companions could have wrought such destruction. Could the Wizard or the Windeye have gained additional powers since she had parted from them? It seemed to her that they must have succeeded in bringing back the Fialan from the Elsewhere, and the notion chilled her. How could she defend herself and her people against such formidable arcane forces, yet who would do it if she did not?

Phaerie magic differed from that of the Wizards. Over the centuries, the Wizardfolk had trained all their people intensively, developing and disseminating their magic throughout their race, whereas Hellorin, jealous of his power, had preferred to hold his subjects in a state of dependence, developing and nurturing most of the Phaerie powers within his own family, and encouraging idleness and indolence among the rest of his people. All had powers of glamourie and could perform basic attack and defence spells using nature and the elements, and some could apport, but only the Forest Lord and his heirs could access the major destructive powers of the elements – which meant that only Tiolani, no matter how much her own warriors assisted her, had any chance of battling the wielders of the Fialan.

So here she was, skulking in this barn while the minutes crawled by like years. Only she could defend Hellorin's steeds (firmly, she closed her mind to any thoughts of them as the enslaved tribe of the Xandim) from theft, therefore she had to be here, for this was where the thieves would strike. Oh, how she had underestimated them! She had considered herself to be in a powerful position, in comparison to her opponents – a small, ill-assorted ragtag group of rebels and dreamers. She had imagined crushing them effortlessly – how could she not with an army of Phaerie at her back? But that was before she had sent out her finest warriors to ambush her foes in the cave with absolute confidence that she would prevail. Only when her force had failed to return had she started to doubt, and when their remains had been discovered, she had known true fear. Now, ablaze with anger at this threat to her people and their property, chilled with terror that she might fail or even die, all she could do was wait, and see what fate would bring.

Unable to bear any more inaction, she rose up on Asharal to the apex of the sloping roof, where a lookout had been stationed at a small window that let in fresh air, to keep watch over the horses that grazed in the paddocks outside. Peremptorily, Tiolani dismissed him. 'I will watch for a while.' She was Hellorin's heir – how could he refuse?

Oh, but it was wonderful to feel the cool night air on her face, and to see the sky, the stars and the horses grazing peacefully below. How she wished that she could turn back the clock to happier times, before the ambush that had disabled Hellorin and killed her poor brother, when everything had been ordered and happy and safe ...

They appeared out of nowhere, materialising in midair with a sound like a thunderclap – a grey horse that Tiolani recognised at once as Corisand, with the Wizard Iriana on her back. The time had come at last. Now she must fight, with everything, including her life, at stake.

Despite the protection of the shadow cloak and magic shield, Corisand felt horribly exposed as she positioned herself above the largest paddock full of milling, uneasy Xandim, facing the barn in which she knew Tiolani and her ambushers lurked. The horses, her own enslaved people, fidgeted below her and lifted their heads, sensing the presence of their Windeye, feeling her power, knowing a strange hope that they could neither define nor understand.

Corisand could sense the tension and confusion within the barn as the ambushers were alerted by the disturbance among the gathered horses. Before they had time to become too suspicious she cast the shadow cloak aside, and felt the explosion of shock among the gathered Phaerie. A few arrows clattered off the shield, shot from the high windows of the building, followed by a lightning bolt spell.

'Stop!' Corisand cried as loudly in mindspeech as she could. 'I know you're in there, Tiolani. I wish to speak with you, and your warriors. You know why I've come. Do you really want a battle? Do you want all the bloodshed, the death? Give me the Xandim, Tiolani. Give me my people, and we'll go.'

'You do not give orders here,' Tiolani snarled in reply. 'You are nothing but an animal, a beast of burden, and you and your people are the possessions of the Phaerie. It's time you learned your place, Corisand.'

'An animal?' Corisand said, in short, dangerous tones. 'We'll see, shall we?' She raised her mental voice. 'Hearken, all you Phaerie, and I will tell you a secret that your Forest Lord has kept from you for hundreds of years. Those magnificent horses you ride are not mere beasts, but a race of shapeshifters: people who look much like yourselves in their other form.'

'Don't listen to her,' Tiolani shrieked. 'She's lying!'

'Am I?' Corisand let herself sink to the ground. 'Get off, quick,' she whispered to Iriana.

'Is this wise?'

'I want the secret to be out. I want all the Phaerie to know.'

Iriana shrugged and dismounted, keeping a hand on Corisand's withers, ready to spring onto her back again at a moment's notice.

The Windeye took a deep breath – and changed. Instead of the great grey warhorse, a dark-haired young woman stood there, all clothed in shadows, with the Wizard's hand still on her shoulder. From within the barn, there came a tumult of voices crying out in shock and amazement.

'Do you see, Phaerie? Do you see now?' Corisand cried. 'These are not true horses that you ride – they are slaves, imprisoned in their equine form by a spell of the Forest Lord. All down these long ages, Hellorin has been lying to his people. These were no lowly mortals like the other slaves, but a tribe of shapeshifters – and that makes them magic users. Do you like the idea that your ruler has lied to you all this time? Can your consciences truly live with the enslavement of an entire civilised race?'

For a moment there was only the uneasy muttering of Phaerie voices, and what sounded like a number of arguments breaking out within the barn, then Tiolani's voice rose up above the babble. 'Lies!' she screeched. 'You fools, you idiots, don't you see? It's all an illusion. That's a Wizard out there, hiding like a coward behind that shield. All she has is an ordinary horse. All the rest is an illusion. *She's* the one behind it all.'

Abruptly, the tone of the voices changed to anger. The barn doors burst open and the Phaerie warriors poured forth, with Tiolani at their head. A storm of arrows came at the Wizard and Windeye, and they were hit by a hurricane of spells. Whirlwinds of soil and stones erupted out of the ground, hurtling upward to strike at them from below, then the sky darkened and hailstones the size of fists came smashing down to shatter on Iriana's shield, sending the horses in the fields, trapped between the two onslaughts, into a frenzy.

'Change back, Corisand – quick!' Iriana yelled. 'Get us aloft.'

Corisand made the fastest change she had ever done, and Iriana, giving herself a boost with her magic, sprang onto her back. Corisand took off like a rocket with a fusillade of arrows and spells bouncing off Iriana's shield. Though the Wizard was desperate to retaliate with her own magic, she restrained herself and stood firm, pouring all her energy into the shield, though she knew that her strength could only hold out for so long. Already she could feel the strains upon her power caused by fighting off the alien magic of the Phaerie.

Corisand was calling to the Xandim; rallying them, telling them that if they followed her, she would free them for ever from Phaerie domination. Hearing the Windeye's call to arms, the steeds of the Phaerie ambushers rebelled against their riders; bucking, plunging and twisting in midair, doing everything they could to rid themselves of their masters. The storm of arrows ceased and the attacking spells faltered, leaving Iriana with a moment's respite in which to catch her breath.

Then suddenly, to Corisand's horror, she heard a shout from her right. The second wave of attackers, led by Cordain, rose up from behind the city walls and came charging down upon herself and Iriana, beginning the attack anew.

The Windeye felt the jolt of shock and fear strike through her friend. It echoed her own. 'Bat turds!' Iriana swore. 'Where in perdition are the others with their distraction?'

'What the bloody blazes do you mean, you can't do it?' Taine's fingers dug into Aelwen's shoulders hard enough to bruise her, his face distorted with fury.

Aelwen quailed, unable to meet the anger and contempt in his stare. Suddenly, when it came to the sticking point, all the doubts and regrets she'd been harbouring since her escape from Eliorand had come down upon her like an avalanche, paralysing her in an agony of indecision. 'I – I can't!' she cried. 'I just can't. When I tried to apport, all that would come into my mind was the Dwelven tearing those warriors apart in the cave. This is my city. These are my people – innocent people who had nothing to do with Hellorin's wickedness or Tiolani's machinations, and—'

'And Corisand and Iriana are our companions,' Taine shouted at her. 'They're committed now. You'll be killing *them* if you let them down. What did you think was going to happen? That we'd just walk into Eliorand and ask that bitch Tiolani to let the Xandim go? I don't want the blood of innocents on my hands either – none of us do – but we have no choice.'

'The Xandim are innocent too, not to mention all the poor Dwelven that were massacred. What of them?' Now Kaldath, grim as death, was also shouting at her. And already, from the direction of the stables, the ghastly sounds of battle had been raised.

With a snarl, Taine thrust her away. 'Come on, Kaldath, we'll ride. They'll be too focused on what's happening in the stables to notice us now, and Iriana needs that diversion.' He turned a fulminating glare on Aelwen. 'You can follow when – or if – you decide whose side you're on.'

With a bound they took to the air, heading towards the city with the Dwelven streaming out behind them. Aelwen hesitated, biting her lip.

'The only chance you'll have of influencing what happens is to go with them.' Dael emerged from his hiding place in the bushes. 'This is not the time for doubts. If you don't make up your mind which side you're on, you'll find yourself hated by both. No matter how things might stand between you and Taine, don't forget that you left Eliorand before you knew he was still alive. Even then, you knew in your heart that what the Phaerie were doing was wrong.'

How could a mere human possibly be so wise? But he was right. With a nod of thanks Aelwen urged her horse skyward. It wasn't too late to play her part. Even if the others never forgave her hesitation, at least she would do her best to make amends.

Suddenly the Wizard and Windeye were at the epicentre of a vortex of spells and missiles as Hellorin's Counsellor urged his fighters towards them. The Wild magic of the Phaerie was centred upon the forces of nature at their most extreme. A howling gale tore across the stable complex, buffeting Iriana and Corisand's shield. More black clouds came boiling across the sky to blot out the stars, and lightning bolts came sizzling through the air to strike Iriana's magical barrier. Petrifaction spells impacted the shield, seeking the tiniest chink in Iriana's defences so that they could turn Wizard and Windeye to stone, and still the hail came hammering down. Great ropes of thorny bramble, thicker than a strong man's arm, erupted out of the ground amid the screaming, terrified Xandim, and reached up to wrap themselves around the field of magical force that enclosed the companions, tightening their grip and trying to pull Corisand and Iriana down.

The Wizard was being battered between her own magic and that of the Phaerie, beaten between the two like a sword blade between a hammer and an anvil. She reeled, knocked forward across Corisand's neck as a renewed fusillade of spells crashed into her shield.

'Grab hold of the Fialan and use it to reinforce the shield,' the Windeye urged her. Iriana, her face already buried in Corisand's mane, reached down to snatch at the leather pouch that swung on its thong round the arching grey neck, but she was hampered by her lack of vision. She was sharing the Windeye's eyesight, but Corisand had a blind spot directly beneath her own head.

Corisand glanced back at the city. 'Come on, Kaldath,' she muttered. 'What's keeping you?' Targeting Cordain's forces, she tried to make their mounts rebel, but clearly the Counsellor had seen the fate of Tiolani's warriors, for this time the horses remained under a spell of iron control cast by their Phaerie riders. The Xandim who were penned in the fields, trapped in the midst of the battle, were now a screaming, seething mass of terror and confusion, and the warriors' mounts caught that panic, which only made them more vulnerable to the control of their masters who whipped and spurred them mercilessly onwards. Tiolani's group took their lead from Cordain's forces, and those who remained mounted, including Tiolani herself, were starting to regain control of their horses.

Realising that her attempts were only causing suffering, Corisand stopped trying to subvert the ridden steeds and joined her own magic, the unique powers of a Windeye, to that of Iriana, who was still trying to grasp at the wildly swinging Fialan. She spun the air around the Wizard's shield and, though it remained as transparent as ever from the inside, to the Phaerie assailants on the outside it turned into a globe of gleaming silver with a blinding mirror sheen. Suddenly the Phaerie found their spells being reflected back at them, and before they had time to realise what was happening they were reeling beneath a bombardment of their own magic, and were being slaughtered, warriors and their mounts alike, by their own hail and lightning. Here and there a petrifaction spell would find a target, and to Corisand's horror, both horse and rider would turn to stone in midair and go hurtling to the ground to smash into a thousand pieces.

At the sight of her own people suffering and dying, Corisand's resolution wavered. In her equine form she was susceptible to the instincts of a horse, which did not see the bigger picture, but simply compelled her to protect the herd. Despite Iriana's frantic urgings, the reflective powers of her shield began to falter and fail.

'Corisand,' the Wizard said sharply. 'I know this must be very hard, but it's your one chance to free your people from slavery.'

'But they're dying ...'

'So will we be in a minute, and what good will that serve? I can't keep this shield up for ever. If you don't stick to the plan we're all doomed.'

Iriana dug her heels hard into Corisand's sides, something she would never have dreamed of doing under normal circumstances. 'Pull yourself together! We've all lost people we love. I lost Avithan and Seyka – don't you think I know how much this hurts you? And what about Dael with Athina? My heart goes out to you, Corisand, but you've *got* to keep fighting!'

The urgency in Iriana's voice finally penetrated the Windeye's distress. As if a fog had cleared from her mind, she realised that her friend was right. She pulled her reflective spell back into place – then suddenly she heard the sound she'd been waiting for. From the city itself came the wailing and screaming of a thousand voices in agony and terror.

The Dwelven were taking their revenge.

With a curse, Cordain called his troops away from the fight and wrenched his horse around, heading back with all speed towards the city. But the sound of that fearful screaming had weakened the warriors' concentration on their control spell. Corisand called to their mounts again, and this time the steeds responded in an explosion of violence, rearing and bucking, doing everything in their power to unseat their riders. Many of the Phaerie, taken by surprise, fell screaming, littering the ground with dead and dying, while some of the horses, riders stuck firmly in place, bolted towards the trees, using the branches to dislodge their unwanted burdens by knocking them out of the saddle. Cordain, however, had no intention of being thrown. With brutal force he turned his mare back towards the city, raking cruelly at her sides with his spurs until the blood ran, and wrenching at her head until the bit cut into her soft mouth.

By this time Corisand was striking the Phaerie attackers with a new weapon: javelin-like bolts of solidified air that could pierce a target as efficiently as a normal spear. The missiles could barely be seen, and so it was impossible to block or evade them. The Windeye could sense the fear of the warriors as their comrades toppled, bleeding and screaming, from the saddle. Amid the chaos, she began to hope. Could she possibly win this after all?

Corisand's all-round vision was so encompassing that Iriana found it easy to concentrate on different areas of the fight, so it was she who spotted Hellorin's Counsellor, whom she recognised from images she had seen in Aelwen and Corisand's minds, fleeing the field of battle. 'Cordain,' she cried urgently. 'He's getting away!'

Corisand's attention snapped round in the direction of the Counsellor. Quick as thought, she hurled another of her spears which sped through the air, converging on the fleeing Cordain. With unerring accuracy it hit him between the shoulder blades, and the Windeye saw him crumple and fall from the saddle.

With Cordain fallen the remaining warriors looked to Tiolani for further orders – but there was no sign of her, and Corisand and Iriana suddenly realised that they had lost her, and her mount Asharal was missing too.

'Where in bloody demon's bile are they?' Iriana said.

'She must have sneaked back through the tunnel when she saw she was losing.'

Iriana laughed, a sound surprisingly harsh from someone who was usually so kind-hearted. 'If she thought it was bad where *we* were, she'll be in for the shock of her life when she meets Kaldath and his Dwelven phantoms. I really wish I could be there to see it. That bitch sent her assassin after Esmon and Avithan – and me too, for that matter, and my beautiful Seyka. She deserves whatever horrible fate she gets.'

Without Tiolani, the Phaerie gave up the fight to save the horses. Those still able to control their mounts guided them down to the ground and dismounted quickly, letting the horses run free. Others, distracted by the tumult in the city, fell screaming from the saddle as their mounts dislodged them at last. Confusion reigned in the stable compound with animals stampeding around, aimless and terrified. The ground was strewn with bodies. Those Phaerie who could still do so broke and ran, some heading for the mouth of the tunnel and others diving like hunted rabbits into the shelter of the forest.

On Corisand's back, Iriana let out a cry of triumph. 'We did it! Quick, Corisand, the flying spell. It's time to get your people out of here.'

The Windeye needed no telling. It took a lot of power to lift so many horses – the entire Xandim race – but Corisand had the magic of the Fialan to draw upon, and she could also feel Iriana, on her back, sending her a steady feed of bolstering power. 'Stop that, you idiot,' she scolded. 'We just pulled you back from the brink of death, and you've been pouring all your energies into that bloody shield. I can manage the flying spell.'

'But I want to be part of it,' Iriana protested. 'We've come so far together.'

'And we've still got a long way to go. Save your strength, my friend. We may need it later. We're not out of this yet.' Corisand didn't need to see the Wizard's face to know that she was pouting, but at least Iriana reluctantly withdrew her power, and let the Windeye continue alone.

With a huge wave of delight that welled up from the very depths of her soul, Corisand drew on the energies contained in the Fialan and poured out the flying spell upon the assembled tribe of Xandim. The stable doors burst apart as the stallions of the tribe came pouring forth, for once at peace with one another and the world, answering the Windeye's call to accept her benison. The glowing magic flowed across them all; stallion, mare and foal alike, like sparkling starlight, like scintillating diamond dust, shooting out sparks of coloured brilliance as it responded to the Windeye's elation. As one the Xandim arose, taking to the sky in a massive surge of power as they responded to their Windeye's call.

'Follow,' Corisand cried out to them, praying that the strength of her emotions would be enough to communicate with them, beyond the simple language of the horse. 'Follow me to freedom.'

They sensed.

They felt.

They soared.

They followed.

In the forest beyond the stable compound, Dael waited, with Melik in his basket strapped firmly behind the saddle. The minutes had seemed like hours to him, for he had not wanted to distract the others with unnecessary questions, and he could not see what was happening. The fearful magical storms; all the noises he'd heard of screaming and the sound of battle had done nothing to ease his mind. How he hated feeling so helpless; being the only one with no magic! As the suspense grew within him, so did his concern, until he felt that he must call out to one of his friends – then suddenly he saw them, soaring above the trees. All the Xandim, glowing like a comet tail with the flying spell. With a whoop of joy he mounted his own horse and waited impatiently while Corisand swooped down towards him. He felt her spell flow across him like a tingling starfall, and urged his mount up into the air to join his friends. 'You did it!' he cried, and it was hard to tell whether the tears that gathered in his eyes were from the cold wind that blew into his face, or sheer joy at the magnificence of that moment.

They sped away from Eliorand, soaring high above the forest, heading south-west in the direction of the border and the realm of the Wizards. Corisand was brimming with exultation. Against almost insurmountable odds she had done what she set out to do. She had saved her tribe except—

'But what about Asharal?' The Windeye's responsibilities weighed heavily on her. She hated to leave even one of her people behind.

Iriana felt the change in her friend's posture and knew she was yearning to turn back. Brutally, hating herself, Iriana put the images of the Xandim who'd been killed in the battle into Corisand's mind. 'You can't save them all,' she said gently. 'I'm sorry, my friend, but you've freed all but a scant handful, and that's far more than we could have hoped for when we started this. Some of your people made that sacrifice so that the entire Xandim race could be free.'

'You're right,' Corisand replied sadly. 'I know in my heart that you're right, but I hate to think of the lost ones.'

'Even Athina herself couldn't have saved them all,' Iriana comforted her friend. "Besides, Asharal isn't lost yet, you know. Aelwen is carrying the flying spell on her body, and it will spread to him if she rides him. If there's any way she can bring him out of Eliorand, she will.' She paused, then added, 'I wonder what they're doing right now? I hope they're safe.'

28

REVENGE OF THE DWELVEN

Taine had spent all his adult life in the shadow of violence and bloodshed. He had killed – and almost been slain himself – on a number of occasions, yet he had never witnessed anything like the scenes of horror he was seeing now. He and Kaldath had finally reached Eliorand and come riding down like an avenging storm, with the spirits of the Dwelven seething and snarling at their heels. Already the streets were crowded, for the Phaerie, alarmed by the commotion that was taking place around the stables beyond the city walls, had come rushing out of their homes to find out what was happening.

A great roar came from the Dwelven spirits at the sight of their ancient foe; their slayers of old. Overtaking Taine and his companions, they came smashing down like an avalanche, spreading out across the city, tearing and ravening wherever they went. In mere moments, it seemed to the horrified watchers, the streets were awash with blood and littered with the dismembered bodies of Phaerie dead. Screams and howls rent the air as Hellorin's people fled hither and thither in mindless terror, fruitlessly seeking to escape.

Suddenly Aelwen appeared beside them. 'Kaldath, stop them!' she cried in anguish. 'I'm sorry I failed everyone, and I'll do anything to make amends, but please, please, you've got to stop the Dwelven. They're killing everyone!'

'She's right. Make them stop this,' Taine agreed, though his own approach was more pragmatic. 'If they kill all the Phaerie you'll have no leverage to bargain with Tiolani for the release of the Dwelven – and if they happen to kill *her*, they'll never be free.'

Even Kaldath, despite all his endless aeons of suffering, looked sickened by the slaughter, his gnarled old hands clenched into knots upon the reins of his horse. 'I only hope I can.'

Taine and Aelwen heard his mental call go out; felt it impact against a vast wall of reluctance. Kaldath urged the phantoms more strongly, his voice becoming sterner and sterner still, until finally he barked out an order with the force of all the iron will that had sustained his sanity for so long. 'CEASE! I COMMAND YOU.'

The Dwelven spirits moaned with reluctance, and snarled and gibbered with frustration, but this time they finally obeyed him.

'Wait,' Kaldath comforted them. 'Only wait a little longer. The time of our release is coming soon. Round up all of the surviving Phaerie. Herd them like cattle into the courtyard before the palace. Keep them there. Then ...' His voice hardened. 'Find Tiolani, daughter of the Forest Lord. You know her. You will have her image in your minds through me, from Taine and Aelwen. Don't stop looking until you've found her, and bring her here alive, to me.'

Aelwen felt him pluck Tiolani's image from her mind and send it out to the waiting Dwelven spirits, and a shiver ran through her. Despite everything the girl had done, she still shared blood ties with the Horsemistress; was still the little girl that Aelwen had once taught to ride. 'What will you do to her?' she whispered. 'You won't hurt her, will you?'

Kaldath and Taine exchanged a glance, both their faces set and grim. 'Let's hope we don't have to,' Kaldath said.

Aelwen's world was falling apart around her. No more Eliorand. No more of her beloved horses. Taine, who she had loved so steadfastly through the empty years, was a stranger to her now. Oh, how desperately she wished that she could turn back time to happier days, when Hellorin and his Queen, Aelwen's beloved half-sister, had ruled in joy over a united Phaerie land with Full-blood and Hemifae working together, and Tiolani and her brother were youngsters glowing with energy and promise.

There could be no going back, however. All Aelwen could do was to battle forward through the ruins of her life, and hope for better times to come.

She was jolted from her bitter ruminations by a cry from Taine. 'What? Are you sure?'

'That's what the Dwelven say,' Kaldath replied. 'They've found a not-Phaerie in the dungeon. Someone like Iriana, they say.'

Then she too received the image from the Dwelven of a venerable man, his silver hair and beard close-trimmed but beginning to straggle now. She gasped. The form and features were unmistakable. A Wizard? Here? In ragged filthy clothes, and chained up in a dungeon?

'Cyran!' Taine roared, and without waiting to explain what was going on, he sped full tilt towards the palace. Instinctively, Aelwen started to follow, but reined in her horse at the last moment. At any time the Dwelven might find Tiolani. She needed to be here, with Kaldath, when they did.

Guided by one of the spirits, Taine leapt from his mount at the palace door and looped the reins round one of the tethering posts that were there at the side of the steps. The animal, who by now had become accustomed to the phantoms, stood calmly, and made no attempt to flee. Already the courtyard was beginning to fill as the Dwelven herded the Phaerie survivors up from the city into the broad, paved space. Some seemed stupefied with terror, while others howled epithets and curses, or wept or babbled in hysteria. There was no fight left in any of them, for they had seen what had happened to those who had not been so lucky. Taine felt a stab of remorse. Most of them were just ordinary citizens, going about their business, living their lives. They were paying a heavy price for the actions of their former ruler.

On the subject of Hellorin, what was happening to him? Taine threw a quick, urgent question to Kaldath in mindspeech, and shortly afterwards, the reply came back. 'The Dwelven say they found him, but the Healers have still not removed the time spells from him, and so they have no way to reach him.'

'Damn good thing, too,' Taine said fervently. 'The very last thing we want is to awaken the Forest Lord. Hopefully, we can find a way to bully Tiolani into doing what we want, but with Hellorin we'd have a fight on our hands that might just be too much for us to handle.'

Putting the matter out of his mind for the moment, he ran into the great building, following his Dwelven guide. He had another ruler to concern him right now. How in the name of all Creation had Cyran come to be here? It looked as if the stupid old fool had come following the trail of his son, and managed to get himself captured.

Taine hurried through the deserted corridors of the palace, keeping his footing with difficulty on floors that were slippery with gore, ordure, and disembowelled or dismembered Phaerie corpses. The air was thick with the stench of blood and death and he breathed in shallow gasps, trying not to take in more of it than he needed. He could imagine only too well what it must have been like: Hellorin's courtiers asleep in their beds while the servants busied themselves with their nightly tasks of cleaning and refurbishing the endless passageways. Suddenly the Dwelven would have come, erupting from the floor, pouring down from the ceiling, oozing through the walls. Those of the Phaerie who had made it out of their bedchambers had been slaughtered in the corridors.

For a moment Taine felt a surge of pity for the helpless inhabitants of the palace – and then Kaldath's voice came into his mind. 'The entire Dwelven race was slaughtered, right down to the last child. I know that these particular Phaerie, save the very oldest perhaps, were not involved in that massacre, but the Dwelven have endured for many a long age, trapped, unable to live, unable to go to their rest, and all they had to think about was revenge. I'm sorry, Taine, but Hellorin started this.'

Taine sighed. 'Sometimes we walk on a very sharp knife edge between right and wrong. When that happens, blood is certain to be spilled and the survivors are left to live with the consequences.' He shook his head. 'We did what had to be done. I don't want to talk about it.'

The Dwelven spirit, one of the lithe, active Sidrai, led Taine down several flights of stairs and a maze of narrower, unadorned passageways, until they came to Hellorin's little-used dungeons, a single corridor lined with barred doors on either side. The air smelled stale and dank, and the place was badly lit, with only the occasional pale, flickering flame, kept alive by magic, in a sconce attached to the wall. The phantom slipped between the bars of the first door on the right, where a figure, his face unseen, lay huddled in a corner. Taine, lacking the abilities of his companion to slip through walls, was forced to use one of the lockpicks he'd accumulated in his years as a spy, for there were no gaolers or guards in sight. 'Cyran?' he called softly, as he worked on the mechanism. 'My Lord Archwizard, is that you?'

A pale face, smudged with grime, emerged from the shadows in the corner. 'Taine?' The voice, though hoarse and croaking, belonged to Cyran. 'Can it really be true?'

'Unless I have a twin that I don't know about.' Taine gave his wrist a sharp twist and the lock finally clicked open. He ran across to Cyran, who was fettered in the corner. 'Archwizard, are you all right? How in Creation did you end up here?'

At first Cyran's words were lost in a fit of coughing, but when he got his breath back he replied, 'I was captured, isn't it obvious? They killed Nara and Baxian, but one of them recognised me and they brought me back here.'

'Where did they catch you?'

'We were following Avithan's trail.' There was a catch in Cyran's voice as he mentioned his son's name. 'We ended up in a clearing where the ground was all churned up and there were signs of a funeral pyre ...'

With the night vision that was part of his Wizard legacy, Taine saw Cyran's face crease with pain. 'The pyre you saw was for Esmon,' he said hastily. 'Your son did not die in that clearing.'

Like a striking snake, Cyran's hand shot out and grabbed the front of Taine's shirt, the sturdy cotton bunching and twisting in his knotted grasp. 'Then what *did* happen to Avithan, spy? Why did you fail to protect him, as you were sent to do?'

Staggered by the unfairness of this, Taine was about to point out that it was Cyran who'd sent his son out into danger in the first place, but just in time he remembered that the Archwizard was overcome with grief and guilt, and he held his peace. 'Avithan has gone from this world but he did not die.' He kept his voice level and matter-of-fact. 'He was taken beyond the reality we know to try to heal wounds so terrible that they would certainly have killed him, had he remained.' Firmly, he prised open Cyran's fingers and loosed them from his shirt. 'This is neither the time nor the place to discuss this, Archwizard. We must leave, and quickly.'

Cyran's mouth set in a stubborn line. 'I'm not going anywhere before I know—'

Taine's fist lashed out so fast that the Archwizard never saw it coming, and he caught Cyran as he crumpled. 'Idiot,' he muttered, though his voice was gentle with understanding. Quickly, he freed the fetters from the older man and slung him over his shoulder, grunting as he took the strain then, staggering slightly under the weight, carried him out of the dungeon.

He only hoped that when Cyran came round, he wouldn't bear any grudges.

Still guided by his Dwelven phantom he carried the limp form out of the palace and finally saw the dim light of the courtyard outside, shining ahead of him through the great doors. He stumbled out into the open and down the steps, taking grateful gulps of fresh air as he went, glad to be out of that dreadful charnel-house stench once more. He slung Cyran across his horse's back, and led the beast back to Aelwen and Kaldath. Cyran was already starting to stir and moan as he lowered him gently to the ground. Taine laid a hand on his forehead, and gently cast a spell to keep him asleep for just a little while longer. This was not the time to be distracted by explanations.

'This is the Archwizard Cyran, leader of the Wizardfolk,' Taine explained, in answer to his companions' unspoken questions. 'The stupid idiot came hunting his son and got himself captured. Poor sod.' He looked up at Aelwen and Kaldath, who were still mounted. 'How's it going?'

'As far as the Dwelven can tell, almost all the Phaerie have been found,' Kaldath replied. 'The last few survivors are being hunted down as we speak, and as for—'

He was interrupted by a triumphant cry in mindspeech from Iriana. 'We've done it! We're leaving with the Xandim now.'

'Don't wait for us,' Taine urged her. 'Get them over the border and back to Tyrineld as fast as you can.'

'We will. Taine, we lost Tiolani. She's heading your way through the tunnel, I think. Keep your eyes open.'

'Thanks, little sister. I will.' Taine suddenly found a smile on his face, and wondered how it had come to be there. 'Take care of yourself – we'll catch you as soon as we can.'

'You take care of yourself too. Corisand says don't delay. She doesn't know how long she can keep your flying spells going as the distance widens between us.' He heard the worry in her voice. 'Hurry, Taine. Do what you have to do, and get out of there.'

'I will. Stay safe, little sister.'

Taine turned back to the others. 'That was Iriana. She said—'

'We heard what she said.' Aelwen was looking at him with a frown and, belatedly, he realised that the foolish grin was still on his face. He scowled at her. She had no right to criticise anyone. He was about to tell her so, when he remembered the sickening carnage within the palace, and his own reaction to it. Aelwen had foreseen what must happen, and now, whether he condoned it or not, he could understand her hesitation – and besides, the battle had been won despite her lapse. There was no point in bearing any grudges. 'I've sent some Dwelven into the tunnel to look for Tiolani.' Kaldath cut through the tension.

Taine was grateful for the distraction. He and Aelwen could discuss their differences at a more appropriate time.

For a little while they waited in the corpse-strewn courtyard, trying not to listen to the curses and wails of the terrified Phaerie survivors, herded and penned tightly into their corner by the snarling Dwelven spirits. Aelwen, unable to bear the sight of what she and her companions had wrought, turned her back on them all – friends, phantoms and captives alike – and looked up into a sky that had grown dark with stormclouds. She had heard the storm; seen the bolts of lightning and grey curtains of pelting hail, but they had been localised over the stable area beyond the city during the fight to free the Xandim. She could still feel the residue of the magic battle that had taken place scraping her skin raw like a jagged blade.

Far away across the forest, she could see the streak of luminosity that was the escaping Xandim horses; her love, her joy, her life. What would she do now, without them? Was her beautiful Taryn among them? He must be, for he had been left behind with the other mounts when she had been forced to apport out of the city. What would he be like in a body similar to her own? Would he ever be able to forgive her? Would any of them?

Suddenly a terrified Asharal came bolting riderless across the courtyard, and a sudden commotion broke out beside the tunnel: the sound of shrieks and curses in a familiar voice, distorted by a savage mix of anger and fear.

'No, no, let me go. I *command* you!'

Aelwen darted out to catch Asharal, and returned with him to Taine, her mind in a turmoil of anguish and doubt. 'They've found her.'

He nodded. 'Finally. Maybe now we can finish this – if we can persuade her to cooperate.'

'Don't let them hurt her.' There. She had said it. The words were out that drew a line between herself and Taine.

Taine took a deep breath. 'She's no good to us dead, Aelwen. But the Dwelven must be freed; you know that, and having come this far, I don't think they'll be too scrupulous in achieving their goal. If you don't want Tiolani hurt, then you'd better persuade her to be sensible – and you'd better do it quickly.'

A number of the swift-moving Sidrai Dwelven herded the girl towards the centre of the courtyard where Taine and Aelwen stood with Kaldath. Cyran lay beside them, only half-conscious, his head pillowed on a discarded Phaerie cloak. The heir to the Phaerie realm was looking distinctly the worse for wear. Somewhere in her flight from the phantoms she had fallen, probably in the tunnel, for her face and clothes were smeared with dirt, her right cheek was scraped, her riding clothes were ripped on the right elbow with blood oozing through from an abrasion beneath, and her knees were lacerated.

As the Dwelven herded her, step by reluctant step, across the courtyard, her eyes suddenly left her tormentors and rose to meet a face that had been familiar to her since the day she was born. 'Aelwen!' She spat out the name, fury exploding within her at the treachery of one who had always been so close to her, although some part of her heart yearned towards the Horsemistress, the only living family that she had left – unless Hellorin should return.

Aelwen opened her mouth to speak, but the words seemed to be frozen inside her. The tall half-blood beside her – Taine, Tiolani remembered from the meeting in Athina's tower – glanced at Aelwen with a flicker of concern, then he turned back to Tiolani, his eyes hard and flat. 'Aelwen didn't betray you when we left you behind,' he said. 'Not deliberately. When we were ambushed by Cordain she couldn't apport three. She knew they wouldn't kill you, but she and I: our lives were forfeit. We had to be the ones to go.'

'And you return as enemies.' Hellorin's daughter hadn't known that she had so much hatred within her. 'Treacherous filth! What have you done to my city, my people? How dare you bring these – these *things* to attack the Phaerie?' She glared at Aelwen. 'You're no kin of mine. You're nothing but a stinking traitor, and I should never have believed you.'

Aelwen's eyes flashed: she found her voice at last. Deliberately she reached out and took the hand of the old, old man, a stranger to Tiolani, who stood beside her. 'These *things*, as you call them, are the Dwelven. They were also a race; happy, peaceful and hard-working. Your father enslaved them, just as he enslaved the Xandim, centuries before you were born, and set them to work his gem mines in the mountains. When they finally rebelled he slaughtered them all; males, females, infants, the old and the young. You've heard all the stories of the Haunted Isle? Well, that was where Taine and I apported to the day we left you, and there we met the spirits of the Dwelven race and Kaldath here, who was their steward in the mines, and for taking their side was condemned by your father to a half-life, a shadow existence among the ghosts for all eternity. I agree that the revenge of the Dwelven has been a terrible thing, and I have hated and mourned the destruction I have seen tonight – but can you not see that vengeance is the only thing that Hellorin left them?'

She paused and looked straight at Tiolani. 'Are you your father's daughter?' Her voice rang out in challenge. 'Can you truly support his actions?'

'Is it any worse than the vile abomination you've wrought tonight?' Tiolani snapped back at her. 'The streets of this city – your city – are awash with Phaerie blood. Can you say you're any better than my father? Renegades.' She spat out the last word with contempt.

'Call it what you will, we're here to correct Hellorin's atrocities.' Taine stepped forward. 'When he slaughtered the Dwelven he cursed them, preventing their spirits from ever resting and keeping them imprisoned in this world for all eternity. You are the Forest Lord's last surviving heir. Only you have the power to free these poor souls, trapped between life and death as ghosts over so many cruel years. Let them go, Tiolani. Put right your father's ancient wrong. Then the city will be yours again. You can rebuild, and make a new start. You have a chance to take the Phaerie in a new direction, one of peace, fairness and cooperation, instead of enslavement, fear and secrets. You hold the key to a golden future, heir to the Phaerie realm, if you will only free your race from the shadows of the past.'

'Fine talk!' Tiolani scoffed. 'Do you think I'm stupid? What golden future can the Phaerie expect now that you've taken the Xandim from us? Without them and with our dreadful losses tonight we'll be weakened; easy prey for your friends the Wizards of the south.'

Suddenly Cyran, who had been lying by Taine's side, sat up and staggered to his feet. 'You would be right to fear us,' he snarled. 'You sent an assassin to kill my son, an emissary coming to you in good faith with overtures of peace. If I had my way, I would wipe every one of your accursed race from the face of the earth.'

'Cyran!' Taine turned on the Archwizard with a flash of anger in his eyes. 'I grieve for your pain, my Lord, but this isn't helping. You and the Lady Tiolani have both suffered dreadful losses. There is no excuse for what she did – save that she did it when she was out of her mind with grief for her lost father and murdered brother, and under the influence of the poison that a conniving traitor poured into her ears. Surely, even amid all this death and destruction, a way can be found to set things right? For you yourself have foreseen the appalling visions of what will happen if war breaks out. Indeed, is that not why you sent Avithan and Iriana to the Phaerie in the first place? Only think what devastation might come to pass if you take the wrong step now. Only if the two of you are willing to let go of the past can there be any future for Phaerie and Magefolk alike.'

His words fell on deaf ears. Cyran and Tiolani continued to glare at each other; obdurate and united in their mutual hatred. As the silence stretched out, Taine and Aelwen exchanged concerned glances. How could they possibly break such a stalemate?

Then Kaldath let go of Aelwen's hand and stepped forward. The usual kindliness had vanished from his face, and the gentleness from his wise old eyes. Now he looked implacable, his expression cold and hard as stone. 'Enough of this,' he grated. 'Daughter of Hellorin, remove the curse from these Dwelven spirits – for if you do not, I will instruct them to kill all of your subjects, one by one, right here in front of you. You will be left to wander, alone and friendless, the last of your kind in an empty city, with only these phantoms to cluster round you day and night, a constant reminder of how you failed your people.'

Tiolani turned sickly white as all the blood drained from her face. She began to tremble so hard that she could barely stand. 'You can't,' she gasped.

'I can,' Kaldath replied remorselessly. 'I will.'

Tiolani broke. She covered her face with her hands, twisting away from his gaze. 'All right,' she sobbed. 'I'll do it. Just tell me what to do, and I'll do it.'

Almost unconsciously, Aelwen stepped forward with distress on her face, ready to comfort the girl, but Taine took her arm in a grip of iron and held her back. 'I'm sorry, Aelwen,' he said softly in mind-speech, 'but this has to be.'

Kaldath pulled Tiolani's hands from her face and took hold of her chin, turning her face until she met his eyes. 'Say what I tell you to say.' Then he began to speak.

In a shaky voice, Tiolani repeated, 'I, Hellorin's heir, heart of his heart, blood of his blood, bone of his bone, do release you spirits of the slaughtered Dwelven from the curse my father laid upon you long ago. No more are you shackled to this world. You are free to depart, to seek rest, and find peace at last.'

Following her words, there was utter silence across the city. It was as if the very world stood still. Then with a great sigh of joy, relief, release, the spirits of the Dwelven race, captive no more, shimmered brightly then dissolved, like silver vapour blowing away on the cool night wind – and as they vanished, Kaldath crumpled to the ground.

Taine and Aelwen knelt quickly, Aelwen cradling the old man's head on her lap. Kaldath's face broke into a beatific smile as he looked at them, and he raised his hand to gently touch the tears on Aelwen's face. 'Farewell, dearest friends, and blessings be upon you for what you have done this night.' He let out a long happy sigh. 'Now I can rest at last.' Then his hand fell limply away and he was gone, his body crumbling before their eyes to ancient dust that whirled away, like the shades of the Dwelven, on the wings of the night.

'Rest well, my friend,' Taine whispered. 'You have done great deeds tonight.' Then he wiped the tears from his eyes and pulled Aelwen to her feet. 'Quick,' he said. 'Any minute now those Phaerie will realise they're free. We've got to get out of here before they do.'

In the Elsewhere, Hellorin was raging as he watched and listened to the defeat of his people in the mirror-like patch of ice on the floor of Aerillia's great hall. The gigantic Moldan watched with him, repeatedly glancing down into the ice as events unfolded in the mundane world, then up at the Phaerie Lord, watching his wrath with the faintest of smiles on her face. Hellorin did not notice her scrutiny. She might as well have been invisible to him as he repeatedly smashed his fist into the floor, shouting and cursing in impotent fury as he watched the carnage the Dwelven were wreaking among his people, and the escape of the Xandim, enslaved with such trouble so long ago, whose abilities to use the flying spell had increased his power a hundredfold.

Then as Cyran was brought out of the palace by that filthy, half-blood traitor Taine, he leapt to his feet and savagely turned on her. 'Liar,' he snarled at the Moldan. 'You said I would have a chance to get home. You told me there would come a moment—'

'Yes, I did,' Aerillia said coolly, showing no concern whatsoever in the face of his wrath. 'And it will. When the Dwelven spirits are released, such a mass migration between the worlds and through the Well of Souls will weaken the boundaries for an instant, and—'

'*What?*' Hellorin roared. 'You never told me that!'

The Moldan shrugged. 'I didn't tell you a lot of things, nor am I under any compulsion to do so. Be grateful I'm helping you at all. Now calm yourself, Phaerie Lord, and pay attention to what is happening in your world. If you miss the crucial moment, it will not come again.'

Scowling, Hellorin turned back towards the gleaming ice patch that was the window into his realm. He glanced at it then dropped to his knees to look closer, cursing horribly when he saw Tiolani being cornered in the palace courtyard by a horde of hostile Dwelven spirits and herded over to— 'Aelwen!' he roared, as if the Horsemistress could hear him. 'Help my child – she is your own flesh and blood. How can you ally yourself with these foul, accursed traitors?'

But it seemed as if Aelwen had done exactly that. Hellorin watched with horror, spitting out oaths as his daughter was browbeaten into releasing the Dwelven spirits. As soon as the last of them had vanished, Aerillia called out, 'Use the window as a portal. Do it now!'

The Forest Lord steeled himself to make the leap – and saw a sight in the mirror that filled his heart with such horror, grief and rage, he thought that it would burst.

'Nooooo!' he howled – and leapt.

Aerillia smiled to herself once more. In mindspeech, she sought her fellow Moldai and the Evanesar; Denali, Taku and Aurora. 'So far, the plan is working,' she told them. 'All this wretched time I've spent concealing my true feelings and persuading Hellorin to trust me finally has a chance of bearing fruit. Now, everything will be up to your friends from the mundane realm – and the powers we placed in the Fialan.'

29
~

THE MIGHTY FALL

Now that their objectives had been achieved, Taine knew it was imperative to get away from Eliorand as quickly as possible. A sidelong glance saw Aelwen already mounted. She reached for Asharal's reins to take him with her, for she knew that Corisand would hate for even one of her people to be left behind, but Tiolani shrieked a protest. 'Leave him alone, you bitch. He's mine!' She ran forward, grabbing Asharal's bridle and trying to pull the horse away. Suddenly there was a dagger in her hand. Taine turned to help Aelwen – but there was a blur of motion to his right, as Cyran hurled himself forward. A terrible scream ripped the night apart – and there was the Archwizard, kneeling over Tiolani's body, his hands still locked around the hilt of the long Phaerie knife that he had twisted out of her hand and plunged into her heart.

Then from out of the palace came an earth-shattering howl of grief, of rage, of pain. The roof of the massive building burst apart in a hail of splintered wood and shattered tiles. There stood Hellorin, grown to titanic proportions, blotting out the stars. 'Fiend!' he roared. 'Murderer! My daughter, my only child, dead at your hands! You will pay for this with your life, Cyran. Before I have finished with you, you will be begging for death.'

'You dare talk of murderers,' the Archwizard screamed back at him. 'The Phaerie have slain my son.'

'Damn it, I *told* him Avithan wasn't really dead,' Taine muttered, but the situation had already gone far beyond an attempt to reason with either ruler. Quick as thought, he leapt into his saddle, snatching at the reins of Kaldath's mount as he did so.

'You will suffer every torment I can conceive,' Cyran was still screaming at Hellorin. 'Before I am finished, *you* will be the one who begs for death – and then I will wipe the rest of your stinking race from the face of the earth!'

To Taine's utter horror, the Archwizard was also expanding, growing in form into a behemoth to rival the gigantic Hellorin, and hurling curses and epithets at the Forest Lord. Their attention was fixed upon each other.

'Come *on*,' Aelwen urged, and Taine turned his horse and took off, following her into the air as fast as the pair of them could go. Together they sped into the night with Asharal and Kaldath's mount behind them, following the fleeing Xandim.

Save yourself. Get Aelwen away to safety.

Every fibre of common sense, every shred of self-preservation, every instinct of survival, screamed at Taine to escape while the two raging behemoths were distracted. They were certain to fight now; they were committed by rage and grief to destroy one another, and there was nothing he could do to stop them. Yet his loyalty and sense of responsibility kept nagging at him, urging him to go back. Hellorin had exiled him and sought his death, while the Archwizard had given him a refuge and a purpose. Surely he owed it to Cyran to at least *try* to help him.

Reluctantly, ignoring Aelwen's cry of horror, Taine thrust the reins of Kaldath's horse into her hand, then turned and began to loop back towards Eliorand. 'Keep going,' he called to her. 'Don't stop for anything. I'll be following you – I promise.'

'Taine, no ...'

Determinedly he blocked out Aelwen's desperate calls, and sped back towards the Phaerie city. The protagonists were so huge that even from a distance he could see the battle taking place, as spells sizzled and exploded between the pair of titans. Cyran, his shield glittering around him like a diamond, was using the Earth magic that was his birthright: the earth shook and jolted with earthquakes, and great cracks opened up beneath Hellorin's feet, making him dodge and leap to keep his footing. In some ways his powers were similar to the Old Magic, the powers of chaos, that the Phaerie used. Hellorin, whose own shield was a misty-grey nimbus that half-concealed his movements, was using this magic now. Earthquakes, strangling vines that sprung out of the ground and petrifaction spells were at his disposal – but he was far less limited than Cyran. He could also command the elemental forces that spawned tornadoes and tempests, lightning, hail and floods.

The two terrible rulers were locked in deadly combat: spell after spell was launched, only to reflect off the other's shielding and recoil back to strike randomly throughout the city. The palace was already a pile of smoking ruins. Many of the Phaerie who had survived the attack of the Dwelven had been struck down by the indiscriminate magic, while the rest had fled screaming into the night.

Even as he approached the outskirts of the forest, Taine knew that he could do nothing. This conflict had already escalated far beyond his own capacity to intervene. The battle was so fierce, the magic so powerful, that already the fabric of reality was beginning to weaken in the vicinity of the combatants. Eliorand seemed to be fading in and out, its buildings wavering as if Taine was viewing them through a shimmering heat haze. And the circle of unreality was spreading. Taine's stomach contracted into a ball of ice as he realised that he was directly in its path.

He'd been a fool to come back! With a wrench he turned his mount to flee – but one of Hellorin's massive hailstones smashed into his shoulder and knocked him from the saddle, his horse thrown off balance by the vicious gale. He fell, twisting and turning in mid-air and crashed into the topmost branches of a pine. The springy boughs caught him and broke his fall, but he struck his head and his vision exploded into flashing lights, while warm blood from a cut on his scalp poured down over his face. He landed face down across a thick branch, knocking the air from his lungs, leaving him gasping. There was an agonising catch every time he tried to breathe that was the sure sign of a broken rib or two. He could do nothing for the moment but lie there, fighting for breath while trying to shake the stunned confusion from his thoughts, and praying desperately that he could escape in time, before the shimmering circle of unreality reached him.

Aelwen, riding harder than she had ever ridden in her life, was closing rapidly on the fleeing Xandim. As she reached the head of the column, Iriana said, 'Where's Taine?'

'Hellorin is fighting the Archwizard. Taine stayed behind, and—'

'Hellorin's back?' Corisand laid her ears back flat. Though that was the only way she could show her horror in her equine form, they could all hear it clearly in her mental voice.

'Cyran killed Tiolani.' Until that moment, Aelwen hadn't real-ised that tears were pouring down her face for her sister's poor lost daughter. 'Hellorin just *burst* out of the palace. He was gigantic, and was raging like a madman. Then Cyran grew in turn ... We started to flee, but then Taine went back to help the Archwizard.'

'The fool!'

'The idiot!'

Corisand and Iriana both spoke together – and at that moment, they all felt Taine's pain and fear as he fell. It was only a faint echo at this distance, but enough to tell them that he was in serious trouble.

'Quick,' Iriana cried. 'We've got to go back and help him.'

'I'll go.' Aelwen, sick with guilt that she had left him, had let the two mounts that she was leading loose to follow the other Xandim, and was already turning her horse.

'Wait, you can't,' Corisand shouted. 'If Hellorin is on the rampage, it'll take the Fialan to help Taine now.' Automatically she began to turn back, but found the column of Xandim faithfully following her.

'Stop, Corisand,' Iriana said urgently. 'Get your tribe to safety – they'll only follow you. I'll take the Fialan, if you can keep up the flying spell without it for a while.'

'But you can't go alone,' Corisand protested. 'It took both of us to deal with Hellorin in the Elsewhere. Besides, you need my vision.'

'I'll go with you, Iriana.' Dael's voice was shaky but determined. 'I'll be your eyes.'

Iriana gave him a grateful smile. She knew how hard this was for him, how much of his courage it had taken. She turned to the Horse-mistress. 'Aelwen, if you—' But Aelwen was gone. She had used their moment of distraction to slip away from them, and was heading back towards Eliorand as fast as she could go. Iriana spat out a rancid curse that she had learned from Esmon. 'Come on, quick – I'd better get back there before we have two of them in trouble, instead of just one.'

'It's madness, risking the Fialan like this,' Corisand said as they landed to transfer Melik's basket to her back, while Iriana took a horse that had belonged to one of Cordain's warriors, and was still saddled and bridled. 'We have no choice,' the Wizard said. 'We can't let him run amok in this world again. Hopefully he'll be weakened enough by his battle with Cyran to let me send him back.'

'We'd better hope so.' Not without a dreadful wrench, Corisand let Iriana lift the Fialan's pouch from around her strong, arching grey neck, and hang it round her own. As soon as it made contact with the

Wizard, she was flooded with the Stone's vibrant energy, so strong that she felt as if she might be unable to contain it all, but might explode at any second. Quickly she mounted, and she and Dael took off, leaping into the sky.

'Be careful,' Corisand called after her.

'I will. I'm counting on Hellorin being preoccupied with Cyran. You get your people out of there.'

'Just remember that where the Forest Lord is concerned, it doesn't pay to count on anything.'

Though Iriana knew her friend was right, she couldn't let that stop her. Keeping close to Dael, she sped back towards Eliorand as fast as she could go. It felt strange using human sight again, instead of equine or feline vision. Iriana felt a little uneasy, not being able to see what was happening around and behind her, but she told herself firmly that in the present circumstances she'd be better off focusing on what lay directly in front of her. Like Taine, she heard the sounds of the battle, the sizzles and crashes and loud detonations of the spells, long before she reached the city, and saw the jagged flashes of lightning flare across the seething sky, but it was only when she neared the outskirts of Eliorand that the full horror of the conflict came home to her.

Iriana looked on aghast, her hands growing slippery with sweat on her horse's reins, at the rippling circle that denoted the weakening of the fabric of reality which spread out from the warring behemoths that were the Archwizard and the Forest Lord. Hellorin looked to be getting the best of the fight; he was still glowing with the energy and unearthly vigour that had come from spending so much time in the Elsewhere. Cyran was retaliating with everything at his disposal, but sweat was running down his face, and there was a weary sag to his shoulders. Nevertheless he kept on fighting, replying to every attack from the Forest Lord, and giving back as good as he got. The battle was becoming more and more frenetic – and every time they smote each other with another spell, battering away at one another's shields, the rip in the fabric of reality spread wider.

This had to be stopped.

To her frustration, Dael's eyes suddenly swung away from the duel and began to scan the treetops on the edge of the forest, where a lone horse, its reins entangled in the branches of a tree, was struggling and flailing in its attempts to free itself. 'Dael,' she said sharply, 'keep your eyes on Hellorin and Cyran.'

'But Taine – didn't we come to save him? He must be down there, close to where his horse is.'

'We can't spare the time for Taine.' It wrenched Iriana's heart to say it, but there could be no question of her priorities. 'Hopefully, Aelwen will be able to help him. We've got to stop Cyran and Hellorin, before those two idiots destroy the world.'

She felt the split-second hesitation while Dael caught and held fast to his courage, then he brought his horse so close to hers that they were almost touching. 'All right,' he said. 'What do we do?'

'First I'm going to use a spell to take a firm control of the minds of our horses, and make them utterly oblivious to what's going on here, otherwise they'll never be able to stand being so close to all this magic.' Iriana cast the enchantment even as she spoke, and felt the trembling animal grow calm beneath her. 'I want to stay mounted so that we can be mobile, but—'

Then it happened. Suddenly Hellorin found a chink in the defences of the tiring Archwizard. Like a hammer blow his magic smashed through, and Cyran reeled, then came crashing down like a mighty tree, transfixed through his heart by a gigantic spear of ice. Even as he fell, he shrank to normal size, and before he hit the ground, he breathed no more.

The agony of the Archwizard's death, intensified by its closeness to Iriana, almost sent her toppling from the saddle. She doubled over, her head swimming, her every nerve jangling from the shock of such intense pain – then Dael's hand grasped her arm, giving her an anchor point to cling to as she mastered the torment and pulled herself back under control.

'Die, Cyran,' Hellorin howled in triumph. 'Die as your Wizardfolk will die, crushed like insects by the might of the Phaerie.'

Then he turned, and his eye fell on Iriana.

'You!' he roared. 'And with no Windeye friend to help you this time. Prepare to meet your fate, Wizard filth. Nothing can save you now.'

The Wizard took a deep breath and got her turmoil of emotions – the grief and anger at Cyran's death, her dread at the damage Hellorin was causing to the area around him and her fear of the half-crazed Forest Lord – under control. Suddenly calm, she dipped into the leather pouch round her neck and took out the Fialan, holding the glowing green stone aloft. 'Not even *this*?'

Her words were a challenge flung into Hellorin's teeth, and in her hand the Stone of Fate flared with fierce, blinding brilliance, as if recognising its old enemy. She saw the Phaerie Lord flinch, saw the flicker of dread and doubt in his eyes – then he mastered himself. Through Dael's eyes, Iriana saw the slight straightening of his stance, saw his eyes and mouth harden in determination – and so was ready when a split second later a great bolt of utter blackness came hurtling at her.

At her command, the Fialan in her hand flared even brighter, surrounding the Wizard and Dael with a sphere of emerald radiance. The dark missile splattered against this shield and burst into a thousand jagged black shards. As it hit, Dael flinched and looked away.

'Keep your eyes on him!' Iriana snapped.

Dael straightened in his saddle, looking abashed, and in gentler tones the Wizard added, 'You've got to trust me, Dael. I can protect us – but only if I can see him.'

The Forest Lord, however, was looking at the mortal through narrowed eyes. With a chill, Iriana realised that she had given away her one point of weakness. It was imperative that she act before he did.

Quickly, she strengthened the shield around her friend then, without waiting for Hellorin to strike again, she hurled a streak of dazzling white light – the first spell she contacted in the Fialan's memory – at him. As it hit his shield it turned into a gigantic, ice-white serpent that wrapped itself around him, tightening its coils around his shimmering silver shield with increasing pressure. Its vivid cyan-blue eyes glinted dangerously, and its great fangs, each longer than Iriana was tall, glittered like diamonds with the Cold magic of the glacial Taku as they scraped against Hellorin's silvery magical barrier, seeking a weak point.

Iriana's heart leapt to feel that the powers of her dearest friend among the Evanesar were on her side. The serpent's coils tightened still further, and Hellorin began to shiver, trying to cringe away from the searing, deathly chill that the Cold magic wrought. Iriana smiled a grim little smile to herself. The magic of the Wizardfolk was one thing, but the powers of the Evanesar were something that Hellorin would never have expected to meet. Then she noticed something that wiped that smile from her face. Because of her spell, the flickering circle of unreality around Eliorand had expanded a little further, and she realised to her dismay that every time she used her powers, the destruction to the fabric of space and time would be increased.

She had to finish this quickly, before the instability spread too far and too fast to be contained – but there was no more time for thinking. Hellorin suddenly turned into a tornado of wildfire, a spinning column of flame that melted Iriana's serpent into a hissing cloud of steam. Two long tentacles of fire snaked out to snatch at the Wizard and her companion and drag them from their saddles.

Iriana reacted instinctively. Extending her arms in front of her, palms up, she threw them up into the air. 'Earth Rise!' she commanded. A broad section of the forest heaved like a shaken quilt and rose up in a gigantic, cresting wave of soil, rocks and trees, that broke over Hellorin and came crashing down on top of his fiery tornado, smothering the flames.

Iriana slumped over her horse's neck, panting and shaking with weariness after such a gargantuan effort, but there was to be no respite. The mound of earth that had covered the Forest Lord erupted, exploding outwards in a shower of missiles that thundered down on the Wizard's shield, and there stood Hellorin in the form of a gigantic wolf whose body seemed to be made up of savage black storm clouds, with blue-white lightning crawling all over his massive form. His eyes burned with a fearful red light as his fanged jaws opened in an ear-shattering snarl loud enough to echo halfway round the world.

Before Iriana had time to act he sprang at her – but this time Dael kept his eyes fixed resolutely on the horror. The Fialan pulsed like a beating heart in the Wizard's hand, and out of it soared a colossal eagle with outspread wings made of scintillating light. 'Aurora!' the Wizard gasped. Again and again the great bird struck at the wolf, its beak and talons extended, tearing great chunks out of the storm-wrought hide that bled lightning like rivers of searing blue-white fire. The great wings beat at Hellorin's storm wolf, producing blinding lightning flashes that forced him back until, unable to hold the spell together against such an onslaught, the Forest Lord changed again and stood there in his own gigantic form, exerting all his powers of the Old Magic to shield himself against the eagle's attack.

Though hope leapt in Iriana's heart, she knew the battle was far from over. She had him on the defensive now – but how much longer could she contain the power of the Stone of Fate? It burned and blazed throughout her body, wracking her with increasing pain as its power rose to meet the challenge of every spell and counterspell. Her entire body was being devoured by the Stone's blazing emerald nimbus – how long could she hold herself together under such strain? Chill fear ran through her. Now she was fighting a battle on two fronts: to meet and counter the Phaerie Lord's attacks, yet still stay strong enough to act as a conduit for the Fialan's power.

Then suddenly a hand reached out, firm and steadfast, and grasped her own. Iriana felt some of the pain subside as part of the surplus energy drained away into Dael.

He mustn't do this! Frantically, Iriana tried to pull her hand away. The last time Dael had handled the Stone he would have died, save for the intervention of Athina. But there was no going back now. The power of the Fialan linked them, and the tie could not be broken until the battle was done.

Events were at a stalemate. The great eagle that represented Aurora's magic had now been joined once more by Taku's serpent of ice, but Hellorin was concentrating all his power on his shield, and even their conjoined spells could not penetrate the barrier. Iriana wondered if she could finish the fight with one sharp, concentrated blow, but that would leave her exposed and at Hellorin's mercy if she failed. The risk either way was tremendous, for if she simply stood her ground, she risked burning out not only herself but the weaker mortal at her side.

The Wizard had been concentrating so hard on her struggle with Hellorin that there had been no chance to watch the patch of instability that was spreading inexorably out from Eliorand. She reached a decision and gathered in all her will for one tremendous strike at the Forest Lord – and at that moment the circle of unreality reached them, engulfing both Lord of the Phaerie and Wizard in its shimmering wavefront.

For an instant, Iriana was overcome by nausea and disorientation. She felt as if she were about to fly apart. Then suddenly the Stone of Fate seemed to pulse in her hand, and quite clearly she heard the mighty voice of Denali. 'Fear not, little friend. This is *my* moment now. At last I can deal with the upstart Hellorin and his Phaerie folk.'

Like a roaring torrent, the power of the Great One surged out of Iriana, engulfing Hellorin in blazing green light and spreading beyond him to encompass Eliorand and all its inhabitants. Then, as if the torrent had reversed direction, the massive magical force turned back and poured in the opposite direction – back through the Stone of Fate. Iriana felt herself expanding, diffusing into the great nimbus of emerald light that became a portal, a gateway into the realm of the

Evanesar. Now she could feel the colossal power of Denali working through her, reaching out to Hellorin and his Phaerie realm, drawing them through her, back into the Elsewhere. Then suddenly the torrent was gone, the portal closed – and reality reasserted itself.

Utterly drained, limp with exhaustion, Iriana looked through Dael's disbelieving eyes at the place where Eliorand, the heart of the Phaerie realm, had stood. Now there was nothing save a great, craggy, tree-covered hill that reared proudly above the surrounding forest – the only remaining memorial to a lost civilisation.

Then suddenly everything went dark. Dael's hand slid limply out of her own, and Iriana felt him slip from the saddle and heard the muted thump as he hit the ground. All through the staggering transition that had just occurred, he had been linked to her by the power of the Fialan, and, as she had feared, the power had proved too much for the frail form of a mortal to bear.

Aghast and stricken with grief, Iriana switched her eyesight to that of her horse. Unaccustomed to this close rapport it fought her, but the Wizard was so desperate to reach her fallen companion that she was in no state of mind to be gainsaid. Ruthlessly imposing her will upon the animal, she used its vision to guide them both down to where Dael lay, limp and broken, on the ground.

30
~

DEPART IN SORROW, RETURN IN JOY

Before Iriana began her desperate battle with Hellorin, Aelwen found Taine by searching the area of the forest's edge near his trapped horse. Even with all her years of equestrian experience and skill, it took the Horsemistress a long time to persuade her terrified mount to come anywhere near the horrifying conflict that was taking place between the Archwizard and the Forest Lord, but finally she managed to coax the frightened creature up to the tree where Taine lay across a sturdy branch. He was moving slightly, much to her relief, and therefore still alive, but his face was grey and contorted with pain.

Aelwen brought her horse up close to hover at his level, wondering with a flash of concern just how long Corisand's flying spell could last without the Fialan to bolster the Windeye's powers while she was in her equine form. Still, it was pointless to wonder, and she had other matters to concern her at present. 'Taine?' she asked urgently. 'How badly are you hurt? Can you move?'

He turned his head and glared at her. 'I told you to get away.'

'And I ignored you.' A little of Aelwen's relief at finding him alive evaporated in irritation. 'Which is just as well for you, as far as I can see. Now can you *move*?'

Taine tried to hoist himself up astride the branch but his cloak was caught on a splintered snag above him. He collapsed back into his former position with a gasping curse, sweat running down his grimacing face. 'Broken a rib or two,' he said through clenched teeth. 'Might need a little help here.'

'Wait, I'll bring your horse. His bridle caught in a tree, or he'd be halfway to Tyrineld by now, but he looks all right apart from a few

scrapes and scratches.' Aelwen had to raise her voice over the detonations accompanying the battle between Hellorin and Cyran, though
the details of what was happening were obscured by the trees. It was
difficult to untangle the trapped animal and harder still to calm him
down once he had been released. She was forced for her own safety
to take him down to ground level, and had only just managed to get
the creature under control when she heard Cyran's death scream,
and saw the trees whip back and forth as the earth shook with the
impact of his fall.

Taine's strangled dry of anguish brought her out of a frozen
moment of shock. She leapt back onto her own mount, then, leading
the other, hurried back to where her lover was still trapped in the
tree. As she reached him she was shocked to see tears running down
his face, but his voice was steady as he spoke. 'Quick! Get me out
of this bloody tree. Now that Cyran's gone, there'll be no stopping
Hellorin.'

'Don't worry. Iriana's dealing with it,' Aelwen said absently, as she
disentangled the tattered remains of his cloak from the splintered
spike of bough.

'WHAT?' There was a loud ripping noise as Taine wrenched
himself free of the encumbrance and hoisted himself upright, oblivious now to the pain. 'Why in perdition didn't you tell me? We have
to help her.'

'We have to get away,' Aelwen panted as she helped him pull himself awkwardly into his saddle. 'The Wizard is dealing with Hellorin.
She has the power of the Fialan to draw on, but there's nothing we
can do against his magic, or I would help her with all my heart.' Her
voice took on a new urgency as she saw the stubborn tightening of
his jaw. 'Taine, she came back to buy us time – at least, that was one
of the reasons. Don't let this opportunity go to waste.'

'You go,' Taine said harshly. 'I'm not leaving her.'

Hunched over in his saddle from the pain in his ribs he urged
his horse aloft, and Aelwen followed him, cursing under her breath.
When they cleared the treetops a horrific sight met their eyes.
Hellorin's gigantic storm wolf snarled and raged against an immense
eagle, formed of shifting, many-hued radiance, that tore at the wolf's
lightning-laced hide with cruel beak and talons.

They saw Iriana, her jaw clenched with pain and effort, consumed
by the blazing green energy of the Fialan, and saw Dael reach across
and take her hand. They saw her master the power as Dael drained

part of it into his body, taking on that same searing emerald glow, then a gigantic serpent of ice joined the eagle in combat, throwing its coils around the storm wolf's body.

Any thoughts of helping Iriana fled from Taine's mind. There was just no way to interfere with powers of this magnitude. He and Aelwen could only watch as the titanic struggle was played out, and the blind young Wizard faced the terrifying might of the ruler of a puissant, ancient race. Taine felt sick with fear for her. How could she possibly prevail? She looked far too vulnerable and fragile to face such might – not to mention handling the extraordinary forces of the Fialan, which blazed out of her so brightly that the shadows of her bones could be seen within her glowing skin.

In that moment, Taine's heart went out to her – then Aelwen tugged firmly at his sleeve. 'By all Creation, look at that!' With a wave of her arm she indicated the spreading wave of instability that was still expanding, and very close to the battleground in the centre of the city now. 'Don't you think we should move back—'

'I said no.' Taine gave her a savage look. 'I may not be able to help her, but I'm damned if I'm going to leave her. You go if you want.'

'If you're not retreating, then I won't,' Aelwen replied through clenched teeth. So she was forced to watch, in an agony of conflicting loyalties, as the battle unfolded.

Hellorin had always been good to her, yet she had betrayed him. She looked down at the bloodstained body of Tiolani, lying covered with dust in the rubble of the courtyard, and her heart bled for all the potential that had been lost. Yet Taine was her lover and Iriana her companion and friend, and she had no intentions of changing sides now. She understood that Hellorin's ambitions had grown out of control, that there was a dark and ruthless side to his character, that he was dangerous in his grief, and that it had been imperative to free the slave races of Xandim and Dwelven – but oh, whoever won or lost, this night would cost her dearly in anguish!

Then the edge of the spreading area of instability finally reached the combatants, and the entire world seemed to go mad. Aelwen heard Taine's cry of horror as the green nimbus around Iriana flared to blinding brilliance, and expanded until it had obscured all trace of Dael and the Wizard. Then, after what seemed an eternity, the light of the Fialan died – and when the dazzling patches of glare cleared from her eyes, Eliorand, the Forest Lord and all his subjects were gone. Only Iriana and Dael, slumped over the necks of their horses, hovered over what was now an ordinary, forested hill.

The sense of loss was like a knife twisting in Aelwen's heart. She gave a wrenching cry, but before Taine could react, Dael suddenly collapsed and slid limply from the back of his mount, and Iriana's cry of grief was an echo of her own.

But I can't leave Iriana now!

Dael was stricken with horror to find himself standing once again by the great old door that guarded the entrance to the realm of Death. His memories of the moments leading up to his demise were vague, distorted flashes – the fearsome battle with the Forest Lord; taking the Wizard's hand and feeling the searing power of the Fialan flood through him; the vanishing of Eliorand … He was tortured by a feeling of things left undone, help left ungiven, words left unsaid.

Not now – I can't go now. I'm not ready!

Yet he found that, while all these thoughts had been racing through his mind, he had somehow passed through the door and the mysterious tunnel that lay beyond, emerging in the strange landscape with its dim, sourceless light. And there, waiting for him, was the cowled and shrouded figure of Death, whom he had now come to know, following his last visit to this place, as Athina's brother Creator Siris.

'They all say just what you are saying, those who pass this way – or almost all of them. Any life that has ended is like a piece of torn linen, with so many loose threads left hanging.' He shrugged. 'It is the way of things. Your path lies in a different direction now.'

Dael's feet seemed to move of their own volition, following Death across the eerie, unchanging hillside that was crowned by the grove of trees that held the Well of Souls, but his mind was screaming in protest, not just for the loss of his companions and the life he had left behind, but for the severing of his final tie with Athina. If he was reborn he wouldn't remember her, and she would never find him again. She had promised him that she would do everything in her power to reunite them, but how could she, once he had passed through the Well?

He was already mourning his loss so bitterly that when he stepped into the clearing in the centre of the grove he was stunned to see the familiar, beloved figure of the Cailleach, moving with swift footsteps round the Well to embrace him.

'I thought I'd never see you again,' Dael murmured. 'I'm glad they let you come to say goodbye.'

'Goodbye? What goodbye?' Athina held him away from her at arm's length, with her hands on his shoulders, and he realised that her face was glowing with happiness. She looked from Dael to the anonymous, dark figure of Death, and her smile was as dazzling as the rising sun. 'Thank you, Siris, my dear brother, for giving me this one chance to slip past the other Creators.'

There was no sign of a face within the shadowy cowl, but as Death replied, it sounded as if he was smiling. 'The other Creators were quite happy to abandon me to this thankless task down all the endless aeons since we formed this world. Only you still cared about me, and visited me from time to time in my lonely exile. Moreover, now you have given me hope that one day I might be free to move on, to Create again, to bestow life and leave the lonely role of Keeper of the Well to someone else.'

'As I told you, you have something that the Magefolk desperately need,' the Cailleach said. 'I believe an accommodation might be reached to bring your exile to an end.'

Athina turned back to Dael. 'And now a choice lies before you, my dear. You may pass through the Well and return—'

'No!' Dael protested. 'If I go through there I'll lose you for ever.'

The Cailleach smiled. 'There is an alternative.'

Dael's heart leapt. 'Can I come with you? Truly? Have you found a way?'

'Thanks to Siris, yes.' Athina turned back towards the grove and beckoned, and Avithan, healed of all his dreadful wounds, stepped out from between the trees. 'Is everything ready?' he asked eagerly. 'Can I go back now?'

'You should not be going back at all,' Siris said sternly. 'You should be going on – but since you did not actually die, thanks to my meddling sister here, I can stretch the ancient laws and send you back to your old life, in Dael's place – if he consents.'

The shadowy cowl swung round to face Dael. 'It all depends on you, human. You must be very sure that this is what you want. An eternity in one place with one person: are you sure your mind can encompass that? Are you certain you could bear it?'

'An eternity ... ' Dael was staggered. 'But how – I mean, I'm a mortal with no magic. I thought I couldn't ...'

'Twice now you have acted as a vessel for the Fialan's power,' Siris told him. 'The first time it killed you, and you were permitted to return to your mortal life. But when you took on the burden of all that power a second time, it changed you – permanently.'

Smiling, Athina added, 'The Stone has a history of reacting in different ways to different people, and it seems to have been drawn to the sacrifice that you made for your friends – first Corisand, then Iriana. You are no longer mortal, my dear, and who knows what other powers the Fialan might have left within you? You might have magic that none of us could even predict, and what the Fialan has bestowed can never be taken away from you.'

'Because of the Fialan I can send you back to your old life one last time,' Siris continued. 'If you decide to return you will take your powers with you, and who knows what you might do, or become, or achieve. In the Cailleach's realm by the Timeless Lake, however, things are static and unchanging. Would you really want to choose that over a lifetime with so many possibilities?'

'Think well, Dael,' Athina said urgently. 'Though it would break my heart to lose you, I would also love to see you reach your full potential.'

'So you must decide, and decide now,' Siris said. 'And once made, your choice can never be unmade. Also, this is the last time I will be able to return you. There will be no third chances, and should you return to the mundane realm, when you finally quit your life there you *must* go through the Well and be reborn. This is your last chance to be united with Athina. So think well – but think quickly. These possibilities will only exist within a narrow window of time.'

'Hold on,' Avithan interrupted, pushing forward. 'What's all this about decisions and choices? I thought everything was quite straightforward: Athina keeps the mortal, I go back home, and since she still has someone with her in her realm, the other Creators won't notice the difference. Scrying in Athina's lake I just watched my father die.' For a moment the pain and anguish were naked on his face. 'I need to be with my mother and my people now, and they need me. Why are you suddenly asking *him* to decide all our fates? He's only a mortal. Who cares what he thinks, or wants?'

Athina's eyes flashed. 'Dael was never *only* a mortal, and he is the son of my heart. His opinions and desires are every bit as relevant as yours – if not more so.'

'Have you not been listening, Wizard?' Siris added. 'Through the Stone of Fate, Dael is no longer a mortal – yet even if he were, he would have the same rights as you in this place. In *my* realm, all are equal. Whether you like it or not, the decision is his to make.'

While they had been talking, Dael's mind had been racing. All the dear, familiar faces flashed before his eyes: Iriana, Corisand, Taine and Aelwen, and the trusting blue-eyed gaze of little Melik. They had all become his friends. It wrenched his heart to think of leaving them – yet when he looked back at the Cailleach, he suddenly knew he would never miss them half as much as he would regret the loss of this all-powerful being who, astonishingly, had become the only mother he had ever known. In that instant his decision was crystal clear. Unhesitatingly, he reached out and took hold of her hand. 'I thought I had lost you for ever, Athina. I never want to be parted from you again.'

'So be it,' Siris pronounced. 'Then you must return to the mundane realm very briefly, for it is only in your world that the exchange can be made.'

Dael nodded. 'Let's get on with it, then.' He shot a cool look at Avithan. 'I'm very sorry about your father. I was there when he fell, and he died bravely and well, but that's no consolation to you. Before we part, I want to give you some advice. Iriana told me how you always used to overprotect her. I wouldn't advise that now; it won't be welcomed, believe me. You'll find that she's changed a great deal in your absence, and accomplished things you couldn't even dream of. She defeated the Lord of the Phaerie not once, but twice and—'

'I've known Iriana since we were children,' Avithan snapped. 'I don't need advice from an ex-slave who has known her for no time at all.'

Dael shrugged. 'You can't say I didn't warn you.' He turned his back on Avithan and spoke to Siris. 'I'm ready.'

The Wizard's horse didn't like her using its sight, and fought her all the way, but Iriana simply overrode its will and took it down to the ground. She dismounted by Dael's body and tied the reins to a low bough, but the animal tossed its head, fighting both its tether and her control, and Iriana couldn't see Dael except for brief, frustrating glimpses as she knelt by his side. Frantically she groped to feel a pulse, but he lay limp and still, with no evidence of a heartbeat. 'Dael,' she sobbed. 'Oh, Dael, I'm sorry.' She ran her fingers over his face, smoothing back his hair, her heart breaking. He had been so brave and loyal. She could never have defeated Hellorin without him – it was so unfair that death should be his only reward.

Suddenly Taine was beside her and took her into his arms. She buried her face in his shoulder and wept. 'Iriana, use my eyes,' he said softly.

She pulled back from him, giving his hand a grateful squeeze, released the mind of the struggling horse with relief and found herself welcomed into the mind of Taine. His sight was blurred by his own tears, but he wiped his eyes and her vision cleared to see Aelwen kneeling beside her, also weeping. Iriana tried to straighten Dael's twisted, broken limbs. 'Oh, Dael,' she murmured brokenly, brushing her fingers across his face. 'I'm so sorry. You were so brave and loyal – you didn't deserve this.'

Then Aelwen suddenly cried out. 'Look! Look, Taine and Iriana.' Taine swung his head upwards and through his eyes, Iriana saw a hazy vision of Athina, with Dael at her side, unscathed, unwounded, and looking much more solid, standing at her side. And with them – Iriana gasped. 'Avithan?'

'We cannot linger,' the Cailleach said urgently. 'My fellow Creators must not find out about this day's work, but as long as I have one person with me in my realm, they won't be concerned with the identity, so Dael and Avithan are changing places.'

'Goodbye, Iriana,' Dael said. 'I'm sorry to have to leave you like this – but it's my only chance to be with Athina.'

'I understand.' The Wizard smiled at him through her tears. 'I'll miss you, dear Dael – but I'm so happy for you.'

There were tears in Dael's eyes too. 'You and Corisand always treated me like a true companion, and you showed me that I can be someone special, mortal though I am, and that I can make a difference. Thanks to you, I did, and I can never thank you enough for that. Say goodbye to Corisand for me – and little Melik.' He held out a phantom hand to her. 'Farewell, Iriana, my friend.'

'Now,' Athina said. 'You'll find a small crystal phial in Dael's pocket. Unstopper it and trickle the liquid between his lips.'

It seemed strange, after just speaking to Dael, to be rummaging round in the clothing on his battered body, but Iriana quickly found the phial, and did what the Cailleach had said.

'Now.' Athina nudged Avithan forward, and his shadowy figure knelt beside Dael, then lay down exactly where the body was lying, so that their forms seemed superimposed on one another. The Cailleach raised her hand and a beam of blinding blue-white light came shining out of her palm to highlight the two figures. Taine blinked – and when he and Iriana could see again there, in Dael's place, was Avithan, alive and well once more, though looking a little dazed. Dael's body had vanished, but his figure, looking even more substantial now, remained with Athina, holding tightly to her free hand, his face glowing with happiness.

'One last thing, Iriana,' the Cailleach said. 'I have foreseen many things in my lake since I was forced to leave you. Every one of the artefacts of power that the Magefolk are creating will require at least one life to be sacrificed, sometimes more. That phial in Dael's pocket contained water from the Well of Souls. You must tell the Leviathan that the only way to make the cauldron of rebirth that they are creating is to use the water from that Well, in the Place Between the Worlds. They must send a representative to Death's realm – and the only way to get there is the obvious one, I'm afraid. That person must be prepared to give their life for the cause, for a bargain must be struck, and Death will demand this sacrifice.'

'But we can't reach them in time,' Iriana protested. 'Please, Athina, couldn't you get the message to them? Surely there must be a way.'

Athina sighed. 'The things you ask of me. Very well, I will do my best, but I can guarantee nothing. I will summon them back to Tyrineld, for in their northern migration they are the closest of the other Magefolk races. You have much information to share with them that they can pass on to the Dragons and Skyfolk, but if they are not there when you get home you would be advised to send a messenger of your own, in case I fail.' Her face, which had been so sombre as she gave her advice and warning, broke into a smile. 'Farewell, my friends. Thank you for taking care of Dael for me – and may fortune favour you in the terrible days to come.'

'What terrible days?' Taine said urgently. *'What terrible days?'*

Athina made no reply. She looked at Dael and nodded, then the two of them began to fade and shimmer.

And suddenly were gone.

31

A DIFFICULT TRANSITION

Avithan sat up and frowned at Iriana, who still had Taine's arm around her shoulders. 'Maybe I shouldn't have come back after all,' he said. 'You don't look overjoyed to see me.'

For a moment the Wizard was lost for a reply. She was utterly stunned by everything that had happened in such a short space of time, and her emotions were all in a tangle: joy at Avithan's return, a mixture of happiness and sorrow at the loss of Dael. She was elated and astonished that with the help of the Fialan she had defeated Hellorin and exiled his entire race from the world, yet filled with lingering grief and pain at Cyran's death. There was also a good deal of concern and doubt over whether Avithan would have altered much – and would he be able to deal with the ways in which *she* had changed? Then the happiness at seeing him won out, and she slipped away from Taine to embrace this dearest of old friends, miraculously restored to her.

'Of course I'm glad to see you,' she said. 'It was just a lot to take in for a moment – I thought you'd gone for good.'

He hugged her back, his face lit with a smile at last. 'And I can't tell you how glad I am to see you again. There were times when I despaired of ever getting home again.'

Iriana gestured to her other companions. 'Avithan, this is Taine, and this is Aelwen. They—'

'I know about them,' Avithan replied. 'Athina and I have been watching your progress from her world.' He looked across at his father's body, which had not vanished with the Phaerie city, but was lying, as if asleep, at the foot of a tree, and his eyes filled with tears. 'I saw all of it,' he said in a choked, unsteady voice. 'I saw my father fight, and saw him fall. A Mortal slave is permitted to escape Death's clutches,' he added bitterly, 'but there will be no second chances for an Archwizard who gave his life in the service of his people.' He left the others and knelt beside his father's body, murmuring his own private words of farewell.

Iriana and her companions left him alone for a few moments, respecting his grief, though the Wizard was longing to catch up with Corisand. Now that it was no longer needed, the power of the Fialan had died away to bearable measures, and the glow around her was the faintest of shimmers. She felt absolutely drained; light-headed with exhaustion and desperate for sleep, but there would be no chance of that. Instead, beckoning to Taine and Aelwen to come with her, she stepped forward when Avithan got to his feet and performed the spell that would take Cyran out of time, so that his body might remain safely where it lay until arrangements could be made to bring him home.

Avithan took her hand. 'What am I going to say to my mother?'

'She'll already know of his passing,' Iriana reminded him. 'You won't have to tell her that, but she'll want to know what happened. Sharalind is a brave woman. With help from all of us she'll come to terms with this. Tell her of his bravery, and his sacrifice. Tell her he never stopped looking for you.'

Avithan sighed. 'I wish he could have known about my return,' he said. 'I wish I could have talked with him, and embraced him one last time.'

'I wish you could have, too.' Iriana squeezed his hand. 'I'm sorry, Avithan, but it's time to leave him now. He'll be safe here, until we can return for him.'

'I hate to leave him all alone.' There was a catch in Avithan's voice.

'Avithan, he isn't really here any more. You know this better than anyone, now that you have actually met Death and lived to tell the tale. Dael told us of the Well of Souls, after the first time he was there, when he held the Fialan for Corisand in the cave, and was overcome by its power. Cyran will have already passed through, to be reborn into a new life. A part of him will always remain, but not in this empty shell. He'll still be alive in your heart, and in your memory.'

At that moment, Taine and Aelwen approached. 'I am truly sorry for your loss, my friend,' Taine said. 'We can share your grief, for we all have lost people who are dear to us today,' he added. 'If you've been watching, as you say, you'll know what Dael and Kaldath meant to us. With the death of Tiolani and the departure of the Phaerie, Aelwen lost close family members, and I mourn Cyran too, for he gave me a home and a purpose when I was a rootless exile. But we must put off our grieving till later, harsh as that may seem. I have a feeling in my bones that this business isn't over yet.'

'And since Iriana has the Fialan, we don't have much time until Corisand's flying spell wears off,' Aelwen reminded them. 'If we don't get back to her before it does, we'll have a long and dangerous walk in front of us.'

Her words galvanised them all into action, even Avithan. So much had happened in the last hour that Taine and Iriana had forgotten about the risks of being too far away from the Windeye with the Fialan.

'Come on, little sister,' Taine said to Iriana. 'You don't have Melik, so you can share my vision if you want, until we get back to safety.'

'She doesn't need you.' Avithan pushed forward belligerently. 'She can share *my* vision.'

Iriana sighed. Avithan had only been back a little while, and her fight for independence was starting all over again. She also hadn't missed the cold look in Aelwen's eyes when Taine was so friendly to her. 'Thanks to both of you, but I can manage,' she said firmly. 'I'll take Rosina, the roan mare that Dael ri— used to ride,' she corrected herself. 'She's gentle enough to take direction from me and let me use her vision.'

Taine nodded. 'Good idea.'

'But—' Avithan began.

Iriana turned on him. 'Don't,' she said fiercely. 'Just don't start that nonsense again, Avithan. I mean it.'

He opened his mouth, closed it again, then turned on his heel and stalked away, grim-faced. After a moment, Aelwen spoke. 'You'll need a mount, Avithan,' she said. 'You can take the one that Iriana was riding. Corisand won't like it if we leave any of her people behind.'

They wasted no time, and in a matter of minutes they were ready to go. Looking at the horses, Iriana noticed that the bright shimmer of the flying spell seemed to be dimming a little, and frowned. Would they get back to Corisand in time, before the flying spell wore off?

'Remember to hang on tight,' Aelwen was telling Avithan. 'Flying a horse for the first time is quite an alarming experience, and if you fall off, it's a long way to the ground.'

347

'I'll manage,' Avithan replied gruffly, but the Wizard noticed that he looked a little pale.

Rosina was a gentle beast, and to Iriana's relief was quite happy to accommodate the presence of a strange intruder in her mind. As they took off, she used the mare's vision to sneak a look at Avithan, and smiled to herself as he suppressed a yelp of terror as his mount took off. She noticed that he was clinging, white-knuckled, to the pommel of the saddle, but most people did the same on their initial flight. She hoped that soon he would relax and begin to enjoy it.

With tensions seething in the air between them, the quartet made their way back towards Tyrineld. As they headed away from the hill where the Phaerie city had once stood, the Wizard thought sadly about the way in which Kaldath's death, Dael's departure and Avithan's arrival had completely changed the atmosphere in their little group. Ever since Athina had taken Avithan to her own realm to heal him, Iriana had longed for his return, yet now that he was back there was an element of friction and discord in their circle that had not been there before. Suddenly she remembered what she had conveniently forgotten during his absence: that for all her life, she had constantly had to cope with his overwhelming solicitousness, and fight him for every scrap of self-reliance.

The Wizard clenched her jaw. She wasn't about to go through *that* again! There had been a lot of changes in her life since his departure, and she had changed with them. Avithan would just have to get used to that, or … Iriana didn't want to think about the alternatives. With the horse's peripheral vision she glanced beyond him to Taine. *He* had never, from the first time they'd met, treated her as though she were helpless – and therefore when he did offer to give her a hand with anything, it was just the same as him offering to help anyone else.

As for Aelwen … She looked at the Horsemistress, sitting easily in her saddle, so much a part of her mount that the Wizard envied her. Then she noticed that Aelwen was also eyeing her, and not in a very friendly fashion. Iriana could feel herself growing tense with anxiety. What was happening to everyone? The tightly knit band of companions that had worked so well together since the day Athina left seemed to be disintegrating before her eyes. She sighed, desperately wishing that Corisand could be there. At least their friendship would surely stand the test of time. As for the others; well, at least they had done what they set out to do. What would become of them now, only time would tell.

Where in Creation are they?

Corisand led the Xandim in the direction that Iriana had given her, towards the settlement of Nexis, but her thoughts were far behind her, with the friends who must even now be fighting for their lives. There was nothing she could do to help them, however. As Iriana had said, her first responsibility must be to her tribe. Determined to get them far away from Eliorand as quickly as possible, she led them as fast as the slowest ones, the old and the very young, could fly. They had already passed the border, and were heading towards the lake with its isle that had been the site of Athina's tower. Corisand kept looking back over her shoulder, desperately seeking a glimpse of the cluster of specks against the dark sky that would show that the others were following.

But what if Hellorin won? Then those specks could be him coming after us.

Corisand shuddered. She would have to put that notion right out of her head before the other Xandim sensed her unease. 'Iriana will be all right,' she told herself firmly. 'Armed with the Fialan, she can handle Hellorin.' Yet the more time passed with no one in sight, the harder it was to shake off her fears.

They had passed Athina's lake before Corisand discovered that she had something far more pressing to worry about. It was becoming increasingly difficult to keep up the pace she had set. She was slowing down; finding it harder and harder to keep moving through the air. Her body felt heavy and sluggish, and when she looked down she saw with a flash of alarm that the treetops were growing appreciably closer.

She was sinking. The flying spell was wearing off.

Then suddenly, Hellorin was gone. Iriana had won. Corisand felt it; felt the chains of his spell that had enslaved her people fall away at last. Since Tiolani was dead too, there was no one left to enforce the magic. The Xandim tribe behind her faltered as the Forest Lord's iron grip was loosed from them, sensing that something profound had taken place but not knowing what, or why.

Right then, the Windeye had no time for celebration. Her own flying spell was still decaying fast, and it was imperative that she get her people out of the sky – and soon. Frantically, she looked down for a safe place to land the herd. She had a vague recollection that, while on the Wild Hunt as Hellorin's mount, she had seen a cleared space somewhere in this area; an ugly scar across the face of the forest where the trees and vegetation had been consumed by a wildfire, probably from a lightning strike. It couldn't be far away, and it was easily visible from the air.

Yes, after a few minutes she spotted it in the distance, off to the right; a long, black smear across the green of the forest. With a sigh of relief, she altered course, hoping that they could get there before the magic wore off entirely.

The fire must have roared unchecked through these woods for some time before finally being put out by rain, and the Windeye hated to think of all the destruction that had been caused, and the pain and terror of the poor woodland creatures who had dwelt there. Nonetheless, the location was easily visible from the air and had sufficient space to land the entire tribe. Corisand called back to them with a ringing whinny and led them down, for she was out of choices. Behind her, the glimmer of the flying spell was growing so dim that she could barely see the Xandim against the night sky. By the time they reached the edge of the great scar, they were practically brushing the treetops.

It was a risky landing. The devastated area contained so many traps and hazards in the form of blackened snags and stumps, and the charred remains of many forest giants that had come crashing down in flames. Though the fire must have happened some time ago, there was still, to the equine sense of smell, the faint acrid stink of burning vegetation and flesh.

The herd were uneasy; away from their familiar territory, out of their routine, and flying for the first time without riders to control and guide them. They had never known freedom before, and they were finding their first experiences of liberty alarming and strange. Only the power of the Windeye was keeping them grouped together, and Corisand hoped desperately that it would be enough. As long as they stayed together they had a chance to protect themselves from predators, but any who started to stray could be picked off one by one.

Though there had been a few stumbles and a number of scratches and scrapes, everyone had managed to reach the ground without breaking a limb – which was what the Windeye had been dreading. As it was, the smell of blood in the air from the various minor injuries stood a fair chance of attracting any local predators, and the Xandim could not flee over such treacherous, rough terrain. Since she could do nothing about it, however, she decided that there was no point in worrying.

As things stood, there was more than enough to concern her. Corisand was in a dreadful quandary. Would she be able to switch back to her human form without the Fialan? If she did succeed, could she then change back to a horse if the need arose? As a human, it would be difficult to hold the herd together, yet if anyone came along – for she was in the lands of the Wizards now and not sure how far she was from Nexis – she would need a human guise in order to communicate with them and explain that these animals were truly free beings, and not mere beasts to be captured and used.

For the present, at least, the Xandim were easy enough to handle. There was a small amount of regrowth, especially near the edge of the burn, where seeds had drifted from the unscathed areas of forest, and a scattering of grass blades were struggling to force their way through the ashy soil. There were drifts of fireweed with their long stems, their spikes of purple flowers and their long, pointed leaves that had a slightly bitter but refreshing flavour. The herd, weary from all their terrifying experiences earlier in the night, followed by a wild race across the midnight sky, fell to foraging, with the hungry foals being suckled by the grazing mares, and the stallions taking up their up their natural guard positions around the perimeter, but taking time to snatch a quick mouthful every now and then.

Corisand, her equine instincts strong while she was wearing this form, would have liked nothing better than to join them, but alas, as the Windeye, such luxuries were forbidden. She had finally decided that it was vital that she transform to her human aspect while some shreds of the Fialan's power remained, for that would make her own powers as Windeye available, and also she needed to make some kind of signal so that Iriana and the others could find her when they returned – if they returned.

I hope they're safe!

There was nothing she could do to help them, however, so she must concentrate on taking care of her own. If her companions hadn't found her by daylight, it was unlikely that they would be coming back, and she would be forced to take the herd on foot through the forest until she reached the settlement of Nexis. Once there, she would explain matters somehow, and throw herself and the Xandim upon the mercy of the Wizards. They were Hellorin's enemies – surely they would be willing to help some of his victims?

Suddenly, as she thought of Hellorin, she realised with a burst of joy that he was truly dead, and she and the Xandim no longer needed the Fialan to change shape. His evil spell was finally broken, and her people were truly free.

As she didn't want to panic the tribe, the Windeye thought of drifting quietly away into the trees at the forest's edge to make the change into her other shape, then decided against it. If they actually saw her undergo the transformation, they would at least recognise her, and that might make it easier for them to accept her authority.

If only equine communication wasn't so limited! Life would be so much easier if Corisand could only explain everything to them. She remembered what a shock it had been, the first time she'd gone to the Elsewhere and found herself trying to balance unsteadily on two legs instead of four. How the entire Xandim race would cope when it finally happened to them, she couldn't imagine – but she had a feeling that it was time to find out. She would have preferred to wait until she'd brought her tribe to a place that was sheltered, safe and secure, but it had to be now. Even though they would begin their alternative existences cold, hungry, naked and defenceless, she needed them to start remembering their heritage, and using their human minds once more.

She would start with herself. Corisand made the change right in the middle of the herd. The Xandim lifted their heads, tossing their manes, snorting uneasily and backing away, yet the power of the Windeye still held them together – at least for now. After a time they settled back to their grazing, but Corisand knew they were all covertly watching her, unsure whether she was one of their own, or some unknown threat. Her heart beating fast, she raised her arms and sent her power flowing among them like a gentle breeze, easing them through the change – and suddenly where the beautiful Xandim horses had grazed, she had a group of people in front of her, crying out in shock and dismay, overbalancing and sprawling on the ground and knocking one another over. She could see them desperately trying to cope with balancing on two legs instead of four, and the change to a whole new type of vision, with eyes set in the front of their heads instead of the sides.

While they were still overwhelmed by alien emotions and a foreign way of thought, while they were still confused, and groping to express themselves, as they had never done before, in a spoken language that had been long locked away in their unconscious memories, she addressed them.

'Don't be afraid, my friends and herdmates. Tonight, at long last, the Xandim have come back into their heritage. I can see that the memories of who and what we were before the Phaerie enslaved us are beginning to return to you, as they returned to me when I first became Windeye. Before Hellorin's spell chained us within our equine forms we were able to change from one shape to the other at will.'

She smiled. 'You'll still be free to live as you have always lived, if that is your wish; to roll in the summer grass, or race the wind, but this time it will be your choice – there will be no masters to compel or constrain you. We have a new home promised us, far to the south in a fair and fertile land. We must rediscover our true identity and find a way of life that suits us, but we will have friends of other races who will help us. We will not be alone. Now you are cold, bewildered and anxious, but I'll take care of you.' She used her magic to send a warm breeze circulating through the group, so that their shivering ceased.

'For now, please take a little time to find your balance – both on your feet and in your minds. Find your companions and herdmates, and see what each other looks like in their human form. After a while, I'm sure you'll have thought of many questions, and I'll answer them as best I can.'

Though she had tried to comfort and reassure them, Corisand could still feel their nervousness and disorientation, and felt dreadfully disappointed. She had worked so hard and gone through so much to free her people: she had expected them to be delighted – or to thank her at the very least. Then suddenly she remembered what a shock it had been to discover her alternate form – and as Windeye, she'd had the advantage of knowing that possibility existed. She looked at the Xandim – really *looked*.

As she'd suggested they were searching out former companions and haltingly trying to speak to one another. One little filly, now a freshly blooming young girl, burst out laughing at something – and broke off sharply with a strangled squeak of fear at the alien sound that had come out of her mouth, while all the others turned to stare at her. Corisand knew that if they had still been in their equine form, their ears would have been laid back, and their eyes rolling anxiously with the white rims showing.

Suddenly it came home to the Windeye just how many difficulties lay ahead of her people. Even though Basileus had given them a home, they would have to learn to build shelters, to make clothing, utensils and weapons, to hunt or cultivate their food. She looked with dismay at all the pale, naked bodies stumbling around at the edge of the trees. Somehow she found that she could identify her former herdmates, even though their appearances were so different. She saw dark hair, blond and red; faces and bodies showing variations of tautness, sagging, musculature or wrinkles, according to the ages and health of their owners.

I don't know what I was thinking, bringing them back. They looked much more beautiful as horses.

Her wry amusement at the thought was enough to cheer her a little. Everything would sort itself out in the fullness of time, she decided. And after all, the Xandim didn't have to stay in these forms. They could change back at any time. Corisand had simply opened up the choice for them.

Taking a deep breath, she addressed her people once more. 'It's up to you, of course – you're slaves no longer – but you might be more comfortable in the forms that you're used to, for the present,' she suggested. 'We can work on the human side of things once we're safe and secure. I simply wanted you to experience the choices that lie open to you now, and I hope that even when you transfer back to your equine aspects, your intellect, now that it has been triggered with the removal of Hellorin's spell, will stay with you.'

'So what happens next?' someone called out.

'Right now, we're waiting for my companions to get here from Eliorand. As soon as they join us, we're going back to the lands of the Wizards, to ask their help while we discover our true identities once more, and find our new place to live. In the meantime, what do you say to changing back? You'll be warmer and less vulnerable, and there's food here for a horse that a human wouldn't be able to eat.'

'I'm all for that – but how *do* we change back?' another voice asked.

Corisand tried to put into words what she knew instinctively. 'Just think of yourselves as you were before. You'll find that the image is locked into your mind – it's part of what we are. Then imagine yourselves flowing into that shape.'

Oddly enough, it was the older Xandim who found it easier to make the transformation. Corisand had been half-expecting the younger ones, filled with curiosity and expectation, to be more flexible in their thinking, but when it came to recovering their former appearance, the older members of the tribe had worn that equine form for a long time. Reverting to it now came instinctively to them. The Windeye had a feeling, however, that when they became human again, the opposite would be true and the younger ones would shine. Unable to resist the experiment (and surely it was important that they had a little practice in switching back and forth) she called out to them.

'Now, can you please change back into your human aspects, just for a moment? I want to make sure you can move easily from one to the other. Just think of yourselves as you were a moment ago, on two legs and with your eyes pointing forward. Your instincts should do the rest.'

I hope.

It took them longer this time, and Corisand had been right: in general, the younger Xandim managed more easily. But she had found out what she wanted to know. They could transform at will now, without her help. The ability came as naturally as breathing.

'Now what?' an impatient voice interrupted her thoughts. She looked up to see a short, stocky, brown-haired man whom she recognised as Alil, who had formerly been Kelon's horse. 'Well?' he asked again. 'What do you want, Windeye? Back and forth, back and forth – make up your mind.'

He was joined by a chorus of mutters and objections from the others, and Corisand couldn't help but smile. 'See?' she said. 'Your human characters are asserting themselves very quickly – you're already learning how to complain.' A scattering of laughter met her words, though she could feel their discomfort at the unfamiliar sound and emotion. 'I'm sorry I had to pester you again. I wanted to be sure that that you could all make the change without my help, for the time will come when you'll need to. I'll leave you in peace now, to change back if you wish, and eat and rest. Let's make the most of this brief respite until my companions come, for then we must be on our way once more.'

Leaving them to it, she turned away, looking forward at last to assuaging her own hunger and weariness. The basket containing Melik, which had been strapped to her back, had fallen to the ground when Corisand changed shape, and Iriana's cat was wailing his protests from within. She didn't dare let him out when the Wizard and Dael weren't there, so all she could do was pray that they would come soon. Like all her companions, she had been carrying a small bag of trail rations, so she pushed a piece of dried meat through one of the air holes in the basket and hoped that the food would help to calm and quiet him until his rightful owner turned up.

After the battles of that night she was as weary and hungry as the rest of the Xandim, but before she could rest there was one more thing she must do. Summoning her Othersight, she tugged and twisted the silvery air currents, shaping them with her hands and mind until they formed the image of a horse. Lifting her arms she sent it upwards, high above the treetops, to mark her location to her friends. By now the flying spell would also have worn off for Iriana and her companions, so it was vital to have a beacon that could be seen from ground level.

Once she had her image in place, she finally sat down on the ground at the edge of the burn, leant back against a tree trunk and rested her weary limbs. Rummaging in her pouch she found some jerky, a hard and rather elderly piece of cheese and a handful of nuts, and fell on them like a starving wolf. She was desperate for some sleep, but didn't dare close her eyes while the responsibility for the entire tribe was in her hands. Besides, until she'd found out the fate of her companions, she couldn't settle.

If only I could get to Iriana so that she could give me back the Fialan. I won't rest until we're safely back with the Wizards.

Though Corisand hated not being able to fly, she told herself that she had better get used to it. Once the Xandim had been liberated she had promised to give the Stone of Fate to Iriana. She dropped her head into her hands and sighed. No more soaring above those plodding people confined to the ground. No more flying among the stars and racing the wind.

Freedom came with a heavy price. She only hoped that when the time came, she would be able to pay it.

Suddenly she realised that she was not alone, and found a man sitting beside her. His hair, dark with the odd gleam of silver, swept back from his face and down to his shoulders. His chin was square, his cheekbones high and chiselled, and his grey eyes held an intensity and power that immediately made her think of a herd leader. Though he was human now, she recognised him as Aelwen's former mount, the black stallion Taryn.

When he spoke, it was almost as if he had been sharing her thoughts. 'It's not going to be easy, is it, Windeye?'

'No,' she answered him honestly. 'I thought that freeing everyone would be the hardest part, but now all manner of difficulties lie ahead of us – though at least we have a home ready and waiting for us.'

'We do?'

'We do, and it's a lovely place – at least so I was told by the one who gave it to us. Sometime I'll tell you the whole story, but it's far too long and complicated a tale for now. But you're right. We have a daunting task ahead, and so much to learn about surviving in our alternate forms.'

He nodded. 'I thought so. It's a strange thing, isn't it, this ability to think and plan ahead. Strange and wonderful – and frightening too.' He gave her a tentative smile. 'I was wondering – how is it that when you changed you were wearing a covering on your body, as the Phaerie always did, yet the rest of us had nothing but our bare skins?'

Corisand noticed that he was shivering, and gave him her cloak, helping him wrap it round his shoulders, for he was unaccustomed to using human hands, and fumbled clumsily at the fastening. 'I'm afraid,' she said, 'that these bodies are a great deal more vulnerable than our equine forms – to cold and small injuries from such things as thorns or stinging plants – or even sitting on rough ground, such as we have here. They need extra protection, and deck themselves in what they call clothes – layers of cloth or leather.' She went on to explain what she had discovered for herself, that materials made from plant or animal sources such as leather, linen and wool, with fastenings of horn or bone, would transform with her to become part of her equine shape, and still be there when she changed back. 'That's why I advised everyone that it might be better for them to stay in their equine shapes for now. Clearly, we'll need to get clothes for all the Xandim as soon as we can, and hopefully the Wizardfolk, my friend Iriana's people, will help us with that. However, we'll have to learn to make our own as soon as possible – and that also goes for all the myriad other things humans need that equines don't.' She smiled at him wryly. 'Our freedom will mean enormous challenges ahead of us, I'm afraid. You all may be cursing my name and wishing you were back with the Phaerie before we're done.'

'I sincerely doubt that.' Taryn returned her smile. 'It may be a hard road ahead, but at least it will be *our* road, and for that we have you to thank.'

He got to his feet. 'I should let you get back to your rest. I only wanted to come over and be the first to thank you, on behalf of all of us. A lot of them are still too afraid and bewildered to understand

357

what a wonderful and amazing thing you've done for them tonight – but I know that once they've had a chance to settle, they'll be as grateful as I am.' He smiled at her, and she could see the same bafflement in his eyes that must have been in hers when she found her human facial expressions mirroring her emotions. 'I think I'll change back for a while,' he said, handing back her cloak. 'This is going to take a bit of getting used to. Rest a little, Windeye. You look weary beyond belief. I will keep watch for any danger, and the rest of the herd with me.'

'Thank you.' Suddenly Corisand felt much happier, and easier in her mind. As Taryn transformed into the black stallion again and went to rejoin the others, she wrapped herself in her cloak once more, leant back against her tree trunk and closed her eyes, secure in the knowledge that there was someone in her herd upon whom she could depend.

32
~

SIGNS IN THE SKY

Yinze would be happy if he never had to fly again. No matter how long he spent swinging in one of the Skyfolk cargo nets, the result was always the same: he felt sick, cold and uncomfortable. If he could only find Iriana, however, it would all be worthwhile. Where could she have been all this time? All too well he remembered his agony and grief when she'd passed from the world, and his utter shock, followed by relief and joy, when she'd returned. In all the history of the Skyfolk, such a thing had never been known.

What had happened to her in those long, missing hours?

Would she have changed?

Would he even recognise her now?

Her black and white horse had been found deep in the forest by a human woodsman from Nexis, badly injured yet still gamely trying to struggle back to the settlement. With thoughts of fresh meat, the man had managed to coax the mare all the way back to his lumber camp, and luckily Yinze and his winged escort had arrived in time to save Dailika from slaughter, since the camp foreman, a Wizard, had proved susceptible to bribery. The sight of the wounded animal had torn Yinze's heart. Had Iriana suffered the same fate?

'Yinze, stop it.' The clear, chiding voice broke into his circling thoughts. He looked around to see Kea flying alongside, with the flame-coloured undersides of her green wings flashing as she kept pace with the net. She was using mindspeech as they always did when flying, to avoid having to shout over the sounds of wingbeats and the wind, and gave him a stern look. 'I can feel you worrying all the way over here. I understand that it's hard, but you've got to stop all these fruitless doubts and speculations. We *will* find Iriana. We won't stop searching until we do. And when we find her – well, you'll discover whether she's changed or not, and worrying won't affect that outcome. Chewing over and over the whole business might be giving you something to do, but it isn't getting you anywhere, and it's costing you a lot of misery in the meantime.'

Yinze glared at her. 'It's all very well for *you* to say that. It's not your sister we're searching for. Iriana doesn't mean anything to you.'

'I know how much she means to you, so she matters a great deal to me too, even though I've never met her,' the winged girl retorted. 'So let's just concentrate on finding her, shall we? Atka's scrying put her close to Eliorand, but if the Dragon's vision was true and she was actually flying on one of those miraculous Phaerie steeds, she could be anywhere by now. This is a bloody big forest, Yinze. You need to be able to concentrate on looking for her, instead of wondering what she'll be like when you find her.'

'I am looking,' Yinze snapped, 'and I can do without the lectures, thank you.'

'Children, children.' Crombec came swooping down before the impending quarrel could grow into a full-blown fight. 'You'll be better off if both of you pay attention to the search. Yinze, Kea is right. These morbid speculations are getting you nowhere. Kea, I know you hate to see Yinze worrying, but nagging at him is only going to make things worse.'

The harp maker had surprised Yinze. On the ground he'd seemed like an old man, yet once he was in his true element of the air, he appeared to have gained unexpected vigour and strength. He flew along as effortlessly as his apprentice, though she was about a third his age, and though he was always sensitive to the gravity of the situation he looked to be gaining tremendous enjoyment from this exploration of new territory.

Yinze reminded himself how lucky he was to have his Skyfolk friends there to help him. Had it not been for them, he would still have been kicking his heels in the city, wild with frustration waiting for all the endless, tedious logistics of getting an army on the move to be dealt with. He'd been incredibly glad to escape. 'I'm sorry I'm so preoccupied,' he told his companions. 'I'm truly grateful for your help. I'd have gone insane if I had to wait one more day in Tyrineld, with all the unease and conflict, and everyone running around organising rations, tents, weapons and medicinal supplies. What with my mother begging me not to go, Ionor disappearing,

Chathak champing at the bit for vengeance – not that I blame him – Thara tearing herself apart over whether she should go with the army or stay behind and help with food production, and Melisanda working herself to a shadow and miserable about the entire business, I sometimes felt as if I would explode.'

Kea grimaced. 'Not to mention the Lady Sharalind practically chewing the carpets because nothing was happening fast enough for her.'

'I couldn't agree more,' Crombec said. 'Though I am deeply concerned about your sister, Yinze, I was extremely glad to have a legitimate reason to leave the city. Though Sharalind has my sympathy, for let us not forget that she also lost a son, she was hinting at using the Skyfolk in Tyrineld – myself, Kea, our bearers and those who brought Incondor – to help transport goods to the staging area in Nexis, or even act as couriers or spies. Without the authorisation of Queen Pandion I cannot allow my people to become embroiled in the wars of another nation, and since Sharalind never mentioned Pandion giving any such permission, I would suspect that she asked and was denied.'

'But what will happen when we go back to Tyrineld?' Kea asked.

'The war will not affect us, my dear, or Yinze either, unless the Phaerie get all the way to the city. We are under orders to concentrate on our Artefact, and the Lady Sharalind has—'

His words were cut off by Yinze's piercing scream. The Wizard was curled sobbing into a foetal ball in the bottom of the net, his hands clasped to his head, his face twisted in pain and anguish.

'Get him down!' Crombec shouted as the bearers faltered uncertainly. They landed the net as swiftly as possible and knelt around the stricken Wizard as Kea called his name over and over. After a few anxious moments, Yinze's shuddering ceased and his breathing became more even. He sat up and took his hands from his tear-streaked face, his expression stricken. 'Cyran,' he gasped. 'The Archwizard is dead!'

He held up his hands to forestall their spate of questions. 'I don't know,' he said. 'I just felt him die – but what about Iriana? Did he find her? Is she in danger too?' He leapt to his feet. 'Come on, quick – we've got to get moving!'

Within minutes they were airborne again, with the bearers beating strongly to gain height. Yinze gripped the meshes of the net with white-knuckled fingers, and the others, seeing his strained expression, forbore to ask any more questions, but concentrated on forging ahead as fast as they were able.

They had flown on a while, growing ever closer to the Phaerie border, when suddenly Yinze let out another yell – but this time, of joy and excitement. 'Avithan – he's back! Just like Iriana, I felt him return! Come on, come on – can't we go any faster?'

Crombec looked at Kea and frowned. 'Just what in the world is going on tonight in Eliorand?' he asked in very private mindspeech. 'I don't like this – I don't like it at all.'

Kea, however, had her mind on something else. 'What's that?' she cried, pointing. 'Look – a good way ahead and slightly to the left. There's a glowing patch in the sky.'

Yinze squinted into the distance. 'I can't see anything.'

'You have keen eyes, Kea, even for one of the Winged Folk,' Crombec said. 'I see it now that you've pointed it out. I wonder what it could possibly be?'

As they drew closer, even Yinze could see the strange phenomenon glowing against the dark background of the night sky. Then:

'I don't believe it!' Kea gasped. 'Crombec, can you see that? It's a horse – a huge, shining image of a horse, and it looks to me to be some form of unfamiliar magic. Yinze, you said that your sister had the ability to perform all four of the Magefolk powers. Do you think her abilities could even stretch further than that?'

Yinze frowned. 'I don't suppose it's out of the question, but why a horse? I hope and pray it is Iriana – but what if it's some sort of Phaerie glamourie, to lure us into a trap? The ferals said that the Forest Lord was badly wounded, but supposing he's recovered? Supposing it was Hellorin who killed the Archwizard? What if we go over there and find ourselves facing the Wild Hunt?'

'They will find that it's a mistake to attack the Skyfolk,' Crombec said grimly. 'You remember the whirlwind Incondor produced from your harp, and how he almost killed himself?'

'I'll never forget it.'

'Well, *I* don't need a harp.'

With that, the old harp maker picked up the pace, heading directly for the mysterious image that glowed amongst the stars.

The Windeye was awakened from a deep sleep by Taryn's hand gently shaking her shoulder. She could hear a disturbance amongst the herd, and suddenly she was wide awake. 'What is it?'

'Something strange is approaching,' Taryn answered. 'Look – over there in the sky.'

When she saw what was heading towards her, Corisand's jaw dropped. She had heard of the Winged Folk from Iriana – surely this could be no one else? But what were they doing here, so far away from the mountain, far to the south, that was their home? And what were they carrying in that dangling net? Could it possibly be a person?

She remembered Iriana saying that the Skyfolk were friendly with the Wizards – and inspiration came to her in a blinding flash. 'Turn back into a horse – quick, before they get any closer,' she told Taryn. 'I don't want to explain the Xandim to them yet.'

'But—'

'Do it!' she hissed. 'I'm sorry, Taryn, but trust me. I'll explain later.' Muttering darkly, he did as she said.

'It'll be all right, I promise,' she assured him. 'Just take care of the herd.' She left the edge of the forest and ran out into the open, waving her arms wildly and yelling at the top of her voice until the airborne figures noticed her, and began to descend.

As the strangers landed, she felt very nervous. With the exception of the herd, the Evanesar and her own, familiar little group of companions, she had never spoken to anyone as a human. In the end, she decided, she could only be herself. She walked forward, hands held out open and empty in token of peace, and said, 'Thank you for stopping. I'm so glad to see you.' Then she got a closer look at the tall man who was stepping out of the net. She had seen his image in Iriana's mind many times before. 'Yinze? Aren't you the Wizard Yinze?'

He looked at her, completely dumbfounded, then found his voice. 'I am – but who in perdition are you? I don't know you. How do you know my name?'

'I'm Corisand, Iriana's friend. She—'

Before she could get another word out, he had grabbed her by the shoulders; not to hurt her, she sensed, but in excitement. 'Iriana?' he shouted. 'You know Iriana? Where is she? Is she all right?'

'Somewhere near Eliorand. I hope she's all right – I was forced to leave her. Oh, there's no time to explain. Please, I'm going to ask you to trust me. Let me use your net, and if your Skyfolk friends will take me, I can go back to find her. If everything went well she—'

'Hold on. You can't just rush off like that. I felt Cyran's passing a while ago, and—'

'You did?' His words filled Corisand with dread. 'But not Iriana?'

'No, but—'

'I promise I'll explain everything as soon as I can, or Iriana will when I bring her back,' she told him, 'but there's no *time* now. She must be stranded somewhere between here and Eliorand, and she might not be dead, but some of our other companions may be. Please, there's no time to lose. I need the Skyfolk to take me to her. Once I've found her, I have a spell to bring her back to you in no time.'

'A spell?' Yinze scowled. 'What sort of spell? You're no Wizard, nor are you a Phaerie or any other sort of Mage. So what exactly are you, and what are you doing with all these horses?'

Corisand ground her teeth in frustration. Why couldn't she make them *understand*? 'I told you – there's no time for this now. What if Iriana was hurt in the battle—'

'Battle?' Yinze roared. 'You left her in a *battle*? What kind of friend does that? What battle? Where was it?'

'For goodness' sake, Yinze, let her go,' Crombec forestalled him. 'If matters are as urgent as she says then both she and Iriana need our help.' He gestured to the net. 'Quickly now, get in, my dear,' he told Corisand. 'Just tell the bearers where to go and they will take you.'

The Windeye lost no time in doing exactly what he said, wrapping herself in the nest of furs. The net took off with a lurch and suddenly she was in the air, swinging back and forth in the most stomach-churning way. 'Look after the herd,' she mind-called back to Taryn. 'I'll be back as soon as I can. Don't change in front of them, or let anybody else do so either. I want Iriana here to back me up before they find out about us. I think we can trust them, but I won't risk them making use of us as the Phaerie did.'

'You be careful up there,' Taryn replied. 'I'm sure it can't be safe. I'll do my best to keep things under control here, but please hurry back.'

'I'll be back before you know it,' Corisand promised rashly. Then she pointed out to her bearers the direction in which she hoped to find the others, and snuggled into her nest at the bottom of the net to keep warm, keeping a constant lookout over the side as she went.

All at once her concentration was broken by the drumming sound of wingbeats and the Skyfolk girl came speeding up to them, her extraordinary green hair flying like a banner in the wind. She slowed down to a steady pace at the side of Corisand's net. 'Yinze wanted me to come with you, because he doesn't really trust you,' she said candidly. 'After all, we don't really know who you are or what you were doing with Iriana. I'm Kea, a Skyfolk Mage from the mountain city of Aerillia.'

She looked expectantly at Corisand, clearly hoping that she would respond in kind.

'I'm sorry, Kea,' the Windeye said firmly. 'I have my reasons for wanting to keep my origins a secret, and you'll understand why when I finally can tell you about my people. But I am Iriana's friend – she's been my staunch ally and companion ever since we met. All I want to do is find her and make sure she's safe. Please, will you help me call out to my companions in mindspeech? It might go further if both of us are trying together.'

'Of course I will,' Kea replied. 'And for what it's worth I trust you. If you'll give me the names and images of your companions – I know what Iriana looks like of course, because she's always in Yinze's mind – I'll help you call. Hopefully, we'll find them soon.'

'I hope we do. It tore me apart to have to leave them, but I had no choice. I had to—' she caught herself up sharply, having almost revealed more than she intended to this friendly girl. Instead she passed on the images of her other companions: Aelwen, Taine, Kaldath and Dael, to Kea. 'Now, are you ready?' she said. 'I'll count to three and we'll start.'

As Corisand was worrying about Iriana, the Wizard was doing the same thing about her friend. When she and her companions sensed that their mounts were beginning to sink beneath them and realised that the flying magic was wearing off, they began, just as the Windeye had done, to look around for a safe place to ease their mounts gently to the ground. The glimmer of the spell had faded almost to nothing, and they were dodging the tops of the tallest trees, before they finally found a small gap in the thick woodland in which they could land.

Once down they paused for a moment, looking at one another. 'Which way now?' Aelwen said. 'We can't be very far from the border, if only we don't start wandering round in circles.'

'We won't,' Taine said confidently. 'I had a good look round and got our bearings before we came down. The river is that way.' He pointed. 'And there's the north star. As long as we keep it behind us we can head directly south to the border. I've been wandering these forests back and forth for years – I know what I'm doing.'

'Of course you do.' The sneering, muttered undertone came from

Avithan. Iriana scowled at him and Aelwen glared, but Taine chose to ignore the sniping. 'Let's get going,' he said. 'We have very little left in the way of supplies. It'll slow us down considerably when we have to start hunting and foraging along the way.' With that he drew a long, keen knife out of a sheath on his belt. Leading his horse, he began to force his way through the thick undergrowth that surrounded the clearing, using the blade to hack out a path when necessary. Aelwen followed him and Iriana came behind her, holding tightly to Rosina's bridle and still using the mare's eyesight. Avithan brought up the rear, his expression still thunderous.

They trudged on, until Iriana's legs were almost giving way beneath her. Unfortunately, the going was far too treacherous to allow her to ride, and she was utterly exhausted from her fight to free the Xandim, her monumental battle with Hellorin, and all the emotional shocks of the last few hours. Furthermore, the magic of the Fialan still pulsed through her, and she had to struggle constantly to contain so much power. In her current state she felt as though she must either drop in her tracks and fall asleep before she hit the ground, or fly apart into a million fragments.

She did neither. She set her teeth and struggled on until, just when she was sure she'd reached the end of her endurance, Taine called for a halt. He had found a narrow rill that flowed sparkling and clear over a stony bed, and they all drank gratefully, taking the opportunity to fill their water bottles. They cleared a space and lit a fire, and ate frugally from what remained of their trail rations, chewing resignedly at the leathery jerky and the hard crust that had formed on the last of the cheese. Only Avithan ate with relish, show-ing every sign of thoroughly enjoying the meal. When he looked up and caught the surprised reactions of the others, he explained. 'When I was in Athina's realm we didn't eat or drink, and there was no such thing as hunger or thirst. Though I didn't need food, I really missed the pleasure of eating, if you know what I mean.'

'What was it like in Athina's world?' Iriana asked.

'It was extraordinary: strange and wonderful and oddly beautiful ...' He began to describe the forest of stone, the Timeless Lake and the great tree in which Athina made her home, but noticed after a while that they were all, Iriana particularly, struggling to keep their eyes open. 'Listen,' he interrupted himself. 'You three have fought a terrible battle tonight. Since we're not going anywhere in a hurry, why don't you get a few hours' sleep? You desperately need it, and it'll give the horses a chance to rest and graze too. I'll keep watch for you.'

'Thank you,' Taine said. 'That makes a lot of sense. Now that Hellorin and the Phaerie are gone, there's no sense in pushing ourselves into the ground.'

As the others also murmured their gratitude, a great sense of relief washed over Avithan. Suddenly he felt a little less like an outcast and more a part of this group, whose experiences had forged bonds between them that were difficult to penetrate. It felt good to be able to contribute. The other three wasted no time in taking him up on his offer. They were already unrolling the blankets that were strapped behind their saddles, and snuggling down as if the lumpy forest floor was the softest of feather beds. Then just as it seemed as if everyone had fallen asleep, Aelwen opened her eyes. 'Iriana?'

'Uh? What?' the Wizard muttered blearily.

'If Hellorin's flying spell is contained within the Fialan – and we know that's true, because it's how Corisand got hold of the magic – couldn't you perform it?'

Iriana sat up quickly. 'I never thought of that!' She groped in her pouch for the Stone. 'I'm too weary to perform it now, but I should be able to find out whether I can access the magic ...' As she held the Fialan in both hands her face grew taut and rapt with concentration.

Minutes passed, and everyone waited expectantly – then the Wizard dropped the Stone back into its pouch with a lurid curse that had Avithan blinking in astonishment. 'It's no good,' she said. 'It's some kind of tangled bond between Phaerie and Windeye magic, and it's utterly alien to me. I'm sorry, everyone.'

'Sorry!' Taine protested. 'Iriana, don't be an idiot. You've already worked miracles enough tonight. It might take longer but we'll get home, you'll see.'

'Exactly,' Avithan agreed. 'At least we will if you three will all settle down and get some sleep.'

'Point taken.' Taine chuckled.

'I'll drink to that,' Aelwen agreed.

Iriana said nothing. She was back in her blanket and asleep already, and the others were not long in following her. So it was that Avithan was the first to hear the calls in mindspeech. Two voices, both female, neither familiar, calling for Iriana and the others. Were they friends or foes? Was this a rescue – or a trap?

He shook Taine awake – and suddenly found himself with a knife at his throat. Taine blinked the sleep from his eyes and lowered the knife. 'Sorry,' he said with a grin. 'Old habits.' Then he too must have heard the calls, for he leapt to his feet and began bellowing in mindspeech as loudly as he could. 'Corisand! Corisand, we're down here.'

By this time Iriana and Aelwen, awakened by the commotion, were on their feet too. There were a few moments of excited babble that went almost too fast for Avithan to follow, though he thought he caught Yinze's name in there somewhere, then Iriana shouted, 'Corisand, I'm going to send up a signal.' She held out her hand and the longest, brightest stream of magelight that Avithan had ever seen leapt from her palm and shot up into the night sky, taking the form of a gigantic white serpent with eyes of dazzling blue.

Corisand let out a cry of delight that was somewhere between a whoop and a laugh. 'Taku! Trust you – it's his very image, Iriana. Hold on, we're coming.'

Almost before the net had landed, the Windeye was fighting her way out of the meshes. She and Iriana threw their arms round one another, laughing and crying, and both talking at once.

'If hugs are going round ...' Grinning, Taine stepped forward and threw his arms around them both. Avithan hovered uncertainly at one side, and Aelwen stayed with him, looking uncomfortable.

When she had disentangled herself, Corisand stepped back and looked around, her expression growing grave. 'Dael?' she asked softly. 'Kaldath?'

Iriana shook her head. 'Both gone,' she said sadly. 'Kaldath died when the Dwelven spirits were freed, but he was happy to go. He was glad that he could finally rest.' She swiped a hand across her eyes as tears threatened to spill down her cheeks. 'And Dael – when so many Dwelven left our world it created an area of instability between our reality and the others. Athina brought Avithan back to us' – she gestured at her fellow Wizard – 'and took Dael back with her to her home beneath the Timeless Lake.'

Now there were tears in Corisand's eyes. 'I'll miss them both,' she said, 'especially Dael. Though he was a mortal with no magic, he was just as much a part of our group, and just as valuable, as any of us.'

'I'll miss him too,' Iriana said. 'And he'll really miss us, but he was so happy to be reunited with Athina. He'll be better off with her, too. Because he'd handled the Fialan, twice, and survived, he was special and different from the other mortals, but I would have had a hard time explaining that to Sharalind and all the other Wizards at home.'

'He could have come with us to the Wyndveil,' Corisand said – and was suddenly reminded that the Xandim might not be safe enough yet to be offering to shelter others. 'What happened to Hellorin?' she asked Iriana. 'I felt his passing, and you're acting as if there's no risk of the other Phaerie pursuing us.'

Iriana grinned so fiercely that it made Avithan take a step backwards. 'You'll never have to worry about Hellorin and his Phaerie again. When I fought him, Denali put some kind of power into the Fialan that snatched the whole of Eliorand and all the Phaerie with it, including their Lord, back into the Elsewhere.'

'*What?*' The Windeye's mouth fell open. All at once, she turned very pale and began to tremble. 'Then we're truly free?' she whispered. 'What about the Wizards? Will they follow Hellorin's example and try to enslave us again?'

'They won't.' This time it was Avithan who spoke. 'My mother would never allow such a thing to happen. We thought the Xandim were only a legend, or a race who'd been lost long ago. When they see you, the Wizards will welcome you, I'm certain.'

'Then, having said that, I think it's high time we were going,' Corisand suggested.

'Just give me a few more minutes, will you?' Iriana asked. Taking the pouch with the Fialan from around her neck, she gave it back to Corisand, who slipped the thong over her own head. 'Will you come with me, my friend, and be my eyes? I just need to do one more thing before we go.'

Avithan made as if to follow, but Iriana shook her head, gesturing him back. With the Windeye at her side, she walked out into the open and gave a shrill whistle. Boreas, the great eagle of the north, came sweeping down from the skies to alight on her arm, while his mate perched warily in a tree nearby.

Iriana stroked the sleek white feathered head of the mighty bird. 'My dear, dear friend and joy of my heart,' she said softly. 'Thank you for returning when I was in desperate need. You saved my life, and I can never repay you – except by letting you go once more, to your mate and your wild, free life in the skies above the mountains.' Her voice broke, but she made a determined effort to steady it. 'Wherever you fly, a piece of my heart will always roam the skies with you.'

The eagle turned his fierce golden gaze upon her, then dipped his proud head to rub it along her cheek. Then, with a shrill farewell call, he took to the skies, with his mate behind him. He circled once over Iriana, then winged away into the north, heading back to the mountains of his home.

It was as well that Iriana was using Corisand's vision, for her own eyes were flooded with tears. The Windeye turned to hug her. 'That was well done, my friend,' she said softly. 'One day we will travel back here, you and I, and we will see how he fares, and all the broods that he will father.'

Comforted by her companion's words, Iriana wiped her eyes and straightened her shoulders. 'Come on,' she said. 'Let's head for home – wherever that may be.'

In the Elsewhere, the Evanesar strove to contain a raging Hellorin and his people behind barriers they had hastily erected around the newly emerged city of Eliorand. Having learned a great deal about working together when they had helped Corisand and Iriana create the receptacle to take their magic back to the Fialan, they had enclosed the city beneath a dome formed from a combination of Taku's Cold magic, Aurora's powers of Air and an addition of Denali's spells of Earth that made the barrier harder than diamond.

At present the Forest Lord was coordinating what remained of his demoralised people to strike in concert at the shield, trying to find a weak spot, and Taku and Aurora were keeping a wary watch over them. Though there was little enough danger of Hellorin breaking free, they were taking no chances.

Taku sighed. 'Remind me – whose idea was it to bring the Phaerie back to the Elsewhere?'

'Denali's of course,' snapped Aurora, 'though I notice that the Great One is quite happy to leave the dirty work to us, as usual.'

'And the Moldai,' the serpent reminded his companion. 'Aerillia played her part to perfection, keeping Hellorin here until our trap could be laid.'

'I still can't believe that it succeeded,' Aurora said. 'It was a risky move, to place all our hopes in the hands of two outsiders from the mundane world. Had they failed ...'

'But they did not fail,' Taku replied proudly. 'I had every confidence in them, and as it turned out, they played their parts to perfection.' He sighed. 'I only wish that it had not been necessary to keep the plan from them. That does not sit easily with me, and it never did. I only hope that they will forgive us if they ever find out the truth.'

'If they ever do. They would need to return to the Elsewhere first.'

'Oh, I think we may see them again. I hope we do. I became very fond of them in the brief time that we knew them. It was a risk sending the Fialan into the mundane world, but while Corisand and Iriana hold the Stone, it will be safe.'

'Indeed, Iriana almost made me change my mind about trusting the Magefolk.'

Taku and Aurora looked around in astonishment to see Basileus. Once more he had come among them in his form of a gigantic bear.

'Basileus! What brings you here?' Taku asked in astonishment.

'I came to tell you that the Moldai have decided to return our consciousness to the mundane world, at least for the present.'

'But why?' Aurora asked. 'You are so much more limited there, in your great forms of stone.'

'We have dwelt here for long ages to avoid the Magefolk and the Phaerie after the betrayal of our Dwelven. But now that they have finally been freed and sent to their rest, thanks to our friends from the mundane world, we have decided to return. Aerillia, in particular, has no wish to stay here to face the wrath of Hellorin, whom she tricked so neatly, and I—' His eyes twinkled. 'I would like to be back in my mountain, to help Corisand and her people settle into their new homes.

'There is another reason, too. Due to the weakening of the barrier between our two realities by the passing of the Dwelven and the capture of the Phaerie, Ghabal is a constant danger. Had he passed through that barrier yet we would have felt it, but we know that he is no longer in his mountain of diamond, and we cannot find him. He is searching desperately to get through and reach the Fialan, and if he succeeds, the Wizard and the Windeye may need our help.'

Behind his barrier, the Lord of the Phaerie threw back his head and laughed, the sound harsh and mocking. 'What think you of your plan now, my enemies? Your little plot has backfired. In removing me and my people from the mundane world, you have left it open to a far worse threat.'

33
~

PERILOUS HOMECOMING

While Corisand, Iriana and their companions old and new were returning to the vast burned-out area where Corisand had left the Xandim, they decided to take few hours to rest there. Some of them had been in battle and, Iriana especially, needed to recover their strength, while all of them had been travelling hard. They needed some time for reunions, and for those who were strangers to be introduced to one another. There were so many tales to tell, so much news to be caught up on and some of them needed time to grieve for the passing of the Archwizard Cyran, and for those lost companions, Dael and Kaldath.

Corisand was extremely distressed that she had missed the chance to bid these friends farewell, and Iriana was glad that her friend had her Xandim to take care of, and distract her from her grief. As Windeye of the enslaved Xandim, Corisand had been desperately lonely and isolated, but now that they were free to change shape as they chose, hopefully those days would be over. Iriana herself was deliriously happy to be reunited with her foster brother and, once she felt safe to turn her attention to her own concerns, was questioning Yinze about her other close friends, and all the news from Tyrineld.

Kea and the Skyfolk bearers had been stunned when Corisand found her missing companions and, having taken the Fialan back from Iriana and performed the flying spell, turned into a beautiful grey horse. The others had had their work cut out on the journey back to the burn, explaining the history of the Xandim, and how they had been freed. Suddenly, now that the secret of her people was becoming more public, Corisand felt nervous. How would they be received by the other races? How would they adapt to their human forms? Would the Wizards offer them help, or consider them a burden? Who would teach them all the skills they would need to exist in their human forms? At least they would never starve, she thought wryly – not if there was plenty of grazing around, and if times were hard they could always change into their equine aspects. It was just that she wanted them to have a choice – and a chance to build their own culture on the Wyndveil; a society that would be uniquely suited to themselves.

The Windeye felt the joy and relief among her tribe when she returned, and though she was interested in getting to know the handsome Yinze better, having heard so much about him, she could hardly wait to rejoin her own kind. She went over to them. 'I've told the others all about us now,' she said. 'These people are all friends, so we have no need to conceal ourselves any longer in equine guise. Those of you who wish to change back into your human forms, and come and meet my friends, are most welcome to do so.'

Though one or two hung back, a great many of the Xandim followed her lead, and transformed into their alternate shapes. The first to do so was Taryn, who came running towards her with a smile on his face. 'You found your friends, then,' he said. 'I'm so glad.'

From the corner of her eye, Corisand noticed Kea staring at him appreciatively, and realised that she was going to have to do something about clothing her people – and soon. Though they were utterly lacking in self-consciousness at being naked, the customs of others should be respected – and besides, the human body, so much more frail and fragile than its equine counterpart, needed a lot of extra protection, both from cold and the forest environment in general. For the present, she turned to her Othersight and spun warmed air and shadow into loose robes for her people. The shadow garments would provide them with warmth and dignity, but it wouldn't help them much if they sat down on something sharp or prickly! Still, it was the best she could do. Maybe some proper clothing could be found for them in Nexis.

Slowly, shyly, the Xandim began to mingle with Corisand's companions both old and new, but suddenly the Windeye noticed an absence. Where was Aelwen?

She finally tracked the Horsemistress down a little way into the forest. Aelwen was sitting in the cavelike depression beneath the riven roots of a fallen spruce, all hunched up, with her hands clasped around her knees. Her eyes stared bleakly ahead of her, as if they saw a future filled with no hope, and there were smudges on her face where she'd wiped away tears with a grubby hand.

As understanding came to her, Corisand felt her heart go out to Aelwen. This woman had devoted her entire life to the care and well-being of the Xandim steeds. Even though she'd understood, once the Windeye had revealed the truth, that those she'd always looked upon as dumb beasts were anything but, the truth must only have hit home to her today, when she saw all the tribe turn into people; individuals who could make their own decisions and were no longer in her charge.

It was probably easier for her to explain me away, because I have a Windeye's magic, but today she came face to face with the brutal truth.

Poor Aelwen! Not only had her great love and her whole life's purpose been removed at a single stroke, but she must be wondering how she would be received by a race which she had trained, curbed and controlled; had bred to one another according to her own wishes, not theirs. No wonder she was here apart, uncertain of her welcome among them.

Corisand approached the former Horsemistress and sat down beside her. She didn't speak at first – oddly, she found herself remembering the calm, unhurried patience with which Aelwen had always treated the Xandim when they were young, rebellious, hurt or afraid. So she waited quietly for her companion to speak, but when Aelwen, looking harried, muttered an excuse and leapt up to leave, the Windeye could wait no longer. She rose too and restrained the other woman with a hand on her arm.

'It's all right,' she said. 'They won't blame you.'

'How could they not?' Aelwen flung back at her. 'All these years I've treated them like animals. I'm the last person they'll want to see right now.'

'You're wrong, you know. Don't you understand, Aelwen? At that time the Xandim *were* little more than animals in their habits and ways of thinking. They didn't understand, as I came to understand when I became Windeye, that they could be anything else. They were all instinct and very primitive emotions, fear being paramount. Horses are prey animals, herd animals. Their instinct is to run, fast and far from anything they perceive to be a threat, and once one starts running, the rest will follow.'

She swallowed to moisten a throat gone dry from talking. 'You kept that fear at bay, Aelwen. You taught them when they were young that they didn't need to spook at shadows, or leaves that the wind blew across their path. You nurtured and cared for them, and because your standards were so high, you and Kelon, you made damn sure that everyone in your employ did the same.'

'So I was a thoughtful gaoler?' Aelwen snapped. 'It makes no difference. I was a gaoler nonetheless.'

'If you'd known the truth about the Xandim, that would be correct. But you didn't. You spoke up for those who were considered mere animals. As far as you could, you didn't let the other Phaerie abuse us. And you instilled those same standards of care and respect into every Phaerie child you taught to ride.'

She stopped and took a deep breath, wondering what else she could say. Plainly, Aelwen was still unconvinced.

'Look, why don't you come back with me and talk to them yourself? You'll soon see that I'm right.'

'I can't,' Aelwen whispered. 'I can't face them.'

Corisand scowled at her. 'I've had enough of this nonsense. You're worrying yourself sick over something you don't even know is true, and that's just plain stupid. After all we've been through together, do you really think I'd put you in a position to be reviled and abused?' Her voice softened a little. 'When I was young, you were always leading me into unfamiliar situations that I was afraid of: having a bit put in my mouth, a saddle strapped around me and a rider on my back, to name but a few. In the end you invariably made me see that there was nothing to fear at all.'

'Is that so? Well, why were you always so bloody difficult?' Aelwen shot back. 'Only Hellorin could ever ride you – I've never come across a more impossible horse to train.'

Corisand grinned at her. 'I said you made me see that there was nothing to fear about being ridden. I didn't have to *like* it, though. I suspect that there was some vestige of the Windeye in me long before Valir died and the responsibility passed to me. Somewhere inside I just knew that this situation should not exist. The others didn't, though. It was different for them. Please, just come and talk to them. You'll see.'

Taking her companion by the wrist, the Windeye hauled her back towards the forest's edge where the Xandim had taken shelter. By now, many of them had turned back into horses in order to graze a little, and rest more comfortably, but as Aelwen approached there was a collective shimmer in the air as they all transformed at once.

'Aelwen,' a voice called out. It was the copper-haired Rosina. The slender young woman ran forward and threw her arms around the startled Horsemistress.

'Aelwen, Aelwen,' the cry echoed through the assembled Xandim. Then they were all around her. Some, like Rosina, who had been spending a great deal of time with people lately and understood the correct way to act, wanted to hug her, or pat her on the back, or shake her hand. Others, less versed in how to act in these new forms, hung back but smiled at her or looked on with shining eyes.

'When my foal was turned the wrong way you helped me, and saved both our lives,' an older woman with a shock of brown hair called out. 'Now, at last, I can thank you.'

'You did everything in your power to stop Tiolani abusing me,' Asharal said. 'I can never repay you.'

'When I was a colt and stumbled in that rabbit hole and broke my leg, you wouldn't let me be destroyed,' another man called out. 'You said, "He's young, the break is clean, I think we can save this one." You covered the break in some hard stuff till it mended, and held me up in slings, and fed me herbs to dull the pain. Thanks to you I can run again. Thanks to you, I lived.'

'You walked me back and forth all night when I had colic.'

'You wouldn't let Ferimon breed me to his vicious white stallion.'

'When my mouth proved too tender to take a bit, you made a special bridle, just for me.'

'When Hellorin said I was ugly and wanted to cull me out, you saved my life.' That was Alil.

'You always gave us the best of food and shelter.'

'You took care of every one of us when we came back filthy, aching and exhausted after the Wild Hunt, no matter how long it took or how tired you and the other grooms became.'

'Thank you.'

'Thank you.'

On every side the voices rang out. Aelwen, with tears in her eyes, was surrounded by her Xandim; horses no more but finally able to express their love for her. 'There's no need to thank me,' she said in an unsteady voice. 'I loved taking care of you. I love you all.'

Smiling, the Windeye slipped away.

It took them four more days to reach Tyrineld. When Corisand asked them, the Xandim readily agreed to convey everyone back to

376

the city, and they had all agreed to miss Nexis completely, avoiding any further delays, and hurry back. They were driven by anxiety to reach safety at last, and also by Avithan's desperate need to be with his mother, who must be grieving over Cyran's death. Sharalind was still assembling her army, too. It was important that she know there was no longer any need.

By the time the city came into view Iriana, her companions, the Winged Folk and all the Xandim were dragging with weariness. Even though they had taken a number of brief rests on the way, the pace had told on all of them. The Skyfolk bearers had been spared a great deal of effort, as Yinze had ridden back on one of the Xandim, but they all, Crombec and Kea included, looked pale with exhaustion.

Corisand was worst off, for she had the burden of maintaining the flying spell for her entire tribe. Though she had the Fialan to help her, and Iriana, who was also attuned to the Stone and could bolster the Windeye's power with some of her own, Corisand's movements were becoming increasingly slow and stiff, and her elegant grey head was beginning to droop. The Xandim who followed her were in a similar state, and the foals and older members of the herd were struggling to keep up at all.

'Oh, thank providence for that,' Iriana said. 'I was so desperate to get away from Tyrineld – I never thought I'd be so glad to see it again. Just a little further now, Corisand, and we can all rest.' But as they drew closer, they heard the alarm go up in a great blowing of horns and ringing of bells, and suddenly there was a rainbow glimmer in the air above the city as a great magical shield snapped into place.

Iriana clapped a hand to her forehead and spat out a curse. 'They think we're the Phaerie! Stop, Corisand. Stop, everyone, before they start firing spells at us.'

Avithan rode forward. 'We should land,' he said. 'We won't look so threatening on the ground. If Crombec and Kea are willing, I'll get into Yinze's net and fly into the city with the Skyfolk. My mother won't attack them, and we'll soon make her understand what's really happening.'

Crombec nodded. 'That's a good idea. You had better hurry, Avithan, because if Sharalind has sensed your presence here she may think that Hellorin has captured you.'

Avithan nodded. 'I'll get into mindspeech range as quickly as I can, and straighten this thing out.'

The Windeye began to lead the Xandim quickly down, and their other companions, including the Skyfolk, landed with them. The bearers spread out the net, and Crombec and Kea came forward. 'We'll wait here with Yinze,' Crombec told the winged girl. 'Our Artefact must still be created, and if there are any misunderstandings as we near the city, there's no sense in putting ourselves in the line of fire until we must.'

'I'm sure it won't come to that,' Avithan said.

'I wouldn't be quite so confident if I were you.' Taine gestured towards Tyrineld. Spreading out like a great dark stain from the city's inland gate was an army of Wizards. Though their appearance was distorted by the shimmer of magical shields, the glitter of sunlight on more conventional weapons could be clearly seen.

With a curse, Avithan leapt into the nest of furs in the centre of the net, just as Yinze scrambled out, carrying his precious harp that he had brought with him in case he'd needed it to help Iriana. The bearers left the ground in a thunder of wings and took up the slack. As fast as their weary wings could go, they headed towards the swelling ranks of the Wizard army.

As he neared Tyrineld, Avithan began shouting out in mindspeech, as loud as he could. 'This is Avithan – Avithan! You felt my return last night. You felt my father's death. These flying steeds are not the Phaerie – *not* the Phaerie! There are no hostile forces here. Hellorin has been defeated and all the Phaerie have been wiped off the face of the earth by our own Wizard Iriana and the other people who came with me. This is Avithan – Avithan! Where is Sharalind?'

Suddenly he heard his mother's voice in his head, so choked with emotion that her mindspeech was barely comprehensible. 'Avithan? Avithan? Is it really you?' There was a thunderclap of displaced air and Sharalind appeared below him. Avithan's eyes widened. She *hated* apporting! Quickly he gestured his bearers to the ground. Almost before he had time to disentangle himself from the net, she launched herself into his arms. 'Oh, Avithan,' she sobbed. 'Where have you been? Are you all right? We all felt your passing – what happened to you?' She turned a ravaged face up to his. 'Your poor father ...'

'Alas, there will be no returning for him,' Avithan told her as gently as he could. 'He came all the way through the forest trying to find out what had become of me, and was captured by the Phaerie. Taine – one of the people I came with—' He gestured back towards the Xandim and their handful of riders. 'He rescued my father from the Forest Lord's dungeons in Eliorand, but when Cyran was free, he slew Hellorin's daughter, Tiolani. Then he battled with Hellorin, but Hellorin proved too strong.'

He took a deep breath. 'It's too complicated to tell you all at once, for I don't understand it all myself, but Iriana fought the Phaerie Lord and somehow defeated him, then Eliorand and every one of the Phaerie – they just vanished from the world. They've gone, Mama, really gone.' Suddenly aware that he was babbling, he wound down into silence.

'Gone? Truly gone?' Sharalind seemed to be struggling to understand. She pointed at the Xandim, still shimmering from the flying spell. 'Then who—'

Her words were drowned by a shattering roar. The massive, misshapen, nightmare form of Ghabal was suddenly towering over the city, drowning the shining white buildings in black shadow. 'Give me back the Fialan,' he roared. 'The Stone of Fate is *mine*!'

Iriana, still on Corisand's back and watching through her eyes, clenched her fingers tightly in the Windeye's mane and cursed. 'He must have known we'd come back here. He's been lying in wait.'

'Denali did warn us,' her friend replied grimly. 'We knew we'd have to fight him again.'

'But not *here*,' Iriana protested. 'The damage—'

Her words were drowned in a great roar as the gigantic Ghabal stamped down hard, and a section of the city walls and the buildings behind them vanished in a cloud of dust, ground into a powder by his colossal foot. The earth shook and the tallest structures collapsed, including Ariel's Tower, which toppled from its promontory into the sea. The death agony of dozens of Wizards struck all at once, and Sharalind's army was thrown into disarray, with many being knocked off their feet by the psychic shock of so many simultaneous deaths.

Iriana cried out in agony, slumping weakly over the Windeye's neck. Quickly, Corisand summoned her Othersight and spun a reflective shield around her companion. Though it would be unseen by anyone but the Windeye herself it would ward off the worst of the pain and trauma for Iriana. Sure enough, the Wizard gathered herself after a moment, though she was still shaking. 'What did you do?' she said gratefully.

'I'm protecting you from the pain,' Corisand replied. 'But don't ask me to do it for all the others – one is all I can manage.' She rose a little way into the air, so that they could see better. 'We're going to have a fight on our hands, my friend.'

'GIVE ME THE STONE!' the Moldan roared, drowning the screams of terror and anguish coming from the city. He reached out, and the great twin-bladed axe that Corisand and Iriana remembered from their battle in the Elsewhere appeared in his hand. He took a great swing, and smashed the weapon down into the midst of the city. Great chunks of white masonry flew into the air, and a cloud of dust arose. Even above the shattering noises of destruction, the screams of Wizards rent the air as more and more of them died.

Ghabal took another step, crushing more of Tyrineld into rubble, and his axe came down once more – right on the Luen of Warriors. The sight seemed to free Sharalind's army from its trance of paralysed horror. With a howl of outrage, they began to hurl spells at the Moldan. Massive vines caused further damage in the city as they erupted from the ground through pavements and buildings. Huge chunks of fallen structures, turned into projectiles by the enraged Warriors, hurtled through the air, impacting Ghabal's rocklike hide with so much force that they shattered into pieces, doing more damage to fellow Wizards than to their target. Beneath the Moldan's feet the earth was quaking and cracking, causing him to teeter and flail for balance, causing more destruction to his surroundings.

'The idiots!' Iriana fumed. 'They're just making matters worse. And Avithan's down there with his mother.'

Thoughts started to fly faster than arrows between Wizard and Windeye.

'Take the Fialan,' Corisand said urgently to Iriana. 'Show it to him. We've got to lure him away from the city.'

The Wizard reached down into the leather pouch around the Windeye's neck and grasped the Stone of Fate, which glared like a baleful green eye as if it recognised its ancient enemy. 'One to shield, one to attack as we did with Hellorin?'

'No, we need to split apart, so one can distract while the other attacks.'

'I'll need eyes then. Can't use yours if we're splitting up.'

'Who?'

'Taine, if he will. And we need to be Ghabal's size.'

'You have a plan?'

'Take me to Taine, then go round to the north-east but stay this side of the walls. We don't want Ghabal taking any more short cuts across the city.'

'Then?'

'We make it up as we go along.'

As soon as Iriana and Corisand had returned to their companions, who still waited on the hilltop that overlooked the city, the Wizard wasted no time. 'Taryn?'

'Lady?' The black stallion changed to his human shape so fast that Iriana blinked in surprise.

'You and Aelwen get the Xandim back out of danger. Yinze, go with them—' She looked around for her brother, only to find that he had vanished. 'Where in perdition is Yinze?'

'He went to help Avithan when the Moldan came,' Taryn said. 'We couldn't stop him.'

'*What?* That bloody idiot!' Fear lodged in her gut like a dagger of ice. Having been parted from her beloved foster brother for so long, was she to lose him already? With a wrenching effort, Iriana forced herself to put him out of her mind. 'Rosina?'

'I'm here.' The pretty roan mare came forward and turned into the slender, red-haired girl who was equally lovely.

'Take Melik and make sure he stays safe.' Iriana scooped up the basket that Yinze had left on the ground, and put it into Rosina's arms. 'Get back to a sheltered place away from the fighting with Aelwen and the others. Kea, Crombec, will you call your bearers to help the injured in the city? When Corisand and I attack the Moldan, use any Air spells you have that might help distract him – but if his attention swings towards you, stop at once. Taine, will you come with me and be my eyes?'

'Of course I will.'

Aelwen opened her mouth to protest, then closed it again at the savage expression on Taine's face.

'No heroics, any of you,' Iriana warned them. 'Corisand and I can do this. You can't. We're attuned to the Fialan and we've fought Ghabal before. Now everybody stop wasting time and get into position.'

'That told them,' Corisand said, as she took Taine and Iriana, two up, to a place near the north-western curve of the city wall and dropped them off. 'Good luck, Iriana, and take your own advice. Stay safe.'

'You too.' Iriana hugged her friend's arching grey neck, and the Windeye sped away to get into her own place on the other side of Sharalind's beleaguered forces, and change shape. Iriana had helped to save her people. Now she would return the favour.

34
~

VENGEANCE OF THE MOLDAN

Already the army's attack had backfired. Ghabal let out an earth-shattering roar and took a great step forward, away from the uncertain ground. His next step would bring his foot down on Sharalind's army, stamping them out like ants. The Wizards scattered. Some escaped, others were trampled by their fellows, but a number vanished beneath the Moldan's colossal foot, and another wave of death-agony hit the survivors. Before the next footfall came crashing down, Warriors tried to run – or, if they had kept their heads, apport – out of danger. It was a rout, a shambles, a charnel house, and the survivors were being buffeted, over and over, by the psychic shock of their comrades' deaths.

The mortal component of Sharalind's forces were even less fortunate. They could not apport out of the way, or run fast or far enough to escape the Moldan's trampling feet. Aelwen, riding the hovering Asharal who had agreed to convey her in Taryn's absence, was about to pull back with the Xandim when she saw the horrifying carnage taking place. She had been told to stay with the Xandim and get them to safety – but who in blazes did Iriana think she was, giving orders as if she had some kind of right?

Aelwen looked at Taryn, who had retained his human form but was now riding another of the Xandim. 'Taryn, we can't let this happen. Please ask your people if they'll help.'

'But Iriana told us to get them back to safety.'

'Who put Iriana in charge? I'm not going to obey her orders, and neither should you. The Xandim are free now – or are you?' Aelwen goaded.

Taryn, though he looked reluctant, nodded. He turned back to the herd of Xandim and called out in mindspeech. 'Please, if you will, help to rescue these people. Soon they will be our allies. Only those who are willing, or able, may do this, and there is no compulsion on any of you. You are free people now, and you must choose.'

Though some – the young and old and a handful of others – hung back, most of the remainder rallied at his call. Glimmering with the flying spell they came swooping down from the heavens to pick up the stricken warriors, Wizard and Mortal alike, bearing them to safety in the hilly area north of the city.

Suddenly Aelwen heard a well-loved voice, and looked down. Her heart almost stopped as she glimpsed a familiar face in the thick of the crowd, far too close to the mad giant. 'Asharal, quick – it's Kelon,' she shrieked, and the stallion took her down at breakneck speed.

Even as she descended, it happened. One of the Wizards' vines, thick as a tree trunk, came erupting out of the ground within feet of her old friend, in an explosion of dirt and stones. One of the rocks struck Kelon, and she saw him fall beneath the feet of the stampeding troops.

Aelwen acted without thinking. Kelon was in peril and she had to save him. But she, who had never even taken part in a Wild Hunt, could never have guessed how terrifying it could be in the thick of a battle, with dust blinding her and getting in her nose and throat so that she choked and wheezed. The gargantuan figure of the Moldan towered above her, far more huge and dreadful than anything she could ever have imagined, casting a thick black shadow. There were people, wild with terror, pushing at her on all sides.

Once they saw the horse, her fate was sealed. Everyone saw a faster way to escape the horror, and everyone wanted to take it. Asharal struck out with hooves and teeth, and Aelwen threw a hasty shield around them while frantically scanning the ground for Kelon. He couldn't be far, she knew. Asharal had landed almost exactly where they had seen him go down.

Suddenly there he was – just a glimpse – an outflung arm, a shoulder, a face turned half into the mud. Straining with all her might, Aelwen extended her shield in his direction until she had used it to literally push the panicking mob aside. She did not dare look up, but she could hear that the Moldan was coming closer, his heavy footfalls making the earth jump and shake beneath her. Even as she leapt from Asharal's back she could feel the Xandim trembling, his newly discovered human intelligence at war with the equine instinct to flee the danger, far and fast. 'Stay with me,' she begged him. 'Hold on just a little longer.'

Kelon was barely conscious. He mumbled and let out a groan when she tried to wake him, but his eyes wandered, unfocused, across her face. What injuries had his body taken from those trampling feet? What more damage would she do by moving him? But there was no choice. She had to take the chance. Aelwen was very strong from a lifetime of handling horses, but she couldn't lift the weight of an unconscious man. 'Kelon,' she shouted, slapping his face. 'Wake up! You've got to help me get you out of here.'

She still wasn't sure that he recognised her, but somehow the slaps and frantic shouts drove the message home. Even though she was taking most of his weight, his effort was enough to get him unsteadily to his feet. Somehow she managed to get him onto the stallion's back, though he'd screamed with pain as she'd heaved at him, and she felt as if she had wrenched every muscle in her body.

With one last effort, Aelwen got up behind Kelon's swaying form and held him tightly around the waist to steady him. 'Now,' she shouted, and let her shield fall. Asharal leapt upwards, pushing off hard from the ground to climb high and fast, even as Ghabal's massive foot came down in the midst of the mortal conscripts, right where Kelon had been standing.

They weren't out of danger, and who knew how grave Kelon's injuries might be, yet Aelwen, even in the midst of all the terror, the death and devastation, felt her spirits lift. With Kelon perched in front of her, with her arms around him tightly, she felt her world, which had been tilting, sliding, out of her control, settle back onto an even keel. For the first time it came home to her how much she had missed him; always at her side, faithful, steady and sure. She had been so accustomed to his loyalty, his unquestioning support, his unspoken love for her, that she had barely noticed them until they had been taken away from her, but she had come to miss them dreadfully since the day she and Kelon had parted so bitterly.

Iriana took Taine's hand. 'You ready? I'm going to match us to his size, so hold on tight.'

'Always.'

Corisand had taken human form and Iriana could see her growing, and beginning to tower over the city, away on the other side of Ghabal and the beleaguered army. Her eyes had taken on an uncanny silver glow as she used her Othersight to spin a shield around herself. Iriana did the same, combining her powers of Earth and Air to form a translucent, adamantine shield around herself and Taine, who was growing alongside her.

The Wizard magnified her voice to match the bellowing of her ancient enemy. 'Is this what you're looking for?'

'You!' Ghabal bellowed. 'I will crush you, little insect.'

Iriana laughed scornfully. 'Didn't you learn your lesson in the Elsewhere? We defeated you then; we can do it again.'

'Ah, but this time there is no Hellorin to interfere, or the meddling Evanesar to come to your aid. In this world, *I* will rule!' He left the remnants of the Wizard army and lumbered towards her, the giant axe lifted high.

Iriana let him get almost within reach of her, and apported the Stone across into Corisand's waiting hand. The Windeye lifted the Fialan aloft, and it blazed into blinding brilliance in her hand. 'Hey, Ugly! Look what I've got!'

With a howl of frustration the Moldan left the Wizard and lumbered towards Corisand. Iriana looked at the northern gates of Tyrineld, to reassure herself that the remnants of the army had fled to safety, and to her horror saw the last of them disappearing into the city, rather than away from it, as she had planned.

It's my own fault. I never thought to tell them *the plan. But may providence help Tyrineld if they decide to attack again.*

She let the Moldan get almost within reach of Corisand, who had thickened the air between them to slow his progress, then shouted in her loudest voice: 'Over here, stupid. Remember me?' and launched a searing fireball at him. She had the satisfaction of seeing him flinch, and dodge clumsily out of its path. Clearly he did remember her – and what she had done to him last time. Quickly she hurled another flaming missile, trying to steer him away from both Corisand and the city. The first one had startled him and his response had been pure reflex – but this time she had lost the advantage of surprise. Since their last meeting, the rogue Evanesar Katmai had clearly been teaching him a few new tricks. Almost contemptuously he flicked the fireball aside with one great hand.

Suddenly there came a shrill cry of challenge from Iriana's right, from within the city itself.

'Monster. Fiend. Foul creature of dirt and stone. Leave my city. Begone!'

There stood Sharalind, towering as tall as Iriana and Corisand, flanked by Avithan and Omaira, head of the Warrior Luen, who were standing behind her shoulders. Beyond them was a phalanx of warriors, all grown to the same gargantuan proportions.

A chill ran through Iriana. 'Stinking bat turds,' she snarled to Taine. 'Just when we'd distracted his attention away from the bloody city!'

The Wizards began striking at the Moldan with all the Earth magic they could muster, focused this time through Sharalind at the head of the phalanx, but if they thought this method would be more effective, they were sorely mistaken. They hurled missiles that shattered against Ghabal's stony hide, and their strangling vines slowed him hardly at all. Turning away from Corisand he ploughed back into Tyrineld, crushing, shattering, killing, grinding everything beneath his feet into dust. As he moved towards Sharalind and her diminished band, he raised his gigantic axe with its deadly trail of oily black shadow that followed the path of the blade.

Suddenly Iriana saw Yinze, his harp in his arms and playing fever-ishly, rise up on a pillar of air to the height of the enlarged Avithan. She could not hear what he was saying, but she could see from his expression that he was begging his friend not to do this. Avithan, his white face grim and set, would not even look him, but swatted him away as though he were a fly. Yinze went spinning through the air, out of control and falling. Iriana caught her breath – she was too far away to help, but suddenly Kea came soaring up from below. Her wings working furiously, she caught and steadied Yinze, giving him an instant to collect himself and start to play again. Once more he was supported in the sky, but too far away now to be any help to Avithan.

'All together,' Sharalind shouted. '*Now!*'

Time seemed to freeze for Iriana as the scenario and its inevitable result flashed through her mind. It would be a petrifaction spell – that was all they had left – and on a Moldan that wouldn't work.

'No!' she cried, even though she knew that she was too late to stop them. The Wizards cast their spell – the focus was so intense that she could see the magic sizzling through the air – and nothing happened. Ghabal continued his inexorable advance. The sinister axe swept down upon the helpless Wizard forces – and Iriana sent forth a blunted missile of air that she'd learned from Corisand, straight at Avithan. It knocked him back, away, and off his feet. As he fell his concentration broke. He shrank to normal size and was lost somewhere among the buildings as the Moldan's axe mowed down his mother and the pitiful, valiant remnants of her army in a single stroke.

Ghabal laughed and looked around at the destruction he had wrought, baring his teeth in a menacing, twisted grin. 'Little town.' He laughed, and the sound was blood-chilling. 'Little people. What can save them?'

He turned and was across Tyrineld in three great strides, crushing another area into rubble every time his massive foot came stamping down with a force that shook the earth. His eye fixed on the slender southern peninsula, containing the Luen of Bards and the graceful rows of former merchants' houses with their air of dilapidated grandeur. Then, with another spiteful glance at Corisand and Iriana, he lifted his axe and brought it down with all his force across the neck of the promontory. Rock crumbled and split with a tortured groan, like a human soul in torment. The entire headland, Luen, houses, inhabitants and all, crumbled into the ocean with a mighty splash that sent a fountaining spray of salt water right across the city.

The Moldan turned back to the horrified Corisand. 'Give me the Stone,' he bellowed. 'Give it to me NOW – or more of your city, more of your people will be destroyed. Their blood will be on your hands!'

Corisand shot Iriana a glance filled with anguish and doubt, but the Wizard, though tears were streaming down her face, tightened her mouth and shook her head. 'Don't give in to him,' she called in shaky mindspeech. 'We can't, Corisand. If he can do this now, think of the damage he'll be able to wreak with the Stone. We have to stop him – somehow.'

The Moldan raised his axe once more and, looking around for his next target, headed towards the next headland where Ariel's Tower had formerly stood.

Unaware of the dramas that were unfolding in the city, Aelwen took Kelon back to the stretch of moorland where a small tarn gleamed at the bottom of a vale. The Xandim not involved in the rescue – the elders, the youngsters and the others who had no wish to become involved in a war not their own – had settled. Those in equine form grazed in the sheltered dell, with a stallion keeping vigil on the hilltop above, with all his attention on the distant battle lest the fighting started to move their way. One or two were trying out their human bodies, but they looked pinched and cold, and Aelwen was sure that they would soon revert. None of them could take care of Kelon, or even make a fire. She would have to stay and tend him herself.

Kelon had passed out again, whether from pain or his injuries she didn't know. Gently she helped to ease her old friend from Asharal's back. When he was on the ground, the stallion turned briefly back to his human aspect so that he could speak with her. 'I'll stay with you, just in case you need to get out of here in a hurry.'

'Thank you,' Aelwen said. 'Will you help me to carry him over there, by the bushes? That looks like the driest, most sheltered spot that I can see.'

'Of course.' Like his equine counterpart, Asharal was strong. Soon they had Kelon settled, with a gorse thicket behind him to shelter him from the chill moorland wind. They wrapped him in a blanket from Aelwen's pack, and she rolled up an old tunic to pillow his head.

Asharal shivered. 'I'm changing back now, if it's all right with you. It's easier for a horse to be comfortable out here than it is for a human.'

'Of course,' Aelwen said. 'I only wish that Kelon and I could join you. Thank you for everything, Asharal.'

'You did your best to protect and help me when I was at Tiolani's mercy.' He smiled at her. 'I'm glad to be able to return the favour.' He looked down at Kelon. 'I hope he'll be all right. He was good to me, too.' The air shimmered and the handsome bay stallion stood there once more. Staying close, he lowered his head and began to graze.

Aelwen covered her friend with her own cloak, then looked around for something to make a fire, but found nothing save a gnarled old hawthorn close to the mere, and clusters of gorse on the slopes of the dell. All prickly, and they'd burn in no time. She shrugged. She'd have to make do. Fire first, and set some water to boil. By then she'd have summoned the courage to look at Kelon's injuries. Pulling her leather gloves from her belt and shivering in her shirtsleeves, she set off determinedly towards the solitary tree.

Back in Tyrineld, Yinze, his head spinning, managed to get himself aloft again, and went in search of Avithan, plucking frantically at the strings of his harp to keep himself in the air and on course. Sweeping low across the wreckage where Sharalind's forces had made their valiant, futile last stand he saw the bodies of the Wizards, shrunken to normal size in death, amid the ruined buildings. The Moldan's axe, with its evil, roiling black shadow, had left their bodies blackened and twisted, their faces contorted in agony so that they were as deformed as Ghabal himself.

Yinze was sickened and grief-stricken at the sight. He wanted to flee; to get far away from this horror that would haunt his nightmares for many years to come, but he could not. He was searching, amid all this death and destruction, for one living Wizard, and would not leave until he had found him.

In the end, it proved easier than expected. Yinze had been looking for an unconscious form, half-buried, perhaps, beneath the debris of fallen walls, beams that had been snapped like kindling and even fallen trees from once-beautiful gardens. Instead, he found a filthy, ragged figure, its face bruised down one side and a lip that trickled blood, that was clambering its unsteady but determined way back to where the bodies of the fallen warriors lay.

Yinze's heart leapt to see his friend alive. Calling frantically for Kea and her bearers, he swept down to land – and his heart froze to see the stony mask of anguish, rage and grief that had transformed Avithan's features. He was overwhelmed with pity. To lose both parents so close together, in such violent circumstances! No wonder Avithan looked so desolate. 'Come on,' he said, putting an arm around his friend's shoulders. 'Come with me. You don't want to go over there, Avithan. You don't want to see what I've seen. Let the memory of your mother stay untarnished, and remember her as she was.'

Only when Avithan allowed himself to be led away without a word of objection did Yinze realise how deeply traumatised he must be. Just then Kea and her bearers arrived. 'Thank providence you found him,' she said. 'Poor man! We'll take him to the Xandim, and let Taryn take care of him for now. Get Avithan to safety,' she ordered her bearers, and they took off with the Wizard dangling in his net beneath them.

'Now,' Yinze said. 'If I don't have him to worry about, I can help Iriana—'

'Yinze!' Kea seized his arm, her face twisted in anguish. 'Please come with me. Iriana said she can manage but I can hear Atka, the Dragon who came with Chathak. She's desperate and she needs help. *Please,*' she begged when he hesitated. 'Her egg – she says she just laid it. Nobody knows except me.'

Yinze cursed. 'Hurry then!' Running his fingers over the strings, he was up and away, following Kea to the building on the northern peninsula that housed the Dragon.

The fishing fleet had all been offloading in Tyrineld port before the Moldan materialised. They were working quickly, anxious to be gone. Though Sharalind's plans for war with the Phaerie had brought them unexpected prosperity, being in the city made them uneasy now – especially on this trip, when the wharves were buzzing with the news of the Archwizard's death and the astonishing resurrection of Avithan, and plenty of rumour and speculation regarding both. The Lady Sharalind had assumed her soulmate's mantle of authority completely now, and was all the more eager to press north to wreak vengeance for her husband's death, and find her son.

Many mortals had already been conscripted, including the ferals from the forest. The fisherfolk were taking no chances.

The offload was almost complete when the alarm went up. The shimmering mounts of the Wild Hunt had been seen high in the skies, heading straight for the city. It looked as though Hellorin's daughter Tiolani had stolen the march on Sharalind and brought the fight to the Wizards.

Word passed quickly from ship to ship along the dock. Valior and the other Captains had no intention of waiting around for the outcome of a battle, and the fish left in their holds would be needed for their own people in the days to come. They raised sail, slipped their hawsers and headed out.

They had barely left the dock when the colossal figure of a warped and deformed giant materialised. Even at this distance he was a blood-freezing sight. Brynne, standing close to Valior at the helm, was frozen in horror and dry-mouthed with fear. Suddenly she felt the older man's hand take hers in a strong, warm, comforting clasp. 'It's all right, little mermaid. That thing won't get us. Let the Wizards deal with it. We'll head home as fast as we can and spread the alarm. We'll get everyone who'll fit onto the bigger boats and make a flotilla of the smaller vessels. By the time anyone, Wizard, Phaerie, or monsters, get round to thinking about us, we'll be far away.'

Brynne knew enough about the sea by now to realise that it wouldn't be so easy. The elements were calm at present, but rough weather would mean trouble for the smaller boats, and even the larger vessels if they were overloaded with passengers. But it seemed that there was no alternative. They would have to take the risk. By the time the fishing fleet had cleared the northernmost point with its Academy buildings and the Healers' complex, and were turning for home, the sounds of screams and suffering, death and destruction, were coming clearly over the water. The hideous monster was bellowing something about a stone, and other giant figures – Wizards, Brynne assumed, who had grown to match the size of the behemoth – had begun to appear, so large that they were easily visible, even at this distance. As she looked back she was seized with a desperate need to escape. It seemed that the *Venturer* couldn't move fast enough for her.

When the first Wizard apported onto the deck in a thunderclap of displaced air, she knew her instincts had been right.

Avithan was scarcely aware that he'd been loaded into the net, but gradually the shock of Sharalind's death was ebbing. He came to his senses with the city walls below him – and there was Iriana, towering tall with that accursed Taine at her side. She and the Windeye were working together to keep the Moldan confined, Corisand with a barrier of solid air and Iriana with a wall of fire. Ghabal had bypassed the Ariel's Tower headland, as if he realised that there was little more damage he could do there, and they were holding him at bay just before he could reach the northern promontory with the Academy and the Luen of Healers – the last headland before he reached the northern city walls, beyond which Taine and Iriana stood. The trapped monstrosity, howling obscenely, was throwing petrifaction spells, first at one foe then the other, and the Wizard and Windeye were alternately shielding if they were under attack, or maintaining the barrier if they were not. It required split-second timing and tremendous concentration, and he could see the strain beginning to tell on both of them. Surely, sooner or later, one of them must fail – and fall.

Iriana was the only loved one Avithan had left.

Seeing her battling the giant, his only thought was to save her.

Ever since they'd been children, they'd played games of getting past one another's shields, until they both knew each other's magical defences – and how to get through them – as well as they knew their own. With her attention elsewhere, Iriana would not be expecting an attack from the rear. On impulse, he threw a sleep spell at her, and saw her crumple, shrinking as she fell.

'Hey!' came an outraged shout from Taine. 'What the bloody blazes are you doing?' He took a gigantic stride towards Avithan, who grew in stature to meet him, forgetting that he was still in the net. The meshes burst apart and the bearers dropped the impossible weight. Avithan fell the short distance, dropping to his knees, then sprang up to meet the advancing Hemifae.

'Let her *go*, you imbecile,' Taine shouted. 'That thing will go after Corisand now.'

With a snarl, Avithan launched himself at this meddling interloper, knocking him off his feet. The pair of them rolled and grappled, losing their concentration and shrinking to their normal size. Beyond all reason now, Avithan groped for his knife and the two of them struggled for control of the blade for a moment, before Taine took it off him and sent it spinning away. That moment of distraction cost him dear. Avithan ploughed a fist into his face that sent the back of Taine's head smashing into the ground. He sprawled on the grass, motionless, pale and limp as a corpse.

When Iriana fell, her barrier vanished, and suddenly the Moldan, now with only one foe to fight, was free once more. Raging, he took the last stride to the Academy and brought his weapon smashing down again and again amid the buildings, then he turned and lumbered towards Corisand. He had only one target now – and she would pay.

It was as well that Healers were taught to shield themselves from the psychic shock that accompanied the death of a Wizard, for now citizens of Tyrineld were dying in their hundreds. Melisanda, trying with all her might to maintain her shield, had been watching the battle from the window of Tinagen's study in the Healers' complex. She saw the giant appear; saw the other figures grow to match it, and gasped to see that one of them was Avithan – and another was Iriana.

Melisanda was gathering her will to apport across to help her friends – the ban on such acts within the city was insignificant now – when she was stopped by Tinagen's hand on her arm. She started, and her gathered powers dissipated. She turned on him angrily. 'Leave me alone. I must go to Iriana.'

'I'm sorry,' the Luen Head replied. 'Melisanda, you must stay here. Everyone's reeling from the shock of so many deaths. We'll be getting a flood of injured soon, supposing we don't have to evacuate this place. The people of Tyrineld need you here. *I* need you.'

With a curse, Melisanda pulled away from him. 'I can't. My friends ...' She was desperately torn. She thought of all her friends in danger: Chathak and Thara, thank providence, were safe in Nexis helping set up supply caches for Sharalind's army, and had taken Iriana's dog Bear and the small white cub from Aerillia with them, but the others ... Yinze she could sense nearby but couldn't see him, and grieving Avithan and blind Iriana were all set to do battle with a colossal fiend, horrific beyond all imagining. How could she not go to them? Yet as a Healer she had made vows, and her duty was clear. Though she might curse Tinagen, she knew in her heart that he was right. She must stay here and help those who needed her.

Yet she couldn't seem to drag herself from the window, and now Tinagen was at her side, unable to pull his own eyes away. She saw the Moldan mow down Sharalind's forces with its sinister axe; saw Yinze pull Avithan to safety. Saw that Iriana, who stood on the hilltop to the north of the city, seemed to have help already from two strangers. Then she saw the Moldan begin his rampage. The southern promontory vanished in one axe blow, and he was heading towards the Ariel's Tower headland.

She knew they would be next.

Already, as he drew closer, she could feel the building shaking, and a crack snaked up the study wall from floor to ceiling.

'Quick,' Tinagen shouted, grabbing her arm. 'We've got to get everyone out.'

'But where to? Where can they go?' Melisanda said. 'We haven't the strength to apport those critical patients right out of the city – it's too far from here.'

As they fled out onto the landing and past the window that looked out onto the ocean, a movement, a flash of colour, caught her eye. 'Tinagen,' she cried, pointing at the fishing fleet. 'Could we shift them there?'

'To a moving target? At that distance, heading away from us? Have you lost your mind?'

'Is there any choice? Send the ambulatory ones away now, they must take their chances and get out of the city as best they can. If they stay on this side and get off the headland, they might have a hope. But the bedridden ones are doomed unless we try something.'

Tinagen hesitated – but only for a heartbeat. 'We'll have to do it in teams then ...' While they had been talking, they'd been racing down the staircase to the next floor. All the while the booming footsteps were coming closer. The Moldan must have been smashing and destroying as he went, or he would have already been here, but the whole building was shaking now. Great cracks were appearing in the walls and the ceilings.

Tinagen stopped at the bottom of the stairs and flung out an arm. 'Go that way and start with Incondor. We don't want a political situation—'

His words were cut off in a shattering rumble and crash as the entire stairwell collapsed on top of him. Melisanda, already racing away to do his bidding, was enveloped in clouds of choking dust, and spun to see the hallway half-filled with a pile of rubble. The death of her Luen Head hit her like a hammer-blow, driving her to her knees.

'Tinagen!' She gasped his name out on a sob, but there was no time for grieving now. Brushing tears away she got to her feet, braced her shoulders to take the load, and rushed away to organise the Healers – her Healers now – shouting out instructions in mindspeech as she went. There might be little they could do and barely any time left, but they would do their best to save what lives they could.

With Yinze close behind her, Kea reached the Dragon's dwelling and wrenched open the rooftop door, gliding down into the spacious chamber below without bothering with the stairs. She had seen the Moldan escape from the barriers that were confining it, and it was now laying about the city with its immense axe – far too close for comfort. Inside the building the wide doorway that Atka used for an exit had been choked by falling debris when the adjacent structure had collapsed, and there was no way out for her. Her golden scales dulled by a film of dust, she was curled protectively around a gleaming egg that was large enough to hold a small human child, if it was curled up tightly inside the shell.

'Kea!' Atka cried. 'Oh, Kea, I'm so glad to see you. My egg – you have to get it out of here.'

The winged girl, with Yinze close behind, landed near the Dragon's head. 'A plague on the egg!' she snapped. 'What about you? Atka, we have to get you out.'

Though she could not see outside, she could hear ominous crashes and howls, and a chill ran through her. It sounded as though the Moldan was coming even closer. Kea could feel the earth shaking from his heavy footfalls, and could hear the screams of his victims.

'There's no time for me,' Atka said. 'The weather is too cold, and

I'm too sluggish to escape that monster, even if you could get me out of here in time. Unless someone stops him soon, I'm finished. Please, for my sake, take the egg. Maybe the Wizards can keep it warm enough to hatch.'

'I'm not leaving you,' the winged girl cried fiercely.

'It's that or die here with me,' the Dragon replied implacably. 'It would take a miracle to save me now. Hope for that miracle, Kea – but take my egg to safety.'

'Yinze, you take it.' Kea turned to the Wizard. 'I'll stay here to help Atka.'

'I can't. I need both hands for the harp.'

'*Please*, Kea,' Atka begged. 'It's the last thing I'll ever ask of you.'

With a curse, Kea capitulated at last. 'All right; hand it over. I'll take it somewhere safe – then I'm coming back for you.'

The egg, large, smooth and heavy as it was, proved impossible for the winged girl to hold. She and Yinze hastily improvised a kind of sack from the Wizard's cloak, lashing the four corners together with the egg contained within. Kea laid a hand on the Dragon's face. 'I'm coming back for you, I promise.' Then, her wings labouring hard to lift the extra weight, she took off with Yinze, unable to look back for the shimmer of tears in her eyes.

35
~

CATACLYSM

With horror, Corisand saw Iriana fall, and the Moldan's deadly focus swing towards herself. If she couldn't revive her friend – and quickly – they were both doomed. Hastily she changed back to a normal-sized equine form, then used the flying spell to speed across the city. While she was moving so fast it was hard to shield, and Ghabal was throwing petrifaction spells at her as hard as he could. The Windeye zigzagged, back and forth, high and low across the sky. There were near misses where she felt the giant's unclean magic sizzling past, but she kept on heading back to where the prone forms of Taine and the Wizard lay, along with the idiot who was responsible for this mess.

Shock at his own deed brought Avithan back to his senses. He got to his feet – only to be ploughed down again by something large and solid. He rolled over, and saw a grey horse, ears back, teeth bared, looming above him. Before he could move, the animal planted one of her forefeet on his chest, right above his heart, pinning him to the ground. The Moldan was coming closer now. All of Corisand's concentration had to be focused on her shield so that she could not use her powers for anything else, but there were other ways to get the sleep spell off her friend.

'Take it off,' she ordered Avithan in mindspeech. 'Take your bloody sleep spell off my friend.'

'No,' Avithan shouted. 'Get off me, you foul beast.' He could find no missiles nearby to hurl at her by magic, nor could he crack the ground beneath her feet without endangering himself. He threw up a strangling vine, but it scraped harmlessly against her shield, and a petrifaction spell bounced harmlessly off the same barrier.

'Take the spell *off*.' Corisand pressed her weight down harder on his chest, and Avithan screamed in pain. The Windeye spoke again, her voice cold and hard as iron. 'Take it off or I'll kill you.' Without waiting, she pressed down again, feeling Avithan's ribs bend a little beneath the weight.

'All right,' he screamed. 'Stop, stop! I'm doing it!'

Chiannala fell onto the pitching deck of the boat with a jolt that knocked the breath from her body. She could scarcely believe that she was still in one piece. Her first apport, and she had survived it! Ignoring her aches and bruises she got to her feet, balancing uncertainly on the tilting surface, and looked around for Incondor. The Skyman was sprawled across the deck nearby, but the splints and bracing on his wings were cracked and splintered, and his wing bones had been further shattered and mangled in the apport.

Two other bedridden patients had followed her onto the pitching deck, and another of the Healers: she recognised Lameron, looking pale and haggard, tending to them. There was all sorts of shouting and commotion going on among the fisherfolk, with much hauling of ropes and massive movements of sails going on above her head. It seemed that someone else had missed the target and was in the ocean, and the crew were trying to turn the boat in time to pick them up.

Then a groan from her right turned her attention back to Incondor. She staggered over and knelt at his side. 'What's hurting?'

He reached out and clasped her hand. 'Everything,' he groaned.

'I'll take care of it.'

'It's no good – we lost them.' Someone's voice broke into her concentration as she worked to block Incondor's pain. She looked up in some irritation to see a tall woman, the one who had spoken, in the bows looking out across the sea, where several sails from other boats could be seen. Judging from her clothing, she was part of the crew. Someone else busied themselves with ropes around the mast behind Chiannala as an older, blue-eyed man shouted, 'Bring her about! Let's head for home.' He turned to Lameron. 'I'm sorry, Healer, but it's very hard to pick up someone who fell off a moving boat, and in this case, your folk were never on board in the first place so we had that extra distance to cover. We did our best but ...' He spread his hands.

'Are you certain, Captain Valior?' Lameron pleaded. 'You do know that Wizards can breathe underwater, don't you?'

Chiannala's heart stuttered, stopped – then started beating again at breakneck speed as panic twisted in her guts.

Had Brynne survived?

Her half-blood prevented her from feeling the deaths of fellow Wizards, so there had always been that tiny shred of doubt – but she had put it aside. Surely no one would survive such a fall into the ocean? But living so far inland in Nexis, no one had ever told her that a Wizard couldn't drown. If the truth about what she had done ever came out, she would lose everything …

Firmly, Chiannala told herself not to be stupid. If Brynne had survived, she would surely have turned up by now. She put the matter out of her mind, afraid that Lameron might catch a fleeting hint of her guilty thoughts. To avoid attracting his attention, she pulled the hood of her robe up to shadow her face, and bent solicitously over Incondor, though she still listened carefully to everything that was going on.

'You said that your sick people were wrapped in blankets,' the Captain was saying. 'They simply must have sunk, and there's no way to bring them back. The cold will likely finish them off, but there's just nothing we can do. And there's no sign of your other Healers. Maybe the other boats picked them up – we'll try to signal them.'

'You did your best, Captain,' Lameron replied with a sigh. 'After all, we came bursting onto your ship without leave or invitation, yet you've agreed to help us. We're all deeply in your debt and I'm very grateful, but I'm afraid that when we performed the apport, those other two patients were targeted on this boat, so they must be lost. You're right, though – the rest of the Healers and patients may be on the other ships.'

He swallowed hard. 'I can't tell you how glad I am that you were here. You've no idea what it was like in the city, with that abomination on the rampage. Had you not been offloading in Tyrineld today, it's certain we'd all have died a hideous death.'

Valior put a comforting hand on the shoulder of the shaking Healer. 'A monster like that creature I saw in Tyrineld puts all folk, Wizard or mortal, on the same side. I'll relieve the helmsman now, and we'll be on our way. I want to put as much distance between us and that – *thing* – as I can.'

As Iriana began to stir, Corisand removed her hoof from Avithan's chest and rapped it smartly against the side of his head. As he lolled, unconscious, she glanced at the limp form of Taine and thought, 'Tit for tat.' Though her sharper equine hearing could detect the Hemifae's heartbeat, he showed no sign of waking, and there would be no time to heal him now. Meanwhile, Iriana was sitting up. 'What happened? Taine? I can't see!' Her voice rose in panic.

'It's all right.' Corisand was busy reverting to her human form. 'Here, link with my mind. Use my vision.'

The Wizard scrambled to her feet as she found that she could see again – and the first things that caught her eye were the prone forms of Taine and Avithan. 'Taine! What the blazes …' Then she gasped. 'The Moldan! Where is he?'

Corisand's voice was grim. 'He's coming for us now.'

Melisanda was the very last to leave the Healers' complex, with the Moldan so close that his vile, black shadow cast a pall over the shells of the shattered buildings. She had done her best to save her Healers and those they cared for, though a number had been lost under fallen walls and ceilings, and though her heart was breaking from the losses she knew that she could do no more. As she stood amid the dust and wreckage, she saw the malformed giant looming above. One more step—

Desperately she summoned the image of one of the ships and with all her will she threw herself, magic, body and spirit, towards it. Then the Luen of Healers was gone, and she found herself face down on a wet wooden deck that pitched up and down in an increasingly rough sea.

'*Another* one?' a voice beside her growled. Weary and shaky she pulled herself up to see a big, bearded man with piercing blue eyes and dark brown hair escaping from a rough braid, who stood at the tiller of the fishing boat. On the deck in front of her were two of her healers, Lameron and Brynne, doing their best to make a trio of patients, including Incondor, comfortable.

Is that all? What happened to the rest of them?

Melisanda let out a moan. Surely these couldn't be the only survivors! It had been a long shot at best, but to have saved so few …

Suddenly she jumped as a strong, work-hardened hand patted her arm. 'Don't take on, lass.' His voice was honey poured over gravel. 'Using flags, we've ways of signalling to one another, and quite a few of them made it to the other boats. You know, it's a miracle that any of you got out of there, and from what Healer Lameron's been saying, that's all down to you.'

Melisanda, braced by the gruff kindness in his voice, pulled herself together. She knew he was right. She had done her best. There had never been a hope of saving everyone. She turned to the helmsman and offered her hand. 'My name is Melisanda. I'm Deputy Head – no, I'm Head now,' she corrected herself with a grimace of pain, 'of the Luen of Healers. This invasion of your vessels is my fault, I'm afraid. I'm sorry, but we had no choice. That monster ... I had to save as many as I could.'

Now that the ordeal was over, she could hold back the tears no longer. Turning to lean on the rail, she buried her face in her hands and sobbed. As a Healer she understood the value of such a release and, for a moment, let herself give in to it, letting the weeping wash away a little of the grief, the pain and the terror.

The helmsman – he had good instincts for a mortal – let her get it out of her system before he spoke again. 'You've had a bad time back there, it seems,' he said gently. 'We'll take you to safety, never fear. My name is Captain Valior and—'

They were interrupted by a piercing scream.

Brynne had been told by Valior to check on the Healer, the one in the pale blue robes. The girl was keeping her head bowed so low over the groaning winged man that the captain, solicitous for all his Wizardly passengers, was afraid she was feeling ill, or had hurt herself during the apport. She went over and tapped the kneeling girl on the shoulder. 'Excuse me, but are you—'

The Healer looked up, her hood falling away from her face, and Brynne's words broke off as if she had bitten her tongue. There, in front of her was an identical image of herself. Were it not for the fact that the other was clad in rumpled, sea-splashed blue robes, while she, Brynne, wore the high boots and layers of rough, seaman's clothing, she could have been looking into a mirror.

The Healer girl sprang to her feet, her face turning chalk-white. She reeled back from Brynne as if she had received a mortal blow – and suddenly the wall in Brynne's head was shivering, falling, splintering into shards to the sound of her own scream, as if the mirror had been shattered ...

Behind her closed eyes she saw a clifftop, with the ocean heaving below. Cold, cruel eyes and a mouth twisted into a vicious sneer on a pretty face that suddenly transformed into her own, plainer features. A hand that shot out, pushing her so hard that she lost her balance, staggered backwards and lost her footing on the cliff edge ...

She was falling, falling, her scream of terror ripped away by the wind – then the water hit her – a massive blow striking shock and pain all through her. The icy grey sea closed over her head ...

She was sinking, down, down, her lungs filling with seawater as her consciousness left her ...

Brynne's eyes opened again, and she looked her impostor full in the face. 'But a true Wizard wouldn't drown,' she said in a cold, clear voice. 'Didn't you know that? What are you, Chiannala, that you didn't know?'

'Brynne?' Valior came rushing to her side and put a protective arm around her, puzzlement in his voice. But the tall, blonde Wizard in the sapphire robes of a high-ranking Healer looked, from the shock and disgust on her face, as if she had been picking up the images from Brynne's mind, and had seen what she had seen. Her grey eyes blazing with anger and contempt, she turned on her former student, who was cowering against the rail like an animal in a trap.

'You pushed her? You tried to *kill* her?'

'No, Melisanda, no,' the girl whined. 'She's lying.'

Valior stepped forward, between Brynne and her double, looking from one to the other with incredulous eyes. '*She* was the one?' he asked Brynne. 'She was the reason we found you all but dead of cold in the sea?'

'Cease!' It was Incondor, who had eased himself up on his elbows, though his face was an ashen grimace of pain. 'Healer Melisanda, this girl, Chiannala, is under *my* protection.'

'My Lord Incondor,' from her tone, Melisanda was clearly far from impressed. 'This is an internal matter for the Luen of Wizard Healers, and is none of your concern.'

'You want to risk a diplomatic incident with Queen Pandion? While Tyrineld is being reduced to a heap of rubble and you will need the help of the Skyfolk as never before?' Incondor snarled.

And then suddenly the world dissolved into chaos.

With Avithan's spell removed, Iriana struggled to her feet and saw what Corisand saw. The Moldan had left the northern headland and was coming towards them, menace glaring red in his eyes. Already he had almost reached the city walls. There was no time to be staggered by what Avithan had done to her, and she scarcely had time to check that Taine still lived and breathed, but she could feel the anger building inside her – at Avithan's betrayal, at all the death, the waste and bloodshed, at the destruction of her home. With a snarl, she grasped Corisand's hand so that they were both holding the Fialan, preparing to strike out at him with all its power – but when Ghabal saw the blazing gem he flinched and turned suddenly turned back, casting a look of pure malice over his shoulder at the Wizard and Windeye.

Then he roared: a shattering blast of sound that shook the earth and flattened Corisand and Iriana to the ground. 'KATMAI! I CALL UPON YOU! BE MY INSTRUMENT OF VENGEANCE!'

All at once the Wizard and Windeye felt a new power, a new deadly energy blazing out of the Moldan – and he could move faster, much faster than before. Before they could act, a huge incandescent fireball appeared in his hand. He lifted it high over his head and hurled it down with all his force to smash against the ground. As Corisand and Iriana looked on, numb with horror, a vast fissure appeared in the earth at his feet, snaking from west to east and cutting all three of them off from the city. He stretched forth his hand again, spreading his fingers wide, and the gigantic fracture in the surface of the earth widened quickly, like a vast maw that consumed the remains of Tyrineld as the ocean rushed in, with earthshaking explosions and billowing clouds of steam, to fill the gap.

The spreading chasm consumed buildings, streets, and people alike. Any Wizard who had not already fled was doomed, and swept away into the churning water; the archivists and scholars working frantically to apport priceless volumes and scrolls to safety, the stallholders and merchants in the market trying to save valuable foodstuffs and implements, any Healers who had stayed behind to help their patients to escape. As for the Mortals – not one of them stood a chance.

The wind howled and dark clouds raced across the sky as all the lands to the south of the city sank, fell, crumbled into the hungry waves, with what sounded like a roar of anguish, and more and more ocean came pouring in. Tyrineld, queen of cities, gleaming jewel, home and sanctuary, cradle of learning and throne of power, was lost for ever.

Though the ships were some distance offshore by this time, the hideous figure of the monster could still be seen, looming over the shattered skyline of Tyrineld. Suddenly he cried out in a mighty voice, and a searing ball of fire appeared in his hand, which he hurled down with colossal force to strike the tortured ground. As the crew of the *Venturer* watched in horror, the earth split apart with a hideous rending sound, and Tyrineld vanished into the widening rift as the ocean rushed in.

The fishing boats were tossed about like toys as the sea heaved and massive waves reared up like walls of green glass that broke over the bows in a welter of foam, as Valior struggled to keep the ship heading straight into them. There was a scream as one of the recumbent patients was washed overboard. The *Venturer* was seized and buffeted by the powerful flow as the waters surged in to fill the chasm which gaped wider with each passing moment. The sails were ripped from the rigging by the rising gale and went kiting off in tatters, into the boiling black clouds above.

The vessel's timbers were creaking from the strain. Planking sprung up from the decks as she groaned and shuddered like a wounded creature in pain. Working on pure instinct, Brynne threw out a spell to hold the straining timbers together. Single-handedly she battled the forces of anarchy and destruction all round her, her eyes glazed, her jaw clenched and her face pale with strain. Brave as a warrior, obdurate as stone, she fought on, desperately trying to hold the *Venturer* together, pitting herself against the raw, elemental forces of nature gone mad.

Brynne's powers, however, were immature and untrained, and exhaustion was taking its toll. The edges of her vision began to darken, and her entire body shook like a leaf in a hurricane, yet still she refused to give in, her fingers grasping Valior's arm so tightly that they dug into his flesh as she drew power from the big man's strength.

All this time the Healers had been in a state of utter terror, clinging frantically to whatever they could find to stop themselves being swept overboard, but Melisanda, looking up, caught sight of Brynne and realised her plight. She threw all the force of her disciplined and practised power behind the younger girl's magic, taking her lead from Brynne's understanding of the ship and its structure.

Miraculously, Brynne felt the load become lighter, and the forces that threatened to tear her apart were eased. Finally, she could take a grateful gasp of salty air and look around her, but what she saw shrivelled her courage. The *Venturer*, along with the others in the fleet, was being pulled inexorably into a heaving maelstrom as the waters were sucked into the gap where the city had once stood. Before her horrified gaze, Mordal's *Intrepid* was pulled towards the rim of the great torrent where the seas poured down, and vanished over the edge to be lost for ever.

The rest of the fleet were drawing closer and closer to disaster ... Brynne turned and flung herself at Valior and clutched him tightly as the gallant *Venturer* neared the brink, and buried her face in his chest as his arms locked round her in an iron grip ...

Then suddenly the Leviathan were there, their forceful Water magic enabling them to cut through the strongest current with ease. They thronged around the ships, putting themselves between the vessels and danger. Though their abilities differed from her own, Brynne could feel their spells that fought to calm the seas and negate the ferocious currents, as all the while they pushed the cluster of fishing boats northward, away from danger, and back towards their home. Weak with relief, Brynne finally let her own powers relax. But she kept tight hold of Valior, and he held her to him as if he never meant to let her go.

Was it possible to die of a broken heart? As Tyrineld was destroyed the pain of Iriana's grief took her breath away; tore with ravening fangs at her mind. She was paralysed, transfixed, barely able to comprehend the horror before her and the scale of the disaster.

Then, like the breaking of a storm, came the anger. The Wizard gripped Corisand's hand so tightly that she seemed about to drive the Fialan into their very flesh, and once they were conjoined, she began to pull in power, taking it in from all around her: from the crumbling earth and raging sea; from the tearing wind and roiling sky; from the death throes of all the lost, Wizard and Mortal alike. From the survivors she took it, gathering all their anger, anguish and pain. She drew upon the Air magic of Kea and Crombec, Phaerie glamourie from Aelwen and the still half-stunned Taine, the shifting, fluid powers of Water from the Leviathan and Ionor with them.

Corisand, joined to her, melded with her, unable to draw away even if it had been her wish, gave the magic of the Windeye freely, pouring it into her friend through the medium of the Stone of Fate. She and Iriana were no longer two separate entities, two friends and comrades; they were fused together by the might of the Fialan into a single force that combined all the gathered powers and joined them with the magic of the Stone of Fate. Then through the Stone came the powers of the Evanesar; the inexorable Cold magic of Taku, the fierce crackling energy of Aurora – and finally the spell of Denali, with her powers of Earth, eternal, obdurate and vast.

When all had been amassed, Iriana, fused with Corisand and seeing events through her eyes, their blood beating through their veins as one, power singing through every nerve and fibre of their conjoined minds and bodies, gathered all the magic, all the energy, into a single missile – and struck.

A tangle of luminescent fibres wrapped themselves around the Moldan, and though he fought and raged and struggled, he could find no way out. Then Corisand and Iriana lifted their conjoined hands that held the Fialan. Power blazed out of the Stone in blinding rays, and for the first and last time in the mundane world the majestic voice of Denali echoed forth. Though her language was unknown, the authority, the meaning and the menace in those implacable syllables could be heard like the grating of the lock in a prison door.

Ghabal's raging cut off abruptly as the interweaving fibres that trammelled him flared and expanded, forming a great sphere of effulgent radiance all around him, so bright that the Moldan shrieked and clamped his hands across his eyes as the dazzling light lanced into his head. When the brilliance faded, the globe had turned into solid, glittering diamond, an immense stone of sparkling beauty that held the cold glitter of Taku's magic, the scintillating, changeful colours of Aurora's energy – and the eternal, unbreakable, adamantine permanence of Denali's power. Imprisoned in its very core was Ghabal, reduced from a slayer of uncounted multitudes and a cleaver of worlds to nothing but a dark, twisted, smoky streak of ominous shadow.

Iriana turned to Corisand. 'Now,' she said. 'We finish it. We bring him down to size.'

She tightened her fist round the Fialan, so hard that the Windeye gasped with pain but followed suit, tightening her own grip around the Stone. And before the stunned eyes of the terrified survivors of Tyrineld, the Moldan's glittering prison began to shrink, down and down, and as it diminished the walls of the crystal grew increasingly dense, so that the sparkling jewel turned clouded and opaque – until finally, lying in the grass, was a stone no bigger than the Fialan; dull, dark and dead with its prisoner visible no more.

Utterly drained, Iriana and Corisand collapsed against each other and sank to the ground, still linked by their hands that were clenched tightly around the Fialan.

That was how Taine found them when he awakened with a pounding headache and an aching jaw. Both of them lying so terrifyingly still, with the Stone of Fate's power surrounding them in a blazing emerald aureole. Alive? Dead? The sight of Iriana's unmoving form and still, lifeless face punched through his heart as though a dagger had been driven into it, with such force that it literally knocked him back a step or two.

Iriana?

When had he started to feel like this about her?

There was no time to wonder. He had to help them. But no matter how hard he tried to reach them, the power of the Fialan kept driving him back – until finally, it faded of its own accord and the green glow died away, leaving Wizard and Windeye lying with their hands still linked, and clasped tightly around the Stone.

The sound of Taine's voice brought Iriana back from some faraway place, and as she opened her eyes she felt Corisand stirring beside her. The first thing she saw was Taine, kneeling at her shoulder, clinging to her free hand, his face contorted in anguish that suddenly transformed into a smile as he saw her awaken.

'Taine?' she whispered.

'I'm here.'

As the storm wrack blew away from the sky, a glowing sunset blazed in the west, the last farewell to a city of magic, beauty and grace, the like of which would never be seen again. And as the light began to dim, a pale, clear new moon became visible, like the clean, sharp blade of a sickle cleaving past and future. The churning waters thundered and crashed against the cliffs of the newly formed coastline: it would take some time to settle, this new-made ocean that separated the north of the continent from the south.

'Who would have believed that such a day as this could end with such a glorious sky?' Iriana murmured. 'At least all the beauty in the world has not died with Tyrineld, and out of all the death and destruction we must somehow forge a future.'

At her side, Corisand stiffened. 'Iriana?' she said in a small, strangled voice.

'Yes?'

'Whose vision are you using?'

'Why, yours of course.'

'I have my eyes closed. Whatever you're seeing, you're doing it on your own.'

Iriana sat up abruptly, and the change of perspective left her giddy. She turned to her friend, stunned and disbelieving. 'I can *see*? Oh, by all Creation – I can see!'

'This is wonderful!' Taine, his face bruised but his eyes brimming with joy, caught her up in an embrace that made her heart beat faster. When he released her Iriana looked around, wide-eyed in awe and amazement, taking in her world for the first time through her own eyes. Even though ruin and tragedy lay before her, even through her grief and bone-deep weariness excitement sang through her mind and body. Her world had suddenly grown so large; had gained so much depth, movement and colour, it seemed that she just couldn't stop looking.

Only the Fialan could have wrought this miracle. Somehow, while she and Corisand had been fused, there had been a sharing – or was it an exchange?

'Corisand, can *you* see?' she asked in sudden alarm.

'Don't worry,' the Windeye said. 'I can see just fine. I don't know what else we shared when we were merged within the Fialan's power.' She turned to Iriana, and for an instant, through the sorrow, the strain and fatigue, her face was brightened by a smile. 'But it's going to be really interesting finding out.' Suddenly she hugged her friend. 'Oh, Iriana, this is wonderful. I'm so happy for you. You can really see!'

'I know, I know – and it's all thanks to you and the Fialan.' Her heart brimming over with an effervescent mix of astonishment and joy, Iriana returned Corisand's hug, then turned the other way to hug Taine. 'It seems a dreadful thing to say, after all the terrible things that have happened today, but this is the most incredible moment of my life.'

Taine tightened his arms around her. 'Despite everything that's happened today, take this moment and treasure it, dearest Iriana. You've deserved it.'

36
~

ΛFTER THE STORM

Because of the waters pouring into the immense fissure that the giant had created, the coastline had altered beyond recognition as the fishing fleet made its way home. Long stretches of seabed lay exposed; acres of high rocks, some as tall as cliffs, clad in barnacles, limpets, and dying anemone, interspersed with long flat stretches of sand, mud or stinking, drying weed. Crustaceans scuttled for cover from the blizzard of feasting seabirds that whirled and screamed above them, and fish flopped and gasped in the shallow pools left behind by the receding waves.

The battered fleet made their way northward, surrounded and propelled by the guardian Leviathan, but the thoughts of their crews were still very much with the devastation they had witnessed in Tyrineld, and the monster that had caused it. The same thought was in everyone's mind:

Will we be next? When that abomination has finished with the Wizards, will it come for us, and for our families?

On the *Venturer*, no one spoke. The shock and terror was all too recent; they could still barely believe that they had escaped the maelstrom, but they were still fleeing for their lives. No one dared voice their thoughts aloud – as if, by speaking of the abomination that they feared, they might somehow attract its attention and bring its wrath down on their heads. Chiannala was still huddled beside Incondor, a creature at bay, her face sheened with a sickly pallor. Lameron, with one arm injured in a fall when the ship had rolled and lurched, was ignoring his injury to tend to the other remaining patient, though his face was contorted with his own pain. As for the rest of Valior's crew, Melisanda was sealing a bleeding gash on Seema's cheekbone, which had been sliced open by a flying splinter from one of the sprung deck planks, while Derwyn, treading carefully to avoid the gaps, tried to clear the tangle of ropes and wreckage from what remained of the decks.

Valior was at the helm, though with the Leviathan steering the boat he really had no need to be there, save to reassure himself that his vessel was still in one piece. He still had one arm around Brynne, who was watching Melisanda at work while her mind, torn and confused by the conflicts between her new life and her old, flicked back and forth between her parents on their farm, all the ambition that had burned within her to attend the Academy and become a Healer, and the new family and profession that she had come to love. They were not even her kind – they were merely mortals – but there was no 'merely' about them in her mind. They had become as much a part of her as the flesh and blood kin she had left behind on the farm.

Suddenly Brynne was jolted out of her thoughts by a great wave of relief that passed through the Leviathan. At the same time Melisanda sagged against the rail, so that Seema had to put out a hand to stop her falling. 'It's over,' she cried. 'They've got him. Iriana and her friend have destroyed the abomination.'

With the news of the monster's defeat, many of the Leviathan turned and sped back towards the former location of Tyrineld, now lost beneath the turbulent, turbid ocean. Wizards would not drown – there still might be survivors who could be rescued. Brynne, her powers newly awakened with the return of her memory, listened to their mindspeech in awe. Apart from the injured winged man on the deck, this was the first time she had encountered any of the other Magefolk.

With Melisanda's words the terrible strain that had gripped the ship dissolved. Suddenly there was a future again, yet the Healer herself did not share the relief of the others. Though the battle had been won, the fight was far from over. Now the survivors must start to rebuild their lives, to mourn their losses and survive through the coming winter, and all the years beyond. The real work was only just beginning – and as Head of the Luen of Healers, she would be right in the thick of things. Suddenly she felt very lonely, isolated out here on the ocean. How she wished that she could be with her friends now! After the battle for the city they might be in dire need of her skills, and she was in desperate need of their support. If only ...

She blinked. Surely she must be dreaming. She had been longing to see Ionor, and for a moment, she was sure she'd heard his voice, a faint echo of mindspeech that had been barely discernible against the background murmur of her thoughts. Wishful thinking, she told herself ruefully – then suddenly she heard him again.

'Mel? Melisanda? Are you there? Are you all right?'

By the side of the ship a Leviathan surfaced, with Ionor riding on its back. Helped by a willing hand from Derwyn, the Wizard scrambled aboard the ship and ran to hug Melisanda, and wipe the tears of joy that flooded her eyes. 'Oh, Ionor, you don't know how happy I am to see you! I've missed you so much. But how did you get here? How did all the Leviathan know to come, just when we needed them?'

Ionor smiled. 'I had the strangest dream a few nights ago. There was a colossal tree, in a forest made of stone and a woman ...' He paused, frowning. 'Mel, I can't describe her, but there was *such* an aura of power around her. She told me in no uncertain terms that Iriana needed me back here in Tyrineld immediately, and all the Leviathan with me, to give me some vital information about the making of our Artefact. Then I woke up and knew, absolutely knew, that it wasn't a dream. There was such a sense of urgency in her message. So I talked to Kahuna, the Leviathan leader – and he'd had the woman in his dream too! I don't have to tell you, we set out as fast as we possibly could.'

His voice grew thick with emotion. 'We arrived in time to see that monstrosity, and the fall of Tyrineld, and then some of the Leviathan spotted your plight, and came to the rescue. But my heart nearly stopped when I saw Iriana battling that thing. I couldn't leave until it was all over, and she had prevailed. She made us all proud today, Mel. She made every one of the Wizardfolk proud.'

The Magefolk of the ocean found a safe haven for the fleet in a newly formed inlet where a steep drop-off in the former seabed had formed a deep, curving bay. Leaving their vessels under the guardianship of the Leviathan, the crews set off on the lengthy tramp back to their homes, with the injured – there were nine in all, spread out among the fishing boats – carried on makeshift stretchers made from ripped-up decking, and attended by the surviving Healers, who had been likewise distributed throughout the fleet. Melisanda and Ionor, however, managed to combine their powers to generate a mind-call that would reach their friends, who even now were heading to Nexis. Some half-hour later, as they were nearing the fishing village of

Independence – the natives of which had suddenly, to their shock and dismay, found themselves dwelling some distance inland – they were astonished to see a group of horses heading towards them – *flying through the air*!

Chathak and Thara had come with the Xandim, for their companions who had taken part in the battle were too exhausted to travel further that day. It took a good while for the terrified fisherfolk to be soothed, and explanations shared all round, by which time everyone was settled in the village's inn, much to the consternation of the innkeeper. Chiannala had been left with Incondor, who was being treated by a reluctant Lameron, but the door of their room was guarded by Wizards who could use their powers to prevent an apport, should the girl contemplate or be able to perform one.

Brynne had returned to the home of her foster family, to be welcomed by a tearful Osella, who, when the sea suddenly retreated, had been convinced that her entire family must have been lost. She was so glad to see them that it took a few moments for the grave faces of the others to register.

Valior took matters into his own hands. 'Osella, it's a long story, but our Brynne got her memory back today. She was a student Wizard on her way to the Academy when another girl – the one upstairs at the inn – tried to murder her and stole her identity.' He turned to Brynne, and put his hands on her shoulders. 'And now it's time for her to go home,' he said softly.

Brynne stared at him in horror. What was he saying? Did he *want* to get rid of her? But he had always been so good to her. He'd made her one of his family and for a time she had belonged here. She'd come to love them all – and one especially. 'Valior, do you *want* me to go?' Her eyes grew wide with dismay and filled with tears.

Suddenly he gathered her into his arms. 'Little mermaid, it'll tear the heart out of me when you go,' he said thickly. 'But you know yourself that you belong with your family, with your people.' He drew back from her and tilted her chin up with one finger, so that she looked into his eyes. 'I know you love us – and I bless you for that – but you had plans, and a future. You were going to the Academy to learn to be a Healer, and I'll wager you'll make a bloody good one. You can't stay here as a deckhand and spend the rest of your life regretting the opportunities you lost. And because I know your good heart, I know how very much you want to see your parents right now. You love us all, and that's why you're torn, but really there's only one direction for you. All I'm doing is making the choice as easy as I can.'

'You say I have a good heart,' Brynne said softly, 'but Valior, your heart is as big as the ocean itself. And I know you're right. I have to go and I want to – but oh, it's hard to leave you all. So right here and now, I'm going to make you a promise. When I'm trained, I'll come back. Fishing holds so many dangers, this community could use a Healer.'

Valior smiled at her. 'Don't bind yourself to such a promise yet, Brynne, for who knows what your future may hold, and you might change your mind, and want a new direction during the years you'll be training. But if you ever want to visit, we'll always welcome you as one of our own, and when your training is done – well, time will tell.'

Brynne nodded her agreement, but inside herself she made a vow. *I will come back, Valior. I'll come back to you – you'll see.*

Though she ached with exhaustion, her heart was leaden with grief for her city and those who had been lost in its fall, and she longed with every fibre of her being for the comfort and company of her friends from whom she had been parted so long, Melisanda, the Luen Head's new mantle sitting heavily on her shoulders, left Ionor catching up on events with Chathak and Thara, and made her way to the inn of the fishing village, which was being used to shelter the injured from the boats.

She knew from Chathak and Thara that more wounded from Tyrineld's fall were being brought to Nexis by the Xandim, and the Healers that Tinagen had sent away from the Luen Hall before the monster had struck were working at full stretch, some in a cluster of tents where they treated lesser hurts, and some in the settlement itself, where kind people had offered shelter to those in most need. She was needed back in Nexis and would be returning soon, but first she had to deal with Incondor and Chiannala.

Melisanda knew that Lameron had already given the dread tidings to Incondor that the apport had destroyed the last small chance of ever mending his wings, and that he would be forever flightless. Much as she disliked him, her heart bled for his plight, and for the way he must be feeling at present. If there was any way she could help ease him through this painful time, then of course she would do it. As for the girl who had apparently taken Brynne's identity – the Luen Head wanted very much to get to the bottom of that mystery.

It was not her place to punish the girl – her crimes were so grave that only the Archwizard could deal with them – but Melisanda was determined to find out who she was, where she had come from, and why she had done such a terrible thing.

A blast of heat from the blaze in the inn's fireplace met her as she entered. The low-beamed common room was seething, with every space at the tables taken, and people standing crammed into the spaces between. The couple who owned the inn seemed to be everywhere at once, sliding with practised ease between the crowded bodies as they served drinks, collected empty glasses or carried plates of grilled fish and warm bread, or bowls of soup that tilted at perilous angles but never quite seemed to spill. Everyone was talking at the tops of their voices about the destruction of Tyrineld and the fleet's narrow escape; in this closely packed space the din was tremendous.

Over the heads of the throng, Melisanda saw Lameron on the stairs, gesturing urgently to her. From the glowering expression on his pale, strained face and the dark glint of anger in his eyes, she didn't need mindspeech to tell her something had gone seriously wrong. Determinedly she pushed her way towards him, thanking providence that people made a deferential space for her when they noticed the robes of a high-ranking Healer.

Lameron had turned back, and she caught up with him at the top of the stairs. 'I'm sorry, Melisanda,' he said wretchedly. 'I just couldn't stop him.'

'Stop who doing what?' But Melisanda's sinking heart was already one step ahead of her exhausted brain, and when her assistant opened a door into a room that looked as though a hurricane had passed through, she knew her instincts had been right.

'Incondor.' Lameron closed the door behind them and rubbed his hands across eyes that were bloodshot with tiredness. 'When I broke the news about his wings he went plain crazy, shouting and screaming, and piling curses on all Wizards. He was flailing about, striking out with blast after blast of his Air magic, and I couldn't get close enough to stop him. As you can see he's wrecked his bedchamber – I don't know what we're going to say to the landlord. Then he called in mindspeech for his bearers, who turned up so quickly that I reckon he must have had something up his sleeve all along. They brought Crombec's porters with them too, who were plainly unhappy, but too scared of Incondor to say anything.'

Lameron paused for breath. 'The long and the short of it is, they blasted a hole in the wall with their Air magic to enlarge the window – I can't imagine why the people didn't hear all the commotion downstairs—'

'Because they're making too much noise of their own,' Melisanda said. 'It's deafening down there. And Incondor's room is at the back of the inn, so there's a good chance that no one saw them in the dusk.'

'That must have been it. Anyway, they wrapped him up and pulled him into one of those nets and took off into the night – and what's worse, that bloody girl went with them.'

'Why in perdition didn't you mindspeak me when it happened?'

'I tried,' Lameron protested, 'but we were both so tired and there were so many others who needed your attention at the same time that I couldn't make you hear me. It wasn't your fault – I know you were trying to reach your Healers in Nexis.'

With an acrid curse, Melisanda sat down on the clothes chest – the only unbroken item of furniture in the room – and dropped her face into her hands. Then all at once, her shoulders straightened. 'Do you know something, Lameron? After everything that's happened today, I just can't bring myself to care about Incondor. If the idiot wants to leave, then that's his mistake. In truth, he's done us a favour. We have better uses for our limited time and facilities than to waste them on that ungrateful, arrogant pig.'

A fleeting frown crossed her forehead. 'I really did want to get my hands on that girl, though. I wouldn't be at all surprised if she put him up to this, to get herself out of trouble. He would have been very vulnerable to manipulation just then, having just received the most shattering news of his life. Still, at least we've found the real Brynne, and that's a comfort.' She smiled wanly. 'On first impressions, she seems much nicer than the imposter too. She's packing now – I've just been talking to her. Though she's longing to see her parents again, it's breaking her heart to leave these mortals who've been so kind to her.'

Melisanda got to her feet. 'Right now we have far more important things to do than worry about either girl – the nice one or the nasty. I'll try to get a couple of Wizards from the Luen of Artisans over here from Nexis, to get this room patched for the landlord.' She looked around at the splintered furniture, the shredded curtains and bedding, and the gaping hole in the wooden wall where the window had been. 'What a mess – and what a waste when everything is in such short supply. Really, I could strangle that Incondor.'

'But under the circumstances I pity him too,' Lameron said. 'What a dreadful thing for him, to be denied the skies for ever.'

'A lot of people were denied their lives today,' Melisanda said sharply. 'I'm saving my pity for them.'

Chiannala had pity for no one but herself. Her life had reached its lowest ebb. Her mind was in turmoil as she huddled by Incondor's side in a swaying net borne by eight struggling Skyfolk bearers. She was worn out from keeping the winged man's pain under control single-handed, her hopes and dreams were in pieces, and her future uncertain. Despite the furs in which she was wrapped, she was shivering with cold, and her jaws and ears ached from the rush of the icy wind.

The massive rift that the crazed giant had opened in the earth was now filled with mile upon mile of dark turbid ocean that heaved and swirled with colossal waves, splitting the continent in half, and she only prayed that the bearers would make it across before their strength gave out. The cataclysmic shattering of the land had also produced wild weather – with savage gusts of wind, rain and hail, and pockets of turbulent air that taxed the bearers' endurance to the utmost, so that Chiannala could feel their terror beating on her, filling her mind with dreadful images of plunging downward, out of control, and drowning beneath those huge and ravening waves.

Incondor stirred and moaned fretfully, and Chiannala, who'd been far too preoccupied with her own plight to have any patience with his wretchedness, was surprised to feel a sudden stab of remorse and a rush of pity. She was not the only one who had lost everything.

'I'm sorry.' She stroked his brow and, exhausted though she was, strengthened their mental link to still his pain. At least she'd learned that much at the Academy, she thought bitterly. Yet she knew that, in helping the Healers care for Incondor, she had absorbed some far more advanced techniques than her fellow students, even when the Wizards involved had not consciously been teaching her. She had learned how to still pain, bring down a fever, stop bleeding, seal wounds, knit torn muscle and broken bones, and stimulate the growth of healthy tissue. Furthermore, she was certain that, with some trial and error, she could learn to extrapolate and adapt the techniques she had learned to other areas of her Wizardly powers. Maybe all was not lost, despite this setback. Why, if any of the Aerillians could be prevailed upon to teach her their arts, as they had done with Yinze . . .

At this point Chiannala's hopeful thoughts ran into a wall. What would it be like in Aerillia? Would she fit in? Would she even be accepted? What if Queen Pandion, wishing to remain on cordial terms with the Wizards, decided to send her straight back to Nexis?

'She won't.' Incondor's mindspeech was faint as a whisper. 'She'll feel so sorry for me, crippled as I am, that she won't deny me your healing abilities and the comfort of your company. I'll tell her I need you to take care of me.'

'And I *will* take care of you,' Chiannala promised.

Too bloody right, she would! He was her only hope for the future. And if she could get through this night, and the difficult days that would follow, who knew what fate might bring? One day she might still be able to bring her vengeance down upon the Wizards, and make them sorry for rejecting her because she was born a half-blood.

37
~

LOOKING TO THE FUTURE

The frontier settlement of Nexis did its best to shelter the survivors from Tyrineld. Many were lucky to be alive. Without the Xandim, the small handful of visiting Winged Folk, the mortal fisherfolk and the Leviathan, many more Wizards would have died in the disaster. The Windeye had called her people together and used the Phaerie flying spell once more. Some of the Xandim had ferried Wizards to Nexis with the news, to find them already preparing for disaster, since the backlash of so many Wizard deaths had travelled all that distance.

The injured Tyrineldians had been left behind in the settlement, and the Xandim had returned with Nexian helpers carrying ropes, nets, blankets and medical supplies. All the next day the Xandim, each of them carrying a Wizard, had flown back and forth over the heaving, debris-littered stretch of sea where Tyrineld had once stood, searching for survivors, along with the Leviathan, who were strong enough to withstand the turbulence beneath the surface.

By nightfall, the rescue attempts had finally been abandoned, and the exhausted Xandim flew into Nexis to find the rescued Wizards huddled in small, shocked, shattered groups around massive bonfires that had been kindled outside the town, where a village of tents and temporary shelters had been erected to house the refugees who could not be accommodated in the Nexians' homes. Luckily, Sharalind had been in the process of setting up advance supply caches for her army in Nexis, so tents, blankets, clothing, food and weapons were all available.

While others had been seeing to the rescue and well-being of the Tyrineldian survivors, Avithan, unopposed in his assumption of the rank of Archwizard – even most of the natives of Nexis accepted him as such, perhaps out of respect for his parents, or because of the grim, obsessive mood that had overtaken him since the loss of his family and home – had been giving thought to the future. While his heart was still reeling with shock and grief, and barely able to take in the magnitude of the catastrophe that had befallen his city and his people, his training as the son of the Archwizard took over, submerging his emotions beneath the need to act; using the necessity to secure a future for the surviving Tyrineldians as a shield against the anguish that threatened to overwhelm him.

He spent the hours after his arrival in Nexis meeting with the most wealthy and established traders and merchants in the settlement, with a proposal to make Nexis the new capital of the Wizard realm. All but a handful, who were easily outvoted, had welcomed his plans with open arms, foreseeing all the possibilities that would suddenly become available for expansion, and the amassment of far greater wealth. Their informal cartel constituted the closest thing to a ruling council within the settlement, and they were more than willing to become co-founders of the new regime.

While the able-bodied Wizards scurried to organise supplies and sleeping places, and settle the refugees into their encampment, most of the Xandim found it easier and more comfortable to remain in equine form as grazing was available, whereas human food was at a premium. Corisand made sure that they were settled comfortably, a short way upriver from the settlement where a cluster of scrub willows grew along the waterside and provided a nominal windbreak and shelter. Aelwen and a bruised and battered Kelon were more than happy to perform their traditional tasks of rubbing down cold and weary muscles, and finding their charges comfortable places in which to rest. Following yesterday's glorious sunset, the weather had deteriorated to cloudy and damp, with a raw chill in the air. Nightfall had been hastened by the heavy sky, and swirling wisps of ground mist threaded between the furze bushes and clumps of stunted trees that lined the river. The scent of autumn and the smoke from the encampment fires drifted in the air, along with the clamour of the settlement, muted by distance.

'Almost like old times, isn't it?' Aelwen said.

'Almost – except it's strange to think that these aren't animals but people that we're caring for.'

'It took me a while to get used to the idea too,' Aelwen admitted. 'I thought they would hate me but I couldn't have been more wrong. They were appreciative and grateful for the care we showed them, Kelon. Just as they're appreciative of what we're doing for them now.'

Suddenly Kelon turned to her and, though still keeping her at arm's length, put his hands on her shoulders and looked into her eyes. 'I'm appreciative of what you did for me yesterday, Aelwen. So far as I know, I was the only one of Sharalind's mortal forces who escaped. Had it not been for you, I would have perished just like Danel and all the rest.'

'I would never have left you there to die – never.' Aelwen took a deep breath. 'Kelon, I'm sorry for everything. I'm sorry I always took you for granted. I deeply regret that I always ignored your feelings for me because I thought I was in love with a memory from my past. I'm—'

'Just a minute,' Kelon interrupted. 'Did you say you *thought* you were in love?'

Alwen pulled away from him and began to pace. 'When Taine returned I was overjoyed. I couldn't believe we'd been reunited after so long. And it was wonderful at first. But as we began to travel together, I soon began to realise how much he had altered; become harder and more pragmatic. All those long years of living on his wits had left him changed, and while at heart he was still a kind man and a good one, he could kill, if need be, without the slightest compunction.'

She stopped pacing, and sat down on a tree trunk that had been washed up onto the riverbank by last winter's floods. 'He just wasn't the romantic, idealistic youth I'd fallen in love with, and made future plans with – and Kelon, once I was exiled from Eliorand, I found that I had changed too. My priorities were different, I enjoyed stability and security. My life had been completely uprooted, but I wanted somewhere new and safe to transplant myself. I liked my work, and my everyday routines. I could never be a wanderer – and in Taine I saw an adventurer who would never be content with the kind of life I craved. It was nobody's fault. We were torn apart and plunged into very different circumstances. We both grew up, and grew apart.'

Kelon came over and sat beside her. 'And does Taine know all this? Have you spoken to him?'

'Not yet – but he knows.' Aelwen dropped her face into her hands. 'In his heart he knows as well as I do that we no longer belong together.' She looked up at Kelon and smiled. 'I don't think he's realised that his heart lies elsewhere, but it's only a matter of time. The two of them are more than halfway in love already – they just haven't quite worked it out yet.'

'Which two?' Bless him, Kelon sounded indignant that Taine might prefer another over herself.

'Never mind.' Aelwen smiled. 'Someone kind, and lovely, and as brave as he is. I hope it works out for them. They both deserve to be happy.'

'And you?' Kelon asked quietly. 'Where does your heart lie now?'

Aelwen reached out and took his hand. 'Where it has lain for many years – but I was so wrapped up in Taine's memory that I never saw it. Can you forgive me, Kelon?'

The expression on Kelon's face was like the sunrise. 'If you'll forgive me for being such an ass and running off with those mortals, we'll call it quits.'

They were in a strange land; they were tired, hurt and homeless and the future was uncertain, but as they embraced in the midst of the Xandim they had loved and tended for so long, Aelwen thought that she and Kelon had never been happier.

Unheard, unseen, Iriana slid back into the shadows among the willows. She hadn't meant to overhear the conversation between Aelwen and Kelon – she'd come to the area where the Xandim were settling down for the night to look for Corisand, but plainly the Windeye was elsewhere.

As she backtracked towards the refugee camp, she replayed what she had overheard with mounting ire and indignation. Poor Taine! After everything he had been through, to be so callously abandoned by someone he had loved for so long. It wasn't right. It wasn't fair. How could Aelwen just cast off such a fine, brave, kind and handsome—

The Wizard stopped dead, her hand pressed to her open mouth. When had her feelings for Taine become so strong? How could she have been so unaware of the secret her heart had been keeping?

Don't be ridiculous. He calls you little sister. That's how he sees you. He's fond of you, it's true, but no more than that.

It was a relief to feel her common sense take over – even though it cost her a pang of unhappiness that showed every sign of increasing over time. She should forget this nonsense – but how could she? It was in her head now. Aelwen herself had put it there:

'I don't think he's realised that his heart lies elsewhere, but it's only a matter of time. The two of them are more than halfway in love already – they just haven't worked it out yet.'

Could the Horsemistress have meant Iriana? Taine was already fond of her. With Aelwen out of the picture, maybe ...

'Iriana! There you are. I've been looking all over for you.'

Avithan. Hearing the accusatory edge to his voice, she felt her guts churn with anger.

He had a nerve.

She turned to face him, glowering. 'What do you want?'

'It's true, you *can* see. I heard the rumours, but ... I'm so pleased for you, Iriana.'

It rang false. Oh, he was smiling, but the expression was plastered on his face, like a mask. She looked into his eyes, and suddenly she could comprehend, all too clearly, his thoughts. He didn't want her independent, free, and out of his control. All the years he'd been there, helping her at every turn, even when she didn't want or need it, always ready to reach out a hand in case she stumbled or strayed – and it had all just been a way of controlling her.

And the worst of it was, he probably didn't even realise what he was doing. He had persuaded himself that she needed him and couldn't manage without him. Indeed, he'd almost had Iriana convinced until Athina had taken him out of the mundane world, and she'd discovered just how well she could do without him.

Don't be hard on him. He just lost his mother; so close to the death of his father.

That was her soft heart speaking. Iriana the Nurturer, she thought, with a touch of self-mockery. It didn't change a thing.

Yesterday he had betrayed her. Yesterday he could have killed her.

'Iriana? Why don't you answer me? I was worried about you.'

'Were you?' Her tones were glacial, her fists clenched at her sides. 'And were you worried when you ambushed me with a sleep spell right in the middle of the battle, and very nearly killed us all?'

The false smile dropped from Avithan's face. 'I was protecting you.'

'Is that what you call it?' Iriana snapped. 'Well, you don't have to *protect* me any longer, Avithan. I'm sorry, so sorry about what happened to your mother, but it doesn't alter the fact that you attacked me, as a Wizard and as a person.'

'*Attacked* you? I was trying to save your life, you stupid girl.'

Iriana took a deep breath, forcing down the anger. '*Girl?* I'm no girl, and haven't been for some time. I'm a woman and a warrior, and it's time you accepted that. Only I could defeat the Moldan, along with Corisand, and that's what I did – no thanks to you.'

'And I suppose you'll be throwing that in my face for the rest of our lives together?'

'We don't have any lives together, and if—'

Her words were cut short as Avithan grabbed her by the arm. 'I say we *will* be together. I'm the Archwizard now, and you'll do as I tell you, or—'

Even as Iriana lifted her hand to strike him down with a spell, a voice interrupted.

'Is everything all right here?' Taine stepped out of the shadows, with an expression on his face as cold and dangerous as the sword that he had drawn.

While Avithan was distracted Iriana made a small fireball, and hit him on the hand. With a cry of pain he leapt back, letting go of her, and Taine stepped up beside her. 'I don't think Iriana wants your company right now.'

Avithan's look was pure venom. 'And you have no place here, you half-breed with your filthy Phaerie blood.'

'Avithan!' Iriana protested.

'His foul kind killed my father.'

'Your father welcomed me,' Taine said. 'For years I risked my life as his eyes and ears among the Phaerie.'

'That's the only reason I'm letting you stay,' Avithan snarled, 'but not for ever. I want you gone from here. You may have Wizard blood but you'll never be one of us.'

Taine shrugged, but Iriana could see a tightening around his eyes that betrayed his pain. 'It makes no difference to me. Do you think I'd want to be anywhere near you, after what you did? I've talked to Corisand, and I'm going with the Xandim when they leave. They need someone with woodcraft and survival skills to teach them how to live in their human forms.'

Feeling her heart lift, Iriana turned to him. 'You're going too?'

'What do you mean by that?' Avithan demanded.

'I'm also going to the Wyndveil with Corisand and the rest of the

Xandim,' she said. 'Corisand is my friend. We've been through so much together, I don't want to be parted from her just yet. I want to see the story of the Xandim through. They'll need a lot of help to settle into their new home, and adapt to their human forms, and ...'

'And your own people won't need help? When did you plan to tell *me* about this?' Avithan's voice was cold and hard as stone.

'When I was ready,' Iriana replied icily. 'After you attacked me, you forfeited the right to any say in my comings and goings.'

She fought to control her temper. 'We won't be leaving right away. Corisand and I talked it over with the Xandim, and they decided to stay here over the winter if you want them, to help the Wizard refugees get back on their feet, and then leave for the Wyndveil in the spring. When they do, I'm going with them. I'm sorry, but my mind is made up. I'm going with Corisand.'

'Well, if you leave you can stay away – for ever,' Avithan snarled.

Iriana felt the blood drain away from her face. Never to come here again? To her friends, to Zybina and Yinze?

'You would do *that* to her?' Taine almost spat out the words.

Avithan folded his arms. 'It's her choice.'

'It certainly is my choice, and I won't be blackmailed,' Iriana told him. 'If you want to keep me exiled, it's your loss.' With that she turned and walked away without a backward look.

'A word of advice: under the present circumstances, you'll find it's not a good idea to be making any more enemies.' With that, Taine pushed his way past Avithan, who stormed off towards the encampment, and followed Iriana along the riverside.

When he caught up with her, Iriana's anger was already abating. She sighed. 'I hate to quarrel with Avithan like this. He's been a friend all my life, and he's lost so many people that he loved and cared about. But I'm not ready to forgive him for what he did to me – and he's not ready to give up his controlling ways. I think we need some time apart so that maybe, in the future, we can be friends again.'

'Just friends?' Taine lifted an eyebrow.

'That's the way I feel, though I know he feels differently. Before he was wounded and we were separated he kissed me for the first time – but while we were apart I realised how much time I'd spent fighting his constant attempts to keep me safe, and how much he had undermined my confidence in myself. I suppose I outgrew ...'

As the words struck a chord in her memory she looked at Taine, suddenly struck by an uneasy thought. 'How long were *you* lurking in the willows?' she asked him.

He smiled at her ruefully. 'Long enough. I came down to look for you, as a matter of fact, but before I found you I heard what Aelwen said.'

'Taine, I'm so sorry.' The Wizard put a hand on his arm; all she could offer in the way of comfort. 'What a horrible way to find out.'

'One way's just as good – or bad – as any other.' He shrugged. 'It all amounts to the same in the end. Besides, it came as no surprise. There's been a distance widening between us ever since we were reunited. We did our best, but Aelwen's right – we grew up, we grew apart, and we changed. I'm sad and sorry, but it's the love we had long ago that I'm regretting, not the feelings we have now.'

He put a companionable arm around her shoulders. 'Maybe it's all for the best. Some things are just meant to be. I'll talk to Aelwen about it later. Unlike some people, I can let her go without making an ass of myself.' He smiled at Iriana and took her hand. 'Come on, little sister. We need to get back to the camp and talk to Corisand and the others. We have lots to do, and we won't be the only ones making plans for the future.'

It took Iriana only a heartbeat or two to make up her mind. She had defeated the Lord of the Phaerie and a mad giant from the Elsewhere – surely she had enough courage for what she needed to do now. Instead of moving with Taine she remained still, so that their linked hands pulled him back to her. Iriana looked searchingly into his eyes. 'Somehow,' she said softly, 'I don't feel like a little sister any more.'

Taine smiled. 'Somehow, you don't feel like one to me, either.' He lowered his lips to hers and kissed her.

They might not have moved from where they were all night, if Corisand had not come to find them. Tactfully she waited for them to break from their embrace – and waited, and waited. After a few moments, seeing that they showed no signs of coming up for air anytime soon, she cleared her throat and spoke. 'Well! I wondered how long it was going to take the two of you to work it out.'

Their heads came up like two startled deer, and Corisand laughed. 'I'm so happy for you both.' She ran to hug them, first one then the other. 'I hate to interrupt you, but unfortunately Avithan has called a meeting back at the camp, and he wants everyone to attend.'

*

The summons to the meeting was going out quickly, passing in mindspeech from one Wizard to another, from the encampment into the settlement. The new Archwizard wanted to address his people. Most of the Nexians, bundled up in cloaks and coats of warm wool or fur against the cold, dank night, came out to join the newcomers, for they were anxious to hear what he had to say. All evening, rumours had been flying back and forth that Avithan now planned to make Nexis the major city of the Wizardfolk, and that the independent, libertarian aspects of the settlement were about to vanish for ever. Though many were angry and resentful at having their home usurped, there were also the greedy majority, who saw nothing but opportunities and potential in such a move. Meanwhile those Nexians who had loved the little town because of its remote position on the frontier, far away from the city, and revelled in its rough and ready ways, muttered and cursed quietly as they saw with dismay the claws of so-called civilisation reaching out to snatch at them. Some were already packing, others planning to leave in the spring. Now that the Phaerie had gone there would be plenty of space in the northern wildwoods where folk could build log cabins and be free to live as they pleased, at one with the wilderness.

One by one or in small groups, the refugees came to the campfire; hurt and bereft, grieving, shocked and bewildered. The Nexians had done their best, lending out all the old clothing and blankets, furs and skins that they could spare, but the Tyrineldians huddled together, as much for warmth as for mutual support.

Iriana and Taine stood hand in hand in a group of friends: Corisand, with Taryn, Rosina, and several other Xandim clad in a ragtag medley of borrowed clothing; Yinze, who had Kea and Crombec beside him; Ionor, Chathak, Thara and Melisanda, who had just returned from Independence, with Aelwen and Kelon standing close by. Avithan, grim-faced, walked out in front of the bonfire and began to address the assembled crowd.

'My fellow Tyrineldians and the good citizens of Nexis, yesterday was a day that will forever be recalled in the annals of infamy and tragedy. At this time we survivors of the fall of Tyrineld are all shocked and grieving too much to consider how we will carry on through the days to come, and with the tragic loss of my beloved parents—' His voice thickened, but he brushed a hand across his eyes and squared his shoulders, making a visible effort to keep his grief under control. 'With the loss of my parents, Cyran and Sharalind, the burden of Archwizard, for the time being at least, has fallen upon my shoulders. First and foremost, I must thank the Nexians who have made us welcome and given us this so desperately needed refuge. I would also like to pass on our utmost gratitude to the non-Wizards who have aided us today: the Winged Folk, the Leviathan, the newly rediscovered race of the Xandim, and even the humble mortal fisherfolk. Any who wish to return to their homes will go with our thanks for what they have already done, and such help as we can spare them. Any who wish to stay with us and share our hardships are welcome to remain, if they will continue to help us rebuild our city and our lives. I have been conferring with the respected merchant leaders of the settlement—'

At this a wave of jeers, boos and catcalls drowned him out for a moment, but he raised his voice above the outcry of the objectors. 'I have decided that Nexis will become the new capital city of the Wizards' realm. There will be no more Tyrineldians and Nexians: we will all be as one. We will build new homes here, new workshops for our crafters, a new Academy and new marketplaces for our merchants. We will mourn our lost loved ones, then we will set to work to make this place a fitting monument to their memory, and we will see the Wizard race flourish and thrive once more.' This time he was drowned out by applause and cheering. In this dark hour his people desperately needed hope – any hope – to cling to, and his words had provided them with exactly the optimism and moral support they needed.

As Avithan walked away between the tents, Iriana, despite their differences, felt proud of him. The old Avithan she had known and loved was still there – and in that moment she realised that he would go on to be a great Wizard and a fine leader.

About an hour later, Iriana and her own Wizard family – Ionor, Chathak, Yinze, Melisanda and Thara – were sitting round a smaller fire of their own, sipping thin soup, together with Corisand, Taryn, Rosina, Taine, Aelwen, Kelon, Kea and Crombec. Though they were all exhausted, they needed this time together, drawing comfort from their bonds of friendship, for their relief and gratitude at being alive and reunited was tempered by anxiety and sorrow. Zybina, Yinze's mother and Iriana's foster mother, had been among those who'd been rescued, and was resting in a house in the settlement as comfortably as could be expected with concussion and a broken arm, but all of them had lost other friends that day, and Chathak and Kea were both mourning the death of Atka.

Chathak, his blond hair flopping over his forehead and glinting in the firelight, cradled the Dragon's egg on his lap as he sat with the others. Iriana and Corisand had combined their powers to enshroud it in a blanket of warm air that would retain its temperature and stay in place no matter how much the egg was moved, and Kea and Crombec were planning to help him return it to the Dragonfolk at Dhiammara.

'Though I don't know how we'll make it without our bearers,' Kea was saying. 'I can't believe that Incondor used his authority to call them away from the rescue work to take him and that girl back to Aerillia.'

Melisanda's mouth tightened at the mention of Chiannala. She had already told the others about finding the real Brynne, who had been taken by the Xandim back to her home, to be reunited with her parents until some provision could be made for training the student Wizards now that the Academy was no more.

'Talking of Healing – in a roundabout way – is there nothing you can do for Avithan?' Yinze interrupted. 'He's shocked and grieving and he's bearing so many burdens just now, yet when I tried to talk to him a little while ago, he just brushed me off; said he didn't have time.'

'He did the same thing to me and Chathak,' Ionor said.

'And to me,' Thara added.

'I had a fight with him,' Iriana told them. 'That couldn't have helped.'

'That fight wasn't your fault, it was his,' Taine said firmly.

'It was, really. I just couldn't get over my anger at the way he ambushed me while I was fighting the Moldan. Of all the stupid, dangerous, irresponsible things to do—'

'And you're still just as angry,' Melisanda interrupted. 'Iriana, you have a right to be. No matter how unhappy Avithan is right now, that doesn't change the fact that he behaved so badly to you. You're both going to need to put some time and space between you before you can become friends again – but hopefully, one day you will.'

'Well, that makes me feel better, but what about Avithan? No matter how angry I am with him, I hate to see him suffering like this. Can't you help him, Mel?'

The Healer sighed, and rubbed a hand across her face. 'I tried when I came back, but he wouldn't listen. He kept saying that he was too busy to talk; that he had too much to do, that the Wizardfolk are his responsibility now – though I wonder at the motives he won't admit to himself. Most of his closest friends now have other friendships with outlanders. I know it's not fair, and without the Xandim, the Skyfolk and the Leviathan, not to mention our Hemifae friends, we would have been lost indeed today. But with his family gone, Avithan feels that he needs us more than he ever has before.'

'And there was nothing you could say to change—' Yinze said – and cut himself off abruptly. 'I'm sorry, Mel. I know what you've been through. I can't imagine how weary you must be.'

'Not as weary as Iriana and Corisand,' the Healer pointed out. 'They gave their all for us, and with little thanks for it. Yet without them none of the Wizardfolk might have survived.' She smiled at her old friend. 'Iriana, you deserve your new gift of sight. I can't explain it and I don't understand it, but I'm so happy for you that I don't care.'

'We think we can explain it, Corisand and I,' Iriana replied, as she nursed Melik on her lap. It was wonderful to look down and see the cat with her own vision, instead of using his eyesight for herself – not to mention the great black dog Bear, who lay protectively at her side, along with the white cub, Yinze's gift to her. By this time, thanks to hours of loving care from Thara and Melisanda, it was out of danger, weaned onto milk and finely chopped meat, and growing fast. Iriana was delighted with it. Yinze couldn't have brought her a more perfect gift, and looking at the size of its paws, it was going to grow up to be absolutely enormous … And her mind was wandering. With an effort, she forced herself to concentrate on what she'd been saying.

'We think that we linked so closely with each other through the Fialan that we almost became one being for a time. I believe I might have more than Corisand's vision when we come to examine the phenomenon closely. I may have picked up some of her powers too, and she might share some of mine.'

'Only time will tell,' Corisand added, smiling at her friend. 'Where the Fialan is concerned, anything is possible.'

'Ah, the Stone of Fate,' Ionor said in wonder. 'I can't believe the adventures you two must have had. And to actually be befriended by one of the Creators – not to mention that she gave you a message for me, of all people.'

'You have a close tie with me, and also with the Cauldron that the

Leviathan are trying to build,' Iriana explained. 'Athina saw the link, and used it to pass the message on to you.'

'It was just as well she did,' Ionor replied. 'She came to me in a vision, and it meant that we set out south without delay, so that I could talk to you. If it hadn't been for that, and if I hadn't been in such a hurry, we'd never have made it back here in time to help.'

'What about Aldyth?' Melisanda asked. 'I'm surprised he didn't come back with you.'

Ionor smiled. 'The old man is utterly content where he is, delving into the lore and history of the Leviathan. It's a good thing we have that spell to survive indefinitely in the depths, because I don't think he plans to come back any time soon – in fact, he's helping them with the Cauldron too.'

'And are you going back?'

Hearing the strain in Melisanda's voice as she fought to hide her sadness, Ionor took her hand. 'I'm sorry, Mel, but I must. I hate to leave you again to face all the burdens that will be put on you as the Tyrineldians try to build a new life – but I'm needed by the Seafolk. It was you I had in mind, when I first suggested to them we might try to make an artefact that would heal, instead of harm. I was in this with them from the very start. We had reached an impasse with our work, but now that the Creator has given me a clue—' He looked warily at Iriana, tacitly imploring her not to tell Melisanda what Athina had said. 'I feel I have to go back and help them. Please forgive me, Mel. It won't be for ever. Or better still, why don't you come with me? Or go with Iriana, or one of the others.'

'Are you *all* going, then?' Melisanda was wide-eyed with dismay.

'Well, I am,' Chathak said. 'I was so obsessed with Esmon's death that I neglected poor Atka. Without you, Kea, she would have felt very lonely and isolated in Tyrineld. I'm committed to returning her child, at least, but I'd like to stay on in Dhiammara, if they'll let me, and be part of their quest to create their artefact.'

'And I'm going back to Aerillia with Kea and Crombec, to work on the Skyfolk artefact, the Harp,' Yinze said firmly. 'I'm sorry, Melisanda, to leave you with this mess on your hands, but—'

'Nothing to forgive,' Melisanda said lightly, though Iriana saw her straighten her shoulders as if to take on an extra load. 'We all have our duties now. Our world has been torn apart, and we must do what we can to piece it back together.'

'Yinze, is it wise to go back to Aerillia?' Thara asked. 'If that swine

Incondor has gone back home, then surely all the trouble between you will begin again. I thought that was what Queen Pandion wanted to avoid.'

'I'm hoping Incondor has learned his lesson, and he'll stay out of Yinze's way this time,' Crombec said. 'If not, then we will deal with him. Last time, we had no idea what was happening, because Yinze was so close-mouthed about the whole business. Cyran, may he rest in peace, wanted to avoid any controversy. But this time the Queen is already aware of the situation, and no such restrictions will apply. We should be able to avoid trouble – if I didn't believe that, I would not take Yinze back. But with all the will in the world, we cannot stay here. We need the facilities a city can provide to make our Harp, and it ought to be Aerillia. This is, after all, the Skyfolk Artefact.'

'Besides.' Yinze glanced across at his foster sister. 'I want to be within visiting distance of Iriana.'

'Because I'm going with Corisand and the Xandim to help them settle into their new lands on the Wyndveil,' Iriana finished for him. 'But I've been talking to Corisand, and she and I, not to mention the rest of the Xandim, have decided not to go until spring, if we're needed here to help the Tyrineldians get back on their feet. With the flying spell, there are a hundred and one ways that we could help build a proper settlement for the refugees, and make a start on the wonderful city of Avithan's dreams.'

'Then I won't leave until spring either,' Yinze said. 'I'm sorry for the delay, Kea and Crombec, but right now my mother needs me, and so does Avithan. I want to be here for both of them. And we've all been apart for so long' – he gestured at the other Wizards around the fire – 'that I want to spend some time with all of you, too.'

'If it's so important to you, of course we can wait.' Kea turned to her mentor. 'Can't we?'

'It seems I've been outvoted,' Crombec said. 'Very well, Yinze, if this is what you need to do, we can at least begin our work here, and return to Aerillia in the spring to complete it. Besides,' he added wryly, 'it will give Queen Pandion time to send back our bearers that Incondor stole.'

'If Iriana and Corisand, not to mention you, Mel, will help me take care of Atka's child – before and after the egg hatches, then I would like to stay and do my bit too,' Chathak said. 'Everything here reminds me of Esmon, and I wanted to use the egg as an excuse to escape, but I'm not the only one grieving. Hearing you talk, I'd rather share my grief with all of you, especially Avithan. Maybe we can help each other.'

'I was longing to return to the ocean,' Ionor said. 'I think that for the rest of my life I'll be torn between my friends on land and those in the sea. But for now the sea, and the Leviathan, can wait. If Avithan needs our help to build his dream, then I'm quite happy to postpone my own dreams for a while, to help him out.'

'I didn't know whether to stay here, where I would be needed to try to get some emergency foodstuffs growing, or go with Iriana to help the Xandim learn how to cultivate their crops,' Thara said. 'After what they've done for us today, they deserve all the help we can give them, and I wanted to be part of that.' She grinned. 'Now I'll have a chance to do both, and spend the winter with my best friends in the world.'

Avithan had been standing in the shadows, no longer sure of his welcome among these people who, before they'd all been parted, had been his best and closest friends. He had listened with growing bitterness to the beginning of the conversation, when they had all been planning to desert him to pursue their own concerns – then suddenly Iriana had turned everything around, and everyone was agreeing to stay for the winter, to help and support him. All at once he realised that, no matter how long they were separated, or how badly they quarrelled, deep in all their hearts, when they needed one another, they would always be bound together in friendship.

Taking a deep breath, he stepped out of the darkness into the warm, bright circle of firelight, and held out his hands. 'Thank you,' he said simply. 'Thank you.' Then his eyes went to Iriana. 'I'm sorry. What I said before – I didn't mean it. I owe you; all the Tyrineldians owe you a debt that we can never repay. You and Corisand should be honoured in song and story for ever after, Iriana – and no matter what happens in the future, this will always be your home.'

38

~

HOMECOMING

Over the winter, the tents and temporary shelters were gradually replaced by roughly constructed log houses, and both the Xandim and the Wizards of Tyrineld learned new skills by the day: construction and carpentry; hunting with bow and snare; skinning and butchery. Those who already possessed skills such as pottery, blacksmithing, spinning and weaving found themselves in great demand to teach their crafts to others. The remnants of the Luen of Nurturers had been forcing grain and root crops to grow unnaturally fast in the areas of forest from which the timber had been cleared for building materials, and though the results were not as good as nature would have provided in season, at least the food supplies were increased.

Work helped the refugees come to terms with their grief, but to look at any of them was to see the haunting shadows of horror and pain within their eyes. Nevertheless, most of them made a gallant effort to rebuild their lives, though some died from their injuries or insupportable loss. Gradually the differences between Nexians and Tyrineldians were diminishing, and Avithan, who worked himself into a state of exhaustion trying to be everywhere and do everything at once, could finally see the beginnings of the community that Nexis would one day become. For the future, he had grandiose plans: he wanted to take the island where the river divided in the middle of the town and construct a massive eminence where he would one day build the new Academy. For now, however, that was still a dream.

The fisherfolk were also building a new settlement, further west of Independence, where an indentation in the newly formed coastline made a natural harbour. They traded timber with the Nexians for the fish they caught, and the new community of Norberth was slowly taking shape. To everyone's surprise, Aelwen and Kelon had gone to live with the fishing community, and had been made welcome. Taryn and Alil had taken them back to Athina's tower to pick up the Wizard mounts and packhorse that had been left there in safety. Esmon's warhorse was a stallion, and though Avithan's mount had been a gelding, the packhorse had been a mare. Iriana had also given them Dailika, who would never be fit to ride again, but could be used for breeding. They hoped eventually to set up a trading circuit that took in farms, fisherfolk, outlying solitary Wizards and the growing town of Nexis, and also to breed more horses to sell and trade.

Iriana never found out what had been said between Aelwen and Taine, but they still seemed to be on amicable terms, content to remain friends though they were no longer lovers. She herself kept a greater distance from Avithan, determined to keep their relations cordial and civil over the winter months. Though things remained awkward and tense between them, somehow they managed to get through. When the seasons turned at last, however, and it was time for the Xandim and those Wizards and outlanders who were leaving to finally depart, Iriana felt positively giddy with relief.

It was on a cool, sparkling clear morning in spring when Corisand finally caught her first glimpse of the Wyndveil. She and her fellow Xandim, along with Yinze, Thara, Taine, Kea, Crombec and new winged bearers sent by Queen Pandion – who had carried Chathak, the young Dragon and the larger of Iriana's animals, Bear and the young white cat whom she had named Frost – had flown through the night across the new stretch of ocean that Ghabal had created to split the north of the landmass from the south. Now, though weary from keeping the flight spell in place all the way across the new ocean, she drank in the sight of the peak, its upper levels still covered by a crown of snow, that reared its craggy head through the clear morning air.

It was such a relief to be here at last. The winter, spent in Nexis, had been long and hard. Sometimes she'd thought it would never end. Out of gratitude to Iriana, and because they wanted the Wizards as allies in times to come, the Xandim had opted to remain and help the refugees from Tyrineld, but they had found themselves working harder, far harder, in more primitive shelter and on shorter rations, than when they had been slaves of the Phaerie.

The difference was that this time they had been doing it voluntarily – and now, finally, they were about to reap their reward.

As they neared the mountain, Corisand felt the Fialan, within

433

its pouch around her neck, pulse once, in welcome, then the deep, echoing voice of Basileus resounded in her mind. 'Welcome indeed to you, O Windeye; and to all of the Xandim. Welcome to your new home, the Wyndveil mountain. May your lives here, and the lives of all your descendants through generations uncounted, be happy, prosperous and secure.'

On her back, the Windeye felt Iriana grow tense with excitement. 'It's so good to hear Basileus again. Doesn't that voice take you back to the times we spent in the Elsewhere?'

'It does indeed.' Corisand sent her friend the image of a smile. 'Basileus,' she called out to the Moldan in reply. 'I can't tell you how glad we are to hear your voice once more. We Xandim will be eternally grateful for this beautiful home. Truly, it is a gift beyond price.'

'You and Iriana released the Dwelven, so it is I who owe a debt to you,' Basileus replied. 'I am very glad that you have both come back here. And who are these others you bring? More Wizards, and Winged Folk from my fellow Moldan Aerillia. There are even Leviathan in the waters around my feet, and a baby Dragon. Truly, all the Magefolk are represented – even if one is very small as yet,' he added wryly. 'Any guests of yours, of course, friend Corisand, are welcome here, but I am curious. Have they come to help the Xandim settle in their new lands?'

'Some of them are simply passing through,' Corisand replied, 'on their way to Aerillia or Dhiammara. With your permission, others are staying with me for a little while to help the Xandim build a home for themselves.'

'These lands are yours now, Windeye – my gift to you. You need not ask my permission – except when it comes to delving and mining in my bones. All friends of yours will be friends of mine. Now, there are one or two places I would like to show you before you settle in. Fly a little higher, Corisand. Partway up my slopes you will find a wide green plateau.'

Afire with curiosity, the Windeye led her people higher up the side of the Wyndveil, looking in delight at the green meadows around the feet of the mountain, the dark forests of fir and spruce that clustered around the lower slopes and climbed up the steep-sided valleys, and the waterfalls, like endless threads of sparkling silver that plunged down from the heights. All the while she was marvelling at such resplendent beauty, Corisand was keeping her eye open for the broad green plateau described to her by Basileus. Finally she saw it – a deep shelf of green grass that clung to the northern slope of the peak, cloaked in a tapestry of vibrantly coloured wild flowers that rippled in the wind. About two-thirds of the way along, closer to the western end, the plateau was divided by a stream that ran out of a narrow vale that drove deep into the mountainside, crossed to the precipice at the plateau's edge, and fell down in a slender waterfall of shimmering white foam. The entrance of the vale was guarded by a pair of tall standing stones, and Corisand looked at them in surprise.

'Within that valley lies your own, private place, O Windeye; a slender spire cleft from the mountainside where you can read the winds and watch the world, and keep guard over your people.'

'Basileus, I don't know how to thank you. You've made everything so perfect for us – but how did you do it?'

'This mountain is my body in this world, friend Windeye. I can transform it through my powers and my will, to suit my purposes – and yours.'

Corisand was longing to see her very own tower, but the Moldan called her back.

'Wait a while, if you will. I have another surprise for you, and this one is a gift for all your people. At the eastern end of the plateau you will find a cliff path curving down around the mountainside. Follow where it leads.'

Led by the Windeye, the Xandim found and followed the steep path as it curved down and around to the eastern face of the mountain. It led to a deep embayment in the mountainside, and there, extending out of the encircling cliffs, was a massive fortress that seemed as if it was formed from a single block of stone, an organic formation from the very bones of the Moldan.

'It is much roomier than it appears,' Basileus said. 'It extends far back into the mountain itself; a labyrinth of rooms and corridors; enough to house many times your number in, and be a secure defence should trouble ever come to the Xandim.'

'But where did it come from?' Corisand gasped. 'Who built it?'

'O Windeye, can you not guess, after I told you about your tower?' The Moldan laughed. 'I formed it myself; it is made of my heart, my body, my spirit. And for those who would not care to live in such a dark, intimidating structure, I have made smaller shelters – see?'

The green slope below the massive edifice was scattered with smaller dwellings looking like mossy boulders that had fallen from the cliff above.

'Each of those structures are small houses that extend a little way underground,' Basileus said, and Corisand could hear the pride in his tone. Clearly he was enjoying making his new guests welcome on his mountain. 'Each of them have simple fireplaces and surfaces that are raised or indented to form stone beds, benches, storage alcoves and tables – as far as I can understand your needs,' he went on.

'Basileus, it's marvellous,' the Windeye said. She spiralled down to land outside the gate of the fastness and, having let Iriana dismount and unstrap the basket that contained Melik, changed to her human aspect, while the other Xandim followed suit.

While Corisand was transforming, Taine drew Iriana a little way apart from the others. 'No Avithan.' He grinned at her.

Iriana grinned back. 'No Aelwen.'

'I've been waiting all winter to do this.' Taine put his arms around her, held her close and kissed her.

'It was worth waiting for,' Iriana murmured happily, and kissed him back.

Pleased for her friend, Corisand smiled to see them – and suddenly felt eyes upon her. She turned and there was Taryn.

'Look good together, don't they?' he said. 'Do you think we would look as good as that?'

'Maybe,' Corisand replied with a secret little smile. 'I think it's going to be fun finding out.'

'The last time I tried anything like that, you nearly kicked me to pieces.'

'I was much too busy to bother with males back then,' Corisand said. 'I had a whole race to free – and besides, we were horses then, and you were Aelwen's choice, not mine.'

'And now?'

'I promise I won't kick you to pieces this time.' Corisand laughed, and took his hand. 'Come on, let's go and explore our new home.'

It was a busy day, but at sunset, Iriana and Corisand stood together high on the battlements of the fortress, looking at the wide plateau and the airy view of the lands beyond, all illuminated in the golden glow of a lovely sunset. This was their moment: the culmination of their friendship, the battles they had fought together, the hardships they had suffered. Iriana smiled at her friend. 'You know, I think that today, of all days, we have the right to be proud of what we've accomplished.'

Corisand touched the wall of the sturdy fortress, wrought from the bones of the mountain, then looked out across the open spaces of the new Xandim realm. 'After all those centuries of slavery, the Xandim have been freed at last.' Her voice was choked with emotion.

'It's so wonderful to see it all begin.' Iriana smiled wistfully. 'I only wish that Dael could be here. Without his help, none of this could ever have happened.' She smiled wistfully. 'You know, I really miss him.'

'I miss him too, but he's where he wanted to be, with Athina,' Corisand replied.

'I know, and I'm really happy that, against all the odds, he found his way back to her. I only wish that he could share this moment with us. He was one of us.'

'Maybe he can,' the Windeye said thoughtfully. 'Maybe he can.'

Looking into the timeless lake with the Cailleach, watching the Xandim arrive at their new home and listening to Iriana and Corisand, Dael felt a wonderful, warm glow of pride. 'Did you hear that?' he asked Athina. 'They miss me. I was one of them. Not a lowly slave, or a mere mortal, but an equal with a Wizard and a Windeye.'

Athina put an arm around his shoulders. 'It comes as no surprise to me. Didn't I always tell you that you were special? And now that the power of the Fialan has flowed through you, who knows what you may become? I don't know how the Universe will cope with a new Creator – but I've a feeling we're about to find out.'